MURPHY'S LAW

Damaged Heroes – Book One

Sandy James

ROMANCE

BookStrand
www.BookStrand.com

A SIREN-BOOKSTRAND TITLE
IMPRINT: Romance

MURPHY'S LAW

ISBN-10: 1-60601-271-1
ISBN-13: 978-1-60601-271-0

First Printing: June 2009

Cover design by Jinger Heaston

Printed in the U.S.A.

PUBLISHER
www.BookStrand.com

DEDICATION

This one's for Judie Aitken with much love.
I thank you from the bottom of my heart for being a mentor and a friend.

Hugs!

Sandy James

MURPHY'S LAW

Damaged Heroes – Book One

SANDY JAMES

...the only redemption is when a person puts himself aside to feel deeply for another person.
Tennessee Williams

Chapter 1

"Unreasonable old bastard."

Seth Remington would never understand his father. Just because the Old Man thrived on working eighteen-hour days didn't mean his son should have to follow in his footsteps. Remington Computers had done just fine without Seth's involvement, and he had no damned desire to enter the corporate world now.

"C'mon, Baby," he encouraged his pristine Porsche Cayman as he pressed harder on the accelerator. He needed the rush that came when the speedometer hit the century mark. Seth eased the car between lanes, weaving through the sparse traffic crawling along the highway, obeying the ridiculous speed limit. He craved the excitement that came with each mile marker he left in his wake. Driving the Cayman was like flying, and God, he was addicted to the thrill.

Thoughts of the looming deadline entered his mind, making his neck muscles tense again. His father had given him one more month to sow his wild oats. After that, Seth's future mapped out like some yuppie wet dream. The job. The marriage. Grinding his teeth at the mere thought of riding a desk and wearing a tie like all of the other corporate monkeys, Seth reached for the Bose stereo and cranked Metallica's "Fuel" louder. But even the thrumming beat of the heavy metal music couldn't drown out his thoughts.

I'm not like everyone else. I'm different.

The idea of marriage wasn't much more consoling than the notion of working. Seth had chosen the pick of the litter when he proposed to Kirsten Scott, but even her sophisticated good looks and regal bearing gave him no comfort. Marriage was nothing more than a way to appease his father, a way to beget an heir to the dynasty. The simple truth was he didn't love her. Had he ever really loved any woman? No, that emotion was completely foreign.

I need to fly!

The snow began to fall in big, thick flakes, quickly covering the road in a layer of white. Seth found a familiar comfort in the way the Porsche responded to his slightest command, even on the slick pavement. His fingers caressed the steering wheel. Zipping around several cars slowing in his path, he felt his tension finally begin to ease.

He took his eyes away from the road for a second as he flipped on the windshield wipers. He glanced back up, and the brake lights that suddenly appeared in front of him caught him off guard.

"Holy shit!" Seth frantically jerked the steering wheel to the left, trying to prevent a collision with the rusty sedan sliding into his path. He jammed his foot on the brake as his mind screamed thoughts that offered absolutely no help in his precarious situation.

The Old Man's going to kill me. If I don't kill myself first.

The Porsche passed over the rumble strips on the shoulder, hit the grass and mud of the median, and began to fishtail as its speed rapidly dropped. As if watching the scene like a slow motion movie, Seth saw the approach of the large yellow barrels through the passenger window. They were the only things standing between him and the enormous concrete pier supporting the overpass. He braced for the impact, well aware of what would happen.

In an eruption of sand and water, the containers exploded from the force of the crash. The car slammed to an abrupt halt as the front passenger fender and door disintegrated into nothing more than pieces of crumpled sheet metal.

Airbags deployed with a bang and a shower of white powder. Seth blinked his eyes against the fine particles now filling the inside of his car. His right hand swelled, throbbing in rhythm with his rapidly beating heart. His chest hurt, but at least he could draw a full breath. No broken ribs. His right knee already felt twice its normal size as he tried to ease away from where it was wedged against the dashboard. A sharp pain sliced across his neck and shoulders as he tried to turn his head. Flipping down the visor to look in the mirror, he yanked the collar of his shirt aside and saw a bruise forming where the seatbelt had restrained him.

He breathed a sigh of relief.

Knowing it was only a matter of time before the police arrived, he let his aching head fall back onto the headrest and tried to relax. Things were definitely going to get crazy in a few minutes. Thank God, no one else had been hurt. The rusty sedan was probably several miles up the highway by now.

He was in deep shit now. No way around it.

Oh, yeah. The Old Man's definitely going to kill me.

* * * *

The police cruiser rolled through the front gates. After a few moments watching the car work up the long snow-lined drive, Sterling Remington let the heavy drape fall back into place. His heart had been pounding a fast and furious rhythm since the phone call informing him of Seth's latest accident. Marching out into the cold, he waited on the front steps for his prodigal son.

Watching Seth ease his way out of the patrol car and carefully walk over to the marble porch, Sterling thought his son looked more than a little fragile. The usual cocky swagger had vanished.

Sterling glared down from his lofty perch. "How bad is the Porsche?"

"Huh?" Seth frowned then shrugged. "Can't hear you, Pops," he explained in a voice much louder than necessary.

Seth slowly worked his way up the stairs, his cautious steps betraying his pain. *I won't baby him.* He'd been down that path too many times with his son. Any display of emotion, relief or anger, would only start another family confrontation.

"What's wrong?" Sterling shouted when Seth reached his side.

"Air bag." Seth pointed to his ear. "Can't hear a damn thing."

"Thank you," Sterling called to the state trooper.

"You're welcome, sir." The trooper had already returned to his squad car.

Taking Seth by the elbow, Sterling helped him into the foyer, surprised his son didn't resist his assistance. Sterling leaned in to get closer to Seth and raised his voice. "Why didn't you go to the hospital?"

"Didn't want to waste my time. I'm fine. Just sore."

"How bad is the car?"

"Totaled."

"How many is that?" Sterling asked, trying to control the fury quickly bubbling to the surface. All the relief he'd felt when he saw his son in one piece and not on a coroner's slab evaporated. He already knew the answer, but he wanted to gauge Seth's reaction.

His son appeared more than a little proud when he tucked his thumb to his palm and held up four fingers. Then Seth folded his arms over his chest and leaned against the intricately carved oaken banister.

"Are you *ever* going to grow up?" The volume of Sterling's words had little to do with his son's impaired hearing. He didn't realize just how loud he'd yelled until he saw Seth flinch.

"Love you too, Pops."

"What am I supposed to do with you?" Sterling had reached his boiling point. Passed it.

Seth shrugged his answer before one of his patented smug grins crossed his face. "You could always give me my inheritance now. I'd take it and get out of your hair."

"You'd burn through it in six months. You've done absolutely nothing with your life. Nothing! I'd hoped the plans for the wedding would settle you down, but..." Judging from the shocked look on Seth's face, he'd forgotten all about Kirsten. "You didn't even call her to tell her about the accident?"

Seth shook his head. "You know what, Pops? I'm going to my suite. Why don't you call her and tattle on me? She's more important to you than me anyway."

Seth withdrew slowly up the staircase to the second floor. Entirely discouraged at his son's prospects for the future, Sterling retreated to the study, his sanctuary.

The fire had ebbed, and the only light in the room came from the desk where he'd been reading the legal papers his friend and attorney Arthur LaGrange had sent. Heading to the oaken bar, Sterling flipped on the track lighting and then poured himself a scotch. He walked over to sit in one of the black leather chairs, stretched out his legs, and nursed his drink for a moment. The liquid burned a trail down his throat, but at least he finally felt himself relax enough to sit back and sink into the soft leather. Balancing the glass on the armrest, he leaned his head back and closed his eyes.

Seth still didn't know what was to come, nor did Sterling have the intention of telling him any time soon. His son had enough trouble dealing with reality. Finding out about Sterling's prognosis would only exasperate the situation. No, Sterling would keep his diagnosis to himself. He took a long pull on his drink.

What's going to happen to my son? An amusing but highly disturbing picture of Seth dressed in a polyester uniform and asking if someone wanted fries with his order crossed his mind. *What I'd give to see him drag in after working his ass off for one damn day!*

Sterling felt the guilt drape over him like a shroud. He'd raised Seth since the boy was four, spoiling Seth rotten because he looked so damned much like his late mother. God, how he missed Brenda. She would have known what to do. She would have known how to fix this.

"Soon, Bren. We'll be together again soon."

Finishing the last finger of scotch, Sterling tried to formulate a plan, Seth's last hope for a good dose of reality. Somehow, someway, he would figure out how to save his son. Seth needed to learn what life was like for people who had nothing, people who worked from before the sun rose until long after it set—just like the people who took care of Sterling's racehorses. Suddenly thoughts flew through his head like shooting stars.

In his mind's eye, a face appeared. Her face.

Katie Murphy.

"Now why didn't I think about this sooner?"

Putting his empty glass on the desk and picking up the phone, Sterling dialed the familiar number. "Arthur? Yes, I know it's five in the morning.

Of course I know you're home. I called you. I don't care if you are... Please, will you just listen to me for a second? I'll be at your office at nine. We've got work to do."

Chapter 2

God, he was tired of the press.

The damn media had set up shop a week ago just outside the compound's security gates when word of Sterling's imminent death had been released. Their numbers doubled when the Old Man had passed a few days later. All the Schaumburg police would do to control the chaos was keep the reporters off private property.

Looking out of the window of his suite, Seth scowled at the big vans with their satellite dishes and broadcast equipment mounted on the roofs. Scurrying around like cockroaches, correspondents held microphones and told their version of the events to the news-hungry public. The talking heads all dressed like "Stepford" reporters, and each told the same story, the same half-truths—there was no heir to the throne.

Seth let the heavy drapes fall back into place and allowed his attention to wander to the plasma television. A blond bimbo in a navy blue dress drawled, "The future of Remington Computers now rests in the hands of the late Sterling Remington's playboy son, Seth. Wall Street's reaction has been swift and severe."

"Screw you."

The obligatory pictures of Seth as a boy appeared. Brenda Remington's face suddenly crossed the high-definition screen, and Seth could feel the tears forming. God, he didn't want to think about his mother now. Fighting the wave of sorrow, Seth scrubbed the tears away with the back of his hands and swallowed the memories.

He'd had enough grief to deal with for one day.

The bimbo reporter just wouldn't shut up. "Often described as a young Mel Gibson, the twenty-nine year old Remington heir has been named one of Chicago's most eligible bachelors."

"You've got to be kidding me."

As the correspondent droned on and on about Seth's less than savory activities, the pictures showed him aging to adolescence. By the time the shots of his car wrecks or the pseudo-celebrities he'd dated in the last few years had their turn on the screen, Seth had seen more than enough. He grabbed the remote and banished the reporter to ratings hell.

He finally answered the insistent ringing of the phone when the caller ID flashed Kirsten's cell. He refused to offer a polite greeting. "I can't believe you didn't show."

"I wanted to, Baby. You know I did. I just hate facing the press."

"Why, I'm doing fine, Kirsten. Thanks so much for asking."

"Stop being sarcastic. You know I didn't want to see myself on CNN. I'll try to come over later tonight if you want. Maybe I can sneak past the press. Will you call me when you get back from Chicago?"

Chicago. He'd almost forgotten he had one more ordeal on this miserable day. "Yeah, I'll call." He ended the call and pitched the phone next to the abandoned remote control.

The Old Man's funeral had been a circus, and Seth wanted nothing more than to have a couple of beers and collapse. If he tried to sneak out and go for a long, relaxing drive, the bloodhounds would just follow him. Judging from his dark mood, he'd probably wreck another car.

None of his friends or his fiancée had come to be by his side. He'd stood in the cold cemetery with only Arthur LaGrange offering moral support. Seth had done his father proud—no tears, no display of emotion, nothing embarrassing to report. He stood straight as an arrow when the hundreds of bereaved paid their respects. Most of them he didn't even know. Probably his father's business associates who wanted to curry his favor. He would, after all, be inheriting Remington Computers. They'd have to get used to kissing Seth's ass now instead of Sterling's.

His father was gone—the last of Seth's family. Sterling now lay entombed in the big Remington crypt in the Mount Hope Cemetery alongside his beloved wife. The enormity of Seth's loss hadn't entirely hit him, but he knew it would. Eventually.

A loud knock drew him away from his thoughts. He walked across the large room and opened the door to face his father's closest friend.

"Are you ready?" Arthur asked.

"As ready as I can be under the circumstances. We're heading to your office to read the will?"

Arthur nodded. "Let's hope we can sneak by the reporters. It took forever for me to get through the damn gate. I think we ought to go out by the stables."

"Good idea. Only the servants use that entrance." Seth suddenly thought about the horses in the big barn. He'd never even stepped foot in the place, but arrangements would have to be made to sell the Old Man's racehorses. The profit didn't matter, but the idea of his father's beloved animals being neglected for even a day didn't sit well with him. "Did Pops leave any instructions about his racehorses?"

Arthur shook his head. "No, your father took care of them before he died. Most of the horses left last week."

Seth hadn't even noticed. "Where'd they go?"

"He wanted to thank his trainers for all their hard work, so he gave the horses to them. He didn't want his animals to end up with strangers. The last one is getting picked up tonight."

One less thing to worry about.

Seth sent the enormous limousine out of the front gate to lure the paparazzi on a wild goose chase. He and Arthur simply disappeared through the back entrance in a much less interesting Honda Accord. Seth found enormous satisfaction in fooling the few reporters camped out near the rear gate. They'd never even bothered to take a good look through the tinted glass. He assumed the media thought they were servants leaving their jobs for the day. Once they had reached the inbound Chicago traffic, he felt as if he could finally breathe again.

"Couldn't this wait a few days?" Seth finally asked the gray-haired attorney as he watched the approaching skyline with very little interest.

"Your father never waited for anything. Told me that he wanted to go out the way he lived. Organized and prompt."

Seth almost laughed at the statement. His father had truly lived by those rules. "I guess you're right. I just don't see why we couldn't do this at the compound. I'll have to run the gauntlet when we get back. Those damn vultures will be there for the next month."

"Seth, if you weren't rich, what would you do? For a living, I mean," Arthur asked as he negotiated the increasing flow of traffic.

Such a strange query, one Seth had never expected. Why in the hell would he ask something like that? Seth's stomach tightened. The old lawyer was up to something. "Why do you ask?"

"No reason. Just... curious."

Arthur sounded a little too sincere. Seth finally answered honestly. "I have absolutely no idea. Never had to think about it before."

"Why didn't you want to work with your father?"

"I studied psychology. Remember? It's not like it set me up to do much at Remington Computers." He gave a sardonic laugh. "Besides, that was his realm, not mine."

"There's nothing you'd want to do if you had the choice?"

Seth wondered for a moment if the lawyer's insistence on an answer should raise any alarms. Nothing about the question seemed too sinister, so he decided to indulge the man. "I suppose I could always race cars or paint houses. I could even do landscaping. Who the hell knows? I'm glad I don't have to worry about it."

Arthur visibly winced at his remarks. Seth chose to ignore him for the rest of the trip.

Pulling into the underground parking garage, Arthur steered the Honda into a reserved space next to the private elevator leading directly to the thirtieth floor law offices of O'Connor, LaGrange, Rowland, and Associates. Exiting the car, the two men rode the elevator in silence.

A pert brunette receptionist greeted them both and handed Arthur a thick stack of pink phone messages. Seth watched her gaze drop to her desk and then return wide-eyed back to him as if she suddenly recognized his face. Then she plastered on one of the smiles he'd seen too many women use as an invitation. Since she wasn't his type, he tried to look bored. Hell, he was bored.

Arthur rifled through his messages and voiced his appreciation to the receptionist, but she had already answered another call. "Let's go to the conference room," he said as he gestured toward a long hallway.

They arrived outside the ornate glass enclosure. Two people sat inside at the conference table. He'd never seen either of them before. Perhaps they lingered around from a meeting that had ended, but they couldn't be there to hear Sterling's last bequeaths.

The will would be simple enough. He was the sole heir.

The brown-haired man dressed in Armani sitting next to the woman leaned toward her as if absolutely absorbed with what she was saying. Seth knew that kind of body language; the man found her attractive. The guy was built like a football player, which made the woman appear tiny in comparison. The closer he leaned in to hear what she had to say, the smaller he made her look. Seth almost felt sorry for her.

Arthur opened the door and ushered Seth inside. The Neanderthal stood in greeting. The woman just sat looking entirely bewildered and a bit out of place in her tight green polo shirt and khaki pants.

Now, she's more my style. She had enormous eyes. Green eyes. And her hair held the most incredible mixture of red and blond. Long, wavy tresses brushed her shoulders, and the light picked up some the blond, making her appear to have a halo surrounding her oval face.

"Ross, nice to see you," Arthur said as he shook the man's hand. "Miss Murphy, thank you for coming on such short notice." He gave the young woman a quick nod.

She returned the gesture. "You're welcome, but I still don't know why I'm here."

She's nervous. Perhaps the thought came from watching her teeth gently pulling on her bottom lip. Perhaps Seth hoped he might be able to offer her comfort. Either way, he was a bit surprised he could so easily understand her thoughts.

Captivated by her, he lost track of how long he'd been gaping until Arthur loudly cleared his throat. The other people in the room now stared at Seth. "Sorry," he offered, walking to the huge mahogany table to wait for the reading of his father's last wishes. When the man and woman didn't make any move to leave, he drummed his fingers on the polished wood. Turning to Arthur, he said, "I assumed this would be private."

"Seth Remington, I'd like you to meet Ross Kennedy and Kathleen Murphy," the lawyer replied.

The woman smiled at her introduction, and Seth took all of her into his mind. She was small but looked to have the type of physical strength most men would kill to possess. Not overtly muscular, but her arms reminded him of a starlet he'd once dated who hired a professional trainer to prepare her for an action flick. The redheaded angel obviously worked out. A lot.

Reaching out to shake Ross's offered hand first, Seth immediately noticed the man liked to use intimidation from the start. He applied a forceful grip, but Seth gave back as good as he received.

Seth reached across the table to take the angel's hand. She gave a small chuckle. "It's Katie. Please. My grandfather is the only one who ever calls me Kathleen, and that's when he's mad at me."

Seth grinned at her, pleased when she offered him another of her alluring smiles in return. Her voice had a slight twang to its soft lilt.

This one was his type. Exactly his type. He figured he'd invite her out for a quiet supper after he found out the extent of his inheritance. They could go to Vivo—it served great pasta. And then afterward maybe they could get his usual room at the Palmer House.

Perhaps she was exactly what he needed to help him forget this wretched day.

"It's nice to meet you, Katie. I know your meeting is done, but if you're not in a hurry, I'd love to take you to dinner. I shouldn't be too long."

Katie shot him a puzzled stare. "This *is* my meeting. We've been waiting for you."

That was the last thing Seth expected to hear. He'd been concentrating so hard on his plans for the redhead, it suddenly dawned on him that he hadn't been paying much attention when Arthur had introduced them. He whirled on Arthur, not even trying to hide his frustration. "What's she mean? Waiting on me?"

Closing the conference room double doors and walking to the head of the large table, Arthur replied, "Sit down, Seth, and I'll explain. Ross, please have a seat."

As Seth and Ross settled into their chairs, Arthur picked up a remote control from the table. He pointed it at the wood-paneled wall and pushed a button. In response, the wall opened, revealing a large flat screen television.

"I used to say 'open sesame,' but my secretary told me no one got the joke anymore," Arthur said.

Katie was the only one to laugh. Arthur favored her with a kind smile and a wink that made Seth think the old codger liked flirting with her.

Seth couldn't conceal his growing irritation. The day had already been trying enough. "Arthur, I just don't—" He stopped talking when Arthur pressed another button and Sterling Remington appeared on the screen. Seth's heart pounded like a jackhammer as he stared at the face he hadn't expected to see again so soon.

Arthur paused the image. The still picture jerked from time to time, but the Old Man simply sat there with one of his determined expressions. Seth felt a shiver run the length of his spine. This just wasn't right. "When did he make this tape?"

Arthur put the remote down on top of a large file sitting on the tabletop. "Calm down, Seth, and I'll explain." Arthur slowly glanced around the room. "I've brought you all together because it was Sterling's wish you meet before we go over the provisions of his will. Ross is an attorney at this firm who's handled more and more of Sterling's business dealings lately." A melancholy smile crossed his face for a moment. "I was going to hand all of Sterling's legal matters over to Ross when I retired next year, but..."

"Like I told you on the phone," Katie interrupted, "I hardly knew the man. Why am I here?"

"Patience, Katie. Please. I'll get to it," Arthur replied. "Seth, Ross is the one who helped me draft your father's will. His new will."

"New will? Pops never told me he wrote a new will." Seth's stomach clenched and a wave of nausea quickly followed. His father had gone to the effort to write a new will. He knew Sterling had been angry after he'd wrecked the Porsche, but why a new will? *Shit! Did he cut me off?* The cryptic question Arthur posed earlier flew through his mind. *What if I'm left with nothing? Where will I go?*

Ross answered Seth. "Your father asked us to tape it. He came to us a few months ago. I think it was right after you totaled the last Porsche."

His father had been keeping secrets. The Old Man had made the new will because he knew he was dying months before he'd shared the news with his son. "He already knew. He was sick, and he didn't even tell me. Shit, I've only known for three weeks." That would be just like the Old Man to play his cards so close to his vest.

Arthur intervened. "Yes, Seth. He'd already heard the news from his doctor. After the accident... Well, let me allow him to explain it." Arthur picked up the remote and hit another button. Sterling Remington's image came to life.

"I hate these things." Sterling's booming voice filled the room. "I never sound like myself and I sure don't look like myself."

Seth couldn't suppress a rueful laugh. God, how he would miss the Old Man.

"Well, looks like my time is just about up. Before I go any further, I want to say something to my son. Seth, you're not going to like me very much when this tape is over. In fact, I'd guess you're going to hate me. But what I'm doing is for you. I love you, son. I do. Your mother loved you too. We waited so long to have you. Maybe I never told you enough how important you are to me. Maybe I could have been a better father. But I won't live with regrets. Hell, I'm not going to live long enough to have too many more things to regret. Water under the bridge anyway.

"Ross, thanks for helping me get this put together so quickly. You know what to do and how to handle it. I'm putting a lot of trust in you. See that you don't disappoint me."

Ross stared at the screen and whispered, "Yes, sir." Seth caught the respectful response.

Sterling continued. "Katie, you're probably thinking you're in the wrong place—"

"Got that right," she quietly replied. She leaned into the table, plucked a loose pen from its surface, and twirled it through her fingers like a tiny baton. Seth figured she was nervous again.

"—but you're not," Sterling continued. "Do you remember what we talked about... about me putting some horses in your stable—colts I wanted you to train? I'm sorry I didn't get that done, Sweetheart. But I'm going to do you one better. You're going to get the best thing I have to offer. Katie, you're getting my son."

The pen suddenly flew from her fingers and sailed across the table.

Katie and Seth both looked at the screen with dropped jaws.

"You can both close your mouths now," Sterling's voice said with a small chuckle. "Katie, Sweetheart, I've never met anyone quite like you. We haven't known each other long, but I know quality when I see it. Your horses are treated better than most people and your talent for training good racehorses is second to none. You know your business like I know mine, and you've been training long enough to have earned the respect of everyone I've talked to. I need you to take Seth under your wing. Teach him. Train him. Just like you do your horses."

"*What?*" Seth had rapidly reached his boiling point. Now his beloved father was comparing him to a large smelly beast of burden. He pushed his chair away from the table, preparing to bolt at the next provocation. "How long do I have to listen to this?"

"Seth," his father's voice continued, "it's time for you to learn what life is all about. Hell, son, you're almost thirty. It's past time for you to grow up. You'll walk out of this office with nothing. No mansion. No cars. No money. No name. No company waiting for you to take it over. The Remington fortune will be put into a trust so you can't have a dime of it now. You can go home tonight, but just for one night. When you leave the compound tomorrow, you can take two suitcases of clothes, but nothing else. And the Remington name stays behind too. While you're with Katie, you'll use a different name. Arthur is working on an alias for you."

Seth whirled his chair around, jumped to his feet, and shouted at Arthur. "What the hell is he talking about?"

"Seth," his father continued, "sit down and hear me out."

Shocked at the insightfulness of his father's posthumous statement, Seth instantly obeyed.

The old lawyer hit the pause button, put the remote down, and picked up the file folder. He pulled out three stapled packets and handed one to each person at the table.

"This is the agreement. Katie and Seth, you've both got to read and sign it for it to be legally binding." Arthur put the file folder down and picked up the remote again. Pointing it at the television, he said, "Just listen to what he wants, Seth."

Sterling said, "I couldn't give you a position at Remington Computers because there would be no challenge for you, no way to show you what hard work is like. And everyone there knows you. Son, you're going to work for Katie Murphy as a groom. You'll work from now until the end of the racing season. You'll live at the track dormitory like all the other grooms. For the first time in your life you're going to learn what it's like to work, to really work."

Katie looked up from her paper and asked a question. Arthur hit the pause button again. "I'm sorry, Katie. What did you say?"

"Why me? I don't understand. Why does he have to work for me? I don't have time to train a new groom. Especially one who doesn't know squat about horses. I wish Mr. Remington would've asked me first."

"It's what Sterling wanted," Ross responded. "He told me he was going to buy some yearlings for you to train, but his illness progressed too fast. He said this would help you out."

Katie was clearly confused. Seth wasn't far behind her.

"Help me out here. How does making his son work for me equal to putting horses in my barn? Seems to me I'm getting the short end of the stick. I'm supposed to pay him too?" She shook her head. "No thanks, I'd rather have some horses."

"All of Sterling's horses were too high profile," Ross explained. "Everyone would recognize them, and then they'd recognize Seth. Sterling didn't want Seth relying on the Remington name to get through this easily." He flipped to a page of the papers sitting in front of Katie. "Besides, *you* don't have to pay Seth. The estate will pay his salary—a groom's salary. Plus you'll get two hundred a week as a stipend as long as he's with you. It'll be up to you to let us know how much he's earned. He's free help for you."

"Free help I have to train," she replied. Then she seemed to mull the whole idea over for a long moment. "Two hundred a week?" she finally asked. Ross nodded. "How long did you say I'd have to put up with him?"

"You can both stop talking about me as if I'm not sitting right here," Seth grumbled. He glared at Katie. "You don't have to worry about it anyway, Princess. I've got no intention of working for you."

"Fine with me," she replied as she leaned back in her chair and crossed her arms over her chest. "Jerk."

The word was barely more than a whisper, but it hadn't escaped the notice of anyone in the conference room. Ross coughed a laugh into his hand. Arthur cleared his throat.

Seth decided to ignore her for the moment and deal with the more immediate problem. "Arthur, this is ridiculous. I'll just challenge it in court."

Ross replied, "You can't... Well, I suppose you can, but Sterling put a provision in the will that disinherits you if you file a civil suit. If you do take this to court, you lose all the money." Ross laughed and added, "Plus you'll pick up some hefty legal bills."

"I've already lost everything according to this asinine tape!"

Arthur intervened. "Please, let's all calm down. Just listen to the rest, shall we?" He started the tape.

Sterling's voice filled the room again. "If you're able to show that you can become a valuable member of Katie's team, you'll inherit Remington Computers—lock, stock, and circuit boards. It will be her decision at the end of the season whether you inherit or not. She'll let Arthur and Ross know if you've fulfilled your obligation. You refuse to work for Katie, you get nothing."

"Son of a bitch," Seth muttered as the tape played on.

"Now, I know you think you're a ladies' man, Seth, so I have one more condition," Sterling cautioned as he grinned and waved his index finger in front of him as if scolding a naughty child.

Seth released a heavy sigh. How could this possibly get any worse?

Sterling's voice took on a note of severity. "If you try to seduce Katie or use collusion to get her to give you the money, you'll get nothing. There's no cheating your way out of this. And just to be sure you don't try to take advantage of her, if Katie decides you've earned your money at the end of the season then you can't have any kind of contact with her again for five years. And Katie can't get a dime of your inheritance, only the colt I've bought for her and the salary I've put aside for her as payment for taking you in. If you transfer anything of value into her name in the next five years, my pit bulls will go after you. That'll keep you from trying to trick her into some kind of plot to split the money. If you violate the five-year-no-contact rule, the money will be taken away from you, and believe me, my lawyers will know if you cheat."

Looks like the angel and I won't be checking into the Palmer House after all.

Sterling leaned in to put his face closer to the camera. The unshed tears in his father's eyes made Seth's throat close up, choking him with grief. "Seth, please believe me. This is really for the best. All you've got to do is work hard. Show the world what you can do when you stand on your own two feet. I believe in you, son. I really believe in you."

The image faded to black.

Chapter 3

All Seth could do was sit and stare at the blank screen as a mixture of anger and grief twisted through his mind. The Old Man had really done it this time. Sure, he'd threatened before. Lots of times. But he'd damn well done it this time.

Arthur's voice finally worked its way through Seth's mental haze. "Seth, it's not so bad. You just have to be like everybody else for a while. Not long. Just a season."

"How... how long's a season?" Seth asked even though he wasn't really certain he wanted to know the answer.

"We're training for it now. We race from the beginning of April to the middle of November," Katie answered even though her attention didn't seem to be directed toward Seth.

She appeared to be every bit as disturbed by the turn of events, but instead of becoming catatonic, she busily flipped through the pages of the packet Arthur had handed her. She'd drawn her lips so tight, they were nothing but a thin line. "I don't get it," she said each time she turned to a new page.

Ross finally took Katie's packet off the table. He turned to a specific page, put it back in front of her, and pointed out an important passage. She read it. "So that's all I get for doing this? That's it?"

"That and the weekly stipend," Ross replied.

She'd piqued Seth's curiosity. "Well? What does she get?"

"A horse. A stakes horse," Katie responded. Her eyes slowly scanned Seth from his head to his feet. "A two-year old Indiana-sired stakes horse. I'm not sure you're worth it."

"What the hell is a stakes horse?" Seth asked. If it was some multimillion-dollar champion, at least it would make him feel as if his life had *some* value.

"It's a horse that's paid up to race in special races. But it's a two-year old. It might not even make it to the track this year. Or ever," she explained, still flipping through the papers.

Even though he wasn't entirely sure he wanted to know the answer, Seth had to ask, "What do you mean about not making it to the track?"

"Some two-year olds aren't mature enough to race well. You spend a lot of time getting them ready, and all you get for your effort is massive frustration," Katie replied. She looked as aggravated as he felt.

"Beautiful. Just beautiful." Seth used his fingertips to massage his now aching forehead.

Katie didn't appear much happier. Perhaps his father had insulted her when he implied she was the kind of woman whose common sense and business practices could be influenced by a handsome face.

Ross leaned toward Katie, put a hand on her shoulder, and said, "Katie, it's a really good horse. Sterling knew you wanted to stay in Indiana, so he had some of his people check around for one of the best two-year olds out there. He probably paid more for the animal than it's worth to get it for you. Plus, you get a new groom you don't have to pay."

"That's it? I still don't get it. Why me? Why'd he pick me?"

"Sterling called you 'quality.' It was the highest compliment he'd give to anyone, trust me," Arthur replied.

"A whole season? What if he doesn't work hard? What if he's not good with my horses?"

Although he understood Katie's concern about the impact this would have on her stable, Seth cared more about what was happening to him. Thoroughly pissed off at the whole proceeding, he scoffed a laugh. "What if we just pretend I work for you? No one would have to know anything." Once said aloud, the ridiculous suggestion didn't sound so farfetched to him. Then he realized he was grasping at proverbial straws. His father's will had left no wiggle room.

About the time it appeared everyone had mercifully ignored him again, Katie spoke up. "There are no secrets in the barn."

"Excuse me?" Seth asked. This woman seemed to have a language all her own, and he hated realizing she could make him feel so ignorant.

"Everyone would know. There are no secrets in the barn," she answered as if that explanation should suffice.

Ross arched an eyebrow. "What do you mean?"

Katie's heavy sigh conveyed her frustration. "I *know* you don't get it. You guys have never been in racing. Everyone at the track always knows everybody else's business. We're together almost twenty-four seven. If you were around a track, you'd understand. It's absolutely impossible to keep anything a secret."

Arthur chuckled. "Reminds me of this office."

Ross smiled and nodded at Arthur. He turned back to Seth. "Can we get back to the business at hand? It's entirely up to you, Katie. When it's all said and done, you get to decide if he's earned his money."

"I don't want that kind of responsibility," she replied, shaking her head.

"You don't have to take him, Katie, but this is a fantastic opportunity for you. Let's go talk in my office." Ross pulled her chair away from the table. Katie stood up, grabbed her papers, and trailed him out of the conference room without a backward glance. Seth's eyes followed her closely as she walked past the glass walls and disappeared.

After Ross and Katie left, Arthur sat down next to Seth and put a comforting hand on the young man's shoulder. "Seth, I know this is a shock."

Seth snorted in response to the obvious understatement. "A shock? Damned right, it's a shock."

"Your father wanted to help you, that's all. Will it really be that terrible?"

"Let's see, Arthur. I've got no home, no car, no money. I can't even use my own damn name. Tomorrow morning, I'm allowed to reduce everything I value into just enough to fill two suitcases. Then I'm homeless. I've got to go to... Where does she work?"

"Dan Patch Raceway. It's in Indiana."

Seth felt no need to hide his rage. "I've got to go to Indiana and work with horses. Isn't that special? I *hate* horses. I *hate* Indiana." He wanted to throw something. "You said I've got to sign. What if I don't? What if I just ignore the Old Man's request? What if I tell you all to go straight to—"

Arthur interrupted. "Then Remington Computers gets divided among the employees as stocks and profit sharing. The personal wealth goes to charities. You'd lose every penny." He patted Seth's shoulder. "Think before you do something stupid, son. Less than nine months. That's all he's asking. If you work hard, then the money is yours."

* * * *

Ross opened the door to his office and strode inside with a confidence that radiated around him like an aura. Katie had never seen a place reek so much of affluence. The enormous room was decorated entirely in black and chrome—not a single item seemed useless or out of place. She immediately felt awkward in her casual clothes and stood in the doorway a little hesitant to walk inside. Something nagged at her, telling her that once she crossed the threshold, her life would never be the same.

Ross patted the back of one of the black leather client chairs, and she swallowed hard and mustered up her courage. Katie marched to the chair, plopped down, and waited for Ross to try to talk her into the whole ridiculous plan.

"How many people would just hand you a two-year old colt?"

"Murphy's Law," Katie replied.

"I beg your pardon?"

"Murphy's Law. 'Everything that can go wrong will go wrong.' With my name, it's obvious I'd be skeptical," she explained with a quiet laugh. "Plus you know that old saying about the gift horse. Nothing comes without strings attached."

Ross chuckled and leaned back against his enormous black desk. "Yeah, I suppose I can see where you're coming from. But I helped design this agreement. There aren't any complications, aren't any hidden strings. Sterling put a lot of thought into this. He told me he had big plans for you. He wanted to make you one of the leading trainers in the country."

"He didn't."

"He did. He said you're already well on your way."

"I'm surprised he'd say something like that. You know, it wasn't like I spent much time with the guy."

"Where'd you meet him?" Ross asked.

"At a horse auction. He sat beside me and we talked about some of the horses in the sale." She shrugged. "Must've liked what he heard because he took me to dinner. We agreed that he'd put a horse in my barn to see if we worked well together, but then he just disappeared." She kept waiting for

Ross to sit down so she'd stop getting a stiff neck looking up at the extraordinarily tall man. "That must be when he got sick."

Ross continued to stand there as imposing as a skyscraper. "Probably. But you obviously made an impression. You know, Sterling went to a lot trouble and expense to find out everything in the world there was to know about you, and the man liked everything he found."

"Incredible. I'm still not sure I want to do this. I just don't see how I can turn it down. The two-year-old is good?" She wasn't about to waste her time and turn her business upside down for no good reason.

Ross stretched over to reach for the thick file resting on his desk. After shuffling through some of the contents, he pulled out the animal's green and white ownership paper and placed it on top of the file. "Come over here, Katie, and read this. I'll be back in a minute." He headed out of his office.

Katie jumped out of the chair, hurried to the desk, and grabbed the paper. She studied the pedigree and sighed. Lord, did she want that animal. The colt had impeccable bloodlines and was bred in her own hometown of Goshen by one of the best breeders in Indiana. Most trainers would drool just to think of training a horse like that, and she'd been given the opportunity to own it. Her own stakes horse.

If the colt lived up to his potential, he could easily have a career that brought in hundreds of thousands of dollars. If the horse turned out to be as talented as she hoped, she could use his earnings to buy her own farm and stop renting stalls at the training center.

She really wanted that colt. But did she want it enough to take on a nuisance like Seth Remington?

Katie thought about the man, and in a rare moment of letting her guard down, she had to acknowledge what she'd realized the moment Seth walked into the conference room. He was the most handsome man she had ever seen. Almost too pretty to be a guy.

He had perfect features—straight, white teeth, a small cleft in his chin, and long, dark eyelashes most girls would kill to possess. Those hazel eyes were hypnotic and the ebony hair wavy, not hopelessly unruly like her own mop. He wore it a little longer than Katie usually liked to see on a guy, but for some odd reason even that trait called to her.

She remembered his less than subtle attempt to ask her out, and wondered for a moment if she'd made a big mistake turning him down. But

Katie didn't usually go for guys like Seth. Handsome and spoiled weren't a good combination. Men like that were typically nothing but a peck of trouble.

And guys like Seth didn't ever go for girls like Katie, girls who played men's games.

Curiosity got the better of her, and Katie put the ownership paper aside and flipped through the thick file clearly labeled with her name. Her stomach churned as she read page after page and saw how much of her life had been laid bare.

Ross walked back into his office. Katie slammed the file shut and was about to tell the man what he could do with Sterling Remington's "request" when he handed her a large stack of pictures. She bit her tongue, took them, and began to flip through them one by one.

Good God. Every picture was of her jogging horses, harnessing them, moving a sulky out of the barn, or standing in a bath stall with an animal. Some snapshots showed her talking to people in the paddock and even standing in the winner's circle. Her heart pounded and her mouth suddenly went dry. Some stranger had been watching her like a Peeping Tom.

"I don't understand," Katie told Ross as she continued to shuffle through the pictures. She tried to control the shaky timbre of her voice. "He had someone following me?" She wasn't sure whether to be complimented or insulted at the prospect. She settled on pissed.

"Sterling always made sure he only worked with people of... quality. His word. He used it with your name almost every time I talked to him. I promised him I'd do anything to make sure you took on Seth. I wanted you to see the pictures so you'd know Sterling didn't jump into this without any kind of thought about how it would affect you. He knew your schedule like the back of his hand. The man could name every horse in your barn."

Katie finally came to the last photo in the enormous pile and glanced back at Ross. "You know, I hate that you know so much stuff about me. Why in the hell would he need all of this?" she asked, brushing the file with the back of her hand.

"I told you, Sterling wanted to know everything about you."

Katie shuddered at the notion. "I guess so. Do you have my shoe size? It's a six."

Ross chuckled and winked. "No, Katie, I don't have your shoe size, but

I'll be sure to add it now." His gaze fixed on her and the humor in his eyes vanished. "So you'll take Seth?"

"How in the hell do you expect me to make that guy a groom? They may have the worst job in the world, but even most of them have some talent and know what they're doing. Seth Remington wouldn't have a clue." From the dubious look on Ross's face, the lawyer had obviously never been around horses.

Ross walked around to sit in the client chair beside the one where she'd been sitting. He patted the empty seat as an invitation, and Katie calmed herself enough to sit down again. "Worst job?" he asked once she had settled in.

"They do almost everything that needs to be done. They have to take care of all of an animal's physical needs. Cleaning stalls. Feeding them. Taking care of minor injuries. Getting equipment on them before races and taking care of them afterwards. It's like... Did you ever hear the old kids' fable about the elves and the shoemaker?" Ross nodded, so she continued. "Grooms remind me of the elves. They do so much work, but no one really notices them. Unless they screw up. Then they catch hell. And they get paid next to nothing while working really crappy hours. You really expect me to get this Remington guy to muck out stalls and clean harnesses?"

Ross nodded again. He leaned forward and reached over to put his hand on the arm of Katie's chair. "I know this is going to be a big change for you, but you've got to think about what a great opportunity this is. The colt is good. From what I've read about you, I know you can make him better. I can't believe how many winner's circle pictures I saw you in. You'll get the salary too. And there's always..." He stopped mid-thought as if censoring himself. "Let's just say there's a bonus when the season's over."

"Bonus?"

"I can't tell you how much now, but if you nurse the guy through the season, you'll be rewarded. Well rewarded. So, will you do it?"

With a resigned sigh, she finally nodded in response. "Fine. I'll do it, but just 'cause I *really* want that two-year old. When will I get my new groom?"

His enormous smile told her Ross was pleased with her decision. "I'll bring him down to your farm tomorrow afternoon."

"It's not really *my* farm. It's the training center where I rent some stalls and my room. I just call it 'my farm.' It's easier than explaining everything. But I suppose you already knew that."

He nodded; she wasn't surprised.

Katie immediately began a mental list of things she would have to do to prepare for Seth's arrival. What a nuisance. "I'd really like to tell my friends. Surely it wouldn't hurt if I told—"

Ross's eyes looked stern as he shook his head at her and interrupted. "No, Katie. You can't. You saw the nondisclosure clause. All you'd need is for one person at the track to get wind you're sheltering Seth Remington. He'd call the press and you'd have cameras camped out at your farm. I mean, he is a member of the Boys' Club."

"The what?" And they'd made fun of the things she'd said.

"The Boys' Club. You mean you haven't heard of the Boys' Club?" Katie shrugged at the ridiculous question. "You must not watch much television."

"Don't even own one. Besides, I wouldn't have time to watch TV anyway. What's the Boys' Club?"

"A bunch of rich guys who like to party hard. A couple of senators' sons, the ex-governor's son, and a few guys from Grosse Point. All of them spoiled kids like Seth who come from money."

"Why would anyone care about what a bunch of losers like that do?" Katie asked, feeling a bit confused.

It was Ross's turn to shrug. "I honestly don't know, but for some reason, the paparazzi love them. It's like Paris Hilton. Who suddenly decided she was famous?"

"Who's Paris Hilton?" Katie felt like a hick.

Ross shook his head and chuckled. "No one important. You know, Remington isn't even one of the bad ones. Most of them have been arrested at some time or another."

That was the last thing she wanted to hear. "Arrested? For what?"

"DWI. Drugs. Assault."

"And you want a guy like that around my horses? You can just forget it!"

"Calm down, Katie. Seth's kept himself out of that kind of trouble. The guy actually tries to help out his moron friends when they're in a jam. I think the only reason he gets so much attention is because he's the

Remington heir."

"And he's cute," Katie added before realizing how adolescent she sounded. Ross's scolding eyes told her he'd caught her comment, and her cheeks flushed hot. "Well, he is. Doesn't mean anything though."

Ross appeared a little annoyed, and Katie wished the filter between her brain and her mouth worked better. One of these days she'd learn to stop thinking aloud.

"Worst thing Seth has done is wreck a bunch of cars. The guy probably has more speeding tickets than all the people in Cook County put together. He tried to drive Indy cars for a while."

Katie stopped for a moment to consider the whole absurd situation. "Let's see if I've got all this straight. He's a spoiled rotten, egocentric, rich pretty boy. I've got to make him work like a slave and hope he doesn't screw up my stable in the process." With a heavy sigh, she finally gave in. "Bring him to my barn tomorrow." She pointed at the thick file. "I don't suppose you need directions."

Ross relaxed back in his chair and laughed.

She stood up and he immediately followed suit. "And the two-year-old damn well better be something special."

Ross laughed again and walked her to the lobby.

* * * *

The long drive back to Indiana that night was rough. Even though the end of winter was close, the lake effect snow piled up rapidly, and Katie's ancient pickup had a nasty habit of sliding around. Ross had offered to put her up in a hotel for the night, but Katie wanted to get home. Besides, the ride would give her plenty of time to think about her bizarre situation.

She shoved one of her favorite Michael Bublé CDs into the stereo and cranked the volume. She fervently hoped some of the singer's soft jazz would soothe her frayed nerves.

Seth Remington was her new employee—a bother in her otherwise organized and orderly life. She worried obsessively about how he would be around her horses. Her thoughts churned in such a state of turmoil, even her beloved music wasn't giving her any relief.

How in the hell am I going to turn that guy into a groom?

All Katie really wanted was to get home to her horses and back to her routine.

After five hours of slipping and sliding through snow, she finally parked her pickup next to the rented barn she called home. As soon as she hopped out of the truck, Katie put a finger and thumb to her lips and whistled. The responding chorus of whinnies and nickers made her smile. Her horses were happy to know she'd made it home, and she finally relaxed.

* * * *

The law offices were quiet and dark, just the way Ross liked them. Nights were always the best time to work.

He shoved some papers he needed into his briefcase. His phone rang. At first, he thought it would be fine to let the answering service take the late call, but his workaholic personality couldn't resist the itch to answer. "Ross Kennedy."

"Ross, it's Arthur. I figured you'd still be at the office."

"What can I do for you, sir?"

"Are you ready to take care of things tomorrow? Seth won't be in the best of moods when you pick him up."

Ross continued to overload his briefcase with work he still needed to complete at home. "I figured as much. You explained all of the rules?"

"Yes, but I'm still not sure he'll go along with using a different name. I hope he realizes it's the only way to protect him. The second someone catches on he's a Remington, there'll be no way to keep the press away. What name did we use on the license?"

"The race officials approved 'Seth Reynolds.' You know, we should probably give him a nickname too. 'Seth' isn't all that common a name and anyone who'd seen a photo of him... People could catch on. Do you think anyone will recognize him at the track?" If Seth wanted to screw up the whole operation, he could simply get someone to identify him. Sterling had wisely made contingencies for that possibility, but it wouldn't be what the old man had wanted.

"I really doubt it. Even if they think he looks like himself, do you think anybody would ever believe Seth Remington is working as a groom? Not likely. Plus, it's Indiana. Not exactly a Chicago journalist's usual place to prowl," Arthur responded.

"I'll make sure he gets there tomorrow," Ross promised. "One way or another."

* * * *

The phone was ringing when Seth walked in the door of his suite. He picked up the handset, glanced at the caller ID, and recognized the number. "Yeah?" he answered as he groped to loosen the tie that had been strangling him all day.

"Seth. Why didn't you call me? Did you get done at Arthur's office?" Kirsten asked. Her words sounded a little too eager and a little too much like scolding. She had no right.

Seth gave a small rueful laugh. "Oh, yeah. I'm *done*."

"What do you mean? There's a problem with the will?"

How did you tell your fiancée you would be broke and homeless as of tomorrow morning? "Kirsten, we really need to talk. Can you come over?"

He could almost see her irritated expression. "The press still there?"

"What the hell do you think? Of course they're still here. Are you coming over or what?" He massaged his throbbing forehead with his fingertips. *Where's the aspirin?*

"No, I'm not coming over there. And you can quit sounding so pissed at me. This isn't easy on me either, you know."

Seth couldn't remember a single reason he had decided to marry the woman. "Thanks for being so supportive. Good night, Kirsten."

"Will I see you tomorrow?"

The day just kept on giving.

When he'd finally made his decision about the demands his father had given him, Seth had easily anticipated her reaction. She'd play the wounded party because of her nature. It was time to set himself free. "No, you won't see me tomorrow. Kirsten, I'm leaving in the morning."

"Leaving?"

"Leaving. You can keep the damn ring."

"You're breaking up with me? With *me*? Why?"

Because you didn't even come to my father's funeral, you selfish...

"We wouldn't work anyway. I was just going through with it for Pops, but he's... gone."

"Seth, can't we talk about this? I know we hadn't set a date, but do you have to break the engagement? What will my friends say? God, it'll be in the papers."

"Yeah, it probably will. But you know what, Princess? They'll say you caught a lucky break. Goodbye, Kirsten." He disconnected the phone before she could even reply.

Seth put the handset back into its cradle and stared at it for a moment. Then he grabbed the phone, jerked it out of the wall, and flung it across the room.

No more calls tonight.

He had to go pack two suitcases.

Chapter 4

The silver Lexus slowed and turned off the winding country road. Seth shook himself out of his near-sleep, wishing he was somewhere else. Anywhere else.

The interminable trip from Chicago to some backward town in Indiana had finally come to an end. Ross steered the car toward an enormous barn standing at the end of the gravel road.

"You can't be serious," Seth groaned. "This place looks like a third world country."

Sheets of corrugated aluminum formed the roof, skylights periodically interrupting their orderly pattern. Similar panels lined the exterior with only a single small window breaking the long brown wall that could be seen from the road. The barn and facilities weren't anything like his father's stable—at least not like the little he'd seen of it.

"It's a nice place," Ross replied. "It may not be up to your standards, but... what is?"

Nice? What was nice about a barn full of horses? "Do I have to stay here? In the barn?"

Ross shook his head as he pulled the Lexus alongside an open sliding door at the end of the barn. "Katie got you a room at the track dormitories."

At least that didn't sound so bad. Maybe it would be just like college.

Seth furrowed his brow as he glanced at several two-wheeled carts lined up in a neat row along the barn's outer wall. Everything around him looked so strange, so foreign. "What the hell are those things? Rickshaws?"

"Ask Katie."

Ross obviously wasn't much of a conversationalist.

"Is that an outhouse? A real outhouse? Good God! Does the health department know about this? It's got to violate some law."

Ross shook his head. "People use port-a-johns every day. It's not against the law. It's fine, Remington."

Nothing's fine, Matlock. Seth had a hard time not giving voice to the insult. Four hours in a car with a stoic lawyer who obviously didn't like him hadn't done much to cool the grief and anger still bubbling through his mind. All he wanted was to go home. Instead, he was being dropped off at a barn in the middle of nowhere to work with people he didn't know. Priceless.

Seth opened the car door, stepped out, and found his foot in a pile of manure. "Damn it!" He looked around desperately for some remedy to fix his defiled Italian loafers. With few options, he finally walked away from the car and began to wipe off his shoe on some frosty grass. "Doesn't anyone clean up after these animals?"

"That's your job now," Katie answered, walking toward them through the open barn door. Dressed in a thick blue flannel jacket, she'd pushed her hair into a gray knit cap. A few red curls escaped their restraint, peeking out from beneath the material. "But we don't clean up the manure in corrals or on the road. Nature takes care of that most of the time."

As if to prove her point, a flock of small brown birds descended on the place where Seth had dirtied his shoes and methodically picked through the pile.

"Disgusting. This place smells like a... like a..."

"Like a barn?" Katie asked with a laugh. "Get used to it." She glanced at Ross with wide eyes as if to plead one last time to be spared this trial. "Did he gripe like that all the way here?"

Seth scowled at the question and pulled his coat tighter against the late winter wind.

Ross warmed to the question. "Gripe? Classic understatement. He bitched about everything. Let's see... Did you know that horses are stupid animals?"

Katie shot Seth an angry glare.

"Wait, there's more. Indiana is a barren wasteland. Only Thoroughbreds are *real* racehorses. Women have no place in sports. Ever. And... um..." He snapped his fingers as if trying to refresh his memory. "Oh, yeah. Horse racing is run by organized crime syndicates." He glanced at Seth. "Did I leave anything out, Remington?"

"You don't say more than ten words for the whole trip, but *now* you want to make conversation? I hate lawyers." Just what he needed. Piss off the new boss on the first damn day.

Katie's eyes narrowed to thin slits as she stared at Seth. She turned back to Ross. "Are you sure he's up to this? 'Cause he sure as hell doesn't act like he is."

Ross shrugged. "Beats me. But he's all yours now."

Seth bristled when neither of them seemed to have an inkling of what he'd been through in the last few weeks. "I'm standing right here. And I'm getting damn sick and tired of you two talking about me like I'm some little kid."

She glanced back at Ross.

"It'll be okay, Katie," Ross said. "We'll try to make it worth your while. Jacob Schaeffer is going to pick up the colt next Monday."

Seth was confused. "Who's Jacob Schaeffer? Why's he getting *your* horse?"

"He's an old friend, and he's going to train the horse up in Goshen," Katie replied in that no-nonsense tone she'd used in Chicago.

Seth's confusion wasn't getting any better. Didn't she know he had no idea how things worked in this business? "Why don't you train the horse if you're so great? My father got the stupid nag for you, didn't he?" The woman made no sense. Why would she take a horse that was supposed to be important to her and then give it to someone else?

She narrowed her eyes again. "I *will* train him, but Jacob is really good with young horses. His two-year-olds almost always make it to the track. I'll have him bring the colt down here when it gets warmer."

Seth snorted. "It'll *never* get warmer."

Ross took a couple of steps toward Katie. "Maybe we can show him where he's going to stay. Get him settled in and all."

"Fine," Katie replied. "But it's already noon. I still have some stuff to do here. I'll take him over to the track dorms in a bit. Is he ready to work?"

"Should be," Ross answered as he moved closer to Katie. "But then again..." He shrugged.

Seth tried to rein in his temper at their banter. He'd resigned himself to his new job as a horse shit scooper, but he wasn't about to clue either of them in on his decision. He'd make their lives as miserable as they were making his. "I'm freezing my ass off here. If you want me to work, I've got to go shopping to get some warmer clothes."

"Gets mighty chilly out here the way the wind whips across the fields. The farm always feels ten degrees colder than the rest of Indiana," Katie said, obviously hoping to lighten the mood. Seth just glared at her.

She took a few strides toward him, crossed her arms over her chest, and stared up at him. "Where'd you get that outfit? Saks Fifth Avenue? Those clothes probably cost more than the last horse I bought. If you wear those around the barn too long, you'll trash them."

Seth closed the remaining distance between them in two steps. He leaned over her to emphasize his superior height and measure whether she intimidated easily. "I hate the crap they sell at Saks. I get all my clothes at Armani."

Her eyes threw enough sparks to light a fire. "You look like a smart guy to me, so I'm assuming you wore that stuff on purpose to make me or Ross mad. I mean, you did know you were coming to a barn."

"Look, lady—"

"Katie. My name's Katie."

"Whatever. I've had the worst couple of days of my miserable life. I've got two suitcases of clothes that look exactly like what I'm wearing. If you don't think this'll work, send me back. We can say we tried, and we can both go back to our lives." He gestured with his thumb over his shoulder toward Ross. "Matlock here can take me home, I can get my money, and we'll call it a day."

"Seth, that's not happening," Ross replied with a shake of his head. "Katie, give me a list of what he needs. I'll head back to town and get some warm clothes for him. He can stay here with you. We can meet back at the dorms later."

"Fine. Let's go into my office." She motioned for them to follow and led the way inside.

The barn had looked huge on the outside and was just as large inside. A wide tarmac aisle ran the entire length of the building. Stalls lined both sides and the smell definitely screamed "horse."

Swinging metal gates opened to allow animals and people access in and out of each stall. The horses all dangled their heads over their gates and nickered at Katie as she walked by. Seth took in her happy reaction and tried not to smile. She almost seemed more comfortable around the horses than she did with people.

They reached the center of the barn. Katie opened a small door across from some large bath stalls and invited the two men inside.

Her office was spartan. As he followed Katie inside, Seth glanced at her gray metal desk. Slips of paper, several pairs of black gloves, some yellow protective glasses, and a white helmet stenciled with some intricate green designs littered the desk's worn surface.

Ross stopped just inside the room, leaned his shoulder against the doorframe, and stared at Katie. It dawned on Seth that Ross couldn't seem to keep his eyes off her. Remembering the man's body language in the Chicago law office, and noticing that Ross constantly tried to get closer to her, Seth realized the lawyer had developed an infatuation with the trainer. Seth didn't have any claim on her, but the notion of Ross staking one made his stomach knot. He tried to push the uncomfortable thought away.

A tiny bed covered with a colorful patchwork quilt rested against the longest wall directly under a small window. He pushed on the mattress and the bed frame let out a complaining squeak. "You keep this here for afternoon... *naps*?" He caught Katie's glance and wiggled his eyebrows. Her eyes threw fire again, and Seth had to turn away not to smile at her reaction.

"Hang on a minute, Remington. You've got no right—" Ross began before Katie stopped him with a wave of her hand. Seth watched them lock gazes for a moment, and then Ross nodded. A flash of jealousy shot through Seth at their ability to understand each other so quickly and so well.

An oak dresser stood nearby, but the only other pieces of furniture were the desk and chair Katie used. A dormitory-sized refrigerator covered in a small pile of clean dishes occupied a corner. Some clothes dangled from hangers lined up along a metal pole suspended from the ceiling with baling wire. This was more than just her office. The bleak room was her home.

A bathroom was accessible through another door, but when he peeked inside, Seth saw nothing more than a toilet, sink, and a small shower stall.

The only form of entertainment appeared to be a small stereo poised on the dresser next to a fairly large stack of CDs.

"You live here?" Seth asked. When she looked up at him and nodded, couldn't believe it. "And you're happy here?"

Katie nodded again and smiled that alluring smile he'd seen in Chicago. "I *love* it here. I'm close to my horses."

He shot her an incredulous frown so she'd know he didn't believe her. Women hated places like this. He wondered if she'd relocated here simply to make his ordeal more difficult to endure.

Seth shuffled through the CDs on her dresser.

"Feel free to have a look around," she said, her voice dripping with sarcasm.

He glanced back at her. The heat in Katie's eyes could melt metal. She might sound calm, but behind that gaze lurked a temper she couldn't hide. A hot temper. He amused himself by pushing a few more of her buttons. "Not like there's much to see." Seth continued to sort through her music.

Katie produced a pad of paper and a pen from one of the ancient desk's drawers. "Let's see. Did you bring jeans? A warm jacket?" Her eyes dropped to his ruined loafers. "Boots?"

Seth shook his head. She sighed and began to scribble out a list.

"What size shirt?" she asked without looking up.

"Large. I'm always... *large*."

"Yeah, yeah. That's what they all say," she added without taking her eyes off the paper, but she couldn't hide the blush spreading over her cheeks.

Ross chuckled and shifted his bulk to the opposite side of the doorframe.

Seth busied himself sauntering around the small room to study the dozens of pictures tacked to the walls.

Each photograph showed a group of happy people standing by a horse with one of those rickshaw things hooked up to it. Although taken at many different tracks, the pictures had one thing in common—Katie proudly smiling while holding onto the animal's bridle. That wide smile, that tousled red hair. She made quite a sight.

There was nothing truly extraordinary about her looks. Her red hair might be special, but he usually preferred buxom blondes like Kirsten. Why the strange attraction? Working as hard as she obviously did, Katie had developed a tight body. But he'd seen better. Perhaps it was her eyes—those large emerald eyes. Or her freckled nose that creased whenever she smiled. Or even her cocky, no-nonsense attitude. She was unique, and that fact alone made her attractive.

Ross took the list Katie offered. "Seth, you want to look at this? See if you want to add anything?"

Seth turned his attention away from the pictures. "What I *want* is to go home."

Watching her lips draw thin and her eyes narrow, Seth quickly realized Katie had reached her limit. "And what your father wanted was for you to grow up. I don't like this any more than you do, but we both need to make the best of it."

Ross smiled and nodded his approval, which only served to piss Seth off a little more.

Katie smiled back and waved the lawyer away with her hand. "Go on, Ross. Go shop. I'll finish here and get him to his dorm. You can meet us there after lunch."

"Fine. I'll catch up with you at the track." Ross made a quick exit from Katie's tiny room.

She was already on her feet, pushing the chair back to the desk. "C'mon, Rookie. I've got to finish filling water buckets then we'll head to the track."

"Right behind you, Boss. I'm just dying to shovel horse shit." Seth knew he was baiting her, but he simply couldn't resist the temptation. She disappointed him when she ignored the remark and didn't rise to the challenge. The woman was all work and no play.

Striding down the aisle of the barn, Katie stopped at a hose wrapped around a metal hanger and attached to an old-fashioned spigot. "You're going to stay in the dorms close to Chris."

"Who's Chris?"

"Chris Harris. He works for me. You can catch a ride with him in the mornings. I took over some of my furniture so you'd have a few things in your room." She flipped on the faucet and hauled the hose from stall to stall, filling the large buckets hanging just inside each gate.

Seth watched her work. He figured he should probably offer to help. It was his job now after all. But he wasn't going down without a fight.

Katie went about her chores with practiced ease, looking back to stare at him with almost each step. "Hard work won't kill you, you know."

"Never said it would."

"I won't feel sorry for you."

"Didn't ask you to."

She laughed at that.

"All right. What do I have to do?" Seth finally asked.

Katie became all business so quickly, he felt like he had to catch his breath to keep up.

"Check the water buckets at least twice a day. Best times are when we feed in the morning and at night. When it gets warmer, you'll check them more often."

Seth stood at attention, clicked his heels together, and saluted. "Twice a day. Yes, ma'am, Boss."

Katie rolled her eyes and moved the hose to the next stall. "And Jack likes to dunk his hay in his water, so you'll have to clean his bucket every day."

"Who's Jack?"

"Monterey Jack. Third stall on your right. See the names?"

Seth's gaze followed to where she pointed out the small plastic plates mounted on each stall with the horse's name printed across. "Monterey Jack? Why would you name a racehorse after cheese?"

Katie laughed. "Trainers don't name them. The breeders or the owners do. And, yes, some of them are terrible. I like the funny ones best."

"What's your favorite name?"

Without any deep thought, she responded, "All Night Long. Obviously named by an overconfident man."

"Sounds more like a woman's idea to me. A guy would have named him No Foreplay Necessary." He glanced over at her, surprised she was blushing again. In this totally uninhibited world, he didn't know women did that anymore.

She pointed to a large green and white dry erase board. "That lists what each horse is doing for each day of the week."

Seth took his time walking over to take a look. He didn't want her to think he was too interested in anything to do with the horses, so he pasted a bored expression on his face.

The top of the board carried a silhouette of a shamrock and the words "Murphy Stables." The rest showed a calendar grid with the names of horses scribbled in and a letter entered for each day of the week. "What's 'J'?"

"'J' is jog. Chris or I usually take 'em three miles or so," Katie replied as she moved the hose to the next stall.

"And 'S'?"

"Stand. The horse just stays in the stall. That's for Miss Daisy. She popped a gravel."

"I beg your pardon?"

"Popped a gravel." Katie entered the stall and crooked her finger at Seth to join her. She picked up the mare's hoof and pointed to a small wound. "A stone got caught in her hoof and has to work its way back out."

"Sounds painful."

"I imagine it is." She put the horse's foot down gently, patted the animal's neck, and exited the stall. Seth followed close behind. "While she's healing she'll stay in her stall. You'll have to make sure you keep the hoof clean. I'll show you how. We also need to give her some attention so she doesn't get too bored and sour."

"How many letters have you got?" Seth walked back over and stared at the confusing green board. He'd never seen a Day-Timer for a horse before.

Katie continued her no-nonsense explanations as she went back to filling buckets. "'O' is outside. Put the horse in one of the corrals for most of the day if the weather is good. 'T' is train, and 'R' is race. We've got two in qualifiers tomorrow morning. You can just watch and get the hang of things."

Good God, he was getting tired of feeling stupid, especially over something as absurd as horseracing. "Okay, I'll bite. What's a qualifier?"

"A sort of practice race that proves a horse is ready to race and good enough to be competitive. They can't race at Dan Patch or any track until they qualify. The qualifiers are Saturday mornings." She never stopped moving, shifting to yet another stall. "We'll take two horses over tomorrow. Once real racing starts, nights get a little crazy. I always seem to pull the thirteenth. Those nights will be late."

"The thirteenth?" Seth had an awfully hard time speaking her language. Was there a damned dictionary for all these stupid terms?

"The thirteenth race, the last race most nights. Post time comes around eleven."

Katie glanced up at Seth as he stared at the board, looking a bit overwhelmed. She continued to wonder if she'd made the wrong decision in taking on the burden of supervising him. The man's knowledge of horses and harness racing was nothing more than a blank slate. Then it dawned on her—that was Seth's problem. All of this was brand new to him.

She chided herself for not being more perceptive in remembering her world wasn't well known to very many people. She needed to give him time to adjust. *Patience, Katie. Just like your grandpa had patience when he taught you.*

Katie turned off the spigot, wrapped the hose back around its hanger, and walked over to Seth. She put her hand gently on his arm. "I'm really sorry about your father. I was so shocked yesterday, I forgot to tell you. He was a nice man."

Seth just nodded. She thought she saw him swallow hard, like he had a lump in his throat.

"This isn't what you're used to," she continued. "It's all so new. I'll teach you, Seth. Just stick with me."

Seth knit his brows and stared at her for a moment before his eyes suddenly softened and the tension he'd held in his shoulders since his arrival relaxed. He appeared genuinely touched at her concern. "Thank you," he whispered.

"I know this'll be a huge adjustment. If you need me to explain something, please ask. I'd rather you ask than try to fake your way through—especially when we're racing. If things aren't rigged right, it can be dangerous... even deadly."

"Dangerous? Deadly?"

At least she'd finally gotten his full attention.

"Drivers are going thirty miles an hour on nothing but a light-weight metal sulky while they're straddling the butt end of an animal that weighs a thousand pounds. If any of the harness is rigged wrong, it could cause an accident."

The look in his eyes told Katie that Seth was finally starting to catch on. "I used to work around race cars, so I understand dangerous. I promise. I'll ask for help when I need it."

Katie ushered Seth out of the barn, closed the big door behind them, and led the way to her truck. "Let's go to the track."

Chapter 5

She should have seen Seth's angry reaction coming. The dorms really weren't much to look at.

He stood in the middle of the room, his nose wrinkled in obvious disgust. "You know, I'm not sure what's worse. The size or the smell. What did they clean this place with anyway? Something scented with dirty sweat socks?"

Katie waited in the doorway next to Seth's suitcases, watching him glance around his new ten-by-ten painted cinderblock home. The worn but comfortable chair and a small chest of drawers she'd donated joined the twin bed the track provided. He probably didn't notice that the warm green of the chair matched the soft blanket she'd put on his bed. No doubt he saw nothing more than Salvation Army rejects. She bristled at the thought.

Katie had sacrificed the furniture from her own room, imagining after the major changes he'd been put through, he probably needed things that felt like "home" more than she would. Some of her sheets and towels were stacked neatly on the bed next to the fuzzy blanket she'd brought for him to use.

Although she was accustomed to living in a similar dwelling, the pinched expression on Seth's face made it plain he'd lived in much more comfort.

Katie figured some people might feel sorry for the guy. He had, after all, been snatched from the lap of luxury and thrust into what many people would consider a hovel. Everything about his manner told her he considered this a step down in life, a giant step. But this was her world, and she was fiercely proud of it. She wasn't about to allow Seth to look down on her or any of the other people at the track. It might not be his choice of a lifestyle, but many people lived here, thrived here.

"Showers, washers, and dryers are down the hall. Here's your key,"

Katie said as she extended her palm to him.

Seth took the few steps necessary to cross the room and reached to grab the key. He arched an eyebrow when she curled her fingers to keep him from taking it.

How can I make him understand?

"I need you to know something from the get-go. You may not feel like you belong here, but you *are* here. You're just going to have to learn to adapt. It'd be nice if you learned to like it. But, hell, I don't want to push my luck. I'll be happy with some simple courtesy."

"I'm not polite?" Seth asked with an irritated tone as he put one hand on his hip and rubbed his forehead with his other.

Katie's frustration grew by the second. "You know, you're acting like a big fat snob."

Seth shot back an angry scowl; Katie wasn't the least bit intimidated, glaring right back at him. "You've done nothing but turn your nose up at everything since you got here."

He might feel her lifestyle was repugnant, but that didn't matter to her in the least. People often looked down on horsemen, assuming they were drawn to the track for the gambling or to avoid a more difficult job. She shook her head at the notion that horsemen didn't work hard. Pure and simple ignorance.

"Seth, this is a way of life for these people. You need to treat them with respect. Your father was a horseman. Remember? He loved these animals as much as everyone else at this track does. You can't keep acting like this is all... beneath you. If you can't get along with the other horsemen, it reflects on me." Katie took a long glance around the room. "I know this dorm isn't the Drake, and this town isn't Chicago. But it's your home for a while. Think you can stop acting like you're being led to your execution?"

Watching emotions shift on his handsome face, Katie wondered if he would eventually realize he had been laying the griping on way too thick. She wasn't a whole lot happier about the situation, but he was only stuck at the track for one racing season. Just nine months. And then he could return to being Seth Remington again. Whoever that really was.

Seth finally plastered a Cheshire cat smile on his face. "I'll be good, Boss. May I have my key now?"

Katie slowly uncurled her fingers, but she still didn't trust him. She wasn't exactly sure what possessed him to do so, but he extended his fingers and placed them on her bare wrist. Stroking a slow path from wrist to palm, he paused for several suspended moments before he tried to snatch the key. His caress unnerved her so much, she dropped it.

Both quickly bent down to retrieve the key, and their heads collided with an audible thud. Katie sprang back up, rubbing her sore forehead with her fingers. Seth plucked the key from the floor before he did the same.

"You're hazardous to my health," he complained.

She hated that he made her feel so clumsy. "You're not the greatest addition to my world, either." She couldn't understand how this man could make her stomach do somersaults with something as simple as a touch. *You're twenty-six, Katie, not thirteen. Get him out of your head.* She fled the room to put some distance between them.

Seth followed her to the hall, grabbed his suitcases, and haphazardly tossed them into the room. He slammed the door, giving her a naughty-boy grin.

She shook her head at him and sighed. "C'mon. Let's go find Chris."

* * * *

"Katie!" a booming voice called as soon as they reached the dormitory's front door. "This the new guy?"

Katie turned around to meet a tall, sturdy young man with light brown hair who didn't appear to be more than a teenager. She greeted him with a hug, and Seth was shocked to discover their embrace made him uncomfortable.

Katie made the introductions. "Chris, this is... um... he's... um... crap."

Chris chuckled. "Crap, huh? Nice to meet you, Crap."

Ross clearly hadn't told her about the nickname. Seth laughed, extending his hand in greeting. "It's *Crash*. Crash Reynolds."

Katie stared back at him, eyes wide with surprise. "Crash? You're *Crash*?" She started to giggle. "Who came up with that name?"

"My friends back home." Seth shot Katie a scolding glare when she continued to laugh. She sure didn't seem properly chastised. She didn't even look as if she was trying to stop.

"Not exactly a great name around horseracing," Chris commented with a shrug. The young man shook hands with Seth. "I'm Chris Harris, Katie's second."

There it was again. That foreign language. "Second?"

"Sorry. Katie told me you were green. I'm her second trainer."

"Why does she need a second trainer?"

Chris glanced at Katie for a moment as if to see if she would explain. She was wiping tears away with the heels of her hands and taking deep breaths, trying to stop her giggle fit.

Seth doubted the boy always deferred to her. Intimidation couldn't be her strong suit. Hell, she was so short her head barely reached Chris's shoulder. How much danger could come from such a tiny package?

Chris finally looked back to Seth. "Most good stables have enough horses, it takes two trainers to get the work done. Katie bounces ideas off of me too. Why are you learning to be a groom?"

"My father was pissed at me for wrecking a car."

Katie had seemed to be getting herself under control, but laughter suddenly consumed her again. It took her several long moments to regain her composure enough to speak. She held up her hand, tucking her thumb to show four fingers. "Four. You wrecked *four* cars," she squeaked out, barely above a whisper.

"How did you—" Seth began to ask.

"Ross told me."

That asshole. "Ross Kennedy needs to learn to mind his own damn business."

Katie took a couple of deep breaths and finally settled down. "*Crash* is here for one of my owners. The man wants his son to learn about racing from the inside. Wants him to get his hands dirty."

Chris appeared to accept the situation without undue curiosity, and Seth wondered if all racehorse owners had eccentric demands.

"If I can help with anything, let me know," Chris said to Seth.

"Thanks," Seth replied, trying to prove to his new employer he really could be polite. "I'm sure I'll need your help. A lot."

Chris turned to Katie. "Do you need me to ship in tomorrow?"

"No, thanks, Chris. *Crash* can help me bring them." The corner of her mouth twitched like she was about to break out laughing again. She bit her bottom lip for a second and seemed to regain her poise. "I'll just need you to help jog in the morning. For the qualifiers, you can warm them up and paddock the last one."

What the hell was "paddock"? Seth simply listened to her talk, fervently hoping he'd catch on to the lingo soon. He was no better than a tourist and his new situation reminded him of a trip he took to Italy as a teenager; he couldn't understand any of the conversations surrounding him.

When his stomach rumbled and complained at its empty state, he figured the notion of hunger was probably universal. Surely they would both understand the word "lunch."

"Any place to get something to eat around here?" Seth asked.

"Track kitchen is that way," Chris replied, pointing to a green building across the large parking lot. "You two want to eat? I could join you. I haven't had lunch yet."

Katie nodded enthusiastically. "I'm starving. We can catch a bite before we go back to the farm."

The three left the dorm and walked across the grounds.

The kitchen seemed to be the track gathering place. People in sturdy, warm work clothes packed the tables as they contentedly munched on their meals. Seth waited in line and watched as a couple of older women took orders. The menu listed almost every type of food he could imagine. Hamburgers, pizza, and just about anything that could be deep-fried. The place smelled of fresh baked cookies, homemade fried chicken, and cigarette smoke.

Several televisions broadcasting all types of racing from tracks he'd never heard of were mounted on high shelves. The biggest surprise was the self-service betting machine in the kitchen. He tapped Katie on the shoulder. "You guys bet on your own horses?"

Katie and Chris both laughed before she replied, "I don't bet much, but everyone else at the track does. We're not racing yet this season, but these guys will bet on anything with odds. Standardbreds, Thoroughbreds, greyhounds. And some are pretty good at it."

Chris chuckled, pointing to a stack of discarded betting slips. "And some aren't."

They placed their orders, but when the time came to pay, Seth opened his wallet and found three dollar bills tucked inside. The stack of gold and platinum charge cards and the well-used ATM card had been handed over to

Ross Kennedy before they'd left Schaumburg. *Shit, I forgot!* He hoped Katie didn't see his frightened reaction when it dawned on him that he'd entered the ranks of the officially poor.

It appeared nothing escaped her notice. "Until you get on your feet, Louise here will run a tab for your meals," Katie said as she handed several bills to the gray-haired cashier and nodded at both their trays. "Anything else you need, let me know. I'll float you some cash, and we'll sort it out with your first check."

After the ladies gathered their lunch orders, Katie, Seth, and Chris took their trays and sat down at a table with several men deep in an animated discussion. Katie and Chris joined in the conversation without missing a beat as Seth simply listened and tried desperately to keep up. By the time they'd finished eating, he'd figured out they had been discussing an unscrupulous trainer they all knew who was now working at another track.

At least that's what he thought they were discussing.

Katie gathered all of their trash and threw it in the nearest can.

She takes care of people. The woman had talked to Chris in a motherly fashion instead of a boss's tone. *So why doesn't she use kid gloves with me? Hell, the woman gives me nothing but attitude.* A crooked smile crossed his lips. *I like attitude.*

Katie glanced out the window, quickly turned back to Seth, and pointed to Ross. The lawyer stood by the dorms with several sacks from a local department store littering the ground around his car's trunk. "Ross is back. Want to go look at your new wardrobe?"

"Oh, yeah. I'm just *thrilled,*" Seth replied before remembering her warning about his behavior.

Katie narrowed her eyes but said nothing.

"Sorry." At least her pretty eyes grew soft again when she heard the apology. He held the door open as they left as an act of contrition.

Katie led Seth to where Ross waited as Chris excused himself and disappeared into the dorms.

"Did you find everything?" she asked, stooping to peek into a sack.

Ross nodded and a sly smile formed on his lips that made Seth wonder what kind of mischief was coming his way. "All of it." Ross leaned down to pick up a bag. "Let's put this stuff up."

They each grabbed a remaining package and headed into the dorm.

After the bags were moved inside and dumped on Seth's new bed, Katie told him to get changed so they could go back to the farm. She walked out with Ross, closing the door behind her.

Seth took his new clothes out of the sacks to see what Ross had purchased, but when he looked over the garments, he fervently hoped they had both experienced a simple problem with communication. That would be the only reasonable way to explain the ghastly clothing.

There were several pairs of the ugliest blue jeans he'd ever seen with material so thick and stiff it could probably rival plywood. Ross had also bought an Elmer Fudd hat. *I'm supposed to wear that?* He shook his head at some plaid flannel shirts, thick socks, and a one-piece dark gray jumpsuit lined with flannel quilting. It looked like something a demented serial killer would wear. *Matlock probably had a hell of a time picking this shit out.* The whole ensemble was completed with less than fashionable black work boots. The only comfort he took in the situation was knowing none of the Boys' Club members would ever see him dressed like a construction worker.

Once he changed, Seth met Katie at her truck. Ross and his impeccable Lexus had disappeared. The smug lawyer wouldn't have the thrill of seeing Seth looking like "Old MacDonald." Another thought shot into his head causing Seth's heart to skip a quick beat. He was stranded. His last tie to Chicago, to his real life, had vanished.

Shit!

He swallowed the panic and refused to show her any weakness. He sure didn't want Katie to see any of his apprehension and think she'd earned a victory.

"Is this acceptable?" Seth asked as he twirled around to show her his transformation.

She nodded and grinned in obvious satisfaction. God, he liked her smile. Those soft pink lips. Her glowing green eyes.

Maybe being around Katie would make this place bearable.

"Much better," she said with a decisive nod. "You've got to admit, it's a lot warmer than what you had on. We'll get you some cooler shirts for the summer. I'm having some made for the stable. Getting 'em embroidered with my logo."

"Why are we going back to the farm? Aren't we racing here tomorrow?"

Katie nodded and fished a keychain out of her pocket. "Yeah, but I need to get the horses that are turned out back into the barn. You can stay here, but I figured you'd want to see how things worked." She unlocked the passenger door. "Normally, I'd probably tell you to go take a nap. Once we're racing and you start to paddock, you'll need one."

"Didn't Chris say the paddock was a building?"

"The paddock is that big building over there," Katie explained, pointing to an enormous barn standing next to the large racetrack. "The horses have a certain time they need to be there before they race. When a groom works on a horse on race nights, we call it 'paddocking' the horse. You stay with it from start to finish. You take care of its equipment, get it on the track, and take it off. If you win or get specialed, you follow the horse to the test barn."

"Test barn? You mean like drug tests?"

"Yep. Winners always get tested." She walked to the driver's side of the truck as she continued to explain. "Other horses get taken there for special reasons or at random. It'll all make sense soon. Just stick with me, and I'm sure you'll get the hang of it."

Katie opened the door and settled herself behind the wheel as Seth crawled into the passenger's seat.

"I like that you ask questions, Seth." She stopped talking and snorted a small laugh. "Sorry, I mean *Crash*. Asking questions shows you care." Starting the truck, she threw it in gear and steered toward the exit.

"I doubt you'll be saying that for too long. You'll probably get sick of me. Pops used to say I had to know everything. My favorite word as a kid was 'why.'" The weight of his loss suddenly descended on him. Seth turned his head to stare out the window and watch the scenery drift by without any real interest. He didn't want her to recognize what he felt, didn't wish to share his sorrow with her.

Seth had never had a chance to deal with his father's passing. At first, he'd been occupied with the funeral arrangements and the paparazzi, and then he had been too busy being transplanted into this new life for the grief to take hold. Now he felt like he was being smothered by a pillow. He sure as hell didn't want to cry in front of Katie.

After a few minutes, Seth regained some composure and turned back to focus on the road ahead of him. He would have to leave his grief behind and get on with playing his part in this ridiculous charade.

Katie glanced over at him. "I know you're still hurting, but it'll get easier. You might not believe it now, but it will. One day, the memories will make you happy, not sad."

Seth's feelings were still too raw, and he reacted before he thought. "What the hell do you know about how I feel?" The words came out much harsher than he intended, and he wished he could take them back. When he finally pushed aside his anger and looked over at Katie to apologize, she didn't appear the least bit offended by his rude outburst.

"Trust me, I know. I lost both of my parents when I was six. I didn't understand it until I was older though. I miss them at the strangest times." Her face suddenly changed to a half-smile that reached her eyes. Her memory must have been pleasant. "The first time a horse I trained won, I cried like a baby the rest of the night 'cause they weren't there to share it with me. Then, it dawned on me; they *were* there, looking down on me. I just know it."

He didn't know what to say in response. *You up there, Pops? Mom? Are you both watching over me?*

"I understand, Seth. Really, I do." She gave a curt nod as if to reaffirm her own conviction.

"You must think I'm an asshole. I'm sorry."

Her sly grin told Seth he was correct—she did think he was an asshole. He'd have to show her otherwise.

"No need to be sorry."

The truck quickly covered the few miles between the track and the farm. Seth had been too angry to take a good look around the first time he'd been there, but now he noticed more than a barn and some corrals.

An oval track extended behind Katie's barn. The surface was smaller than the racetrack at Dan Patch Raceway, although still impressive. A second barn the same dimensions as Katie's stood on the opposite side of the practice track, and all around were dozens of fenced areas full of horses. "You own all of this?"

Katie laughed. "God, don't I wish! I'd give my right arm for my own farm. I rent some stalls and my room from the owner of the place."

They hopped out of the truck, and Katie began to teach Seth his first task—how to move the outside horses back into the barn. When she explained the halter and lead rope and the mechanics of the chore, he figured it was as simple as leading a dog on a leash. Then Katie let him lead his first horse.

She slipped into a corral and whistled at the large brown horse. The animal came right to her. After she attached the green lead rope to his halter, she motioned for Seth to join her. After she gave him several tips that he didn't pay much attention to, Katie let him try on his own.

Seth attempted to lead the horse the short distance from the corral to the barn, but the horse ended up dragging him instead. He tried talking to the horse and jerking on the lead rope. He even went so far as to put his body in front of the contrary animal, but the horse didn't stop until it reached a large patch of untouched grass running alongside the barn where it dropped its head and began to graze.

Seth figured watching him struggle with the horse had to be highly entertaining to Katie. After a few frustrating minutes of losing the wrestling match with the horse, he was grateful when she took pity on him. She marched over and took the rope out of his hands.

"Watch," she ordered like a drill sergeant. Seth couldn't tell if she was scolding him or the animal. Katie took the lead rope and gave a sharp tug to get the animal's attention. Once the horse raised its head from the grass it had been munching, she gave the rope another quick snap and led the now compliant animal to the barn.

"I'll be damned," Seth said, putting his hands on his hips. "How'd you do that?"

"Horses are smart. They can tell when you're afraid of them. I'm not. They respect me 'cause I let them know who's in charge. Don't feel bad, you did fine for a first time."

From the conciliatory smile on her face, he knew he looked as frustrated as he felt. He appreciated her care in trying to suppress her amusement so it didn't appear she was laughing at him, even if she had every right to do so.

"Yeah, right," he mumbled, following her into the barn.

"Be patient, Seth. It takes time to get the hang of things."

Chapter 6

Seth's morning flew by in a whirl of activity. Chris had awakened him at a ridiculously early hour, and they'd grabbed a quick breakfast in the track kitchen before heading to Katie's farm. From the moment they arrived, she had rattled off instructions, and Seth felt like he'd spent most of his time in perpetual motion. He'd tried to follow Katie and Chris as they exercised the horses, turned several out to pasture, and prepared two horses for qualifying races, but he found himself constantly in the way.

As Katie worked with one of the horses, she'd identified each piece of tack and made Seth repeat it back like a parrot. Just about the time he was getting the names correct, Chris came into the barn, leading another horse with a completely different set of harness. Seth frowned. What the hell was all this stuff? He'd never felt so ignorant in his life.

They'd fed the horses in the barn, and set out for Dan Patch Raceway.

Katie pulled her truck to a stop beside the guard shack at the back entrance and rolled down her window. Reaching over, she clipped a small plastic badge onto Seth's collar. He lifted the ID to get a better look at it and wasn't happy with the grim-faced picture staring back at him.

The photo on the groom's license made him look like some deranged man who had just been named as one of the F.B.I.'s "Ten Most Wanted." Of course, he hadn't been in the best of moods the day he'd arrived in Indiana. Ross had stopped at the race office on the way to Katie's farm, insisting Seth fill out the paperwork for his track ID badge. He barely remembered posing for the mugshot while the lawyer had talked with the race officials.

When he noticed the name "Reynolds," the word only served to make Seth a little more irritated. He let the badge fall back onto his chest. *I'm a Remington, damn it.* He couldn't wield the power his name had always represented. Hell, Katie couldn't even get the name right. He didn't think she even realized she called him "Seth" every time she talked to him. If she slipped and used his real name in front of the wrong person, the paparazzi might find his trail. He wondered what his fate would be if they unmasked him before the end of the racing season.

Ross had never discussed any contingencies, and Seth sure didn't want to end up starting all over again in another stable in a different state with a different boss. His anger ebbed as he decided Katie's difficulty in using his alias pleased him immensely. To her, Seth wasn't "Crash Reynolds," he was just himself.

That morning as he shadowed her during chores, Seth realized he would have a hard time keeping this woman out of his thoughts. She was bossy, opinionated, and stubborn—qualities that weren't common to the spoiled, over-privileged women he'd always known. Every one of Katie's traits appealed to him, as did those gorgeous eyes and that alluring smile. Seth shook his head to stop the dangerous path his thoughts traveled. No woman was worth that much money.

"Hi, Katie," the guard called as he passed her side of the truck. He walked to the back of her trailer. As he came back around, he wrote a few things on his clipboard and then returned to Katie. "Who you got with you today?"

"Hi, Joe." She nodded toward Seth. "New groom." The man gave Seth a small wave. "Master Criminal and Heathcliffe are in the trailer." The man made a few more notations on his log and backed up a few steps.

"You're cleared. See you when you leave," he said as Katie rolled up her window and eased her truck past the checkpoint.

Seth's gaze wandered the fence surrounding the track. Tall as the enclosure at any prison yard and topped with barbed wire, it assured the only way in or out was the road leading to the security shack.

"Why the Gestapo?" Seth asked once they'd left the guards behind.

"These are expensive animals, and they race for quite a bit of money. The guards help keep them under close watch. Stops any monkey business."

Katie parked her truck beside one of the dozens of barns lined in military rows. Seth found the sheer magnitude and complexity of the place overwhelming. People and horses moved about as parts of a well-choreographed and oft-rehearsed dance. Much to his surprise, he realized this was a dance he wanted to learn. Some of the people led horses toward the paddock; some came from it. Several pairs of grooms walked around the barns, leading blanketed horses.

Before he could ask about them, Katie offered an explanation. "They're cooling down after a race or training." The woman could read his mind. The entire time they'd worked together that morning, she'd anticipated almost every one of his questions and often answered them before he'd given his curiosity a voice.

After Chris met up with them and Katie unloaded the horses, they each grabbed an animal's lead rope and a large plastic bucket stuffed with a blanket and walked the horses toward the paddock. Seth hefted the heavy canvas harness bags and followed along.

They passed the small guard post, the only entrance to the fence-enclosed paddock. Katie and Chris gave the names of the horses once again and recited their memorized license numbers without even breaking stride. Seth had to set the harness bags down so he could look at the license Katie had clipped on his shirt. He decided to memorize the number quickly so he didn't have to keep gawking at his hideous likeness. Turning to hurry after Katie, he collided with a woman heading in the other direction.

Seth immediately dropped the bags to grab the woman by the waist before she fell. "I'm so sorry. I wasn't looking where I was going." He set her back on her feet.

The woman looked up at him, her lips forming a coy smile. "You can knock me over any time, Handsome." Seth almost laughed aloud at the notion any woman would find his work clothes and Elmer Fudd hat attractive.

He reached down to retrieve the harness bags. "I've got to go." Seth made haste to follow Katie and Chris. If he lost them, he wasn't sure he'd ever find them again in the crowd of people and horses.

The flirtatious woman wouldn't let him escape that easily. "What's your hurry? You haven't even told me who you are." She stepped directly into his path and reached out, trailing her fingers along his forearm.

Seth recognized an intimate invitation when he saw one. He looked the woman over for a minute to see what she offered. Slim and athletic with long brown hair that curled around her shoulders, she wore a little too much makeup. She was attractive in an earthy sort of way, although not nearly as pretty as Katie.

Seth tried to step around her. "Excuse me, I've got a qualification."

"You've got a what?" The brunette laughed. "Oh, you mean a qualifier."

He bristled at the rudeness. He might be ignorant, but he wasn't stupid. *Not dating you with that attitude, Princess.*

"Boy, you're green. How'd you find your way to the track? Most of us are born into this."

"Long story. Did you see which way Katie Murphy went?" Seth glanced around at the multitude of extraordinarily busy people he didn't recognize.

She put her hands on her hips and gawked at him. "You work for Katie? Well, I'll be damned."

"Excuse me?"

"Katie and I are old… *friends*," she replied with an odd sort of smile. "I'm Rachel Schaeffer."

"I'm... um... Crash Reynolds." After the number of times he'd picked up and put down the harness bags, he didn't bother dropping them again to shake her hand.

She didn't seem offended because the invitation remained plain in her eyes. "If you tell me which horse you're paddocking, I'll help you find it. The races are posted over on that big board by the race office. Even numbered races on the right side of the paddock, odd on the left." She pointed to the two long aisles of stalls with small metal plaques indicating the race number and postposition for each animal.

"I don't know which horse. Katie didn't tell me its name. Oh, wait. There she is." Seth shouted at Katie as she came toward them with swift, angry strides. "Hey, Boss! Sorry. I lost you in the crowd. Your friend here was going to help me find you, but you forgot to tell me which horse I'm working with."

Seth caught the distrustful glances exchanged between the two women. Rachel was not only rude, she was a liar. Whatever she and Katie had shared had obviously been far from friendship. For a few long, awkward moments, the three of them stood without saying a word.

Katie finally broke the stilted silence. "Hello, Rachel." The words were icy and said with a clenched jaw. She turned back to Seth. "We need to get moving." Making an about-face, Katie stalked back up the left side of the paddock.

"Nice to meet you, Rachel. I need to go," he said, turning to run after Katie.

"I'll be seeing lots more of you," Rachel called after him.

Seth found Katie in front of one of the paddock stalls. Jerking one of the harness bags out of his hands, she hung it on the stall door, unzipped it, and started pulling out equipment. She didn't say a single word. Earlier in the morning as they'd worked around the barn, she'd chattered nonstop, showing and explaining everything to him time allowed. Now she picked up the tack, marched into the stall, and deftly equipped the horse, ignoring Seth entirely.

She impressed him when she had the horse ready in less than five minutes.

Chris walked up and handed a plastic pad to Katie. It was the last thing she put on the horse, her fingers nimble as she threaded it under the harness.

"What's that?" Seth asked Chris.

"Postposition marker. Big number is the postposition. Small one is the race."

Katie turned to Chris. "He's ready. Get the jog cart and warm him up." Chris dutifully followed her orders.

Grabbing the bridle hanging on the stall door, Katie stopped for a moment and just stood staring at the mulch-covered floor. Seth watched her face as several emotions played across her features, wondering at the dramatic change in her mood.

"There aren't any rules about who you can or can't see."

He couldn't tell if she was talking to him or to herself, but he saw her teeth tugging at her bottom lip the second she fell silent. He didn't understand. "Katie, did I do something wrong?" The huge transformation in her demeanor bothered him, as did knowing he might have caused her emotional shift.

She shook her head. "No, you didn't do anything wrong. Just drop it. C'mon, Criminal." She patted the gelding's neck. "Time to qualify."

Katie slipped the bit into the horse's mouth, secured the bridle, and led the animal from the stall. Chris brought the jog cart up from behind and helped her hitch it to the harness. As he slipped onto the seat and tucked the reins under his legs, she led the animal out of the paddock. Moving out onto the track, Chris urged Criminal into an easy jog.

Seth was fascinated by the movement of the horses. Despite the numerous animals on the track traveling in different directions, everyone seemed to know how to steer clear of collisions. Some trucks dragging large metal grates across the track's surface joined the spectacle, and he expected the horses to leave. Wrong. They all managed to share the track without a problem.

Chris completed a pair of laps and guided his horse off the track. Katie caught Criminal's bridle and led the gelding back to the paddock. Seth watched as Chris managed to deftly remove the jog cart even though the horse remained in motion, wondering if he'd ever be able to do anything except get in the way. He followed Katie and Criminal back into the paddock.

She removed the bridle, replacing it with a halter. Without taking off the harness, she tethered Criminal in the stall and covered the gelding with a blanket. The job done, Katie hurried away.

"Where we heading?" Seth fell in step beside her, thinking the woman never seemed to stand still for even a second.

"Master Criminal is warmed up. We've got to get Heathcliffe ready now."

Seth shook his head and laughed. "Master Criminal? Heathcliffe? I'm never going to get over the ridiculous things people name their horses. Don't people ever call them something like Bob or Joe?" Katie smiled, making Seth grateful to see her eyes sparkle again.

As she crouched to put a piece around the horse's lower front leg, Seth squatted beside her to watch. He decided to try and impress her. "Tendon boot. Protects and supports the leg." Katie glanced over and grinned. Then she grabbed another piece and put it on Heathcliffe. "Knee boot. Keeps him from hitting his front knees together."

"You might learn this yet." She stood up; he followed. Katie grabbed the black leather harness. "How about this?" she asked as she slipped the harness on the horse's back and held up an attached vinyl loop through which she threaded Heathcliffe's thick tail.

"Crupper. And the towel hanging off it's called a shit towel. How am I doing, Boss?"

Katie gave him an enchanting smile. "Great. Better than I expected." She shoved some equipment at him. "Since you're doing so well, you can help me with the hopples."

Chris arrived with the jog cart, and Katie stood back and let Seth lead

Heathcliffe to the chute. "Don't forget the overcheck," she yelled after him.

Seth hoped he'd surprised her by knowing exactly what she was talking about and that he'd figured out how to correctly attach the long strap running from bridle to harness.

Hopping onto the jog cart, Chris steered the horse onto the track. Seth walked back to Katie and waited for her to acknowledge his achievement.

"You did all right for a newbie," Katie said.

Seth decided she wasn't one to liberally apply praise. "Thanks. I think. How long until Criminal runs?"

"He'd better not run!"

Seth scratched his head, feeling like he'd been in a perpetual state of confusion since the moment he'd met Katie Murphy. "I thought he was here to run a qualifier."

"Standardbreds don't run or gallop, Seth. They race at a pace or a trot. If they run, they're pretty much out of the race. It's called 'making a break.'"

Good God, was he going to learn enough to stop sounding ignorant? "Okay, I'll bite. What's the difference between a pacer and a trotter?"

"It's got to do with what their legs are doing." She used her fingers to show him how the animal's legs would move. "Pacers move both legs on the same side of the body at the same time. Trotters move opposites. You know, right front leg and back left leg at the same time. I like pacers better. Trotters break more often than pacers."

After Heathcliffe was safely back in his paddock stall, Katie invited Seth to stand at the fence to watch Criminal qualify. They stood side by side as a blue Cadillac sedan pulled out on the track with two large metal gates tucked neatly along the doors.

As the rest of the horses finishing their warm-up laps vacated the track via one chute, the qualifying horses entered using the other. Seth watched as Chris led Criminal toward the track. The young groom chatted with a tall, thin man buckling the chinstrap on his maroon and gold helmet.

"Who's that?" Seth asked, nudging Katie with his elbow.

"My driver—Brian Mitchell."

"Isn't he using your cart?"

"He uses his sulky... his race bike. It's a lot lighter and a lot faster than a jog cart. Carts are safer, but they're way too heavy to race with." She pointed back at Brian. "Look how much closer he sits behind the horse on a bike." Brian Mitchell practically straddled the horse on the much smaller metal sulky.

The sedan opened its gates, spreading them wide as if they were wings. The Cadillac started to move, going faster and faster as the seven horses picked up their pace and took their positions. Katie pointed out the numbers on the gates indicating which horse should be in which postposition. By the time the line of animals and drivers reached the starting point, they were in full motion. The car sped ahead and the gates retracted. The qualifying race was on.

Katie told him it didn't really matter who won, but Seth had a hard time not cheering for her horse. She reminded him they just needed to complete the mile in two minutes or less to qualify the animal, but he got caught up in the movement of the horses as they circled the track. The race was poetry in motion.

The finish line, Katie called it the "wire," stood in front of the grandstand. The field changed as the drivers jockeyed for position. Some of the horses that had been trailing at the start of the stretch kicked into a higher gear, passing the animals that had led most of the race.

"I can't see who won!" he shouted at Katie.

She smiled, a dimple creasing her right cheek. "On race nights we watch the finish over there." She pointed to a huge television set mounted above a small building standing between the two chutes leading to the track. "They don't broadcast qualifiers. I'm not worried though. I'm sure Brian got him through in under two. You take Criminal back and strip the equipment. I want to talk to Brian."

Ten minutes later Katie caught up with Seth and helped him bathe the horse. After covering the animal with a blanket, she tethered Criminal in a stall and then they repeated the whole procedure with Heathcliffe.

The second race was even more exciting than the first.

* * * *

As they drove back toward the farm, Katie glanced over at Seth and grinned. Poor little rich boy. He was so worn out, he'd fallen asleep. His chin sagged against his chest, and she hoped he wouldn't get a stiff neck.

Seth couldn't possibly know how pleased she was with him. She'd never seen anyone take to the job so quickly—even people born into the racing world.

Chris decided to stay at the track to catch his customary afternoon nap, but Seth had told Katie he felt it was his job to get the animals home before he rested. She liked the dedication he'd shown, and his insistence on helping her with Heathcliffe and Criminal boded well for the long season. He certainly wasn't the nuisance she'd expected him to be.

She wondered what Seth's reaction would be when he saw a real race. He was already hooked, and she couldn't wait to watch him on opening night.

Despite the fact that both of her horses easily qualified, Katie couldn't push aside a feeling of apprehension, although it had nothing to do with Seth's work. Her anxiety grew from her reaction to him. The man's smile intoxicated her, and Katie found herself constantly staring at his mouth. She couldn't take her eyes away from the soft curve of his full lips. And there was that absolutely heavenly butt.

You saw how Rachel looked at him. To her, he's fresh meat.

"Why's that my problem?" she whispered to her traitorous mind.

You saw how he looked at her too, came the silent reply.

"He's just a fickle guy." She glanced over at her sleeping groom. "Just like all the rest of them."

Katie decided she would stop being stupid and decidedly adolescent. She would concentrate on her job, and quit thinking about his... *smile.* He appeared to be learning very quickly and seemed capable of all she'd asked of him. *That's what's most important.*

Maybe things would work out well after all. She forced herself to ignore the nagging notion of Murphy's Law.

Chapter 7

"You're dead meat, Remington."

Seth knew the explosion he should have been hearing in Katie's voice was being carefully contained. She obviously didn't want to spook Monterey Jack as Seth steered him around the practice track. But he knew she meant every hushed word.

As he drew closer, Seth saw her standing on the chute with her hands on her hips, her lips drawn so thin they'd all but disappeared, and her cheeks flushed cherry-red. He decided to take the animal on another leisurely lap, knowing there would be hell to pay. Her eyes blazed a threatening promise, but he could swear he saw panic hiding within her anger. Flashing her an enormous grin, he gave a small wave as he drove by.

"You're toast." Katie's words hung in the air. Not a shout, but he knew the warning remained there nonetheless.

"I know," he called over his shoulder.

After he took his victory lap, Seth steered Jack to the chute. Katie immediately seized the bridle and led the horse back to the barn. As soon as the animal was cross-tied, she turned to Seth in a rage. "Who told you could take this horse, or *any* horse, on the track? This isn't some Girl Scout camp pony, Seth. It's a racehorse. A valuable racehorse. What would Jack's owner say if something happened to him while you were jogging him?" She took a bullying step toward him. "Do you have any idea how dangerous driving is? What in the hell were you thinking?"

Seth held his ground and tried not to grin, but it was hard to feel threatened by such a small woman. Even an enraged one. "I was thinking that Chris has been showing me how to drive when you're working on the books or getting supplies. *And* I was thinking I've watched you every day for weeks and might've picked up a pointer or two." He took off Chris's helmet, shoved his driving gloves inside, and dropped them onto a closed trunk. "I wasn't training, Boss. Just jogging."

Katie seemed to be having a hard time spitting out the words. "Just jogging? Like that's all there is to it!" She whirled around and returned to the horse. As she worked around Jack, she started thinking aloud. Seth found it an endearing habit. "What if Jack spooked? What if he took the bit in his teeth and made for the road?" She hefted the harness off the animal's back and shoved it at Seth. "Did you even think that you could've gotten hurt?"

"Of course I thought about that. I told you, Chris has been working with me," Seth replied as he calmly wiped down the harness and hung it on a large hook by Jack's stall. "I wasn't taking stupid chances, Katie."

She snorted an incredulous laugh and patted Jack. "Thinks he's a driver now," she said to the horse, nodding toward Seth.

While he understood her anger over his brazenness, he was more than a little surprised to hear some genuine concern in her voice. Amused by her apprehension, Seth couldn't resist the desire to tease her. "You were really worried about me, weren't you? Aww... That's so sweet." Seth walked over to her and batted his eyelashes like a flirtatious girl.

Katie's face flamed, her nostrils flared slightly with each breath. He wondered for a moment if she'd slap him. She sure looked like she itched to. "I just don't want to get sued. That's... that's all."

Seth wasn't about to let the highly amusing situation drop. Trying to look as cute and as childlike as possible, he clasped his hands together, put them under his chin, and he pouted his lip. "If I got hurt, would you be sad? Would you come visit me in the hospital?"

"I'd... I'd just leave you on the track where you fell. I'd kick you to the side and train around you if I had to," Katie sputtered in reply as she busied herself taking off the last of Jack's equipment. He could tell she was rattled because she haphazardly threw the knee and tendon boots on the ground instead of habitually putting each piece away.

Seth put his hand over his heart. "You wound me, fair damsel. Can't I get one bit of kindness from your sweet lips?"

Katie rolled her eyes, but the twitch in the corner of her pretty mouth showed she was having a hard time not smiling at him. "Can we get back to work?"

"That's all you're about, isn't it?" He bent down to pick up the discarded equipment.

"Damn straight. What else is there? I've been working with horses since I was a kid. It's what I do, who I am."

"Don't you ever have any fun? Life doesn't have to be so serious all the time, you know." This woman's personality fascinated him. The only women he knew were all like Kirsten—young, pretty, rich, and very selfish. They'd sooner die than ruin a manicure working on an animal. Katie was young and awfully pretty, but she sure didn't live like the Kirstens of the world. He respected the fact she made her own way rather than living off of a wealthy family.

Like I always did, he thought with some remorse.

Seth wasn't sure the word "selfish" was even in Katie's vocabulary. She gave her time freely to anyone who needed her. Whenever they found themselves in the paddock, he knew someone would come to ask for her help with a problematic animal. Plus the patience she'd shown in teaching him about his new job was nothing short of phenomenal.

"Answer me truthfully," he said, dropping the sarcasm. "What was the last thing you did that made you laugh?"

"I went to a lawyer's office and he told me I could turn some rich guy into a groom. Trust me, it was a laugh riot."

"Ha ha. Very funny, Boss. You can't even remember, can you?" Seth wasn't about to let the matter drop. He would make sure she had some fun even if it killed her. Or him.

"I don't know. Maybe you're right. I can't remember, I guess." She flipped her hand at him as if dismissing the whole notion. "I have a good time working with my horses, and I'm sure I'll have a good time on opening night. It's usually a lot of fun."

"So it's a date. You and me on opening night. You can teach me about race strategies. Maybe it's a lot like car racing."

Katie stopped working and gaped at him open-mouthed for a long moment. "A date? You're asking me on a *date*? Have you lost your mind? What about the clause in the will?"

Seth laughed and patted Jack's neck. "It's just an expression. I'm not asking for a lifelong commitment. Can't we both just relax for one night? Maybe have a few laughs?"

She appeared to be giving his suggestion some serious consideration.

"Okay. I'll go. But not on a date. We'll go with Chris."

"Aren't you a little old for a chaperone?"

Katie shrugged. "Call him whatever you want, but if Chris doesn't go, I don't go."

"Fine. I'll take what I can get. Will you let me start helping jog the horses? You can pick up teaching me where Chris left off. I know I can do it, and I promise not to take any stupid chances." Taking care of the animals hadn't turned out to be as unpleasant as he had imagined. Hell, if he was honest, he'd have to admit how much he enjoyed his time at the barn. But Seth wanted to take a more active role. If he had to do this job, be in this barn, he would do it on his own terms.

Katie stared at him, cocking her head as if trying to read his expression. He hoped she realized he made the request with genuine desire to learn rather than a way to not have to muck out stalls. She finally heaved a resigned sighed. "It's against my better judgment, but we'll give it a try." She wagged her index finger at him. "But... just jogging. No training. I don't want to see you going for any speed. Those horses better barely break a sweat. Do you think you can handle that and play by my rules?"

"Absolutely."

As he led Jack toward the bath stall, Seth savored his small victory. He knew he'd be training in no time.

* * * *

Opening night at Dan Patch Raceway heralded the arrival of spring to the Hoosier state, and those in attendance were rewarded with a warm and clear April evening.

Everyone in the paddock had kicked into a higher gear. People scurried about dragging race bikes and jog carts. The drivers stood near the front of the paddock waiting for the horses to be brought forward. Constant announcements droned on the public address system.

Katie pointed out some familiar faces, and Seth noticed the work clothes had all but disappeared. "See the colors?" she asked.

"Colors?" He gazed around at the people in one-piece nylon jumpsuits. "You mean the funny outfits?"

"They're not funny; they're called 'colors.' Drivers and trainers have to wear them on race nights."

"Why haven't I seen yours?"

"Only trainers and drivers wear them, and only on race nights," she explained. "They're expensive, and we'd ruin them if we wore them all the time."

Seth gave her an amused smile, picturing Katie in her colors. "Let me guess. Your colors are... oh, I don't know… green?"

"Like I'd be caught dead in anything else."

He put a finger on his lips as if contemplating an important question. "Hmm. I'll bet you have... *horseshoes* on your colors."

"Shamrocks!" He couldn't help but laugh at her reaction. She blushed and slapped him on the arm. "Where's Chris? He's got to be better company than you."

Seth pointed to the bulletin boards hanging by the race office where Chris stood appearing to be engrossed with the postings. "Said he was checking on tonight's entries. And what's wrong with my company?"

"It tends to be a little... aggravating." Her sweet smile and the laughter in her eyes told him she didn't really mean it.

Seth saw another horsemen dressed in blue colors hurry to Chris and begin an animated discussion. After a few moments, Chris jogged over to Katie and Seth. "Emergency paddock," he said. "I've gotta bail on you two tonight. Sorry."

Katie gave him a friendly pat on the back. "It's okay, Chris. Fifty bucks is fifty bucks. Go for it."

Seth caught the implication. "You mean I'll get fifty bucks when I paddock?"

"Yep," Katie answered. "You've got Jack tomorrow, and his owner usually hands you cash on the spot. Plus a fifty bonus if he wins."

"Gotta run," Chris called to the couple as he turned and raced toward one of the paddock's long halls.

Katie stood craning her neck, looking up the aisle. "There's Brian and Sam." She grabbed Seth's hand and dragged him over to the stall where the couple worked. He was a bit surprised by the intimate action, and he wasn't sure she even knew she was hanging onto him. But it pleased him to feel her small, cool fingers entwined with his as she introduced her new groom.

"Brian, Sam, this is Seth... Crap!" She stomped her foot. The frustrated look on her face was so comical, Seth tried not to laugh at her predicament. "No, not *Crap.* Crash. Crash Reynolds."

Would she ever get the alias right?

"He's my new groom. Crash, this is Brian Mitchell and his wife, Sam. Um... Samantha."

That had to be the strangest set of introductions Seth had ever heard.

He wouldn't have recognized the driver, having only seen Brian with a helmet and work clothes. Dressed in his maroon and gold colors, not a dark brown hair out of place, Brian appeared more than ready to take center stage.

Standing next to the tall, thin driver was a petite woman with honey-blond hair braided into one long plait. She wore a maroon sweatshirt with an embroidered gold logo over her heart that declared "Mitchell Racing."

As Brian and Sam stopped their work to greet him, Seth had to stare down at Katie's tight grasp on his right hand. She'd have to turn him loose before he could offer it to his new acquaintances. After a few long seconds, he realized Katie wasn't even aware she had a death grip on him or that she was nibbling on her lower lip. He finally nodded at the couple. "Glad to meet you both," he offered, hoping they wouldn't think he was too rude.

"Crash? Yeah, right. What's your *real* name?" Samantha asked, her eyes boring holes through him.

Katie answered before Seth could. "Let it go, Sam. We can talk about it later."

Sam studied Katie for a moment then looked back at Seth, the suspicion still plain in her quizzical eyes. "Fine. Nice to meet you too, *Crash.* What brings you to Katie's barn?"

Seth felt Katie's sudden tight squeeze of his hand, and he wasn't sure exactly what she wanted him to say. As he tried to form the right choice of words, Katie beat him to the punch again. "His father used to own horses. Crash wants to see racing from the inside. It's just for one season. That's all."

Brian and Sam exchanged a glance that told Seth the couple could communicate without words and that neither had believed a single word Katie had uttered. Brian spoke for them both. "Interesting." He drawled out the word for a couple of seconds, making Brian sound like Sherlock Holmes assessing a new murder. "If there's anything we can do to help, just holler. I drive most of Katie's horses, at least when one of my own isn't in the same race."

"Brian is the best driver at the track. He's going to win the driving title this season," Katie added with obvious pride.

The man actually blushed at her compliment. How nice to see a good athlete without an overcharged ego. "So you don't own all the horses you drive?" Seth asked.

Brian shook his head. "I wish. I have a small stable I train, and I drive my own horses and some for other trainers who don't like to drive in races. Like Katie."

Sam turned to Katie. "We're still on for Monday?"

Seth's curiosity got the better of him. "Monday? What are you doing on Monday?"

Katie's eyes shifted to Sam. "Nothing." The two syllables held a note of entreaty.

Sam casually smiled at Katie's less than subtle appeal and appeared more than happy to supply the information. "We always go out on Mondays. Since we race Wednesday through Saturday, Monday nights are our weekend, our Saturday nights. We get some dinner, suck down a few beers, and—"

"And that's it," Katie interrupted as her eyes shot daggers at Sam before glancing back at Seth with a tacit plea for mercy.

He granted her no quarter. "And what?" He stared into Katie's eyes and gave her a broad, smug smile.

Sam winked at her husband. "We dance and then we—"

"Don't do it, Sam," Katie warned, but Sam laughed it off with a wave of her hand.

"We karaoke. All of us. It's a hoot."

Katie tensed, but Seth gave her fingers a gentle squeeze.

"Katie sings a mean Barry Manilow," Sam added.

Katie groaned and rolled her eyes. "Thanks a lot, *Samantha*."

"You're welcome, *Kathleen*," she replied in a voice dripping in honey. "Crash, you going with us?"

"Wouldn't miss it for the world," he replied, smiling at Katie again.

So she could have fun after all. Katie Murphy singing in a bar. Who would have thought?

Katie and Seth made their farewells, and she still clung to his hand. He loved the feeling of her hand in his, loved that she tightened her grip ever so slightly whenever she smiled.

He glanced down the aisle, taking in the horsemen and their colors when he suddenly locked eyes with Rachel. She sashayed up the aisle, swinging her hips, and didn't stop until she came face to face with the couple. Katie released her hold on him as if his hand had become molten lava.

Obviously expecting to be acknowledged, Rachel glared at the couple.

Katie's jaw clenched. "Rachel."

Rachel gave an arrogant laugh and looked right at Seth. "Hello, Handsome. I figured you'd be sweeping some other girl off her feet." She drew the corners of her lips down in a counterfeit sad expression. "Aw... I guess its Katie's turn." She glanced over at Katie. "But I got him first."

Katie winced at the comment.

The tension between the two women grew heavy, and Seth figured Katie and Rachel shared something important and clearly divisive. His customary curiosity overrode his common sense. "What's with you two? Did one of you steal the other's boyfriend?"

When he saw the pained response to his words on Katie's face, Seth realized his mistake. His jest obviously hit too close to the truth. Rachel had hurt Katie.

Damn. You've got a big mouth, Remington.

Rachel finally broke the uncomfortable silence. "Something like that." She turned to Katie, a haughty smile spreading across her lips. "Don't you have anything racing tonight?"

Katie's eyes gazed at the bark lining the floor of the paddock as she slid her fingers into the back pockets of her jeans. "Not tonight." The woman's inability to hide what she felt would make her a terrible poker player.

"That's a shame," Rachel replied. "But it's mostly big time horses tonight, so... I'm not really surprised."

Green or not, the statement made things crystal clear. Katie had told him the majority of the races on opening night were for some of the best horses in the country. While she had some fast horses in her stable, none of Katie's animals were at the top of the game. Seth refused to let Rachel's insult pass without a comment. "Our horses just didn't get in tonight."

He wondered if Katie heard the annoyance in his voice and took any comfort from his defense—even if what he said wasn't necessarily the truth.

She pleased him when the corner of her mouth rose enough to give a hint of her dimple as she gently placed her hand on his arm. "We need to go up to the grandstand now." Looking back at Rachel, Katie seemed to be able to muster some bravado. "You know, I'm sure Brian is looking for you. Aren't you paddocking for him tonight?"

"Shit. Gotta run," Rachel replied as she jogged away.

"Thank you," Katie said as soon as Rachel was out of earshot.

"For what?"

"For calling them *our* horses."

"I did?" That took him by surprise.

"Yes, you did. Admit it, you like the horses."

He couldn't stop his smile. "All right. I like the horses. Happy now?"

"Very. C'mon. Let's go up front." Katie took his hand again and led him toward the crowd in the grandstand.

Chapter 8

"That's Dan Patch," Katie said as she pointed out a picture in the grandstand's exhibit devoted to one of the most famous horses in harness racing history. "He set a bunch of world records in the early 1900's. I don't think he was ever beaten in a race. He's kind of like our version of Seabiscuit or Secretariat."

Katie also showed Seth the big board where the photographs of the season's leading drivers would be posted each week once the statistics were compiled. "Brian's always top three," she bragged. "He'll win the whole show this year."

"It's just like car racing," Seth grumbled. "I'm never..."

"Never what?"

"Never... mind." He couldn't admit to her the irresistible pull of that leader board and how the display reminded him he'd never really been "good" at anything. "Let's go see the horses."

Katie and Seth joined the rest of the crowd as they moved to the short fence separating the track from the spectators. The first post parade began, and the starter's car, with its wings neatly folded, led the line of horses and drivers past the crowd as the race announcer introduced each entry.

"Who's the chick riding the horse?" Seth asked, pointing to the far side of the track. A woman wearing a red jacket and a black protective riding helmet sat atop a big palomino, vigilantly watching over the bustle of activity around her.

"That's the outrider. She's there to protect the drivers if there's an accident. Sometimes she helps lead temperamental horses to the starting gate. Her job is weeks of boredom interrupted by minutes of sheer terror."

"Sounds like you know the job."

"I've done some outriding."

"How long have you been around horses?" Her revelation about outriding, small though it was, made Seth recognize just how little he knew about Katie Murphy.

"Since I was six." She chuckled for a second. "I guess that makes twenty years. Damn, it went by fast."

"Who taught you all the things you're teaching me?"

"Grandpa—Kevin Murphy. He's great with horses."

"That explains your obsession with green and shamrocks. It's the Irish in you." Seth chuckled. "Probably accounts for the temper, too."

"It might account for mine, but what about your short fuse? Come by it honestly?"

He had no choice but to acknowledge the truth. "I'm definitely Sterling Remington's son. How many stables have you worked for?"

"After I learned from Grandpa, I worked with Jacob Schaeffer."

The name rang a bell. Or two. "Oh, yeah. The guy who has your two-year-old." Although Seth wondered about a connection to Rachel Schaeffer, after the little scene in the paddock, he wasn't about to ask if Jacob and Rachel were related.

Katie nodded. "Yeah, he's got my colt. Let's go watch the horses warm up."

Seth helped her elbow out a place in the crowd gathered along the whitewashed fence close to the finish line to enjoy the first race of the season. The drivers jogged their horses around waiting for post time, and he wondered what was tumbling through their minds. Did they get the same adrenaline rush, the feeling of flying he always enjoyed behind the wheel of a fast car?

People headed into the grandstand only to return with betting slips like the ones he'd seen in the track kitchen. Across the track, a large illuminated tote board near the finish line constantly updated the odds, betting pools, and possible payoffs.

The drivers were called to post as the Cadillac spread its gates. After working up to racing speed, the field of nine horses was released as they passed the crowd.

It didn't take long for Seth to be hooked. The first race that night did the trick. The rush of watching horses and drivers vie for a win coupled with Brian's photo-finish victory turned him into a fan for life.

As Brian drove the victorious horse back toward the grandstand, he waved for Katie and Seth to join him.

"Winner's circle," Katie said, pointing to the area next to the fence strewn with silk flowers.

Seth finally understood the photos covering the walls of Katie's room. *Winner's Circle.* Remembering the multitude of pictures, he realized once again how good she was at her job.

Katie shook her head at Brian, declining her friend's invitation, but she gave Seth's back a small push to let him know he was welcome to go.

He shook his head as well and turned back to Katie. "When one of our horses wins."

How could something as simple, as normal as her responding smile cause his mouth to go dry? How could something as common as the touch of a hand, as natural as the lacing of their fingers, make his breath catch in his throat?

Sweet Jesus, Seth. You've gone way too long without a woman.

He found himself in uncharted territory, adrift in a sea without a buoy in sight. Katie wasn't just another woman, another potential conquest. She wasn't a one-night stand. This woman called to a part of him he hadn't known existed. This lure more than physical, more than sexual. So much more than lust.

Seth instinctively tightened his grip on her hand and led her back toward the grandstand. "Let's get something to..." He let the thought hang unfinished between them because he was flat broke, and while he wanted to buy her dinner, he couldn't. This predicament was exactly what Sterling had wanted. Seth Remington—officially working class. Even worse. Poor.

Katie watched him with eyes much too full of worldly wisdom for someone her age. She allowed him a few moments of reflection, plainly understanding what churned through his mind. Seth assumed she would throw him a lifeline like she had many times in the track kitchen, but the notion that he constantly needed her help hurt his already wounded pride. He broke the silence first. "If I had any money, I'd buy you a nice dinner, but I can't—"

"I've got an idea," she interrupted. "They've got hot dogs for a buck on Saturdays."

"Sounds good," he replied before realizing he still didn't have any cash. "I don't suppose you'd float me a dollar?"

"Didn't I tell you?" Katie flashed him knowing smile. "It's payday. You can buy your own hot dog."

She pulled a wallet out of her back pocket and retrieved a yellow check she handed to Seth. He took it from her and just stared at the payment for a moment. It was less than he'd paid for the last shirt he'd bought, but the amount didn't matter. This was his. Not handed to him and earned by someone else's labor. *His.*

"Don't worry. Ross set up an account for you at the bank with a branch next to the track, so they'll cash it without a hassle. I already settled your tab at the kitchen." When Seth didn't say anything, she started to talk more rapidly. "Ross always has your money deposited in my account. I can pay you in cash if you want, but I'm not very good at keeping track of things if I don't use checks." A mild, apologetic blush spread over her cheeks. "I'm good with horses, not at bookkeeping."

"It's not that," Seth finally replied. "This is the first paycheck I've ever earned."

"I should've docked you for all the extra feed. I swear I've never seen anyone spoil horses as much as you do. They're all getting too fat to race."

Seth leaned his shoulder against her in a playful shove. She returned the gesture. Seth took her hand, and they walked to the grandstand together.

Katie footed the bill, and the two ate hot dogs and shared an enormous soda before they settled into some abandoned seats to watch more races. He enjoyed the simple meal more than any expensive cuisine he'd ever tasted. "How much does a trainer get when a horse wins?" he asked.

"The purse gets divided between the first five finishers. Everyone else is an 'also ran.' That means they get..." Katie blew a raspberry and smiled.

Seth shook his head. "That's not what I asked. What would *you* get?"

"Whatever the horse wins, its trainer gets five percent. So does the driver. This race, I'd get two-hundred for first place."

"If it's an also ran?"

She blew another raspberry. "Trainers have to make sure their horses are ready to race, or they make zilch at the track."

Katie picked up a discarded program, her eyes scanning a page as her finger traced the entries. She suddenly gave the program a hard tap. "This one is easy. Brian's going to take it."

"Show me how to read that thing," Seth begged, looking at the pages of jumbled names and numbers. After a few minutes of instruction, Seth caught on. "Boss, can you float me...? What's the minimum bet around here?"

"Two dollars," Katie replied as she wiggled to reach for her wallet. "But that's all I'm staking you. You lose it, you're out of luck."

"I won't lose it," he promised, taking the bills in hand and sprinting toward the betting windows before the race went to post.

"That's what they *all* say," she commented loudly, eliciting laughter from several close spectators.

Seth returned with his red and white ticket, but he refused to divulge his wager to Katie. The race was close, but as Katie predicted, Brian's long-shot horse managed to win the mile.

Seth checked his ticket several times to be sure he was seeing it correctly, waiting with baited breath to see the results of the race posted.

"Official" illuminated on the infield tote board, and Seth watched as the payoffs were displayed. Just to be contrary, he made a somber face and shook his head.

Katie must have noticed his expression when she offered a conciliatory comment. "Most people lose. Don't feel bad."

"Oh, I don't feel bad at all. Hell, I just wish I'd bet more."

She appeared confused, which made Seth extremely happy. For once, *she* was off balance.

"I don't understand," Katie said, knitting her brows.

Seth tossed her a smug grin. "If I'd had four bucks on them, I'd be in four figures."

"*Them*?" He savored her puzzled expression, the small tilt of her head, the sudden dawning of understanding. "Let me see that ticket!" She grabbed for the betting slip.

Seth began a teasing game of "keep away" as she leaned over her seat to try to snatch it from his hand. The more she struggled, the harder he tried to keep it out of her grasp.

Katie jumped up, obviously frustrated and way too stubborn to ever admit defeat, and faced Seth as she leaned against him, bracing herself on his chest with her left hand. Her right reached for the betting slip he continued to keep as far behind his head as he could manage even as he realized his actions were nothing more than an adolescent ploy to draw her closer.

Standing on tiptoe, Katie finally caught the paper. She opened her mouth, probably preparing for a victorious comment, and then suddenly snapped it shut. Her face flushed a deep shade of red. Not only was Katie practically in his lap, but her chest pressed into Seth's face. "I'm sorry," she mumbled as she tried to get her balance.

"Oh, you're quite forgiven," he replied with a chuckle. Settling his hands around her waist to steady her, he hoped to keep her near for a moment longer. The whole episode had been the best thing that happened to him in a very long time—winning the bet included. As she moved away, awkward and apologetic, he could still make out the lingering sweet flowery scent of her. A subtle smell that eclipsed even the finest of perfumes. For the first time, Seth seriously wondered if any sort of loophole existed in the ridiculous "all business" clause of his father's will. Perhaps he wasn't entirely barred from pursuing her.

What the hell are you thinking, Remington? The instructions had been clear enough, and his inheritance was obviously more important than any fleeting attraction. Even if it was an extraordinarily strong one.

Taking a good look at the betting slip she now held in her hand, Katie's eyes went wide. "You bet a trifecta?"

"Sure did. First, second, third in correct order. All long shots, too. That two dollars you floated me just turned into five-hundred and eighty," he arrogantly replied, plucking the ticket from her fingers.

"Beginner's luck," she reasoned as she crossed her arms over her breasts.

Seth laughed as he patted her shoulder. "Hell, with the way things have been going lately, I'll take any luck I can get. You want your two bucks back?"

"I'll take it out of your pay." Katie checked her wristwatch. "It's after ten, and we've got an early morning. I'm exhausted, so I'm heading for home. Think you can find your way back to the dorm, Rookie?"

"Oh, I think I can manage." He waved the ticket in her face. "With this I might just call a limo." The stunned look on Katie's face told him she thought he was serious. "Don't worry, Boss. Old habits die hard. But let me walk you to your truck. You never know what kind of shady characters are hanging around a racetrack." He winked at her.

After cashing his ticket, Seth counted out half of his winnings and handed the bills to Katie. She sheepishly accepted the money after he insisted they had shared the bet. Leaving the grandstand, the two headed back toward the barn area to Katie's truck.

Once they reached her pickup, both of them stood awkwardly by the vehicle not knowing exactly how to end the evening. Katie finally fished her keys out of her pocket. "I'll see you in the morning."

He reached out as his hands cupped her shoulders before his fingers traced slow, steady trails down her arms. Was she trembling? "I had a nice time, Katie. It's the best date I've had in a long, long time."

She shook her head, but the gesture did little to alter his opinion. "It wasn't a date. Just a couple of barn rats going to opening night races." Her lips shaped a small, hesitant smile. "I'm glad you won us some money."

"Me, too," he said with a chuckle that sounded more nervous than amused, making him wonder at his own odd reticence. She was, after all, simply another woman. "My clothes need washing and I'm out of detergent."

He finally opened her door and watched as she buckled her seatbelt before putting her keys into the ignition. The truck's warning tone began to chime. Although the annoying sound droned on, Seth wasn't ready to let her go. He had to remind himself Katie was off limits, that no woman was worth losing the Remington fortune. And yet, he drowned in an overwhelming desire to kiss her, to find out for himself if those lips were as soft and warm as they appeared. One kiss would indulge his curiosity, and then he could brush this ridiculous adolescent attraction aside.

Besides, how could a simple kiss be against the rules?

Seth leaned in the truck, placing the most gentle of kisses on Katie's lips.

He pulled away to gaze into her eyes, and he saw her confusion. He understood what she felt because he had the same problem. How could such a simple kiss feel so... wonderful?

For a moment, their eyes locked, their lips only inches apart. How easy it would be to drown in those gorgeous eyes of hers. She would be a woman worth knowing well, a woman who would bring passion to everything she did. Katie Murphy wasn't just another woman.

Suddenly, he wanted her. His body was already responding to the mere thought. Tightening, throbbing, demanding. He wanted to know every inch of her, wanted to taste her skin, wanted to feel her beneath him as he eased himself into her soft body. The hunger overwhelmed Seth as it stole his breath away.

He had to stop this. Stop it quickly. Stop it now.

With tremendous effort, Seth eased away from Katie. "Good night," he whispered. He closed the truck's door, pleased he had found the strength to do so, and stepped back into the darkness.

All Katie could do was stare at her hands gripping the steering wheel and wonder what had just happened. The instant Seth's lips touched hers the world had vanished, and for that brief moment, there had been a void. Nothing.

Nothing but Seth.

Every part of her had taken flight, circled the sky, and then landed without grace or style. She had plummeted back from the void, slammed to the ground the moment he'd pulled away.

Over a kiss? A harmless little kiss? What in the hell was wrong with her?

Katie jumped when someone knocked on her window. Seeing Sam standing with her hands on her hips and throwing one of her patented stern frowns, Katie knew she was about to get an earful. She rolled down her window. "God, Sam, you scared the life out of me. What's up?"

"Just wanted to find out if you think he kisses as good as he looks."

"You saw that?" Katie tried to dismiss Sam's concern with a wave of her hand. "It was nothing. Honest. The guy works for me. That's all." Katie couldn't look her friend in the eye. If she did, Sam would instantly recognize her fib.

"Yeah, I believe that one," Sam said, rolling her eyes. "It looked pretty... *intense* to me. What's his story?"

"It's complicated, Sam. I can't tell you more than I already have. He's only here for the season."

Sam leaned in and put her hands on the truck. "Katie, he'll break your heart if you let him. I know guys like him. When they look like that, they don't stick around long. He's just like Mike. I'd think you'd have learned your lesson."

Katie nodded. "I know. Too good looking for someone like me."

Sam shot her an unyielding glare. "That's not what I meant, and you damn well know it. The season's a long time, and there are no secrets—"

"In the barn. I know. I know. I'll be careful. Go on, Sam. I'm heading home." Katie started the engine.

Sam backed away from the truck and waved as Katie drove away.

Chapter 9

Seth looked up from where he crouched next to Miss Daisy. He'd been wrapping her front legs to prepare for trailering her to the track when a black sport-utility vehicle pulled up to the sliding door. A tall russet-haired man walked around to hold the passenger door open for an attractive forty-something woman. They casually strolled hand in hand into the barn.

"Can I help you?" Seth asked.

"No, thanks. We're fine," the man replied as he and the woman walked over to Monterey Jack's stall. They started talking to the animal as the woman stroked the horse's nose and neck.

Seth had a hard time holding his temper when his favorite horse was being fondled by total strangers. He stood up and leaned over the mare's back. "Hey! Leave my horse alone!"

Katie must have heard him from her office because she poked her head out into the hall. Her face suddenly broke out in an enormous smile, and she hollered a greeting. "Susan! James! It's so nice to see you. I'd hoped you'd come tonight." She jogged the length of the barn to meet them.

"You know these people?" Seth asked Katie as he pointed at them with the roll of green elastic wrap he still held in his hand. "They're bugging Jack."

"They *own* Jack. This is James Williams and his wife, Susan. They own some restaurants in Illinois," Katie explained. "James, Susan, this is Crash Rem... um... Reynolds—my new groom. We were just getting ready to head to the track."

Susan turned her attention to Seth, studying his face for a moment. "Nice to meet you, Crash." Her eyes seemed to sparkle with amusement, but Seth had no idea what she found so funny. "Interesting nickname. How did you earn it?"

Seth winced remembering how reckless he'd been. God, that seemed like a lifetime ago. "Let's just say I had a few... mishaps with some cars."

Katie threw him a smile and a conspiratorial wink.

James took a few strides toward Seth and offered his hand. Seth stood up, wiped his own hand on his work pants, and shook the man's hand. Then Seth went back to squatting next to Daisy to finish getting the shipping wraps on the mare. "Which horses belong to you?" he asked Susan as she watched him work.

"Besides Jack, we've got Postage Stamp and Kitty Kat."

Katie came to Seth, put her hand on his shoulder, and gave him a light squeeze. "Seth is paddocking Jack tonight, but I'll be close by." Seth couldn't tell if she was reassuring the owners or him. He was still a little nervous at the notion he would be paddocking for the first time by himself.

"Good," James said. "Hopefully, we'll see you both in the winner's circle. I think Jack has a good chance tonight, I just worry about claims."

"Claims?" Seth glanced up at Katie for an answer. He wondered if he would ever understand everything said around the barn and the track. While he had caught on to a great deal of the racing business, he still sometimes felt like an outsider looking in.

The sudden tightening in Katie's face bothered him. She looked too much like a person about to deliver some really bad news. "Uh oh. Forgot to explain claims to you, didn't I?" Katie's tone reminded Seth of a parent talking to a child. Had they been alone, he would never have allowed it to go unchecked. "I'll tell you about it on the way to the track. Is Daisy ready to go?"

"Yeah. I'll get her in the trailer," Seth replied as he grabbed a lead rope.

After he walked the horse out of the barn, Katie turned to Susan and James. "He's new, but he learns real quick. I wouldn't let him paddock if I didn't have faith in him." James and Susan might be some of the easiest owners she'd ever worked with, but she also knew owners generally needed constant reassurance their trainer stayed on top of every situation.

Susan crooked her finger at her husband, and he bent to listen to her whisper in his ear. A huge smile spread across his face, and he nodded at his wife before turning back to Katie. She felt like she'd missed something important.

"We trust you, Katie," James said as he reached out to pat her on the shoulder. "If Jack gets claimed, we'll be looking for a new horse right away, so keep your eyes open. Or we can go back and reclaim Jack if they leave him in at eight-thousand."

"We'll talk after the race," Katie said to James as she opened Jack's stall and led him to the cross-ties.

* * * *

"What's this claim stuff about?" Seth asked as he buckled his seatbelt.

"It's a way to handicap races, and it's going to piss you off when I explain it, so be prepared," Katie warned. "When I decide an animal's ability, I pretty much put a price tag on the horse. I decide what it's worth, then I put it in a claiming race that meets that price." She put the truck in gear and started for the track as she waited a moment for the information to sink in. He wouldn't like the rest of the story. "Once the horse is entered in a claiming race, anyone with an owner's license can go to the claiming office half an hour before the start of the race and put cash down to buy the horse."

Seth rubbed his fingertips across his forehead, his frustration and confusion obvious. "Buy him? You mean you sell the horse *before* the race? How can you make any money doing that?"

"It's *after* the race. The horse races for the current owner, and once it crosses the finish line, it belongs to the new guy."

She could tell Seth was still confused. He squirmed around on the seat like an antsy two-year-old. "Why would anyone want to put a horse into a race where any bozo can buy it?"

"Not buy it; *claim* it. It's the only way most of the middle to lower priced horses can race. If we didn't classify the horses by their value, then anyone with a really good horse could sweep in and steal every purse. This way you never race your horse any lower than the animal is worth just to win. You have to risk losing it for that price and hope you make some purse money while you own it."

"I don't like it, Boss. You mean I could lose Jack tonight?" Seth asked with clear dread in his voice.

Katie understood exactly how he felt and wanted to console him, but claiming was simply a universally accepted part of horseracing. Seth would understand in time, but she remembered the anguish the first time one of her favorites had been claimed. She simply couldn't make the situation any easier on him. A horseman's first claim was baptism by fire. She did take close notice of Seth starting to form attachments to many of the animals, and that pleased her immensely.

"He's in for eight-thousand, and he could very well get claimed if someone thinks he's worth that much," Katie replied.

"When... when will we know?"

"They announce the claims right after the race."

Katie tried to watch his face while keeping her eye on traffic. "Don't worry so much. Most people who work with horses are good people, Seth. They take care of their animals."

"And you can make money this way?"

She nodded. "You look for good horses to claim and improve, and you hope people leave your good ones alone. Look, you can't choose who claims a horse, but if they want to race it, they have to stay at the track for thirty days. Jack won't go far."

"They can't leave and race somewhere else? Head to Illinois or something?"

"Nope. They've got to stay in Indiana if they want to race, and why claim if you're not going to race for purse money? The thirty-day rule helps keep horses here. Otherwise people might cherry-pick the best and leave for tracks with higher purses."

"I hope they don't claim Jack," he grumbled.

"If they do, we'll watch him."

She saw the understanding suddenly dawn on him. "We can claim him back? You mean we could play the claim game too?"

He was catching on. "If James wants to. Depends on what tag Jack is put in for. Lots of times people move a horse up to a higher price off of a claim so you don't claim him right back the next week."

"I get it. If you want him back, you'll wait 'til Jack is in for the price we lost him at."

"Bingo," Katie replied.

* * * *

Seth worked mechanically as he readied Jack for the race. Claiming a horse still sounded utterly absurd. What if the new people didn't know Jack liked to have his hay sprayed with water or he wouldn't eat it? What someone didn't pack his hooves right? How could anyone take away *his* horse?

He scowled at horsemen who appeared to be eyeballing the big brown gelding too closely. The whole notion of claiming seemed cruel, and he knew he would worry about losing Jack until the animal was safely back at the farm. How could he face this every week?

Katie leaned against the wall several stalls away from where Seth labored, watching him move around Jack. She tried to give Seth enough freedom to work while also assuring herself he'd secured every piece of tack. The apprehension was written plainly on his face, and she couldn't remember ever seeing Seth so open about his feelings. Maybe the guy had a heart after all.

As the time to warm up the animal for the race approached, she slipped into the women's locker room to put on her colors.

She loved driving onto the Dan Patch oval for the first time each year, and she was more than ready to go to work. Just before she stepped out of the changing area, the full-length mirror's reflection of her green and white jumpsuit caught her eye. Katie uncharacteristically looked herself over to check for any noticeable flaws.

Wondering where the vanity came from, she nervously pushed her fingers through the disobedient curls in her ponytail before sternly reminding herself she would be wearing a helmet that would cover most of her hair. Glancing at her colors, she realized they had faded over the years. And there was that small tear on the right hip. Perhaps she'd have to order a new jumpsuit soon. After all, she wanted to look her best for...

"Go ahead, Katie," she scolded herself. "Just admit it." Who did she want impress? The spectators, the owners or drivers? "No," her whispered words affirmed, "not them. Him."

With an exasperated groan, Katie grabbed her helmet, glasses, and gloves and headed back to the paddock.

* * * *

Seth led Jack from his stall, and Katie attached it firmly to the harness. She sat on the cart and tucked the excess reins under her. Feeling like an authentic groom, he proudly escorted his horse to the chute and adjusted the proper equipment before watching Katie prod Jack into his natural pace.

Chris tapped Seth's shoulder. "Will you bring the jog cart over after she's done?"

"Yeah, sure." As Chris turned to walk away, Seth called after him. "Hey, Chris!"

"What?"

"You don't think Jack will get claimed, do you?" Seth asked, hoping he didn't sound too awfully pathetic.

"Doubt it," Chris replied with a shake of his head. "People don't claim off Katie much."

"Why not? She's got great horses."

"Most people who claim want to improve the horse. Who'd be able to improve on Katie?" Chris explained. "But, all it takes is one person and some cash." He shrugged. "Some people have more dollars than sense."

Seth nodded his understanding, and Chris returned to the paddock.

Walking over to the fence, Seth saw Katie pass by after her first lap. He leaned against the top rail, resting his elbows against the whitewashed wood. His eyes tracked her kelly green colors around the enormous oval. It came as a surprise he felt so content watching her ease Jack around the traffic of tractors and horses.

"Most people don't claim off of Katie," he reassured himself before he glanced around, wondering if anyone standing nearby had heard him. Feeling a bit foolish, he kicked the bottom rail of the fence before hurrying to help Katie when she drove Jack to the exit chute.

* * * *

Katie never took her eyes off Brian's bright maroon and gold colors. Throughout the race, she chattered in Seth's ear, explaining the strategies involved.

The ten-horse field pushed into a single line by the first turn. Brian guided Jack into the fourth position and seemed to bide his time. The animals raced through the first turn to charge the long back stretch where their drivers began to maneuver for the second half of the mile.

Brian eased Jack into the outer flow, the driver behind him following suit. As two even lines of five horses made the last turn, they passed the paddock and headed for home.

"Look! He's moving up!" Seth yelled like a spectator in the grandstand.

Katie wanted to caution him to cool a little of his enthusiasm around the other horsemen, but it was damned entertaining to watch Seth's emotions getting the better of him.

"Shit! I can't see!" Seth shouted as the horses moved up the stretch. Katie grabbed his hand and pulled him over to the television. She knew that in his excitement he'd already forgotten she'd told him about it during the qualifiers.

They watched Brian thread Jack through two slowing horses, pulling within striking distance of the leader. Jack eagerly responded to Brian's last call for strength, besting the horse he challenged by one length.

"He did it! We won! Did you see it, Boss? We won!" Seth exploded in an excited cheer. He picked her up and spun in a circle. "Wahoo!"

"C'mon," Katie said when he finally put her back on her feet. She tugged on his arm. "We need to get in the van."

Katie, Seth and Chris piled into the white van that made constant trips between the paddock and grandstand. The driver zipped them to the winner's circle to meet Brian and Jack.

James and Susan greeted them all with smiles and pats on the back. As Brian slowed the horse to a walk, Katie watched Seth grab Jack's bridle and led him triumphantly to pose for the winning photo. They all quickly smiled for the photographer, and then Seth led Jack back out to the track.

Katie had to laugh when she saw Seth kissing Jack's nose and giving the horse words of praise before allowing Brian to drive away. She always did the same thing with all of her winning horses. Maybe she *would* be able to turn a spoiled rich guy into a useful man.

In the van on the ride back to the paddock, Katie explained to Seth what came next. "He'll have to go to the test barn. Let Brian unhook his race bike, then lead Jack over there." She pointed at a fence-enclosed green barn situated a short distance from the paddock. "I'll bring the wash bucket and a blanket."

"Got it, Boss."

"I'll be there as quick as I can. Chris can warm up Daisy."

"What do I do?" Seth asked.

"The same things you do after a qualifier or training. Put him in a wash stall, strip his equipment, bathe him, but then take him to a pee stall."

Seth laughed and shook his head. "Shit towel. Pee stall. What's next? Copulation corral?" His face grew serious, but his tone didn't. "Please tell me I don't have to hold the damn specimen cup."

"Just get him to the test barn, smart ass," Katie answered. She smiled when she supposed she would have to tell him about a breeding shed one day just to see his reaction.

All of a sudden, Seth's expression changed, concern wrinkling his brow. "Did Jack get claimed?"

"They'll be reading claims any minute. Listen to the announcer."

* * * *

It had been a successful night for the Murphy Stable. One win, one second, and no claims. Seth still beamed as much from the win as from the fact Jack had accompanied them back to the farm. He made sure to give the horse some extra grain, a couple of carrots, and a few affectionate pats to show Jack how pleased he was.

Even when Seth and Chris had finally returned to the dorms well after midnight, Seth had been too full of adrenaline to sleep until the wee hours of Monday morning.

Monday. Katie would sing on Monday.

He smiled before he fell asleep.

Chapter 10

"You're going to love this place," Chris said as he eased his truck into the parking lot of a restaurant called The Place. "Great hot wings, cheap beer, and the owner loves horse people."

Seth followed Chris inside and took a good look around. Two large televisions broadcasting sporting events sandwiched a small stage with a large karaoke machine. A dance floor stretched in front of the stage, and several couples danced to the twang of the jukebox's country song. The place smelled of pizza, barbeque, and stale beer.

Seth's gaze wandered the large room until he finally spotted Katie sitting next to Sam Mitchell. *Sam.* Such a masculine nickname for such a pretty woman. Katie glanced over at the door and waved. Seth and Chris joined her at one of the larger tables.

Katie introduced Seth to several people from the track before she turned back to chat with Sam.

Seth ordered a beer from the waitress making the rounds. He tapped Katie on the shoulder. "Can I get you something, Boss?"

"Ginger ale," she replied. He passed the information to the waitress.

Katie stared at him for a moment before she finally noticed. "You cut your hair!" She reached out to brush her fingers across his now bare neck. His skin tingled from her touch. Just when he felt her fingertips begin to move in a caress, she pulled her hand away.

"It was getting too long. It was either a ponytail or a haircut, and I'm sure not a ponytail kind of guy."

"Did you get the picture I left?" she asked with a luminous smile.

Seth nodded as he remembered the winner's circle picture he'd found taped to his dormitory door that afternoon. "Yeah. Thanks, Katie. When did you get it?"

"Picked it up this morning. Photographer put a rush on it for me. Jim is a real gem. Hell, I practically stood over the poor guy's shoulder while he printed *my* first picture." She took the tall glass of ginger ale and a bowl of pretzels from the waitress. "You know, my first win was at Dan Patch."

"You sure I can't buy you a beer?" Seth asked again as he placed his mug on the table. "You know... to celebrate Jack's win?"

Katie shook her head. "No, thanks. I don't drink much."

Most of Katie's friends spent their time in idle conversation as the group consumed numerous pizzas, bowls full of nachos, and several trays of buffalo wings. Chris's age made him the customary choice for designated driver, and Sam volunteered to pick up any slack. With the amount of alcohol being consumed, Seth figured there probably wouldn't be too many others capable of performing the task. After one beer, he switched to soda in case another clear head was needed later in the evening.

The chatting at the table suddenly fell silent. Following everyone's intent glances at the door, Seth was more than a little surprised to see Rachel Schaeffer walking into the restaurant. From the track gossip, he'd gathered she came uninvited and unwelcome by several in the large party. She was hanging all over a driver who Katie said she used when Brian drove his own horses. Josh Piper, he remembered. Katie said he was Chris's friend.

"Hey, Pipe! Over here," Chris shouted as he waved Josh to their table. Rachel threaded her arm through Josh's and accompanied him. Josh didn't even sit down at the table as he and Chris beat a path to the pinball machine. Rachel settled herself in Chris's abandoned chair opposite Seth.

Seth watched Katie's relaxed demeanor evaporate. He could read the tension in her face. She drew her mouth into a thin line, and she stared at her glass. He was about to ask if she wanted to sit somewhere else, but before he could open his mouth, Sam let her thoughts be known. "What are you doing here, Rachel? No one better to do at the track?"

Seth tried to stifle a chuckle by coughing in his hand. The rest of the table wasn't as subtle. A wave of laughter rose from everyone close enough to hear Samantha's remark.

Rachel was clearly pissed. "What'd you say?"

"Nothing," Samantha replied, taking a sip from her soda and rolling her eyes to stare at the ceiling. The sniggers started up again.

"Kiss my ass, Sam," Rachel sneered. "It's a public restaurant." When Rachel caught Seth's gaze, she perked up considerably. "Hello, Handsome.

Wanna dance?"

Seth tried to find a way out of the trap she set. Josh was so engrossed in playing pinball with Chris that he didn't look remotely concerned Rachel now directed all her attention at Seth. No rescue there. He shook his head, declining the invitation.

"Aw, c'mon." She reached out and let her fingers wander over his forearm. "Please? I mean, you did knock me down after all."

The woman wasn't going to let up. Seth glanced at Katie, but she was talking with Sam again. "All right."

He stood up to follow her, and Rachel led him to the dim lights of the dance floor. He wasn't sure how she managed to walk with as much swing as she put in her hips. As he moved away, Seth heard Katie order a beer. He glanced over his shoulder and saw her nervously nibbling on her bottom lip and staring at her empty glass again.

In what appeared to be well-practiced motions, Rachel gyrated around Seth, and it finally dawned on him exactly why she was there. Rachel didn't like to be turned down. He'd become a challenge for her.

"Wanna come back to my room? I'm the floor below yours." She pressed her breasts to his chest and slid her arms around his neck.

"No, thanks." He subtly extracted himself from the unwanted embrace. As the dance continued, Seth kept putting some distance between their bodies, but Rachel constantly closed the gap.

No matter how many times she asked if he'd leave with her, when he declined, she always offered again. Didn't she have any self respect? "I'm heading back to the table, Rachel." He left her on the dance floor. Josh must have noticed she was alone because he left the pinball machine and joined Rachel. Chris returned to the table and reclaimed his chair.

"Who's responsible for those?" Seth asked Katie, pointing to two empty beer mugs sitting in front of her.

Katie shrugged and sipped from a third almost drained glass.

"You drank both of those? That fast?"

She just shrugged again, grabbed a pretzel from the bowl, and nibbled at it.

Rachel slinked back to the table with Josh at her heels. Seth sure didn't appreciate the daggers Rachel's eyes were throwing at Katie. His gaze shifted to his boss. With her head lowered and her eyes downcast, she looked as if she'd just attended the funeral of a loved one.

After several minutes of profuse begging, Chris convinced Katie to dance. The couple weaved their way to an open spot on the crowded floor.

Watching Chris take Katie into his arms as they danced, Seth had an uncharacteristic flare of jealousy. Funny. It never bothered him when Kirsten danced with another guy. No matter how hard he tried to push the feeling aside, the foreign jealousy clung to him like bug splatter on a windshield.

Seth considered simply stalking out to the dance floor and taking Katie away from Chris. Not wanting to appear too rude, too eager, or entirely too adolescent, he decided to wait patiently for five minutes before he would go cut in. Well, maybe four minutes. He looked at his wristwatch and then back at Katie. Three if Chris didn't keep his hands to himself.

Seth had taken a seat close to Samantha, and she turned to him, leaning closer to be heard above the music. "You know, there's history there."

"Where? Oh, you mean Katie and Rachel. Thanks, but I'd already figured that out."

"Maybe. But it's probably worse than you know. Katie's still kinda... fragile. I can tell there's something going on with you two. I don't want you to hurt her by—"

Seth easily dismissing the idea with a shake of his head as he thought about his inheritance. "I'm not going to hurt Katie. Trust me. She's... Well, she's just... not worth it."

Sam visibly angered at the statement, leaning back and sternly folding her arms across her chest. "Katie's worth her weight in gold, you arrogant son of a—"

"No, no. That's not quite how I meant it. I'm trying to say that she'd cost me more than that if..." He shook his head not sure how much he should or even *could* say about his whole unusual relationship with Katie. "Look, just forget it. I'll leave her alone. Promise." He tried to sound sincere, but he also realized he hadn't been able to take his eyes off Katie the whole time he'd been talking to Sam.

Chris tried to show Katie the steps of a line dance, but judging from the amount of beer she'd consumed, Katie's reflexes weren't at their sharpest. Seth lost track of how many times she stepped on Chris's toes. She looked like she was about to give up from sheer frustration.

The jukebox switched to a slow song. Seth jumped up, almost upending his chair, and made his way onto the dance floor. Katie had her back to him. Seth put his hand on her shoulder, spun her around, and immediately wrapped his arms around her waist. Chris smiled at the couple and snuck back to the table.

Seth could feel every curious eye boring into his back. Gossip probably flew around them at the speed of light, but he didn't care. All he could see was Katie. Her shining eyes, that untamable hair, and those lips were the closest pieces of heaven he would ever possess. Her cheeks flushed with color as she gaped up at him as if seeing him for the first time. He pulled her a little closer. As they swayed to the music, she suddenly surrendered with a sigh and a soft rub of cheek to chest. He nuzzled his nose in her soft hair then indulged a whim and let his lips brush the lightest of kisses to the skin joining neck to shoulder. A kiss over almost before it began. The song ended too quickly to suit Seth, too swiftly to even begin a proper seduction.

The jukebox powered down, and the lights on the stage came on. "No more dancing?" Seth asked, more than a bit disappointed he couldn't keep her in his arms a while longer.

"Karaoke." As if suddenly realizing the intimacy of their stance, she pulled her arms back from where they were wrapped around his ribs and let them drop awkwardly to her side.

"You going to sing, Boss?" Seth asked, trying to strike up a conversation as he led the way back to their table.

"Hell, no."

"Why not?" It was the entertainment he'd been hoping to see, and hearing her sing would be more solid proof Katie had more to her personality than being a workaholic. "Everyone says you're great."

Katie rolled her eyes.

"You're not gonna sing?" Brian asked.

"Not tonight." Katie took the new mug of beer from the waitress and handed back yet another empty.

Chris took the microphone first as he crooned a recent country-western hit. Katie leaned toward Seth. "Chris loves country. The kid worships Tim McGraw."

Seth sat back to listen and sip his soda, taking heart in the fact that Katie had called Chris a "kid."

After a passable rendition of the tune, Chris returned to his table to the sounds of whistles and applause. The restaurant was clearly occupied by quite a large number of country music fans.

Brian walked to the stage. Everyone suddenly stopped talking and started shouting.

Seth glanced over to Katie for an explanation. She leaned closer again, trying to talk above the din. "He only sang for us one other time." She appeared to choose her words carefully. "He wasn't... He couldn't..." She stopped, hiccupped, and then continued. "Brian can't sing very well."

Seth turned back to the stage and watched Brian grab the microphone. Wadded napkins and straw wrappers began to pelt the stage. Seth shook his head and laughed.

"Hey! Come on, you morons!" Brian shouted as he ducked the missiles. "Give me a chance! This is important!"

The crowd quieted, but they eyed him suspiciously, waiting for any opportunity to chase him off the stage with another deluge of paper. If Brian sang as badly as Katie described, Seth figured they might switch to chicken bones and pizza crusts.

"This one is for my Samantha," Brian said as he punched the selection on the karaoke machine. He launched into "She's Having My Baby" done in a style only the deaf could truly appreciate.

Brian paused as if waiting for a response of some kind, and then a roar rose from the crowd. He grinned from ear to ear. "Took you jackasses long enough to figure it out! She really *is* having my baby!"

Friends descended on Brian and Sam to offer their best wishes. Plus, Seth figured it gave them the perfect excuse to get Brian to stop singing.

Katie turned to Seth with tears in her eyes.

"Are you happy or sad?" he had to ask.

"Oh, happy. Very happy."

He couldn't deny the urge to reach out to brush away a tear slowly slipping down her cheek. She favored him with a shy smile. He felt his stomach flip in reaction. "Go on. Go talk to her," Seth encouraged.

Katie shook her head. "Too many people. Sam is my best friend. She'll come to me when she's ready."

Several minutes passed before Sam and Brian extracted themselves from the well-wishers. Sam flopped down in the chair next to Katie who immediately leaned over and hugged her.

"When?" Katie asked as she brushed away her tears with the back of her hand. Seth wondered how long she'd continue to weep over the happy news.

Sam wiped away a few tears of her own. "October. Probably before the season is over."

"I'm so happy for you. I didn't know you and Brian wanted to start a family," Katie said before she ordered another drink from a passing waitress.

"Let's just say... it was a surprise. It'll happen for you too, Honey. I just know it will," Sam said in a whispered voice that raised Seth's radar a notch. "I don't care what that doctor says. Maybe... maybe when the time is right."

Katie gave Samantha a weak smile, lightly placed her finger against Sam's lips to silence her, and shook her head. Seth felt like he'd missed something important that had just passed between the two friends.

"You'd never catch me doing that," Seth proclaimed when Katie finally turned back to him.

"Catch you doing what?"

He gestured his thumb toward Brian. "Making an ass out of myself for some woman."

Katie crossed her arms over her breasts and leaned back in her chair. Unfortunately, she pushed a little too hard, almost tipping over. Seth grabbed her arm and pulled her back as she righted herself. Her face flushed a vivid red all the way to her ears. "That's what you think he did?" she asked with the anger plain in her voice. "Made an ass of himself?"

"Of course. What'd you think he was doing?"

"I think he was showing Sam how much he loves her—how much he wants this baby. I think it's... it's romantic." She released a heavy sigh.

Seth rolled his eyes at the entire notion. "Romance? What a waste. I'd never do anything that ridiculous. Flowers, yeah. And candy, maybe. But get up in front of everybody and sing?" He shook his head. "No, thanks." Picking up the pitcher of soda, he refilled his glass.

From the corner of his eye, Seth could see Katie studying him for a moment. He loved the fact she never had the ability to hide her feelings. She concentrated on him, scrunching up her nose and furrowing her forehead. She stared at him for so long Seth began to wonder if she'd forgotten what they'd been discussing.

"No, I don't suppose *you* would," she finally commented.

He laughed at the lag time between the statement and the response. "No way. There are better ways to impress a chick. I never had to sing to a girl to get laid," he teased.

"I suppose someone like you gets... *you know*... whenever he wants."

"Yep. Just have to snap my fingers." It took every ounce of Seth's self control not to laugh aloud at his own absurd statement. Women might have been easy enough for him to get, but they'd never been quite *that* accommodating.

Katie picked up a menu and started to fan herself. "Is it getting warmer in here?"

They both turned to look toward the stage when Rachel took the microphone. She pushed the stool out of the way and began a unique rendition of "Sexual Healing" which included some very creative and downright lewd choreography. If she would have had a pole, guys stuffing dollars into her panties, and some strategically placed strips of Velcro, she might have made a great stripper. He glanced around and saw Josh and Chris missing the show as they played pinball again.

Katie stared at the stage. "I suppose he's drooling over her," she muttered, thinking aloud again.

He didn't believe the ridiculous statement deserved a response. Besides having no interest in Rachel's little exhibition, he was entirely fascinated with watching Katie. The woman couldn't even *say* "laid"—which probably meant she had never even...

Good God, she might be a virgin! He figured most people lost their ranks in that category by the time they turned sixteen. "How old did you say you were?" he blurted out much louder than he'd intended.

"I beg your pardon?" Her somewhat garbled words were getting harder to understand.

Seth tried to remember what she'd told him about herself on opening night. Hadn't she said she was twenty-six? "How old are you?"

"Old enough." She gulped down the last of her beer and raised her hand to get the waitress's attention. Unfortunately, Brian's head happened to be in the way, and Katie inadvertently gave him a good smack, the slapping sound loud enough to echo over the music.

"Hey! Katie, what the hell?" Brian yelled, rubbing his temple.

"Sorry. Just wanted another drink," she offered with a slur to the words before waving her arm again.

"I think you've had enough." Seth grabbed her hand and pulled it out of the air. "I thought you said you didn't drink much."

"Since when's it your business? Aren't you tired of butting in my life yet? God, what an ego!" Katie pouted like a child for a moment before some thought perked her up. She looked at Seth, a coy smile spreading across her face. "I sing I'll think."

Seth couldn't resist laughing at her. "'I sing I'll think?' You're drunk."

"That's *not* what I said. I *think* I'll *sing*. Got it, rich boy? Geesh." She waved her hand in dismissal and then repeated the action, staring at her fingers as they moved.

Seth shook his head and tried not to laugh at her again, but the woman was plastered.

Samantha leaned toward her friend. "Katie, I don't think that's a good idea tonight." Her voice was downright parental.

"Sure, it is. I even know exactly what to sting... to sing," Katie replied with a giggle and a hiccup.

Brian chimed in as he shook his head. "Katie, I wouldn't—"

She cut him off by waving her hand again. "No, *you* wouldn't, but *I* would."

Seth leaned over the table to get Samantha's attention. "Why don't you want her to sing?"

Sam appeared horribly uncomfortable, and she seemed to select her words carefully. "Katie always chooses... um... appropriate songs."

"What do you mean? 'Appropriate?'"

"She picks songs that match a person, what she thinks he's like. I don't really think she should sing to you," Sam replied.

"She's not singing to me."

Both Sam and Brian snorted a laugh. Seth scowled at them and turned back to watch Katie.

She'd made her way to the stage. From her weaving walk, he was concerned whether she would be upright for too much longer. She grabbed the microphone out of Rachel's hand, pushed the woman out of the way, and then stooped to ponder the selections on the karaoke machine. Rachel actually backed down and went back to the table. Seth had pegged her as too catty to simply step aside. Maybe she'd recognized Katie wasn't quite... herself. Of course the threatening glares Sam threw at Rachel were probably a bit intimidating.

After a couple of tries, Katie eventually punched the correct buttons and she moved to the edge of the stage where she teetered awaiting the song's intro. Turning to face Seth as the music played, she began to sing "You're So Vain" in a less than steady voice. Katie didn't make it through the second verse before she slipped off the edge of the stage and found herself sitting on the floor.

Seth jumped up and ran to her aid. "Are you hurt?"

She shook her head.

"Time to go home, Carly Simon. Where are your keys?"

Katie smiled and clutched his proffered hand as he helped her to stand. "In my pants pocket," she answered before she turned to face him, fisted her hands in his shirtfront, and leaned heavily against his chest. "Wanna play 'Go Fish'?"

"Not tonight, Boss. Let's go." Seth pulled out his wallet and dropped some money on the table to pay for their bill. "Good night, everyone." He herded Katie out of the door before anyone would have time to stop them. Once in the parking lot, she obediently handed over the keys to her truck.

He listened to Katie sing several differing renditions of "You're So Vain" all the way to the farm. She even rolled down the window and serenaded some cows they passed along the way. While the words might never have come out entirely correct, he most certainly got the gist of her message. He knew he should be offended, but he wasn't. She made him laugh, even at himself.

Helping her out of the truck, Seth tried to guide Katie to her office to get her settled in for the night before he returned to the dorm. She would be madder than a hornet when he drove her truck back to the track, but the only other option would be to stay at the farm and sleep on the office floor. Too many people had seen them leave together. Staying at the farm would be a recipe for disaster. With all the gossip he'd heard in his time at the track, he'd grown insight into what Katie meant that day in Arthur's office. There really were no secrets in the barn.

Seth wrapped a steadying arm around her waist and led her down the long aisle toward her room. She wasn't horribly cooperative as she kept dragging her feet and reaching around to put her hand on his butt. "C'mon, Boss. A little help here."

She pulled her keychain from his back pocket and planted her feet. "Come to my room, Handsome." She turned to face him and jiggled the keys.

Seth furrowed his brow. "Don't call me that." He knew the alcohol was talking and not the Katie he knew.

"Why not? It works for Rachel. She had you eating out of her hands. What do you say, *Handsome*?"

She slipped her keys into her pocket, grabbed Seth's arm, and pushed her chest against his bicep. Seth sucked in his breath and tried hard to stop his physical reaction to her teasing. He wasn't successful.

"Katie, don't call me that," he scolded. "You're not Rachel. You'll never be like her."

What he intended to be a compliment was taken as an insult. "I know I'm not as pretty as she is, but I'm a woman too."

"Katie, I never said—"

"I might not come on as strong as she does, but I want you. I want you bad."

Clearly drunk, she couldn't know what she was saying. But she was too close, too feminine, and too willing. He tried to put some distance between them before things went entirely to hell. "Rachel doesn't want me."

Katie put her hands on her hips and glared at him. "Bullshit. She wants you, and you damn well know it. She can't have you, too. Not this time."

Seth had not a clue what Katie was rambling on about. "You need to go to bed, Boss." He tried to take her hand; she jerked it away. Her expression kept shifting between anger and sadness. Her green eyes smoldered then pled for mercy. Seth wished he knew what was hurting her so much because he damn well wanted to make it stop. "You're not like Rachel."

"I could be. If you want me to be. Just watch." Katie dug her fingers into Seth's shirt and pulled him to her. Standing on tiptoe, she kissed him before he could even think to block her action. Not that he would have wanted to.

She retreated before he even had a chance to kiss her back. Katie stood there on unsteady toes, staring up at him with those intense eyes. She still had her fingers clenched in his shirtfront, teetering against him, nothing but her small fists separating them. Then she let out a small, contented sigh. He could feel her breath caress his neck. Such a preposterously simple stimulus to elicit such a response. Just a sigh. All the blood left his brain.

"That was a nice kiss," Katie whispered, relaxing her grip and stepping back.

"Nice kiss, my ass." Pulling her roughly back against his chest, Seth claimed her mouth and showed her what he thought a real kiss should be.

Seth made love to her with his lips and his tongue. Her mouth was so warm, and she tasted wonderful. Katie revealed her true passionate nature to him in her zealous response. He'd known all along what hid behind that wall of protection she'd so carefully constructed. She clearly burned as hot as he did.

Her tongue didn't hesitate to seek his. He thought he heard her growl, and the sound only made his heart pound harder as the primitive rhythm thrummed through him. Again and again their mouths slanted across each other as their tongues exchanged caress after caress. He'd never had a woman react with such openness, such abandon, or such passion. God, he wanted her. *And all because of a sigh.*

She leaned heavily against him. Seth drew her closer in his arms, measured the length of her with his own body. Katie slipped her hands around his neck and laced her fingers through his hair.

Something in the depths of what remained of Seth's tenuous self-control began to shout a warning. *You're playing with fire!* But he couldn't seem to find the strength to pull away. His body betrayed his true feelings, stood at attention, refused to push her away. *A damned sigh.*

In her drunken state, Katie had absolutely no inhibitions. She pulled her hands back scraping her nails along his shoulders, slipped her arms around his waist, and then slowly lowered her palms to his backside.

She broke the magic spell the kiss had spun around them. "I love your butt." Four drunken words ended the enchantment.

Seth slowly came back to Earth, knowing this wasn't how it should be. *Not here, not now, not like this.*

The sigh's spell was broken.

"Katie, stop it," Seth scolded as he finally found enough of what remained of his shaken sanity to pull away from the intoxicated and intoxicating kiss.

"I don't wanna," Katie pouted. "You taste so good." She slowly and seductively licked her lips. "Like... um... you." She stood on tiptoe to try to kiss him again. He groaned as he fought the desire still raging through him, barely controlled, wanting the spell to be cast again.

"Katie, *please,*" he pleaded, grasping her shoulders and pushing her firmly away. It wasn't far enough to do much good. He could still taste her, smell her, want her. "We can't. You know we can't."

"No. *You* can't. I can."

"You're drunk."

"And you're gorgeous." She moved toward him again; he took a step in retreat. Katie gave him a crooked, naughty smile. "Are you afraid of me?"

"No, I'm not afraid of... Look, you need to go to bed."

She licked her lips again. He tried not to watch. "Sounds like a great idea. Care to join me?"

Seth desperately hoped she wouldn't remember any of this in the morning. "Hand over the keys, Katie."

She pouted her lip, but she jerked on the keys in her pocket. It only took her three tries to get them out. She held the keychain out and jingled it at Seth.

He grabbed the keys, and in his befuddled state, it took him a couple of moments to open her office door. When he turned to lead her inside, Seth noticed she had suddenly taken on a green pallor.

Green. Her favorite color.

About to grab her and rush her to the bathroom, he jumped when she threw up on his shoes.

Well, I guess that's what I get for trying to wear Chinellis with jeans.

Katie began to sob. "I'm so sorry."

"Come on," Seth said, kicking off his shoes and pulling her out of the hall toward the bathroom. He sat her down on the closed toilet seat, grabbed a washcloth off the towel rack, and ran warm water over it. With a tender touch that came without thought, Seth gently washed her flushed face. She appeared so vulnerable with her eyes closed, humming to herself as if his touch relaxed all of her worries. For a moment, he wondered if she would begin to purr like a cat if a man was lucky enough to make love to her. "Are you better now?"

She sighed. "Buch metter, Seth. So much better." Then she hiccupped hard enough to bounce.

"Where do you keep your shirts?" Katie pointed toward the dresser. After he retrieved a clean garment, he lifted her soiled shirt over her head and threw it in the sink, trying not to stare at her lacey purple bra. But, damn, those were nice breasts. He ached to caress them. *Rein it in, Remington. You can't have her.* "Come on, Katie. Lift your arms." He helped her into the clean shirt.

Seth took off her shoes, tugged Katie to her feet, and led her to the bed. He dragged back the quilt. "Get in. Time for bed."

"All by myself?"

He patted the pillow. "Yes, Boss. All by yourself. Be a good girl."

After finally getting Katie settled, he returned to the bathroom to wash her shirt out in the sink before hanging it over the shower stall to dry. Then using the wash stall hose, he sprayed down the hallway and his shoes to clean things up.

By the time he walked back into the bedroom to check on Katie, she was asleep. Seth stopped for a moment and leaned his back against the wall. Rubbing his fingers against his forehead, he watched her. Katie's long, red-gold curls fanned around her head like a halo, and Seth counted the light brown freckles on her nose. She sighed once and smiled but slept on. *Another sigh.* But he had sobered.

This one could be more than I can handle.

He'd never known a woman who could be so fiercely independent and still be comfortable with the many different types of people she worked with in and around the racetrack. And she was a giving person. So many times, he'd seen Katie go out of her way to help people when they needed assistance with an unruly animal or had a problem with equipment. Yet she never asked for anything in return.

Katie Murphy was unique—one special woman among millions. Seth suddenly realized he could learn to love this one.

"No woman's worth that much money," he reminded himself, quietly slipping out of the room.

Not even an angel.

Chapter 11

"You look like shit."

Just the sound of Chris's voice made Katie cringe. "Probably because I feel like shit," she mumbled. She could feel her cheeks flame with embarrassment. She still wore her jeans, and she didn't remember changing her shirt. Her hair had to look as messy as an opened bail of hay. "What are you doing here anyway? It's your day off." She whispered the words, fearing anything louder would increase the throbbing in her head.

"I brought your truck back." He tossed the keys to her.

She grabbed them out of the air, wincing at the loud sound they made when they slapped her hand. "My truck? Isn't it parked out...?"

No. Oh, my God, no.

As some memories of the evening came flooding back, Katie fervently wished to be able to pack up all of her belongings and move far, far away. Did she really puke on Seth's shoes? Maybe someplace like New Zealand would be nice. They raced harness horses there after all.

She scanned the barn to see if she'd have to deal with the awkwardness over her actions now or if it could be mercifully postponed. To her relief, Chris came alone. "Seth... um... Crash didn't come with you?"

"Nah. When I saw your truck this morning, I figured he left you here and drove back to the track. I knocked on his door, and he snarled and threw the keys at me. Didn't seem a lot perkier than you are today." He chuckled as he tossed a flake of hay into Jack's stall. "Of course, he's not a morning person to begin with." Chris gave Katie a lopsided smile and began to hum the melody of "You're So Vain" as he continued feeding the horses.

"Chris, you can just kiss my—"

"I can what?" he asked over his shoulder.

"Never mind," Katie groaned.

Brushing her teeth twice didn't seem to take the layer of film off her tongue, but the hot, albeit short shower relaxed her muscles enough to take the edge off of her pounding head. The barn's owner really needed to buy a water heater that provided more than a few minutes of hot water.

Using her damp towel to wipe away the thin layer of condensation from the foggy mirror, Katie took a moment and considered her distorted reflection. "What did you do? God, what must he think of you?" The reflection refused to answer. "I hope you're proud of yourself." At least the face staring back at her appeared properly contrite.

After swallowing some aspirin, Katie dressed and joined Chris as he completed the morning chores.

"Want to catch some breakfast?" Katie asked, hoping some toast and coffee might take the edge off of her aching head and touchy stomach.

"Nah. Already ate, but I'd like a ride back. I've got some plans this afternoon."

She jingled her key ring at Chris. The action brought back more memories of her less than ladylike evening. She vowed that she would never set foot in The Place again. "Let's go."

On the ride to the track, Katie's apprehension grew by leaps and bounds. She didn't know what she would say to Seth when she saw him. What would he think of her now? Would it be best to start with a huge apology? Maybe a better plan of action would be to act as if none of it ever happened.

Is there possibly a large sinkhole that might conveniently open up and swallow me whole?

A complication. That's all Monday night was—another damn complication. Katie was fed up with snags in her once orderly life. Everything about her existence had always been so simple, so regimented. She had a routine to every aspect of her world and a solid plan in place for her future.

Then *he* had arrived.

Sure, Seth did a great job around the barn. He'd turned out to be a really good groom. And she had to admit it was nice to have more time to train now that both Seth and Chris jogged horses for her. But she had an increasingly hard time keeping Seth from sneaking into her thoughts. Her stable and her mind were no longer her own.

How could she possibly repair the damage and get things back to the way they were? Or did she really want her life to return to what it was before Seth Remington arrived?

Katie honestly wasn't sure exactly *what* she wanted anymore. And that scared the hell out of her.

"Is something wrong? Anything I can do?" Chris asked. "You chew on that lip of yours any harder, you'll draw blood." After a few silent moments, he tried again. "Katie? Can I help?"

She sighed. "No. But thanks anyway."

"It'll be all right. It's not like you two slept—"

She grimaced, slapping him soundly on the upper arm. "Don't even *say* it, Chris."

"Well, it's not. He got back to the dorms about the time I did, so I know he wasn't at the farm long. Look, you had a few too many beers, and the guy drove you home. Nothing happened. He was a gentleman. Right?"

"Yeah, nothing happened." Other than puking, the rest remained a tad hazy.

Had they kissed? Katie thought she remembered a kiss. She desperately needed someone to talk to, but she knew Chris wasn't the right person. She wanted Sam.

Katie pulled up next to the race office and parked her truck. "See you tomorrow morning. Enjoy your day off."

Chris got out of the truck, waved, and jogged toward the dorms. Katie went into the office to check that she had the proper horses entered for the next day's draw for races. She checked the postings for future dates and then left the race office, heading for the track kitchen.

"Hey, Katie! Wait up!" Seth called from his window.

There would be no reprieve so she could have some time to think about a plan of action or the right thing to say. She would have to face him now. *Nonchalant, Katie. Just act like it's business as usual.*

"Hurry up! I'm hungry!" she yelled back before realizing the noise would reverberate in her head like the beating of a bass drum. Katie wondered how people who drank as much as some of the horsemen did managed to function at all. The pounding headache alone was enough to make her swear off alcohol altogether.

Seth joined her in the parking lot as she put both hands to her temples, rubbing small circles to relieve the ache.

"Feeling any better?" he asked.

Favoring him with a frown, Katie practically growled her response. "I'm fine." She couldn't think of the right thing to say, at a loss as to what would be her best move. Pretending nothing happened seemed the correct course of action. She started walking toward the track kitchen. He fell in step beside her.

* * * *

Standing at the counter in the track kitchen, they ordered their breakfast. Katie took out her wallet and opened it, and Seth saw a strange expression cross her face. It was only there for a brief moment, but he could swear she seemed frightened. That confused him because she'd never appeared to be afraid of anything. "Something wrong?"

"No," she snapped. "Nothing's wrong."

"Boy, aren't you in a great mood this morning?"

"Kiss my butt, Seth."

Oh, no. He couldn't just let that one slide. He wiggled his eyebrows at her. "I'd love to. Bare it." Her eyes flew wide as she looked properly astonished at his response. God, he loved teasing her.

Gathering their food, Seth led Katie over to a table away from most of the remaining breakfast crowd. She took the dishes from the tray and dropped them on the table before taking a seat. He settled opposite her, staring at her as they ate.

She pointedly tried to ignore him as she sipped her coffee. He watched her closely, seeing the turmoil on her pretty face. The tightening of her lips, the lids that hooded the averted eyes. Was she thinking about their kiss? He wished for a moment he could offer her something, anything, to let her know how very much she'd come to mean to him. The attraction couldn't be shaken. He'd tried to tell himself the tempest had only been a kiss, nothing more. Yet he'd come to the stark realization that he couldn't get Katie out of his mind, out of his senses. Out of his heart.

Damn Pops anyway! This is all his fault. It's about the money.

Seth sat back and rubbed his forehead to work out the dull ache he tended to get whenever he felt frustrated.

It was *always* about the money. Money could buy happiness. Money could buy a future that didn't include shoveling horse shit and getting up at an unholy hour every morning. Money could buy ease. But money couldn't buy a kiss like the one he'd shared with Katie. A kiss that really meant something.

"Hey, Katie!" a blond man in a green baseball cap called as he waved from across the dining area.

Katie turned and then pasted on a fake smile that made Seth suspicious. "Hey, Tom. How you doin'?"

"Doin' fine," he said, walking over to the table. "You got anything in tomorrow?"

"Just one."

"Would you wanna paddock for me? Chris told me you need to pick up some paddocks and warm-ups when you could."

"Which race?"

"Thirteenth"

"Yeah. I'll take it. I'm in the second. And I'll do the warm-up for you," she replied.

"Must be nice to catch the second," the man said with a chuckle. "I never draw the early races. Thanks, Katie. You'll have Chock Full of Steam. I'm in barn twenty this year. Steam will be in stall five. Gotta run. See you tomorrow." He turned and made his way to the door.

Seth noticed Katie had returned to staring intently at the table and nervously shifting her cup of coffee between her hands. When his gaze finally caught hers, she was suddenly engrossed with a winner's circle picture from the disco era hanging on the wall next to their table. "Katie, why would you paddock for him?"

She ignored him, pushed the cup away, picked up a triangle of toast, and nibbled at the crust.

Seth leaned forward and put his hand over hers. "I don't understand. What's up, Boss?"

Katie pulled her hand away. "I'm just doing a favor for a friend. Drop it, Seth."

He wasn't about to take the hint. "Do you want me to take it? He doesn't know me, but—"

"No!" She jumped to her feet and shoved her chair back. "I've got it. Just leave it alone." Katie grabbed the remainder of the food she'd barely touched and pitched it at the wastebasket. "See you later." She rushed toward the exit.

Seth hurriedly disposed of his trash and ran after her. "Katie. Come on. Wait up."

"I need to go," Katie scolded over her shoulder as she quickened her pace to a near jog. As fast as she moved, she might as well have been heading for a one-time-only sale at the tack shop.

"You never answered me." Seth jogged to catch her. Something was wrong, but he couldn't seem to drag a word out of her. He finally caught up with her, matching her short strides with his long ones. "Talk to me, Boss."

Katie abruptly stopped and let out an exasperated groan. "What do you want? Why can't you just leave me alone?"

"It's not in my nature. I live for bugging you." Her irritated scowl told Seth that humor wasn't going to work today. "Tell me what's wrong. There's got to be some reason that guy thought you wanted paddocks."

Katie started to walk away again without a word.

He stepped in front of her. She stopped and glared up at him with blood-shot eyes, but he wasn't going to be put off until he got some answers. "I'm not stupid. I know something is up. What aren't you telling me?"

She threw her hands up. For once, she hadn't tried to mask her pain. Or the anger. "Fine! You want to know why I'm paddocking for Tom? I'm flat ass broke! Satisfied now? I wouldn't expect a rich guy like you to understand."

"What do you need the money for? You've got twelve horses in your barn. You should be rolling in dough."

"Obviously, I blew it on my cocaine habit and those guys from the escort service. I have very expensive tastes." She shook her head at him as she angrily stomped away.

Seth ran after her, but she dodged every attempt he made to talk to her. When she reached her truck, Seth grabbed her arm out of sheer frustration and spun her around to face him.

"What's wrong? Why are you so pissed off?"

"You're an idiot, Seth. You don't have a clue. Not a clue." Katie tried to yank her arm away. "Let me go, damn it!"

"Not until you tell me what's wrong."

"You want to know what's wrong, Mr. Millionaire? Fine. I have bills piling up on my desk. Vet bills. Feed bills. You name it, I owe it. I need money, and if I have to paddock for everyone and their cousin to get it, I will. Happy now?" Katie tried to jerk open the truck door, but Seth slammed it shut again.

"What about training fees? Don't you get some decent money for training horses?"

Katie fixed a glare at him that could ignite a blaze. "James and Susan pay me. And Ross makes sure I get the salary for you being here. But the rest of my owners take their sweet time. The guy who owns Heathcliffe and Miss Daisy is loaded, but he never seems to find the time to send me what he owes me. I haven't had a check from him in three months. Rich people forget what it's like for the rest of the world." Her hands trembled and her eyes brimmed with unshed tears. "Lots of owners are like him. He'll pay. Eventually. But the horses still need to be fed *now*. The rent still needs to be paid *now*. I still need to buy equipment *now*. I'm sorry I'm not the brilliant financial success you seem to think I am."

"When I get my money—" *Damn*. He remembered the five-year barrier to any financial help he could offer her.

Katie narrowed her eyes at him and reached for the door handle again. She obviously hadn't forgotten. Seth held the door firmly closed; she railed at him in response. "Where do you think money comes from anyway? It doesn't grow on some big tree behind the barn. Not everyone has a rich father. Damn you and damn your money. You'll never understand." She pushed his arm away and reached for the door.

He finally understood. Katie wasn't really angry, she was embarrassed. "I didn't mean to make you mad. I was just trying to help." Seth planted his hand against the door again to hold it firmly shut.

"By reminding me how rich you'll be? Must be nice. The rest of the world has to work for a living, so if you'll excuse me... I've got work to do."

"You know that's not what I meant." Seth wanted to help, wanted to share all that he had with her. Maybe he'd get her a really good horse—a champion—when she handed him back his life.

Maybe in five years when she'd forgotten him and didn't need his help. Seth finally released his hold on her truck's door.

Jerking the door open, Katie threw herself into the driver's seat and started the engine. Seth used his body to block her from slamming the door and driving away. "I'm sorry if I said the wrong thing. Can't we talk about this? Please?"

Evidently, Katie's hurt wasn't that easily dissuaded. "Seems like we already have, doesn't it? Can I please go now? Or is there anything else you want to know about me that could be more humiliating than the last two days?"

"Oh, I get it. We're talking about last night now. You puked on my shoes. So what?"

Katie turned her face toward him, and Seth tried to show her one of his smug grins, tried to make her think that the highlight of his night had been her getting sick. He needed her to think their kiss meant nothing to him. Nothing at all. Even if that was a lie.

In Seth's mind, he was throwing her a lifeline. She just had to be wise enough to grab it. The kiss *had* to be forgotten or things could get entirely too hot to handle. "See you in the morning, Boss?" Seth asked, finally moving out of her way.

Come on, Katie. Please just let it go.

"Yeah, whatever," she answered before she slammed the door.

Seth watched her drive away and wondered if she would be able to forget what passed between them. If she could forget, perhaps she could teach him how because he'd always remember.

Always.

Chapter 12

Seth hung the freshly washed harness on the big hook next to Monterey Jack's stall. The horse dangled his head over the gate and nudged Seth as he passed by.

"Ready to get handsome?" He patted Jack's neck, opened the gate, and led the horse to the aisle cross-ties.

As he brushed and curried Jack, Seth let a smug smile cross his lips, remembering the training miles they'd completed together that morning. "I told you she'd teach me to train. And it's only May." He finished his work and returned his favorite pet to the stall.

The sound of a vehicle heading down the gravel road drew his attention. Katie suddenly appeared from her room and sprinted the length of the barn toward the door. Her face glowed and she wore a broad smile. She knew something he obviously didn't, so he followed her outside to investigate.

A truck pulling a two-horse trailer ground to a stop close to the barn's entrance. Two older men stepped out and waved to Katie.

"Grandpa!" she squealed, running to the shorter of the two gray-haired men. He took her in his arms, lifted her off her feet, and spun her in a circle. Her laughter wrapped around Seth's heart like a warm blanket on a winter's night.

When her grandfather finally put her down, she turned to the next man. "Jacob!" The hugging started all over again.

Once turned loose, Katie hurried to the back of the trailer. A chestnut horse moved restlessly inside the cramped space.

The animal had to be the stakes horse the Old Man had bought for her. Seth felt a stab of jealousy followed swiftly by overwhelming envy. *Katie didn't know Pops as well as I did, but they shared something special.* The love Katie and Sterling felt for their horses gave them common ground.

Day after day of working in the barn had finally helped Seth understand how much these animals could grow on a person and why horseracing was so compelling. A wave of grief ran through him as he wished he would have spent more time with the Old Man, wished he could have known him on a deeper level, and wished he could have shared this with him.

Katie moved to grab a lead rope hanging just inside the trailer, but Jacob reached out to lay a restraining hand on her arm. "Best let me get him out. He's a handful and a half."

"I can handle him, Jacob." The hurt was plain in her voice.

"*I* can't even handle him, Red." Jacob opened the back of the trailer and stepped up into the empty side.

Despite every attempt, every trick Jacob used, the stubborn colt refused to budge. Seth had never seen an animal resist leaving a trailer that obstinately. Most horses seemed to hate going in but loved getting out.

"He's ill-tempered. I'm not sure this is a good idea," Jacob cautioned, stepping back outside and shaking his head. "He's fast as lightning, but a real pisser to work with. Why you took a damn chestnut, I'll never know."

"I don't care what people say, they're not bad luck," Katie replied as she walked around the trailer and peered in the side window. "That's such a silly superstition. Besides, if *you* can handle him, *I* can handle him. And he's mine now."

"Still stubborn as ever, ain't ya, Red?" Jacob asked with a smile.

Seth walked to the barn and leaned casually against the wall to watch the fireworks. This looked to be a long siege. Having seen Katie face other willful horses, he knew she wasn't about to give up. And he didn't want to miss a minute of what he was sure would be an entertaining and informative show.

With a good view of the back of the trailer, he watched as Katie leaned her head in the window. He could hear her talk to the colt in a low, gentle voice. The horse calmed his restless movements and turned his head toward her. After several minutes, Katie stepped up into the trailer. After a few more, she backed the colt slowly out. Flashing an arrogant smile to Jacob, she seemed to have the situation well in hand. Then the horse suddenly bolted, dragging her behind as she held tight to the lead rope.

The colt veered toward Seth. He lunged for the halter and caught it. Between their combined efforts, Seth and Katie finally subdued the animal.

Standing on opposite sides, they tried to coax the horse into an empty stall. Despite their best efforts, the chestnut refused to cross the threshold. He backed away then reared, hauling both Seth and Katie momentarily off their feet. She dropped the halter; he held on tight.

This horse wasn't getting the better of him in front of Katie.

As soon as he got back on his feet, Seth jerked the colt's head down until he was eye to eye with the animal. "Listen, I've had it with you. Stop it," he ordered in a calm but firm voice. Miraculously, the colt maintained the eye contact and stopped struggling. "We're going in that stall." Seth inclined his head at the empty enclosure. "Do you want it to be the easy way or the hard way?" The colt gave a slight shake of its head and neck, but Seth wasn't sure if it was the horse's way of answering or just an innocent twitch. Feeling a surge of confidence, Seth led the colt easily into the stall. After releasing the lead rope, he patted the animal's neck and gave him an affectionate rub. "Good boy. Mind your manners from now on."

Seth swaggered over to Katie and handed her the lead rope. He gave her his best arrogant smile. "What was it you said? Ah, I remember. 'Horses are very smart. They can tell when you're afraid of them.'" He winked at her. "I especially like redheads."

From the flash in her pretty eyes, he could tell Katie wanted to smack him. He was tempted to kiss her just to keep her riled up.

Kevin Murphy smiled at Seth, rubbing the gray stubble on his chin. "I thought Kathleen was the only one who could do something like that with an obstinate horse. Nice job, son."

"Thanks. She taught me everything I know."

Katie made the introductions. "Grandpa, Jacob, this is Seth... Shit! Crash Rem... No, it's not. It's... um... Reynolds. He's my new groom." She looked like she wanted to scream her frustration as her cheeks turned ruddy and she stomped her foot. After a few deep breaths, she continued. "Crash, this is my grandfather, Kevin Murphy. And this is Jacob Schaeffer. They taught *me* everything I know."

"Schaeffer. Any relation to Rachel from the track?" Seth asked, hoping to change the topic so the men wouldn't get too worked up over Katie's botched introduction.

"I'll go get his equipment." Katie turned and walked away.

Jacob's gaze followed her before he turned back to Seth. "Rachel is my daughter. You met her?"

"Yeah. I see her in the paddock a lot. It's nice to meet you both." Seth extended his hand to the men. After shaking hands, Seth nodded toward the chestnut. "What's his name?"

"Who?" Kevin asked. "Oh. You mean the colt. He's Spun Gold."

Jacob snorted. "He's a big fat pain in the ass is what he is. Even Red will have trouble with him. Needs to be gelded, but she wouldn't let me cut him."

Seth winced at the idea. The poor colt deserved to keep his family jewels. "Give us a chance with him. Maybe we can help settle him down. Katie works wonders."

"Nice to see she's taught you a thing or two. Where do you hail from?" Kevin asked as he leaned against a stall and crossed his arms over his barrel chest.

"Chicago."

Jacob seemed to perk up at the mention of the Windy City. He obviously assumed Seth knew the litany of names Jacob sent in a barrage. After a never-ending stream of negative responses, Jacob looked frustrated. "Do you even race in Chicago?"

"Not horses. A few cars maybe, but never horses," Seth replied.

"So how the hell did you end up with my Katie?" Kevin asked with a booming voice, the irritation plain on his face. His intense gaze reminded Seth of the look Katie always had when she was pissed, and he suddenly realized Kevin Murphy didn't like him, nor did he trust him. "What's your *real* name, boy? What's your game? Nobody comes to racing this late in life."

"It's a long story," Seth replied before Katie returned to interrupt as she hung up the colt's harness on the hook outside his stall.

"His real name is Seth, but his friends call him Crash. I just keep forgetting, that's all. He's only here for a season, Grandpa. One season. Then he's moving on." She glanced over at Seth, her eyes pleading with him to keep his silence. He accommodated her.

Jacob looked confused as his gaze darted from Katie back to Seth. "I think I missed somethin' here. You're not a horseman, son?"

"No, Jacob. He's not. I'm trying to teach him a few things. Just drop it. Please."

Seth knew there wasn't a chance in the world that would happen with these two men who obviously loved Katie very much. Watching the three of them, he felt as out of place as a skunk showing up at a picnic.

"Sweetheart, can we go to your office for a minute?" Kevin walked that direction without waiting for a reply. With a nod, she bit her bottom lip and followed him before they disappeared, shutting the door behind them.

What he wouldn't give to be a fly on the wall for that conversation. Seth wondered how Katie was going to be able to talk herself out of the mess she'd made with her attempt to introduce him.

Jacob and Seth awkwardly stared at each other for a few moments before Jacob broke the silence. "Red is the best. She'll teach you good."

"Yep. I can't believe all I've learned since I got here. She's... she's... special." *And she's beautiful, and she's wonderful, and she's absolutely off limits.*

What had the Old Man been thinking? That question crossed Seth's mind at least a dozen times each and every day. Perhaps her angelic looks hadn't impacted Sterling Remington the same way they assailed his son. She appeared in his dreams—ready and willing to become his lover, spread beneath him in welcome. And she appeared in his nightmares as he was forced to walk away from her no matter how much he wanted to stay by her side.

"She's worth her weight in gold, that one is," Jacob added.

"If you'll excuse me, I'm going to take a look at Spun Gold. I think he scraped up his knee getting out of the trailer." Seth walked back to his new colt. He was a little chagrined when Jacob followed.

Seth went into the stall and gently reached for Gold's halter. The horse that had been so hard to handle now seemed as docile as a kitten. Seth ran his hand down the animal's leg until he found a small, swollen spot on the knee. The colt reacted to Seth's touch with a shiver but made no move to pull away. "Hang on, Gold. I'll fix you up." Seth stroked the horse's neck, exited the stall, and headed for one of the equipment trunks.

Jacob tagged along like an obedient pet, obviously deeply interested in the workings of the Murphy stable. Seth retrieved some antiseptic balm and a roll of gauze bandaging.

"You asked about Rachel. You seein' her?" Jacob asked as Seth entered the stall again and stooped down to work on Gold's injury.

"No, I'm not." Not that he hadn't had plenty of opportunities. But Rachel wasn't the type of woman Seth wanted to spend time with. How could he tell her father that she'd been passed around to just about every man at the track?

"Good thing."

The words took Seth by surprise. "Why'd you say that?"

"She and Red got history. I 'spose you heard it all already."

"Not much. Everyone says the exact same thing—they've 'got history.' But that's all I've heard." Seth rubbed some ointment on the wound and then wrapped a bandage around Gold's leg as the horse kept rubbing his muzzle in Seth's hair.

"You know who Mike Knight is?"

"You mean 'The White Knight?' Drives at the Meadowlands? He's great," Seth answered, rising from his crouch. He gave the horse a pat. "All better, Big Guy."

Jacob leaned his shoulder against the wall and watched Seth. "He's a horse's ass is what he is. He and Red were engaged."

"Really? Katie was engaged?" *My Katie?*

"Yep. But she broke it off. Couldn't trust him anymore."

Seth frowned as he walked out of the stall and latched it closed. He knew what was coming next, and he didn't like it one damn bit. "Rachel broke them up, didn't she?"

"Red found 'em together in Mike's truck. The windows were steamed up, if you get my drift."

It's worse than I thought. "I see." No wonder Katie acted the way she did around Rachel. It came as a surprise that Katie was able to keep herself from scratching Rachel's eyes out.

* * * *

In the office, Kevin took a seat in the lone chair and stared up at his granddaughter.

Katie paced in nervous circles. He had a flash to her similar childhood reactions when she'd been caught being naughty, and he wondered what kind of problem had made her so anxious.

"Seth is a... project from one of my owners," she finally explained before he'd even asked a question. "His dad owns horses and wants his son to see what working for a living is like, so..." She shrugged. "I've got him for this season. They pay me a stipend, and I get a groom."

Kevin shook his head. "Kathleen, try again. You're not telling me everything here."

"It's all I *can* tell you. It's all on the up and up, Grandpa. Honest. There's this clause... a non-disclosure clause that I can't violate."

Kevin stared into Katie's eyes for the truth. She could never lie to him and look him in the eye. When she let her gaze meet his and didn't flinch, he had his answer. "All right, Katie. He seems to be doing okay. Handled that colt real well." Kevin leaned back in the chair.

Katie finally seemed to settle down as she sat on the corner of her bed. "He's a quick study. I've never seen anyone take to the horses the way he did. He's so much help around here, and he's so... He's really..." She gave a wistful sigh and looked away.

"Uh oh."

Katie's face flushed with color. "No, Grandpa. No 'uh oh.' There's nothing between Seth and me." Then she stared intently at the floor as if it had suddenly morphed into an engrossing work of art.

Kevin knew his granddaughter wasn't a child, and he had no right knowing all of her business. But the whole Mike Knight incident had hurt her. Kevin blamed himself for leaving Katie without someone to watch out for her. "Katie, be careful," Kevin advised as he stood up, walked across the small room, and put his hand on her shoulder.

"God, that's all everyone says. 'Katie, be careful.' You, Sam, Brian, Chris. Can't I have my own life? Listen to me. There's nothing going on. Nothing!" She pushed his hand away, stood up, and started to pace again.

Kevin wanted to point out her obvious overreaction, but her Irish temper had taken full flight. He'd have to save a deeper discussion for another time. "If you say so, Kathleen. Let's go look at your new colt."

* * * *

Seth saw them exit the office. Katie's shoulders were tense, her lips had thinned to a mere line, and her ears flamed red. About to call her over so he could figure out what was bothering her and find out what information she'd shared with her grandfather, he heard a car heading up the gravel drive.

Going to the barn door, Seth spied the familiar silver Lexus. As it ground to a stop, the wheels threw rocks hard enough to hit the barn's wall, sounding like hailstones as they smacked the metal. His parole officer had finally arrived to check up on him. "Son of a bitch."

Ross Kennedy opened his door and carefully spied the ground around him before stepping out of his expensive car. The man looked entirely out of place in his impeccable suit and tie. Seth uttered another curse and returned to his new horse.

Katie and Kevin were still talking near the office when she suddenly squealed in delight. "Ross!" Hurrying the length of the barn, she threw herself into his arms. The lawyer hugged her, lifting her tiny frame off the ground.

Ross Kennedy was touching what wasn't his. Seth wanted to beat him senseless.

"It's so good to see you," Katie said when Ross put her back on her feet. "What brings you out to the boonies? You usually call. How's your mom doing?"

Call? Ross had been calling Katie? And since when did she know anything about his family?

The lawyer smiled. "She's feeling better. Thanks for asking. I came to see you, Katie. When I heard your horse was coming today, I knew I had to be here to see your reaction. Did he get here yet?"

"Yep. Come on, I'll show him to you." Katie linked her arm through Ross's and ushered him toward the stall.

Seth watched them walking toward him and frowned before he slipped back into Gold's stall to look at the colt's bandage again. Why in the hell did that high-priced shyster have to come? And why was Katie hanging all over him?

Ross smiled down at Seth where he squatted next to the horse's leg. "*Crash.* Good to see you. You don't appear any worse for the wear."

Condescending, conceited... Seth gave Ross a nod of his head. "*Matlock.* You appear to be entirely full of shit."

Katie blinked a couple of times. "Seth, what on earth..."

Ross laughed and shook his head.

"Let it go, Boss," Seth replied.

Kevin and Jacob exchanged confused glances. Katie must have noticed as well because she tried to smooth the tense atmosphere. "Ross Kennedy, this is my grandfather, Kevin Murphy. And this is Jacob Schaeffer."

Seth stifled a flash of jealousy that Katie hadn't messed up Ross's introduction.

The three men exchanged greetings and an awkward silence settled on the barn again.

Ross reached out and ran his hand down Katie's arm. Seth clenched his jaw hard enough to crack a tooth.

"Katie," Ross said, "I wanted to see if I could buy you that dinner we missed in Chicago. Would you like to go out tonight?"

Both Seth and the colt snorted. Seth patted his new pet and smiled. Spun Gold was obviously a very intelligent animal.

"Maybe. Depends. Grandpa, you and Jacob staying?" Katie asked.

Both shook their heads in response. "Not this time," Kevin replied. "We need to be heading back. I'm sorry, Sweetheart."

"It's okay, Grandpa. We'll have dinner next time. You'll have to come for some races. Did you leave Gold's equipment card, Jacob?"

He nodded. "Dropped it in the trunk next to his stall."

"Well, you ready to head up the road?" Kevin asked as he turned to his traveling companion and gave him a friendly clap on the shoulder.

"Yep. We can stop for coffee and a doughnut on the way."

Both men hugged Katie, and Seth noticed the tears pooling in her eyes. She clearly missed them a great deal. She walked out of the barn with Kevin and Jacob.

Realizing they were alone, Seth turned on Ross, making no attempt to disguise his annoyance. "What are you really doing here, Kennedy? Checking up on me? Well, I'm being a good boy. So why don't you just trot your ass back home." Seth left the stall and latched the gate.

"I'm not here for you, Remington. I'm here for Katie."

"Bullshit." Seth dropped the remainder of the bandages in a trunk and slammed the lid.

Ross shrugged. "Think what you want. I wanted to make sure she got her payment for dealing with you." He didn't seem to even try to hide his disdain. "Not that it's worth it for her."

"I'll have you know that I do a great job around here," Seth said in his own defense. "I'm a damn good groom. Hell, I pick up pocket money paddocking for other trainers when we don't have any of ours in some nights." Seth didn't bother to tell Ross that the money he earned paddocking always managed to find its way into Katie's desk. The way she handled bookkeeping, she always assumed she'd made a mistake and forgotten the bills had been left there. Her exasperation on discovering the "misplaced" funds always made Seth happy, but he wondered how much longer he'd be able to keep supplementing her income before she'd catch on. Thank God, she was such a bad bookkeeper.

"It's nice to know you're good for something," Ross added with condescension dripping from each word.

Katie returned before their exchange could escalate as Seth assumed it easily could have. She glanced at Seth and then at Ross, her brows knitting in confusion. "What's wrong with you two?"

Neither replied.

She frowned and studied them for another moment before she shook her head. "Fine. Don't tell me. Seth, why don't we drive you back to the dorm? I'll take care of feeding the horses tonight. It's your day off anyway.

"Fine. I'll go hang around my jail cell with nothing to do. Whoopee," Seth replied as he spun his index finger in a mid-air circle and plopped down on the closed trunk. Then an idea perked him up. "Let me stay here. I can get to know the colt."

"You sure? Maybe I should stay too." Katie walked over to Gold's stall and watched him over the gate.

Yeah, Katie. Stay with me.

Ross's disappointment showed plainly on his face. Seth savored the response like fine wine. And then Ross went to stand next to Katie and reached out to wrap his arm around her shoulder. *Touching what's not his.* Seth had to resist the overwhelming urge to break the man's arm.

"I really wanted to take you out, Katie. The horse will be here from now on, but I have to drive back tonight," Ross said.

"I'm sorry, Ross. I hadn't even considered... Okay. We'll go out." She turned back to Seth. "Sure we can't take you to back the track?"

The more he thought about it, the more he wanted to stay. After being cramped in that small trailer all day, Gold needed some attention. And while Katie was gone, perhaps Seth could take a look at the mess she called a desk. Maybe he could do something to help the situation. It obviously couldn't get much worse. By sticking around, he'd know when she got home. Seth wasn't about to let her hang all over Ross Kennedy if she had a beer or two. Not if he could help it. "I'd really rather stay."

"Fine," Katie finally agreed. "I'll leave the office open if you get bored and want to listen to some music."

Seth laughed as he shook his head. "I've seen what you call music. I'll pass."

"If you'll both excuse me, I'm going to change out of my work clothes." Katie headed back toward her room.

The two men just stared each other down for a moment. Seth didn't want to have to appeal to Ross for anything, but he'd thought of a possible way to help Katie out of her financial woes. Since he would need Ross's help, Seth swallowed his pride. For her sake. "Look, Ross, I don't remember what you're paying Katie to have me here, but it's not enough."

"I think three-hundred a week is great for someone who doesn't even have to pay room and board." Ross crossed his arms and leaned against the wall.

"No, Bonehead. Did your mom drop you on your head when you were a baby? I'm not talking about *my* pay. I want to know what the estate pays Katie for putting up with me."

Ross shook his head. "That's none of your business, Remington. She gets paid. That's all you need to know."

Seth scowled at the lawyer. *You conceited prick. Can't you see Katie's struggling?* "Isn't there a way Arthur could arrange for her to... I don't know, get a larger salary? After all, I'm going to have all that money. I'd like some of it to go to Katie. Can't—"

"You'll get the money, *if* you finish the season and *if* you keep your nose clean," Ross interrupted.

It took every ounce of his strength for Seth to keep from smacking some sense into Ross. "We're talking about Katie, not me." He sighed, realizing he had no choice but to share the whole story if Ross was ever going to understand. He hoped Katie wouldn't consider it a betrayal. "I don't want you to tell her I said anything, but she's hurting."

Ross's brows gathered in a concerned frown. "Hurting?"

"Yeah. She's in a little over her head. Some of her owner's drag their feet paying her, and she could really use a boost." Seth couldn't get past the notion she'd be angry at him for telling Ross about her problems, but he wasn't about to let her continue to flounder. Not with the Remington money available. "What good is all that money doing just sitting there? Couldn't you use some of the estate funds and buy a good horse for her? You know, make sure she gets paid training fees on time?"

Ross was already shaking his head. "No. Katie can't get any more money. The will is very specific. Five years, remember? But I could..." Obviously deep in thought, he let the words hang between them.

Katie's office door opened, and when she waltzed through, Ross immediately pushed away from the wall as Seth jumped off the trunk.

While she had always been pretty in Seth's eyes, the transformation was incredible. Work clothes had been replaced with a pink sundress that hugged her curvaceous upper body and billowed around her hips and legs in soft folds of fabric. A lacey ribbon tied her red tresses into a ponytail, and a soft layer of make-up accentuated her green eyes. The high-heeled sandals were much more appealing than her work boots. She looked as utterly feminine as anything Seth had ever seen. He wanted to scream at her to stay with him, to not leave with Ross. *Stay. Stay. Please stay.*

"What?" she innocently asked as she ran her hands down her skirt to smooth it against her legs. "Am I unzipped?" She peered over both shoulders.

Seth finally found his ability to speak again. "You sure clean up nice, Boss." Her blush was his reward.

Ross walked over and took Katie's hand. He pressed a quick kiss to her fingers. "You're beautiful." Her cheeks flushed a deeper shade of red.

Ross held onto Katie's hand. Seth clenched his fists at his side. *If you don't let her go, you're going to die soon, Ambulance-chaser. Slowly and painfully.*

"Ready to go, Katie?" Ross asked. "Choose the restaurant. Anything you want. Sky's the limit."

"I'm happy with anything." She turned back to Seth. "Help yourself to the stuff in the fridge. I'll run you back to the dorm later. Let me know what you think of the colt."

As soon as the couple disappeared, Seth turned to Gold. "Women. If I had a Lexus, she'd be with me. What does she see in that jerk anyway?"

Gold shook his head and snorted. Such a perceptive horse.

After finishing the few remaining chores, Seth went to explore the mountain of debris Katie had piled on her desk.

If she needed a hand, he wanted to be the one to give it to her.

Chapter 13

"What a disaster!"

Seth shuffled through the bills and receipts scattered haphazardly over the surface of Katie's desk. Some were over a year old. As he thumbed through the ledger in her checkbook, he realized it hadn't been balanced in months. Of course the barely legible scribbling probably had something to do with her ignoring it. Heaven forbid the I.R.S. ever took a good, long look into her finances. Katie would never survive an audit.

He couldn't help but think he could bring some organization, *any* organization, to her record keeping. "How does she make any sense out of this mess?"

Once he'd divided the papers into orderly stacks, Seth tried to use some simple accounting to figure out just how far Katie was in the red. He rifled through her desk, but he couldn't even produce a calculator to assist him in balancing her books.

Recognizing the near impossibility of the chore he faced, Seth grabbed the keys to Katie's truck. She'd be furious he borrowed it, but the only way he could help with her problem was to get some important supplies. She'd also be furious he was plowing through her financial records.

Seth weighed her possible reaction against whether he could help her. He held out a slim hope her money worries might simply be a result of her horrendous bookkeeping. Deciding she needed his interference, he risked her irritation. "Time to move into the twenty-first century, Boss."

Seth had some shopping to do.

* * * *

"You sure this is where you want to eat?" Ross asked as he appraised the building's rundown exterior. Wanting to impress her, he had hoped she would pick something more elegant.

"I know it's a hole in the wall, but they've got the best Chinese food in town," Katie answered, reaching for the door handle. Ross gently brushed her hand away and opened the door for her. She obviously wasn't used to men treating her with common courtesy.

Placing his hand on the small of her back and savoring the freedom to touch her, Ross ushered her to a table where he pulled out her chair. "So how is Seth really doing?" He moved around the table and took his seat.

"Much better than I expected," Katie replied over the top of her menu. "Try the cashew chicken. It's to die for."

"Sounds good." He turned to the waiter who had appeared at his side. "Two cashew chickens and an iced tea. What do you want to drink, Katie?"

"Sweet tea would be nice," she replied as she handed the menu to Ross. He gave them both to the waiter and ordered her drink.

"Is Seth pulling his weight?"

"Oh, yeah. And then some. I was going to call you this week to see if you could up his pay. He's wanting to train now, and I'm teaching him. He's a quick study." She grinned so broadly, Ross began to suspect a strong attachment was forming between Katie and Seth. Her face showed pride when she talked about Seth. And, even worse, it showed affection. That notion didn't sit well—not when Ross had set his sights on getting much closer to her.

"Wow. I've got to say I'm impressed. Who'd have thought? How are you handling the whole thing?"

The waiter brought their drinks, and she took a sip of tea before finally addressing Ross's question. "How am I handling it? Day by day. It's... different having him around. I thought I'd be babysitting, but he works so much harder than I ever expected."

"Seth Remington working?" He shook his head. "I'm sorry, but I can't seem to get a good handle on that idea."

"I know. It surprised me, too. He's actually a damn good groom, and he's got a knack for training, too. And he's... fun to be around." She smiled and shrugged. "Who knew?"

With a laugh, Ross shook his head again. "Not me. All right, enough about Remington. Tell me about you. How'd you decide to start training horses?"

Throughout dinner, Katie and Ross shared stories from their lives. She spoke of growing up in Goshen and learning the trade from her grandfather and Jacob. Ross absorbed every word.

He told her his tales about playing college football, going to law school, and the trials and tribulations of working for a large firm. He was thrilled she appeared genuinely interested.

The fortune cookies arrived at the end of the pleasant meal. Katie took one and broke it open. When she laughed aloud, she piqued Ross's curiosity. "What does it say?"

Katie read from the small slip of paper. "'Where there is love, expect the impossible.'"

"Gee, that's specific." He rolled his eyes. "You don't believe that stuff, do you?"

She shook her head and gave him a crooked smile. "No, not really." She picked up the second cookie and set it in the palm of her hand. Looking up through those thick lashes, the challenge was plain in her eyes. "So, Ross. What does your fortune say?"

Ross took the treat, cracked the shell, and retrieved the paper. "'The heart often wants what it cannot obtain.'"

Katie crinkled her nose. "That has to be the most depressing fortune I've ever heard."

Taking several bills out of his wallet, Ross dropped them on the table. "Ready to go? Maybe we could catch a movie."

"I really should get back to the barn. Seth needs a ride back, and I want to see my new colt," Katie replied as Ross pulled her chair back and escorted her out of the restaurant.

Jealousy flashed vivid and strong, but Ross pushed it aside, reminding himself that Katie and Seth only worked together. She was here, having dinner with him, not Remington. And Ross would do whatever it took to keep her close a little while longer.

Once they reached the parking lot, he opened the passenger door of the Lexus. "What would you say if I told you I'm thinking about buying a horse and putting it in your stable?"

Katie had been ducking to slide into the car, but she suddenly popped back up. She knocked her head on the roof and let out a yelp. "Thanks a lot, Ross. That hurt." She rubbed a spot on the crown of her head.

"Sorry."

"Did you just say you wanted to put a horse in my barn?" Katie asked, clearly confused over the prospect.

When he didn't immediately reply, she carefully sat down in the passenger seat as he closed her door and walked to his side of the car.

Once they pulled out into traffic, Ross finally answered her. "I really think I'd like to see what it's like to own a racehorse. And if I get one, where else would I possibly put it than with you? Would you mind taking on another horse?"

Katie shook her head, and Ross watched her soft red ponytail bounce in response. Her pretty face made it hard to keep his eyes on the road. She couldn't possibly know how much he'd been thinking about her since that cold day he'd left Seth at her barn. Even from the moment he first saw her in his Chicago office, he'd been infatuated. Through their many phone conversations, they'd forged a strong friendship. But he pictured Katie as so much more than a friend. The notion that Seth Remington could share all of her time was driving Ross to distraction.

The only thing keeping him from losing his mind to jealousy was knowing Seth couldn't pursue Katie. He'd dealt with lots of men like Seth—guys who believed money was more important than anything else in life. You inherited that kind of money, you sacrificed your conscience. It was a relief to know Katie would be spared Seth's charms.

Ross figured he could be charming too, and he intended to do everything in his power to spend time with Katie Murphy. If it cost him the price of a racehorse, so be it. And Seth had told him she needed the money. Ross desperately wanted to find a way to help her.

"I'd love to work with you. Did you want to buy or claim? Did you have a horse in mind?" She kept talking as they drove, practically bouncing on the seat with her apparent excitement. "How much did you want to spend? Did you apply for an owner's license yet?"

Katie impressed him with the catalog of questions she continued to throw his way, but she didn't even pause long enough to take a breath so he could have a chance to respond. Her enthusiasm was infectious, and Ross pictured himself in a winner's circle with a handsome horse. And with Katie.

This might be a lot of fun.

"You tell me what to do, and I'll do it. How much do you need?" Ross asked.

"It depends on what you want. Easiest thing would be to claim. Lowest claimers are five-thousand. And I can cut you a good deal on training."

"No!" He hadn't meant to shout. "No deals. You need to earn a living, and I know you'll more than make it back for me. Tell me about claiming."

Katie explained the process, and Ross agreed it would be the easiest way to acquire a good horse. "What's the highest claiming level?" he asked.

She gawked at him. "Thirty-thousand, but there are lower claimers. You can—"

Ross interrupted with a wave of his hand. "Thirty is great. I'll have money wired to a track account tomorrow, and I'll get my owner's license as soon as I can."

"You can't be serious," she scoffed. "No one starts at the highest level."

"Of course, I'm serious. When you find what you want, you get it." He reached over to her, tucking his hand around her slim, cool fingers. "And I'll send you an advance on your training fees so you can get anything you need."

"Ross, trainers don't get an advance," Katie said as she shook her head.

"Mine does." He grinned at her like some besotted adolescent before he caught himself and put his eyes back on traffic.

She squeezed his hand. "Are you sure? God, Ross, that's an awful lot of money."

He smiled at her touch and her concern. "I don't know how to say this without sounding like I'm bragging, but I've got plenty of money. I'm single, and I work seventy hours a week." He shrugged. "What else do I have to spend it on? Humor me. Get me a good horse. Let's win some money together."

Katie's face glowed. "I'll do better than get you a good horse; I'll *make* you a good horse."

"I beg your pardon?"

"Turn left on the next street," she instructed as she pulled her hand from his.

Ross did as she asked. "Where are we going?"

She pointed toward a strip mall. "There's a coffee shop with computers over there. It's open late. I'm going to show you how to make a good horse."

* * * *

Ross guided the Lexus into a parking space in front of The Cyber House. Katie didn't even wait for him to work his way around to open her door before she jumped out of the car.

She found a vacant table and sat herself down in front of one of the shop's open computers where she hunched over to stare at the screen. Katie hoped Ross wouldn't recognize the trouble she had as she tried to find the correct website. She'd never learned much about using a computer, and she didn't want him to think she was an uneducated hick. Even if she was.

"What are we looking for?" Ross asked, leaning over her shoulder.

"I'm going to find you a horse we can turn into a thirty claimer."

"Why not just claim one at thirty? Wouldn't that be easier?"

Katie shook her head as she tried to navigate the confusing Internet. "It might be easier, but not nearly as profitable." She looked up at Ross for help. She'd forgotten how incredibly tall the man was. "Do you know how to find a website when you don't know the address?"

Sitting down next to Katie, Ross gave her a few lessons in web surfing. Before too long, they arrived at the correct place. Rows of names and statistics filled the screen, and she took over the role of instructor as he assumed the role of student.

"There!" Katie pointed at the screen. "That's the one. I knew he was in this week."

Ross looked at the information, but seemed confused. "What does that mean?"

She lowered her voice to a whisper. One never knew when other horsemen lingered around, and claiming was best done covertly. "Taylor O'Riley's horse is in for fifteen. I can make him a thirty claimer," she said softly but with confidence. She might not know computers, but she damn well knew horses.

Ross whispered in return. "How can you do that? Make him a thirty claimer?" He sat so close that his breath tickled her ear, but it didn't send the wave of heat through her body the way Seth always did whenever he was near. Katie tried to shake the thought of Seth right out of her head. She wasn't entirely successful. "By the way, why are we whispering?" he asked with an amused smile.

"It's best to keep a good thing under your hat," she softly replied. "I'll turn this horse into a thirty claimer by improving him. It's like buying stock. Buy low; sell high. Taylor's a really nice guy, but he's a terrible trainer. I can improve on him. Trust me." She thumped the screen with her finger. "This is the horse you want."

He nodded and gave her an enormous grin. Katie wondered why her heart didn't beat a little faster like it always did when Seth smiled. "What do I have to do to get this one?" Ross asked.

"You need to come to the race office tomorrow and get your license. You'll need fingerprints," she answered as she continued to search through the information she'd found on the gelding she wanted. She started a mental list of things she would have to do to prepare for the new horse.

Katie felt as excited as a toddler at Christmas. For the first time she could remember, she had the financial backing to choose a really good prospect. Ross was handing her a golden opportunity and serving it up on a silver platter.

But why? Why out of the blue?

Katie stopped looking at the computer and turned to stare at her new benefactor. "Ross, can I ask you a question?"

"Go ahead."

"Why now? Why get a horse now?"

Ross seemed to think about his answer for a long moment before he finally replied. "Because of you."

Katie furrowed her brow. "I don't understand."

Ross took her hand into his. His touch was warm and comforting, but her stomach sure didn't flutter the way it did when Seth touched her. "Katie, you're contagious. Ever since I first saw you, you're all I can think about. It's like I've contracted some type of... virus."

"Gee, thanks." Katie pulled her hand away, leaned back in the chair, and crossed her arms. "I'm a virus?"

Ross looked sheepish. "Sorry. Bad analogy. I'm not really good at... at saying what I feel." He seemed hesitant, which surprised Katie since his style usually came across as much more assertive. "I really like you, and if we get a horse together, it gives me a good excuse to spend time with you."

Although she was flattered by the admission, something in the back of her mind sent a warning flag soaring. It was never a good thing to mix business with pleasure, especially in racing. Acquiring a horse could be a long-term commitment, and too many a romance had fizzled under the high pressure of the industry.

An image of Seth came unbidden into Katie's mind, and she tried desperately to push it aside, to sweep him out of her thoughts. That man was bad news in every sense of the word. Just as soon as he completed the season, Seth would disappear without a backward glance. She imagined he would be so anxious to leave that he would high-tail it out of Indiana at the first possible moment. He might have adapted well, even thrived, but Katie was certain he viewed her way of life as well below his social station.

Ross was here embracing her world with open arms, and his addition to her stable could very well save it. So why couldn't she want Ross instead of Seth? The lawyer was handsome with his wavy brown hair and big brown eyes. He led a successful life. And he acted like an adult instead of a spoiled child.

Damn Seth Remington anyway!

One part of her wished Seth would leave her in peace even as another pushed her to hold onto him with all of her strength. For a woman who desired total control of every aspect of her existence, the duality of her own feelings shook her to the core. Where could this whole mess she called a life ultimately lead?

For now, she would let it lead her to a new horse. And she'd make money for both of them.

"Thank you, Ross. You're sweet," Katie said as she leaned forward and patted his arm.

Ross smiled and covered her hand with his. "Let's have some coffee and talk about what it's like to own a horse, then I'll take you back. It's getting late, and I'll need to find a place to stay tonight."

"I'm sorry. I forgot you had to go back tonight. We can do this another time."

"No way. You know what you want, and we're going to get it. I'll make some calls in the morning. No sweat," Ross reassured with a pat of his hand.

* * * *

It was nearly eleven when Ross eased the car down the long gravel road and parked next to Katie's barn door. He turned off the engine and glanced over at her. Ross reached up and wrapped one of the curls that had worked free of her ponytail around his finger. "I had a really nice time, Katie."

She waited for that feeling of anticipation she got whenever Seth had reached out to touch her, but she felt nothing. No shiver of excitement, no blood rushing through her veins, no visceral thrill. "Thanks for dinner, Ross. And thank you for having faith in me."

Ross leaned over to press a kiss on her lips, and she didn't resist. Katie waited patiently for the lightning bolt, waited for her insides to melt, waited for the ecstasy she got when Seth had kissed her. Despite the sweetness and gentleness of Ross's kiss, those feelings never arrived.

He pulled away to stare into her eyes. She could see he was deep in thought as his gaze searched hers, and she didn't know what to say or do to make things better.

Katie decided she needed to be very sure she wasn't making a huge error in judgment based on one chaste kiss. Maybe she needed to try harder. Putting her hand behind Ross's head, she pulled him into a deeper kiss, hoping for a spark to ignite, wanting Ross to exorcise Seth Remington from her troubled mind.

Seth had buried himself in working on Katie's books, and he'd quickly lost track of time. Hearing the gravel crunch with a vehicle's approach, he glanced up at the clock above the desk.

Damn it! Where has she been all night?

It took every ounce of his self-control to keep from running straight out to the car and jerk Katie out to make sure Ross kept his paws off her, that the lawyer didn't lay claim to what wasn't his. Trying to be as sly as possible, Seth eased his way to the barn door and stared in stunned disbelief as he clearly saw Katie grab Ross and draw him into a zealous kiss. "Damn it!"

He whirled around and marched back into the barn.

Chapter 14

Katie pulled away from Ross. She had her answer. For the second time that night, she damned Seth Remington. Why couldn't she ever be attracted to the right guy? "Ross, I..."

"You don't have to say anything, Katie. I get it. I just wish..." His fingers reached up to stroke her cheek. He was so kind, so attentive, and she felt like a fool for not wanting him.

She heaved a weighty sigh, knowing she'd lost her benefactor. But she wasn't about to string him along simply to get a new horse in her barn. "If you don't want to get a horse now... I understand."

His hand dropped to cover hers. "Don't be ridiculous. Whether we date and whether I buy a horse are entirely separate issues. I want the horse, and I expect you to make a success out of him. But I do hope you'll give me a chance to see if there might be something more between us than friendship. That's all I ask. Just give me some time. I grow on people."

Katie smiled as she felt herself relaxing. "I'll bet you do. Fine, Ross. I'll give you some time."

At the barn door, he took her hand again and pressed a kiss to her cheek. "The money will be at the race office sometime tomorrow. I'll come to get you for breakfast. Maybe around eight? Then we can go to the race office."

"I'm sorry, Ross," she replied with a pang of guilt. "I won't have time for breakfast. We have chores in the morning." She drew her hand away. "Thanks again for dinner. I had a really nice time. I'll get you a damn fine horse. I promise. We're going to make some money together."

"You're welcome, and I believe you, Katie. I believe *in* you, too."

She watched him make his way back to the Lexus. She couldn't help but smile at the care he took in deciding exactly where to step. Some people just couldn't get past their fear of a little manure.

Katie stood for a moment to gather her tumbling thoughts. Ross was handing her a small fortune to get a horse that could pull her and her stable out of a financial crunch. He wanted nothing in return, didn't expect anything except for her to do a good job.

Why couldn't she feel for Ross what she did for a man who would leave her behind in the span of a heartbeat if given the chance? Why did she always have to care for the wrong man? Why couldn't she ever love wisely?

She sighed and leaned her head against the doorframe, watching the Lexus disappear up the white rock drive.

"Did Matlock leave?" Seth suddenly appeared from the shadows, making Katie jump. She put her hand over her rapidly beating heart.

Surprise wasn't the only reason her heart was pounding. She didn't want to, but Katie reacted to Seth being so near. She could feel a flush warming her cheeks as heat raced through her veins, slowly spreading its way through her body. Butterfly flutters assailed her abdomen. Why did things always become decidedly warmer every time he drew near?

She tried to appear nonchalant when she finally answered. "Yeah, Ross left."

"You two seemed awfully cozy." His eyes were hard, his voice strained.

"Were you spying on me?"

Seth didn't answer. Katie let the point drop. It wasn't as if it would even matter. What she felt for Seth could never be returned, and what might happen between her and Ross was no one's business but their own. Seth could assume whatever the hell he wanted.

"You ready to go back to the dorm?"

"Not yet. Come with me." Seth grabbed her hand and dragged her toward her room. Katie stumbled to keep up in her high-heeled sandals.

Seth opened the door and pulled her across the threshold. It only took a second for her to notice what he had done to her desk, and when she did, she reacted in a fit of temper. "Where's my stuff? What in the hell did you do with all my bills?"

"I know you hate change, Boss. But just look for a second."

"Look? Look at what? My bills are gone. How am I supposed to pay them now?" Despite her anger, she looked around, surprised at what she saw. On the middle of the now clear desk sat a laptop computer with a printer attached by a long cable. Standing next to the old desk was a small metal filing cabinet. Katie gawked at them. "What did you do?"

With a smile, Seth pulled the chair out and pushed her to take a seat. "You should've had one of these a long time ago. There's a spreadsheet program so you can print bills for your owners." He pointed at the screen to show her a mock-up of a bill with a cute racehorse logo. "If they get a professional looking bill, they'll be more likely to pay you on time. The laptop has a wireless card, so if you take it to one of those coffee shops, it'll pick up the web."

She was so embarrassed she had a hard time looking at him. "I... I don't know how to use a spreadsheet, Seth. I can barely use a computer. I only have a G.E.D." She let her fingers brush gently across the keys. *My own computer. Seth got me my own computer.*

"So? What does that matter? I know people with PhDs who can't handle a computer. I'll show you how to use the silly thing. I happen to know a little bit about them," he said with a wink. "Did you know you paid Jack's vet bill twice last month?"

"I did?" Katie pulled open one of the drawers in the file cabinet. Hanging green folders with neatly printed labels cradled her now organized paperwork.

He pointed to one of the files. "Yeah. It's in there. And the feed bill was wrong." He flipped to another file. "They charged you for too many bags. I remember because I unloaded them from your truck."

Katie was stunned. How could he have done so much in such a short time? The fact that he'd managed to make some sense of the one part of her life she never seemed to be able to handle confounded her. She wasn't sure whether to be insulted or thrilled with everything he'd done. "Seth, I really appreciate all this, but..." She shook her head in frustration. "I can't afford any of this stuff."

"I took care of it." He leaned over her and jiggled the computer's mouse to navigate the spreadsheet on the screen. His scent drifted around her. So masculine, so enthralling, so... horsey. Fresh hay and leather. "I was just glad they had a laptop I could get my hands on tonight."

Katie rolled her eyes, thinking she understood the whole situation. "Yeah, I'll bet you *took care* of it. I suppose you called one of your friends at Remington Computers and he sent—"

She was entirely unprepared for Seth's angry interruption. "I paid for it! It's a refurbished computer, but it's still good. And, yes, it's a Remington, but I *paid* for the damn thing! Thanks a heap for the vote of confidence, Katie."

She had misjudged him and offered a contrite apology. "I'm sorry, Seth. I really am. I just don't know how you can afford all this stuff."

Her apology noticeably cooled his anger, and he went back to leaning over her and playing with her new computer. "What else do I have to spend my stupid salary on?" He shrugged his broad shoulders.

It dawned on her this was the second time a man had told her the same thing that evening, and she felt overwhelmed at the generosity of both Seth and Ross.

Ross. A man who could offer Katie a future, a stable future. He seemed secure in himself, focused on making his career a success, and had a genuine interest in learning about her way of life.

But Ross's kiss hadn't reached her heart.

Seth. A man who never made plans beyond tomorrow, had a history of being a spoiled brat, and was only a part of horseracing because he had to be. What kind of future could he have other than a continuation of the habits that had forced his father to create such an onerous will? How many more cars would he wreck? How quickly would he return to the ranks of the Boys' Club after he left Katie's employ?

But simply having Seth near made her sigh in longing.

Two very different men, both helping her out of a jam. Each in his own way and neither having an expectation of receiving anything in return for their generosity except friendship. Even though she truly appreciated both of them and what they were doing for her, the emotions running through her mind threatened to drown her.

Katie hated needing other people so much. Relying on others made her too vulnerable. She needed to stand on her own two feet, to handle her own problems. Knowing these men might bail her out of her financial mess was humiliating. She couldn't stop the tears from welling up in her eyes, nor could she stop her throat from closing up as she choked on her emotions. She tried to hide her reaction from Seth, but he put his hand under her chin and lifted her face until she looked up into those handsome hazel eyes. Knowing all the affection she held for him wasn't returned only made it harder to stop weeping.

"Katie? Why are you crying? Don't you like the computer?"

"I'm not crying," she lied even as another tear traced a path down her cheek. He brushed it away with his thumb.

Seth was suddenly drowning in her eyes, smothered by her sweet and very feminine scent. Without a thought to the consequences, he dropped to his knees, cupped her face in his hands, and pressed his lips to hers.

The contact was almost more than he could stand. His head swam and the world rotated around him. Every inch of him screamed for her, demanding and demanding, and when his tongue swept into her mouth, she rewarded him with a low moan that instantly made him hard.

Unprepared for the wave of emotion roiling through him when Katie's tongue returned his caress, he let it wash over him, having no intention of stopping. All he had wanted to do was to make her forget Ross, but she'd succeeded in making him forget everything.

Breaking away from the kiss, Seth wrapped an arm around her waist, sat back on the floor, and pulled Katie from the chair onto his lap. She wrapped her arms around his neck and kissed him again as he threaded his fingers through her soft hair, all but untying her ponytail. He ravaged her mouth, demanding her assent, giving her no opportunity to deny him. He needed to taste her, needed to touch her, needed to consume her.

Time ceased to exist as Seth let one hand slide down her spine as the other boldly moved to claim her breast through the thin material of the sundress. He could hear Katie mewl deep in her throat, and his body responded even more forcefully to the sound, throbbing in anticipation, demanding the interminable seduction come to fruition. Maybe he *could* make her purr.

There had never been a time in his life when he wanted anything as much as he wanted to possess her at that moment. Body. Heart. Soul. She belonged to him and no one else. His touch would brand her, mark her, make others keep their distance.

"God, Katie, I want you. I want you now." He nuzzled her neck and she shuddered in response.

"Seth, we can't," she offered in a weak protest even as she laced her fingers through his hair to press his face closer to her throat.

Seth chuckled lightly knowing the battle was won. He kissed his way up to her cheek and then ran his tongue over the curving lines of her ear.

"Yes, we can, Baby. No one has to know." He returned to placing kisses along the slim, white column of her throat. Her pulse raced against his lips, pounding a fast cadence and telling him she felt the attraction as strongly as he did.

His hand found her knee, and he let his fingers begin to inch their way under the material of her skirt and up her bare thigh. She felt like heaven, her skin soft and warm stretched over trembling muscle. All he could think about was stripping her out of the sundress and kissing every inch of her body. He'd bring her to the edge of ecstasy then he'd bury himself deep inside her, knowing she would come screaming his name.

"Hmm. Yeah," she encouraged. "Ooh, I like that. Do it again. No one has to..." Katie's spine suddenly stiffened. Supple muscle tensed beneath his fingertips. Her hand dropped to cover his where it rested on her thigh, to halt his quest just short of the grail.

Damn. Damn. Damn.

He looked into her eyes, and he sure didn't like the confusion he saw. Where had the passion gone? "Katie? What's wrong?"

"No one has to know," she repeated with a quiver in her voice. Tears pooled in her eyes. He kissed away one that fell from her lash to her cheek.

"I won't tell anyone if you won't." Seth tried to claim her lips again.

Katie pulled away and started to cry in earnest. He'd never been so confused in his entire life. "What did I do wrong?" Suddenly, he thought he understood her resistance. "God, Katie, I really don't want to leave, but I can run to the store and get some condoms if you're not on the pill." Funny, he hadn't even worried about protection, hadn't really even considered it up to that moment. Unfortunately, his statement only seemed to make her more upset. She cried hard enough to shake on his lap. "C'mon, Katie. What's wrong?"

"I'm... ashamed of myself."

"Is that all?" He'd always thought shame was overrated. Seth tried to nuzzle her neck again, to coax her to respond, but she put both hands on his chest and pushed him away. Her skirt tangled around her legs as she struggled to stand. Seth held her firmly in his lap. "I don't understand."

"Let me go! I know you don't understand. You've probably never been ashamed of anything in your whole life. We... we can't do this! We can't!" She fought to break his grasp.

Seth released her and sighed, realizing he'd never understand women.

Katie obviously wanted him as desperately as he wanted her. Why fight it? Then it dawned on him. Perhaps she was frightened. "If it's because you're a virgin—"

"Who told you that?" Katie snapped as she stood up and kicked off her sandals, sending each in turn flying across the room. One of them knocked a stack of CDs off their dresser perch. They hit the floor and the sound of the clatter filled the room. She turned back to him, clenching her fists at her side. "Who in the hell told you that?"

"No one," he calmly responded with a shrug. "I just... guessed. I mean, the way you act—"

"I'm not a virgin!" Her hands flew to her mouth as if horrified at letting her private life slip out.

"Then what's the problem?" The whole situation baffled him. He could understand her reticence if she was inexperienced and afraid, but since she was neither, Seth figured they should simply give in to their obviously strong mutual attraction.

"You don't have a clue, do you? I gave my word to your father. *My word!* I might not have been looking him in the eye at the time, but when I signed that agreement, I... I promised to keep our relationship business. You should be thanking me. If we... if we... You'd lose your money."

Seth scratched his head in confusion. "I wouldn't lose anything. We wouldn't have to tell anybody."

"But I'd know!"

His confusion wasn't getting any better. He stared up at her from where he still sat on the floor, still wanting her, still needing to touch her. "I don't get it. You want me. I want you. There's not a soul around..." He knew he wasn't saying the right things, so he tried again. "I want you, Katie. Trust me, it'll be... wonderful. And no one has to know."

Katie pulled the ribbon from her hair and shook her head. Her long tresses spilled around her shoulders. "I'd know, and I'd be ashamed of myself!" She grabbed the truck keys resting on her bed and hurled them at him. "Go home! Just go away!" She ran to the bathroom and slammed the door.

Seth could hear her crying and felt like a cad; he just didn't have the faintest idea why. "I sure as hell didn't do anything wrong." Rising to his feet, he walked over to the door and knocked softly with the back of his knuckles. “Katie? Are you okay?”

“Go away!” She started to cry louder.

He laid his palm on the door, wishing he could touch her, wishing he could soothe her. “Can’t we talk about this?” He couldn’t stand to see her in so much pain—especially since he clearly caused her distress. The whole situation seemed a bit absurd, but Katie’s weeping was too hard for him to listen to.

“Please just... just go away!”

Seth put his fingers to his forehead and massaged the dull ache. His body was still tense with desire as the beat of his heart echoed in his ears. But every instinct told him to get the hell out of there before he fell in too deep. Katie’s restraint might be the only thing standing between him and a lifetime of abject poverty.

He couldn’t leave her. Not like this.

Seth rested his forehead against the door. “Katie? Please, Boss. C’mon. Come out and talk to me. I promise not to touch you. I promise. I just need to know you’re okay.”

After a few moments, he heard her sniffle and then blow her nose. “You promise?” Then she sniffled again.

“Cross my heart.”

The door squeaked opened a crack, and Katie peeked out. Seth took a few steps back, and she opened the door the rest of the way. She held a wad of tissue and her mascara had streaked, rimming both of her eyes in black.

“Are you okay?”

She nodded slightly and gave a small hiccup in response. Walking over to the bed, she sat on the quilt and pulled her legs up under her skirt.

Seth sat down on the desk chair and stared at her, still wanting her.

“What? What are you staring at?” she asked.

“You look like a raccoon,” he replied with a small chuckle.

Katie ran her fingertip under her eye and stared at the black smudge left behind. “Gee, thanks.” She dabbed at her eyes with the wad of tissues. “First, I’m a virus. Now, I’m a raccoon.”

“A virus?”

Katie breathed a weary sigh. “Never mind.” Her face grew serious. “Seth, we can’t do this. *I* can’t do this.”

Seth nodded. “I’ll behave.” He wasn’t entirely sure he could keep the promise for too long, but it sounded sincere enough to keep from scaring her away. All he really wanted to do was join her on the bed and peel off that pretty pink dress.

What the hell is wrong with me?

While he would admit to an indiscretion or two in his life, Seth had never let lust rule his behavior. Never. But he felt himself becoming aroused, felt his groin tighten, felt his heart pound again at the mere thought of running his hands over Katie's tight little body.

"Don't you understand?" Katie's words drew him back from his thoughts.

"No. Why don't you explain it to me?"

"Seth, I don't have much in this world, but I have my self-respect. If something happened between us... I would hate myself because I'd be breaking a promise."

Self-respect. Such a foreign concept. Had he ever had any self-respect? Had he ever done anything that he would be proud of when he was old and gray?

The Old Man had. Sterling had built a formidable dynasty from a small family business. He'd discovered a love for horses and proceeded to apply his typical Midas touch. Through reading Katie's horseracing magazines, Seth had learned more about his father than he ever had by talking to the man. There were pictures of his high-profile horses. There were interviews about how much racing meant to him. There was an article mourning his death.

Seth had to squash his envy. Sterling had been a success in every aspect of his life—businesses, hobbies, finding the love of his life. Sterling had succeeded at everything he'd ever done.

Except raising his son.

Seth suddenly realized how much he must have embarrassed his father, how much his recklessness must have hurt the Old Man. Between the car accidents, the speeding tickets, and Seth's penchant for dating selfish starlets, Sterling must have felt like he had failed at being a parent.

"Seth?"

He was too angry at himself to talk to her. He was too angry at her, too.

Katie hadn't wanted him, she'd wanted Ross Kennedy. Remembering the kiss he'd seen her give the lawyer, jealousy made Seth's stomach knot.

He felt something for Katie, something more than lust, more than desire. But she didn't return his feelings. She might have responded to his kisses and caresses, but when the time came to follow through, she had turned him down. She probably thought Matlock was the better man. And why wouldn't she? Ross Kennedy didn't demolish expensive cars and whisper sweet nothings into the ears of women who didn't really matter to him.

The passion Seth felt for Katie was smothering, driving him to forget what should have been the most important thing in his life—his fortune. Hell, he wouldn't ever earn it back if he didn't get his act together.

Shame nagged at him, nibbled at him from every angle. He hated the way it felt, hated the way it weighed on his thoughts, and hated that it kept him from simply doing as he pleased.

He was ashamed he'd almost betrayed his father. Even though the man was gone, Seth knew he still held the power to disappoint Sterling Remington—just as he had *always* disappointed him.

Well, this time would be different. This time he wasn't going to screw it up. This time he'd make his father proud.

Seth glanced back at Katie. She still stared at him with those intense green eyes.

She was the problem. If she wasn't so close. If she wasn't so beautiful. If she wasn't so desirable.

If she wasn't interested in another man.

Despite his best intentions, despite wanting to do this job right, Seth couldn't shake what he felt for Katie. But if he was going to follow through and make Sterling proud, he had to let her go. Wouldn't that be what was best for her?

Why did it have to be Matlock? The man was a walking example of everything Seth had wanted to avoid in life. A time-consuming job. A straight-laced, starched-collared approach to life. There wasn't an ounce of fun in him. How could he let Katie go knowing she'd probably run straight into the arms of Ross Kennedy?

Seth had to succeed at this job; he had to finally do something for his father. Seth would do his time, and he would leave Katie Murphy alone. No matter how much it hurt.

"Seth?"

His clipped words came out harsh. "Take me back to my room." He needed to put some distance between them, and the best way to do that was to push her away.

Even if it broke his heart.

Chapter 15

"Is it really that bad?" Samantha asked Chris as they ate breakfast in the track kitchen.

"Oh, yeah," he answered with a vigorous nod. "They've been fighting like cats and dogs for the last month."

Sam shook her head in frustration. Katie had been miserable for weeks, but for the first time since they became friends, Katie wouldn't share her problems with Sam. She knew the fishing expedition might be a little... immature. But Sam was concerned about Katie. She'd never seen her so unhappy—even after Mike Knight's infidelity. "What's the main beef?"

"You know, that's what I can't seem to figure out. It's like *anything* sets them off. If Katie's cell phone rings," Chris snapped his fingers, "that starts a squabble." He took a sip of his orange juice. "I think Spun Gold is most of the problem."

"Katie's colt? She's having trouble training him?"

"*She* isn't training Gold. The colt won't let anybody but Crash drive him." Chris stopped, shook his head, and scoffed. "*Crash.* Katie doesn't even call him that anymore. It's always 'Seth.' What's up with that? Hell, even I call him 'Seth' now."

Sam considered that for a moment. "I've been working on that one, but nada so far. So Gold won't let Katie near him?"

"Oh no, he'll let her near him. She can put on his equipment, bathe him, turn him out and whatnot. But if Katie or I sit in the jog cart, he won't budge an inch. He nickers every time Seth walks in the barn. Trains like a dream for him. Seth treats him like a damn pet."

"No wonder Katie is pissed." Sam squirted some mustard on her scrambled eggs and home fries before she squeezed some over her sausage patties for good measure. Chris wrinkled his nose. "I'm pregnant. Get over it. How are *you* handling it?"

He stared at the paper cup he held between his hands. "I'm ordering my colors this morning."

"Chris, that's great. Your own colors." Then Samantha realized the significance. "You're thinking of leaving Katie?"

He shook his head but wouldn't look at her. "Not right away. But if... Well, if things stay the way they are..." He shrugged. "Who knows? If I have my colors, I can always get a horse or two on my own."

"At least give them a chance to work it out. Katie would hate to lose you," Sam said hoping to convince Chris not to do anything rash. He was like a brother to all of them, and Katie depended on Chris as her second. At least she had until Seth arrived. "He'll be gone at the end of the season."

Chris drained the rest of his juice, crumpled the paper cup, and pitched it in the trash can. "Swish. Two points"

Sam shook her head and chuckled. Men. They never really grew up.

"You know I don't wanna leave Katie's barn, Sam. I love working with her. She's the sister I never had. But this season is getting to be *way* too long. And it's only the beginning of June."

"I understand."

Chris stood up and pushed his chair to the table. "I need to head out. I'm meeting Seth. He wanted to go with me when I order my colors."

Sam nodded. "Pick something nice, Chris. I don't suppose you'll use maroon and gold." She gave him a lopsided smile. "It'll be weird not seeing you warm horses up in Brian's old colors. You grew up so fast."

He laughed as he headed to the exit.

As she watched him leave, Sam pondered Katie's predicament. Trying to make sense of the information she had, Sam was still at a loss. It was like trying to solve a jigsaw puzzle with several pieces missing.

Katie obviously felt something for Seth, and it was just as clear the man harbored feelings for her. Sparks flew whenever they were together. Sam had seen the lingering glances, heard the forlorn sighs. But somehow, some way that attraction had been replaced with animosity. "And I don't know why," she whispered.

The most confusing part was where Ross Kennedy came into the whole mix. Katie had claimed a horse for him, and Taylor O'Riley had been hopping mad he'd lost College Mascot to her stable for fifteen-thousand when she'd turned Mascot into a victorious thirty claimer in less than a month.

Ross was at the track for the big win. The instant Katie stepped out of the van, he'd picked her up, swung her in a circle, and planted a kiss on her in front of everyone gathered near the winner's circle. Sam had been there, closely watching Seth's reaction to the kiss. If there had been any doubt in Sam's mind that Seth had feelings for Katie, that hesitation vanished once she saw the darkness spread over his face when Ross kissed Katie. The air had been thick with tension.

With its customary speed, the gossip spread through the track that Katie had landed herself a rich new boyfriend. Sam was tired of hearing the speculations about Katie and Ross that floated so freely. She was tired of not knowing what was going on between Katie and Seth. And she was tired of her best friend shutting her out.

* * * *

"Red for the leg stripe," Chris explained. The old man taking his order scribbled a few more words on the form. "And I want the 'H' on the forearms, not the shoulders."

Seth watched as Chris carefully selected his colors, realizing the kid would have something that was his and his alone. An envious ache formed in the pit of Seth's stomach. All he'd ever possessed was a well-known family name that he'd done little to deserve. He'd never felt any real allegiance to the Remington dynasty. Hell, he'd never really felt an allegiance to anything.

Once Chris placed his order and the two men were walking away from the shop, Seth suddenly stopped. "I need to go back." Chris appeared confused at the statement. "Look, I just want to ask the guy a couple of things." Seth pulled out his wallet and handed Chris some money. "Please go grab me a breakfast sandwich, some milk, and a banana. I'll meet you at your truck. Then we can go get Gold for his qualifier." Chris nodded and headed toward the track kitchen.

"You back so soon?" the old man asked when Seth came back through the door.

"Yeah. I've decided to order colors for myself." Flipping through the book of designs resting on the counter, Seth considered several different color schemes and logos. Nothing seemed to call to him. Nothing seemed to inspire any kind of pride.

Suddenly he had a brilliant idea. "Did you happen to make Katie Murphy's colors?"

"Sure did. Green with a white shamrock. Green stripe down each leg. Right?"

"You got it. Here's what I want..."

* * * *

Spun Gold wasn't in a cooperative mood when qualifiers began. Even Seth had problems controlling the stubborn colt as Chris took the bridle in hand and led Gold to the track for warm up. Seth figured part of the problem was that the horse had picked up on the nervousness of his driver.

It was the first time Seth had ever steered an animal around the Dan Patch oval, and he imagined the other trainers and drivers looked upon him as an interloper who had borrowed Chris's helmet. He felt like a fish trying to fly and figured he might have made a big mistake in believing that he could ever belong to this world.

But the instant he entered the track and urged Gold into his pace, a feeling of rightness settled over Seth. Despite the fact he had never meant for it to happen, he felt as if he'd at long last come home.

He savored the beauty of the animal in motion and craved the feel of the dirt that hit his face with each stride Gold took. Seth loved how the rhythm of the powerful colt's gait thrummed through him. Hell, he even loved the smell of the sweaty animals and the manure.

Seth loved it all—including the red-headed angel he battled daily.

He saw Katie leaning against the fence and caught her expression as he passed the paddock for his second lap. He could see the envy in her eyes. Spun Gold was her colt. Yet here Seth sat, jogging the chestnut through his warm up. It didn't seem right, nor did it seem fair. Somehow, Seth knew he needed to make this better. Katie had been so unhappy since the night they had almost...

Almost what? Had sex?

No, it had been so much more than that. For the first time in Seth's life, he realized it wasn't about sex. This was more than just physical. Katie had touched him on a level of his heart he didn't know existed, and that was why he now fought her so fiercely. The intensity of what Seth felt whenever he drew near Katie scared him to death.

And always lurking in the background was the damned Remington money. If Seth allowed the bud of what he felt for her to grow to full bloom, he would lose everything. He would disappoint his father. Again.

It was simpler to keep her at a distance—easier to fight Katie than to love her. Besides, Matlock waited in the wings. Ross would obviously make a more sensible match for her. Just because Seth was growing to love her didn't give him the right to ruin her life. Katie deserved someone who could offer her more than a five-year disappearing act. And as much as Seth hated to admit it, Ross really seemed to care for her.

Yet the thought of Ross Kennedy putting his hands on Katie was enough to drive Seth insane. He'd never felt so possessive of anyone or anything in his whole life.

He steered Gold through the exit chute.

Katie grabbed the animal's bridle and couldn't help but smile at Seth's beaming grin. She helped him unhitch the jog cart before they walked back to the paddock with the colt.

"Felt good, didn't it?" She led the horse into the stall and attached a cross-tie. She'd never seen Seth looking so happy.

"Hell, yeah. Damn good. I see why you love this so much. God, I'd love to race." Seth followed her into the stall and pulled the other cross-tie to clip on the colt's race halter.

"It's a lot harder than it looks." They both turned to see Brian leaning on the gate and smiling at his own words. "What do I need to know before I take him out?"

Katie and Seth started to talk at the same time.

"He needs to be under cover—" Katie began.

"No, you need to send him—" Seth disagreed as he turned to face her.

They quarreled for a few moments before a shrill, loud whistle pierced the air. They both stopped talking and turned to stare at Brian, the source of the sound.

"Enough! I don't know what the hell is wrong with you two, but I need to know what to do with this colt," Brian said as he pointed at Spun Gold. "You want him to qualify, don't you?"

Katie nodded in deferment. As much as she hated admitting it, Seth knew Gold better than she did. He'd been the one who worked with the horse for weeks as he put in mile after mile of jogging and training, and she knew he should be the one to give the driver instructions.

Seth nodded back at her before he gave Brian his opinion. "Send him. Take him to the front and he'll take you the rest of the way. And no whip. He'll run if you whip him."

Brian nodded. "Got it." He started to walk away before he turned back with a somber frown. "You both need to get over whatever it is that's causing all this... this friction. You're making my wife nuts and pissing off Chris. Get it together. I'll see you guys when they call his race."

They watched in stunned silence as he walked away.

Katie stared at her boots, not knowing what to say. She wasn't about to tell Seth what she felt for him, even though keeping it bottled up inside ate away at her soul a little more every day. She finally decided to make conversation to get past the uncomfortable moment. "Brian will give him a good trip, but remember Gold is only a two-year-old. You've done a good job training him, but he'll likely need a couple more qualifiers before he's ready."

A smug smile spread across Seth's handsome face. "He's ready now. You can put him in the box to race next week."

She adjusted some of Gold's equipment, trying not to let Seth know just how much he could affect her with that smile of his. "You're becoming a classic trainer," she teased. "Way too overconfident and entirely full of shit. We'll see how he does." Shrugging, she added, "I hope you're right."

"Who'd have thought?" Chris asked as he walked up the aisle pulling Brian's race bike behind him.

"What?" Katie asked.

Chris gave her a haughty smile. "You two *can* spend more than one minute together without shouting at each other. I hope it's a trend." It clearly pleased him to see her a bit contrite. Seth's face bore what had to be a similar expression.

Katie suddenly felt foolish. Chris was right. They'd been squabbling like a couple of bratty kids. She turned to Seth. "Truce?"

Seth nodded and extended his hand. "Truce."

Katie grasped his outstretched hand and gave it a shake. Much to her chagrin, she could feel the heat of his skin as if it was still pressed against hers after they no longer touched. Her own body had become her worst enemy. Every nerve, every fiber wanted Seth, and nothing she could do would put a damper on how she reacted to him whenever he was near.

The qualifiers progressed rapidly, and Gold's moment of trial by race arrived. Both Seth and Katie worked quietly around the horse to check equipment one last time before attaching Brian's race bike to the harness. Seth led the colt to the chute as Katie took a place along the fence and said a silent prayer. One never knew what could happen with two-year-olds. A prayer sure couldn't hurt.

"I'm worried about the start," Seth said as he walked up to stand by Katie's side and rest his elbows on the fence. "I should've schooled him behind the gate more."

"No, you schooled him plenty. He knows what the gate is for. Seth, you did great with Gold, as well as I could've done training him." The smile he gave her in response was so unguarded, so genuine, it made Katie's heart skip a quick beat. God, how she wanted to kiss him right there in front of everyone, gossip be damned. She shook her head and turned her attention back to the start of the race.

They watched helplessly as the field set into motion. Spun Gold's fate now rested in Brian's hands.

Following Seth's instructions, Brian urged the colt to the front of the pack with apparent ease. "Twenty-nine seconds for the first quarter," Katie said as she reached over to place her hand over Seth's where it rested on the fence. She wasn't sure if she wanted to reassure him or bolster herself. "So far, so good."

As the field began to move on the backstretch, a horse challenged Gold's dominance by charging fast on the outside. Just before the half-mile pole, the horses raced neck and neck, eye to eye.

"No!" Katie let out a frightened shriek as she watched her colt suddenly take a bad step and fall. Gold's tumble threw Brian's bike toward the infield grass, and Brian flew for several feet before landing in a motionless heap. The only good part of the horrible spill was that the horse, bike, and driver were flung to their left and away from the other sulkies. If they had veered right, there would have been a major pileup.

People all over the track sprang into motion. The remaining racers had moved on toward the finish as the track workers ran to help the injured driver.

Katie saw Gold back on four hooves and dragging the still attached but now twisted race bike toward the paddock at a quick pace. Seth ran out onto the track. He whistled as he tried to capture the wayward colt. Katie followed at his heels and was relieved when Gold slowed and then ground to a stop next to Seth. At least they wouldn't have to chase the frightened horse.

As soon as she caught up with Seth, Katie struggled to remove the tangled bike from the horse's harness while Seth held the bridle and ran his hand over Gold's bleeding front legs. "Take him to the vet," she ordered. "He's over in the test barn. Let him look Gold over. I'm going to see about Brian and see if he has horses that still need to race."

"They won't cancel the rest of the qualifiers?" Seth asked.

Katie shook her head. "An accident only slows the races down, doesn't stop 'em."

Seth nodded and led Gold toward the test barn.

By the time Katie had dragged the deformed sulky off the track, she could see Brian had regained his feet. Samantha had run to his side, and Brian now leaned heavily on her shoulders as he walked on unsteady legs. The ambulance entered the track, and Katie watched Sam intently saying something to Brian and trying to lead him to the vehicle. She was obviously insisting that he be put inside. Brian didn't seem horribly cooperative as he shook his head. Sam must have won the argument because Katie watched Brian finally step up into the rig. His wife crawled in beside him.

Katie decided the best thing she could do was get the Mitchell's horse ready for the upcoming qualifier. She checked the posted races and then turned to jog up one of the long rows of the paddock.

Several minutes later, Sam joined Katie in the horse's stall. "Thanks, Katie. I needed to see Brian."

"Since you're here, I hope that means he's fine." Katie finished tightening the cinch on the leather harness.

"Yeah, he's fine." Sam gave a small, odd laugh. "He needs to change his tighty-whities, but he's only a little scraped up. God, I hate this. I wish to hell he'd stop driving and just train." She grabbed a tendon boot, crouched next to her horse, and began to wrap it around the animal's lower leg even though it was upside down. Sam's hands were shaking.

"But he's one of the best. He loves it."

"I know he loves it. Hell, he *lives* for it. I just wish he didn't." Sam stood up and threw the tendon boot down in disgust. "I promised myself I wouldn't cry," she said even as the tears fell on her cheeks. She turned and gave the wall a solid kick.

Katie moved to her friend, spun her around, and pulled her into a hug. "He's okay, Sam. He's fine."

"What about next time? Huh?" She sniffled against Katie's shoulder. "We're going to have a baby. He needs to be more careful."

Katie patted her friend's back. "He's just as likely to get hurt crossing the street."

Sam snorted a laugh then pushed herself away from Katie. "That's bullshit, and you know it. But thanks anyway." Sam wiped her tears on the sleeve of her shirt. "Damn, I hate crying. Must be the hormones." She reached down and retrieved the tendon boot. "At least he used the old race bike. I'd kill him if he trashed the new one. Let's get this horse on the track." Sam stomped her foot. "Oh, hell. I've gotta get another driver."

Seth came back to the paddock, leading an uncharacteristically subdued Gold and hauling the harness over his shoulder. The colt now sported long streaks of silver disinfectant spray down both of his front legs and across his chest. Katie walked over to take a look at the damage.

"Just some cuts and scrapes. Nothing major. He should be good by next week's qualifiers," Seth informed her.

Katie patted the horse's neck, relieved the accident had caused no serious damage to Brian, Gold, or anyone else on the track.

"How's Brian?" Seth asked. "I didn't see the ambulance leave."

"He's all right. He didn't have to go to the hospital, but I'll bet he'll feel it tomorrow. Let's get Gold back to the farm."

"I'll get him in the trailer for you, but would you mind if I stayed here?"

Katie shook her head. "No. Stay. Get a nap. We've got two in tonight. I'll bring them in."

Seth helped her gather the equipment and load Spun Gold into the trailer, and then he watched her drive away.

The instant he saw Katie's taillights pass the guard post, Seth beat a path straight to the race office.

Chapter 16

"You did *what*?" Katie shouted, startling the horse she had led into a stall.

Seth had known she wouldn't like what he had to say, and he promised himself he'd keep his own temper in check. "You heard me. I got my Q-license yesterday so I can drive. I'm going to race Gold in the next qualifier."

"The hell you are! What do you want to do, get yourself killed?"

"Thanks for that vote of confidence, Boss." He let an arrogant smile form on his lips. "I might start to believe you really care."

Katie was in one of her huffs, and Seth knew she wasn't about to be charmed out of it. "Seth, you might think you're a groom, and you can make believe you're a trainer. But you're *not* pretending you're a driver. Are you insane?"

"I *am* a groom, and I sure as hell have been doing a pretty good job *pretending* to be a trainer." Seth took an angry step toward her. "And if I want to drive, why should you care? I'll get him qualified. Gold wouldn't have fallen if I'd been the one driving him."

Putting her hands on her hips, Katie threw him an incredulous scowl. "And how could you possibly know that?"

"I just do," was his cocky response as he glared down at her. As if the woman could ever be intimidated.

"You honestly believe that?"

"Absolutely."

Katie rolled her eyes in clear exasperation. "Well, excuse me. I didn't realize all-knowing, all-powerful Seth Remington could see the future." A sarcastic chuckle came from her lips. "Remind me to ask you before I ever bet again. It would help to know the winners *before* the race."

Seth watched her run through a gamut of emotions, her face full of expression, her eyes full of worry. His announcement had obviously affected her deeply.

After a few moments, she stomped her foot. “I won’t let you do it. He’s my colt, and I won’t let you do it.” Whirling around, Katie took long, angry strides getting back to her office. “It’s ridiculous. It’s dangerous. It’s entirely out of the question,” she muttered along the way.

Seth worked quietly around the barn to give Katie time to cool down. Her anger wasn’t going to change his mind, but it did give him some insight into her thoughts. Could it be Katie cared about him more than she let on?

No. She’s just thinking about Spun Gold.

Besides, it was becoming pretty clear she belonged to Ross. That thought tore through Seth, making his stomach churn. No matter how hard he fought them, his feelings for Katie couldn’t be shaken. She remained in his thoughts almost every waking moment, and the little time his mind drifted elsewhere, it focused on racing. This world had become his life; Katie had become his passion.

Several minutes later, he knocked softly on her door and stuck his head inside. “Katie?”

“Yeah.”

“Will you give me a chance? I know Gold. I can drive him. C’mon, Boss. It’s just a qualifier.”

Katie’s heavy sigh was enough to let Seth know he had succeeded. “Get Mascot ready. We need to leave soon.”

“Thanks, Boss.” He ran to do her biding.

* * * *

Ross grabbed Katie as soon as she crawled out of the van and planted a kiss on her lips. From the corner of his eye, Ross saw Seth scowl as he moved out to the track to grab College Mascot’s bridle before leading the horse into the winner’s circle.

They all made nice for the picture before the three of them piled back into the van to head for the paddock as Brian drove the gelding in the same direction.

After the horse exited the track, Seth and Katie worked to remove Brian’s race bike. Ross moved aside to wait for some time alone with Katie, watching Seth glare at Katie over the horse's back.

"I'll take Mascot to the test barn. That way you can spend more time with Romeo over there." Seth inclined his head toward Ross.

Katie glared right back at him. "What's it matter to you anyway?"

He snorted a small laugh. "It doesn't."

Ross waited patiently, watching their exchange and feeling like an outsider. No matter what he did to try to win Katie's favor, she remained aloof. He'd never courted a woman as hard as he had Katie, but then again he'd never wanted a woman as badly, either. Flowers. Candy. Phone calls. He crossed his arms and leaned against the paddock wall, resigned to waiting for Seth and Katie to stop their bickering. Realizing Seth inspired all kinds of emotions in Katie, Ross felt a stab of jealousy. He was relieved when Seth finally led Mascot away.

A brunette sidled up to Ross so silently he barely heard her coming. He had no idea who she was, and when she began to talk, it took him a second to realize she was addressing him. "I'm sorry, what did you say?"

"I said, 'Hello, Handsome.' I'm Rachel." She reached out and let her fingers caress his arm. "What's a nice guy like you doing in a dump like this? A little out of place in a suit and tie, aren't you?"

"Look, I don't know who you are, but I've got no intention of—"

A shriek came from behind them. Ross and Rachel both whirled around to the source of the racket.

"You bitch! You can't keep your hands off anyone's man, can you?" A tall, muscular woman with long bleached-blond hair marched on Rachel with hate clearly in her eyes. The woman reached out, grabbed a handful of Rachel's long hair, and gave it a vicious tug.

Rachel squealed, placed both of her hands on her attacker's chest, and pushed. She succeeded in getting free but lost several strands of hair in the process. "I'll kick your ass!" Rachel shouted.

"Bring it!" was the blonde's response as she spread her arms, narrowed her eyes, and crouched in anticipation of a fight.

With a loud snarl, Rachel pounced first, but the blonde was ready. As Rachel reached for her, the blonde used her foot to trip Rachel who ended up with a face full of the bark that lined the paddock's floor.

The blonde glared down at Rachel. "That's for sleeping with my boyfriend!"

Rachel rolled to her back as the other woman sat down to straddle Rachel's stomach and rain blows to Rachel's face and chest. Rachel held her hands up to ward off the punches, but she was definitely on the losing end of the battle.

Two security guards must have noticed the commotion because they ran from their post at the paddock's entrance to try to separate the fighting women. The blonde struggled against the guards with the obvious intention of getting in a few last licks, but the men finally pulled the women apart. Rachel was led to the race office while the blonde had an escort to the drivers' lounge. The crowd of people that had formed quickly dispersed when a black and white city police cruiser pulled up alongside the guard shack a few minutes later.

Katie had come to stand at Ross's side and observed a good portion of the altercation. She tried not to be pleased to see someone taking a piece out of Rachel. She didn't want to be that petty. But, damn, it was hard not to thank the blonde.

Ross turned to her, looking extraordinarily confused. "Do you know what that was all about?"

"I've got no idea."

"You know them?"

Katie nodded. "The brunette is Rachel Schaeffer. I don't know the blonde, but I think she's dating one of the drivers. I've seen her around the paddock a lot lately."

"Does this happen often? I'd hate to think I'm missing all the fun."

Katie chuckled. "No, doesn't happen often. But everyone here knows everyone else's business. There are no—"

He waved his hand to stop her. "No secrets in the barn. I remember. I see what you mean now." Ross seemed amused by the whole situation. "I think the brunette was hitting on me, and it pissed off the blonde."

Katie watched the people around the paddock excitedly spreading word of the fight, scurrying around like squirrels storing nuts for the winter. She hoped the new gossip would give them something to talk about other than her and Ross.

"I don't doubt she was hitting on you."

"Why? Because I'm so handsome?" Ross teased as he playfully leaned into her shoulder.

Katie couldn't help but smile at the man. He really could be charming. She wished again that she could feel about Ross the way she felt about Seth, but time and again, Ross's kisses seemed nothing more than brotherly. There had been plenty of chances for a spark to ignite, but it never did more than fizzle. But Katie had come to value his friendship, and she needed Ross almost as much as she did Chris and Brian. Admitting it to herself came as a relief. Ross was just her friend. "Rachel and I've had a few... problems in the past," she finally answered.

"Want to tell me about it?" He slipped an arm around her shoulder.

Katie had buried the horrible, humiliating story deep in her mind long ago. It was the only way she could function with Rachel always underfoot. Seeing the blonde attack Rachel brought the whole sordid mess bubbling to the surface. "Do you know who Mike Knight is?"

"Isn't he that hotshot driver from back east? What do they call him? The White Knight?"

"Yeah. That's him." She took a steadying breath. "I used to see Mike. Actually, we were engaged for a while." Katie's voice took on a hard edge despite her best efforts.

"If you don't want to talk about it..."

"No. It's okay. You're my friend. I can trust you. I thought I knew him, and I thought... I thought he loved me. But the only one Mike ever loved was Mike. Rachel got her hooks in him one night and I was lucky enough to find them screwing around in his truck."

Ross pulled her a little closer. "I'm so sorry."

"Yeah? Well, so was I. I threw the ring at him and..." She gave a small shrug. "That was that. He headed to the Meadowlands a few weeks later. Unfortunately, I still have to see Rachel almost every day."

"It's obvious she gets around," he said in a conciliatory voice. She wondered how often he'd used that tone with his clients.

"She does, but this is more... personal. Rachel's dad is Jacob Schaeffer. You met him at the farm the day they brought Spun Gold down from Goshen. Remember?" Ross nodded. "Jacob taught me how to train horses. Grandpa wanted me to learn from the best, so when I turned twelve, he kind of apprenticed me to Jacob."

"I take it Rachel thinks she was neglected, right? Daddy gave you more time than he did her. Way too Freudian. Why didn't Jacob teach her to train too?"

"She's too damn lazy to train. Sleeps 'til noon every day. Can't stand to get sweaty." Katie gave a small, sardonic laugh. "At least not from work."

It seemed easy for Ross to take over the story from that point. "She's still jealous, so whatever you've got, she wants. And right now she thinks you've got me."

Katie nodded, feeling a bit humiliated over the whole situation. "She made a play for Seth when he first got here just 'cause she thought I liked him."

"Do you?"

"Do I what?"

"Like Seth."

She could feel the heat of the blush spreading over her cheeks and looked away hoping to hide the truth.

"Katie, you need to be honest with me. You know how I feel about you, but if you want Seth—"

"I don't want Seth." Katie gave a small wave of her hand, hoping to deflect any further questioning along the same line. *God, I have a hard time keeping my mouth shut.*

She glanced up to see Rachel being escorted from the paddock. One of the police officers leaned her against his car and locked her wrists into handcuffs before she was tucked into the back of the squad car. A second car pulled up, and the blonde was led from the paddock, cuffed, and placed in the back seat.

"C'mon," he said, nudging her with his elbow. "I need to head for home. Walk me to my car."

Once they reached the Lexus, Ross turned and leaned back against the door. Katie joined him.

"What'll happen to Rachel now?" Ross asked.

"She'll probably get suspended from the track for a few weeks. Maybe get a fine. The race officials hate that kind of disturbance happening in the paddock. Makes us all look bad. I imagine one of her lowlife friends will bail her out of jail later tonight or tomorrow."

He turned to look at her with a serious and troubled expression. "Katie, I think we need to figure out what kind of relationship we've got here."

The hurt look on his boyish face tore at her heart, but Katie didn't want to lead him on. She'd given him the chance he'd asked for, but her heart wanted Seth. "Ross, I wish..."

He shook his head and put his hand up to halt her words. "That's what I thought. It's Remington, isn't it?"

Lying didn't suit her, so Katie simply decided not to reply. She wasn't about to put Seth's inheritance in jeopardy because of her unrequited infatuation.

"It's all right. It doesn't change anything if you're attracted to him. The only problem is if he tries to use you to get his money. I'd appreciate it if you'd be honest with me," Ross encouraged. "You can tell me, Katie."

Taking a hard swallow, she finally confided what she'd hidden from everyone else. Even herself. "I don't want to love him, but I do." She'd said it in a whisper, but her own words hit her with the intensity of a scream. *I love Seth Remington. I do. I love him.* She wasn't sure whether she should shout for joy or weep like a baby at the revelation.

"Wow. You've got it that bad, huh?" Ross rubbed the light growth of stubble on his chin as he breathed a weighty sigh.

Katie nodded as a tear worked its way down her cheek. She felt foolish letting her guard down in front of Ross.

He sighed. "Well, at least we're making some good money together, right?"

With a forced smile, Katie nodded again as she wiped away the tear with the back of her wrist. "Yeah. We are, aren't we? At least I'm good at something."

"You're good at a lot of things. I'm sorry Seth is too stupid to know your worth." Ross draped an arm around her shoulders and gave her a reassuring squeeze. "I'm just glad we can be friends. And partners."

"Thanks, Ross."

He smiled, but the expression didn't reach his eyes. "'The heart wants what it cannot obtain.'"

"Excuse me?"

"Just remembering a fortune cookie. See you later, Katie."

She began to walk away as Ross reached in his jacket pocket and produced his keys.

Chris came running across the parking lot with a look of panic on his face. "Katie! Sam needs you! Brian just went down, and it looks really bad!"

Chapter 17

The paddock had turned into organized pandemonium by the time Katie made it back to the building. Chris and Ross followed hot at her heels.

An accident had caused a four-horse pileup, and the track workers frantically rounded up the loose animals. Katie saw the outrider dutifully protecting the fallen drivers, two of whom were already walking. The paramedics busily ministered to the two men who remained motionless on the track, but Katie couldn't tell which drivers had been involved.

She anxiously looked for Samantha but couldn't find her. Trying to manage the problems she could control, Katie quickly scanned the posted races to see which of the Mitchell's horses was in the next race—the final race on the evening's card. Armed with the information and suffering from a bad case of déjà vu, she sprinted to the animal's paddock stall as Chris and Ross followed close behind.

"Won't they cancel the last race?" Ross asked in obvious confusion.

"No. It'll be delayed, but they'll race," Chris replied.

Katie went to work. "Best thing we can do is get Brian's horse ready. We'd just get in the way out on the track. Chris, go see if Josh Piper can take this race for Brian. I don't think he's got a drive, and I saw him in the front of the paddock, so he wasn't in the accident." As an afterthought, she shouted at Chris's retreating back. "And tell him he'll need his race bike."

The horse remained harnessed and blanketed from his warm-up. Katie grabbed the tendon boots out of the canvas bag and squatted next to the horse to put them on.

Seth found her crouching in the paddock stall, and he could see the panic on Katie's face. She looked up at him wide-eyed from where she worked on Brian's horse, and it wounded him to see her so afraid. He saw the question in her eyes, but he didn't have an answer to offer that would soothe her fear. "Four went down. Three are moving. Just bumps and scrapes, but..." He hated being the bearer of bad news, especially something that could hurt Katie so much. He swallowed hard. "Brian is… bad."

Katie's hands stopped moving and her fingers trembled just enough for Seth to notice. "How bad?" she whispered.

He entered the stall and moved to her side to lay a reassuring hand on her shoulder as she went back to equipping the horse. "It looks like there's a bad break. They're bracing his left leg for transport. Word is they're taking him to Methodist Hospital in Indianapolis."

Katie closed her eyes and took a few ragged gulps of air. Seth squeezed her shoulder to bolster her, amazed she stayed strong enough to stop herself from crying. "Where's Sam?" she asked.

"She's with Brian. She's going in the ambulance with him. She wanted to get the horses back to the farm, but I told her we'd take care of it."

He watched Katie take a deep breath and straighten her spine. Her chin rose as her jaw set. "And we will." She slipped her hand under Seth's and laced her fingers through his. "Thank you."

Feeling the tremble in her grasp, Seth recognized just how frightened she really was. She desperately tried to put up a brave front so she could help the Mitchells, and he respected her all the more for it. Brian, Samantha, and Katie were closer than most families, and he vowed to stay near her for the rest of the night. Once the work ended, the shock would wear off. The events would eventually settle on Katie's heart, and she would need someone to lean on. He patted her shoulder again before he stepped out of the stall to get the bridle for her.

"What can I do?" Ross asked.

"Honestly, Ross, nothing right now," Katie replied as she rose from her crouch. Then she began to think aloud. "Brian is going to be out of commission for while, and Sam can't possibly run the stable all by herself. She's a great second. I know she could handle the training, but she's pregnant. She needs to take care of herself and the baby."

The men simply stood by and listened to her train of thought.

Katie suddenly stopped and stared intently at Ross. "Can Seth work anywhere? Does he have to work for me?"

"I see where you're going with this Katie, but he's got to stay with you." Ross shook his head in stern admonition. "You can't pass him off to Sam."

Seth was stunned at how much relief washed over him at hearing the lawyer's assurance he wasn't going to be traded to another team. He wasn't at all surprised when Katie immediately turned her attention to Chris.

"Then you've got to go," she said in that authoritative voice that Seth knew brooked no refusal.

Chris looked confused. "Go where?"

"You're going to run Brian's barn until he's back on his feet." Katie reached for the bridle Seth held out for her.

Chris's reaction was to shake his head in denial. "I'm not ready to run my own barn. Katie, I... I can't."

"You have to, Chris. Seth can't 'cause he has to stay..." Her eyes caught Seth's. For that single second, they communicated without words—she hadn't wanted him to go. "Well, Seth just can't. Sam and Brian need you. You can do this, I know you can." Katie pushed the bit into the horse's mouth.

Seth understood Chris's attack of nerves, but he also knew Katie was right. He tried to offer his support. "Chris, you've got way more experience. And you wouldn't have to listen to Boss fight with me anymore."

Chris smiled, but it was a hesitant, nervous grin. The night had already been a horror, and the idea of having the fate of the Mitchell's prominent stable put entirely into Chris's hands had to be enough to make the guy nauseous. He sure looked a bit green.

Katie continued to insist, kept trying to build his confidence. "Chris, you can do this. I know you can. And Sam will be there to help."

Chris finally nodded. "Fine." He looked absolutely terrified. "Fine."

"Seth?" Katie asked. "You ready to be my second?"

"Absolutely."

* * * *

As Seth sat next to Katie on one of the trunks, he tried to muster up enough energy to move. He checked his watch. *Two a.m.* He wasn't sure he even had the strength to drive back to the track and had all but resigned himself to sleeping in Katie's truck. He wasn't about to ask her to drive him back. She looked exhausted.

The cell phone cradled in the palm of her hand rang. She answered it, jumped to her feet, and began to nervously pace down the barn's long aisle.

"I don't care if you don't want me there," Katie insisted. "No, it's not too late to drive. I'll drink a bunch of coffee. No, I won't fall asleep at the wheel." She paused, probably getting an earful from Sam, judging from Katie's continued frown and the loud buzz coming from the phone. "Your mom is there?"

From the side of the conversation he could hear, Seth gathered that Brian was in surgery.

"Fine. I'll wait, if that's what you want," Katie said. "I'll be there first thing, though. I'll grab a couple hours of sleep then I'm there, Sam."

By the time Katie flipped the phone shut and slid it back into her pocket, she had silent tears rolling down her cheeks. When she turned to face him, he could see the anguish in her eyes.

Seth quickly crossed the distance separating them and took Katie into his arms. She braced her forearms against him, put her forehead on his chest, and began to weep. "It's okay to cry." She shook her head; he pulled her closer. "Let it out, Katie. Go on and let it out."

"What if he's... crippled? What's going to happen to his stable?" Her words came in choked sobs. "And... and Sam's pregnant. She needs... she needs to take care of herself. She can't do it all... all alone." She wept for a few moments before her thoughts again tumbled from her. "I can't let them... let them lose their farm. I... I can't." Katie's fears were all given voice, and all Seth could offer her was the shelter of his embrace.

He'd never felt so utterly powerless. If he had his money, then he could help. He'd make sure Brian had the best doctors. He'd hire the best trainer to help the Mitchells until Brian got back on his feet. That would make Katie happy and bring her some peace of mind. Didn't it always come back to the damn Remington money? "Shh. It'll be okay, Boss." He squeezed her tighter and kissed the top of her head.

Katie couldn't seem to stop crying, and Seth finally decided the best thing he could do for her was to get her to rest. She was physically and emotionally spent. He gently scooped her into his arms and carried her to her room.

"Seth, we can't..."

"Didn't even cross my mind."

Inside her room, Seth stood next to her bed and put her back on her feet. He pulled back the quilt. "Sit down, Katie." She obeyed with no argument.

Seth knelt and removed her work boots and socks. He rubbed her calves for a moment before realizing exactly what he was doing. *Stop it, Remington*. He patted the mattress. "Get in bed. You need some sleep. I'll drive myself back to the dorm."

Katie glanced up at him with red-rimmed eyes, and then she started to cry again. She muttered her thoughts through her sobs. "What if Brian's leg is so... so bad he can't drive again? What if he... he can't train? What's going to happen to his family, Seth?"

Tears had always been Seth's downfall where women were concerned, and seeing the strongest woman he'd ever known so despondent was more than he could bear. He sat down on the bed beside Katie and tugged her back into his arms. She buried her face against his chest and sobbed.

Seth stroked her long hair and whispered reassurances in her ear until Katie finally started to regain some of her composure. She pulled back and wiped away her tears with the backs of her hands. "I'm sorry. God, I feel like such a big baby."

"Stop it. You have every right to be upset."

"I feel like someone ran me through a shredder." Katie leaned forward to rest her elbows on her knees. She suddenly popped back up. "I'm so sorry! I know you're worried about Brian too. Sam said he's got a broken femur. He's in surgery so they can put his leg back together."

"Ouch. How long 'til he's out of surgery?"

"I don't know. Sam said she'd call. Do you think I ought to go to Indianapolis now? Her mom is there but—"

Seth shook his head and interrupted. "Not tonight, Boss. You're too beat to go anywhere without falling asleep at the wheel."

"But I should be there." Katie stifled a yawn. "I guess you're right. And she told me to wait 'til tomorrow. You want to take my truck back?" She glanced up at him and reached out to take his hand as if the gesture was nothing more than natural.

Seth saw so much emotion in those emerald eyes. The need to reach out to her overpowered him. He put his hand under Katie's chin and lifted her face so he could plant a gentle kiss on her lips. She tasted salty from her tears. He wasn't at all ready for her response. Katie threaded her arms around his neck, quickly turning the gentle kiss into one that ignited all the desire he felt for her.

Seth's tongue parted her lips and swept into her warm mouth. Katie stroked her own tongue against his, mimicking his caresses. She pulled away for a moment to gaze into his eyes before she lowered her lips to his neck and began to kiss and nuzzle him. The sensation of her lips on his throat sent fire to his groin, and it was almost beyond his power not to take advantage of her vulnerability. He couldn't remember ever wanting a woman as badly as he wanted Katie at that moment, but he knew it wouldn't be right.

With every fragile ounce of self-control Seth had left, he took hold of her wrists and pulled her arms from around his neck. "Not like this, Katie."

"Not... not like what?" She looked at him with so much wide-eyed trust, he couldn't allow her to do something she might regret later.

"You need some sleep. You're exhausted and you're hurting, and it won't be like this," he replied with much more calm in his voice than he felt. If she so much as leaned another inch toward him again, there would be nothing Seth could do to stop himself.

As if on cue, Katie yawned again. He hoped she wouldn't feel rejected, but she was probably too emotionally depleted at that point to think too much. Seth patted the pillow, and Katie obediently lay down and curled up on her side to give Seth a good view of each and every gentle curve. His imagination saw the hills, valleys, and dimples hidden in denim. *Rein it in, Remington*. Tracing his fingers over her hip, he leaned over, placed a gentle kiss on her temple, and walked to her desk to turn off the lamp.

As he grabbed her truck keys from the desktop, he heard Katie stir, and he saw her glance over her shoulder. Although it was too dark to see her eyes clearly, somehow he knew they were still full of fear. Seth wanted to go to her, but did she really need him as much as he hoped?

"Don't leave. Please, Seth. Please stay," Katie whispered in the dark.

He crossed the room in three long strides, sat down on the bed, and jerked off his boots and socks. Seth stretched out beside her to mold his body to her back as he draped his arm across her waist. Katie plainly needed comfort. He desperately needed to hold her to feel the peace only her warmth could provide. Gossip might damn them both, but Seth decided to wait until Katie fell asleep before he slipped out to go back to the dorm.

Until he'd stopped long enough to think, Seth hadn't realized the accident had taken a toll on him as well. The image of Brian's still form lying on the track flashed in his mind, making Seth's blood run cold. A bond had grown there he'd never expected to form. *Friendship.* His first true friendship. He said a rare, silent prayer that Brian would come out of this accident whole.

Lying beside Katie, Seth could feel the heat of her body pressed so tightly against his, and desire flooded his senses. Despite the honorable notion of not taking advantage of her, it was torture to have her so close and not be able to touch her in the way he wanted to. Every inch of her burned into his flesh as if they touched bare skin to bare skin. *Maybe just a kiss.* But that path ran straight downhill, and he'd never stop the momentum once allowed to start. Seth's yearning wrestled with his conscience, barely allowing consideration to win the match.

Her breathing grew slow and steady, and Seth knew she'd finally fallen asleep. Yet he just couldn't seem to find the strength to pull himself away. Seth nestled his nose into her silken hair and breathed in Katie as he fantasized about every inch of her and what he wanted to do to her, with her. They would recreate Eden.

But she was so much more to him than a feminine means to a passionate ends. Katie touched every part of him. Reached out to his body? *Oh, yes.* Reached out to his heart and soul? *Yes. Oh, yes.*

A smile crossed his face as he thought about his angel. There had never been a woman who could anger him as quickly as Katie Murphy, but there had also never been a woman who could calm him as quickly either. Or who could send fire racing through him.

He reflected on Kirsten for a moment as he compared his former fiancée to the woman who now slept in his arms. Kirsten's outward beauty seemed flawless. Perfectly styled long, blond hair. Cosmetically enhanced face, impeccable no matter the circumstances. A curvaceous figure that made many a man drool. She only dressed in designer fashions and always spoke in a style that showed her breeding and refinement. Men lined up to get just a moment of her attention. Yet Seth couldn't remember a time when he'd ever felt even half the pull toward Kirsten as he felt toward Katie.

Katie—who dressed in frayed jeans and men's shirts, wore more dirt on her face than make-up, and sometimes cursed like a sailor. She was the most desirable woman Seth had ever known.

"Oh, Boss," he whispered. "What have you done to me?" The only response was a quiet, sleepy sigh.

So what's it going to be, Remington? Love or money?

What Seth desperately wanted was a way to have both. He wanted to give Katie all of the things she deserved, to shower her with the nicer things in life. He would take her to Cabo San Lucas, or Paris, or just to his luxury suite in the Remington compound. He would buy her a million-dollar horse and an enormous farm. And he'd put a flawless diamond and platinum ring on her finger.

In his fantasies, he could have both this beautiful angel and his inheritance.

But only in his fantasies.

Seth closed his eyes and pulled Katie a little closer as he promised himself he would only stay a few more moments.

And then he fell asleep dreaming of a fantasy world where a man could have everything he desired.

Chapter 18

What a nice dream.

The first shards of daylight broke through the small window, bathing the room in an orange glow. Katie was surrounded in comforting warmth, and the pressure of a gentle and welcome weight covered her. Seth kissed her as he ran his hands through her hair, tilted her head, and ravished her mouth. She could taste him. It all looked so real, felt so real, was so real.

In the erotic dream, he moved his lips from hers to kiss her checks, her nose, and her chin. Little kisses that brushed against her skin like the flapping of butterfly wings or the caress of a soft, summer breeze. She heard her own voice moan a response low in her throat. After he ran his hands down her arms and laced his fingers with hers, Seth pulled her arms over her head. He turned her hands loose, tracing his fingertips down the soft underside of her arms to her breasts where he cupped each to give a lingering stroke before he let his hands wander to her stomach.

Such a wonderful dream. Katie could feel the brush of his fingertips on her heated skin as he grasped the hem of her shirt and lifted it slowly up her body and over her head. She arched her back and then lifted her shoulders to assist him in the task, knowing this could never be real. His warm lips immediately went to her belly where he kissed her as he slid his hands behind her shoulder blades to release the clasp of her bra. The garment was removed and fell silently to the floor. When Seth's hot mouth and tongue began to work their magic on her naked breast, when he made her want and want, only then did the fog fade to give way to reality.

No, it isn't a dream. But Katie still reveled in the feeling of being outside of herself. Pretending she still slept was easy enough, and she didn't want to apply too much sobering reason to what was happening to her. The sensations racing through every nerve were too new, too wonderful, and much too strong to allow them to die in the stark light of the new day. As

Seth suckled and teased her breasts with his mouth and fingers, the rush of passion, her need of him caused Katie to lose what little will she might have found to deny him.

Powerless to stop herself, she gathered the material of Seth's shirt into her fingers as she tugged and pulled to raise it over his head. Once free, he covered her body with his as her breasts flattened against the hard muscles of his chest. Warmth to warmth. Skin to skin. Man to woman. She lost herself in his kisses and let herself believe the dream hadn't vanished.

Seth had awakened to the intoxicating smell of Katie, and something fierce and primitive had taken control. The instant he opened his eyes and saw her still sleeping in his arms, he needed to possess her body, capture her heart, and imprison her soul. He wanted to wipe out any memory of any other man who had ever dared to touch her. *Mine. She's mine.* All of his ability to reason evaporated as his body cried out to make her his own.

The rush of sensation, the tightening of muscle, the ripple of visceral excitement. Seth drowned in it all as he hungrily took from Katie everything he could. She pushed him past the point of logic. Pulling away from her breast, he took possession of her lips. His tongue swept into her mouth again and again, and her enthusiastic response fueled his already raging fire.

Katie reached for the waistband of his jeans and tugged at the buttons until they opened one by one. Seth reluctantly pulled away from her long enough to stand and shed the cumbersome denim and his boxers.

Kneeling on the bed over her, Seth ran his hands down her rib cage as he kissed the soft, white skin of her stomach. He circled her navel with his tongue and enjoyed the way she trembled in response, savored each feminine cry and gasp. He unzipped her jeans and peeled them slowly down her hips and legs. He stopped to stroke and kiss a thigh, a knee, a calf as each was revealed.

Katie moaned at the alternation of shivers and warmth that washed over her each time his hands and his soft lips touched her legs. Once her jeans were shed, her lacey panties quickly followed.

Once again, Katie felt the delicious length of his perfect body covering hers. The meeting of his strength and her softness. New and exciting, yet old as time itself. Katie could feel the heat of his erection pressing against her, and knowing how powerfully his body had responded to hers only made her burn more. Her blood ran lava-hot, scalding her from the inside out. The core of her throbbed in anticipation screaming, "Now!"

Seth whispered softly in her ear encouraging, promising, and praising. Katie thrilled at the sensations that spread through her like wildfire licking at dry grass with each of his seductive words. She wanted so much to declare her love, wanted to whisper it as he touched her, to shout it when he took her. The dread of his response made her hold her tongue. She wouldn't ruin this. But the three magic words she longed to confess sang through her mind each time skin rubbed skin. Between the way he made her body reply to his caresses and the love she nurtured for him, she feared she would weep. The experience was almost too overwhelming to bear, almost too intense to endure.

Rolling to his side, Seth stroked the inside of Katie's thigh as he slowly worked his way up to caress the part of her he'd imagined a million times in his mind. The feel of her soft heat was more fulfilling than any fantasy, almost exciting enough for him to lose control. He stroked and teased as he drank in her reactions like warm brandy. He felt her shudder and heard her moan when he slid a finger inside her, and he knew he couldn't wait much longer to bury himself in that welcoming warmth.

Katie trembled as his fingers worked magic on her body. Passion so new, so raw, so untamed she almost feared losing herself to its intensity. Her muscles clenched and her hips rose from the bed as she felt herself building toward some release that she didn't know quite how to reach. She cried out in frustration when he moved his hand away.

Seth pushed himself above her and placed his knee between her thighs to gently force her legs further apart. "Katie? Are you sure?" he whispered as he settled over her. If she denied him, he wasn't sure if he could even stop. He wouldn't have been able to explain why, didn't even understand himself, but he needed her assurance that she wanted this just as much as he did.

Katie had never been more sure of anything in her life. She needed him inside her, joined with her, one with her. No beginning, no end, only here and only now. "Yes, Seth. I'm sure."

Lifting her knee to rest against his hip, Seth entered her as tenderly as he could. He tried to hold back, reining in the desire to plunge into her soft, moist heat with all the naked passion holding him hostage. The moment had to last an eternity because now would be all they had, all they would ever have. But her body fit his so perfectly he could hold nothing back. "God, Katie, you feel so good."

"So do you." They were the last coherent words she could form as her body took command of her mind.

Katie arched against him as she wrapped her legs around his waist and rocked her hips up. She could hear the salacious growl in his throat as the tempo of their bodies quickened, making the old bed frame squeak a melody in rhythm with their frantic movements.

Seth tried to be gentle, tried to maintain some kind of control. Katie wouldn't allow it as their bodies met again and again in a rough race to find release. The warmth in her body settled firmly between her legs as she teetered on the border of rapture.

He could feel the tensing of her muscles as her legs pulled him closer, and knowing she was as frenzied as he was almost pushed Seth over the edge. With what little control he had remaining, he urged her on. As she began to tighten around him, he whispered, "That's it, Baby. Come with me now."

Katie's body exploded, a thousand rays of warm sunlight shimmering through her veins. She dug her nails into Seth's shoulders as he buried himself inside her one last, glorious time. When he breathed her name hoarsely as he shuddered, Katie felt a delightful aftershock run the length of her body.

Both were entirely spent, breathing as if they'd run a great distance. As if they'd changed the rules. As if they'd held back time for one incredible moment.

Seth reluctantly rolled from her. Sprawled on his back, he pulled Katie close to his side. He held her cradled to his shoulder as he marveled in the rightness of the moment. His body had never been so relaxed, his mind so bathed in contentment.

Katie rubbed her cheek against his shoulder and sighed in satisfaction. Her heart wanted to sing her love for this man, to shout it from the rooftops. When she loved him, there was no last will and testament, no fortune to claim, and no way to lose him.

The insistent ringing of her cell phone intruded on their private and satisfied world. Katie grudgingly rose to answer, knowing reality could no longer be held at bay.

Seth watched her leave the tiny bed they'd shared and had to fight the urge to drag her back into his arms. She grabbed her shirt, shyly turned her back, and pulled the garment quickly over her head. He chuckled at her modesty. She grabbed her jeans off the floor and yanked her phone out of the pocket.

Lord, looked she pretty in the early morning light—especially when her cheeks were still flushed and her creamy legs were long and bare. The shirt barely covered her pretty backside, and Seth loved the tease of seeing the roundness of her bottom playing peek-a-boo every time she moved. He felt himself getting hard in response. *So quickly, so soon.* Katie absolutely bewitched him.

Catching the gist of the conversation from listening to her words, Seth figured Brian was out of surgery. He waited patiently for her call to end so she could give him the details.

"We'll be there as soon as we can," Katie promised before she flipped the phone shut. Seth wondered if she even realized that she'd included him in her pledge to Samantha. "Brian is in a room now. They put his thigh back together with nine pins, but the doctor thinks he'll be fine. It's just going to take time and lots of therapy."

"That's good to hear. I know you want to see him. We could drive to Indianapolis after we get the horses fed." Seth knew there was work to do, and he wondered if for once she'd put personal ahead of business.

"Yeah, I promised Sam we'd go. We'll just feed 'em and clean the stalls. We can train tomorrow." It almost sounded as if she was talking herself into making the trip. "I want to go."

"Then we'll go." Seth threw his legs over the side of the bed and stood up. Katie blushed and turned her back to him again. "I can't believe you're embarrassed. I mean after what we just did..."

"I'm not used to seeing guys... you know... naked."

Seth laughed. "Good." He slipped on his boxers. "It's safe to turn around now."

All of a sudden, Katie looked like someone had hit her with the force of a heavyweight title fighter. Her face contorted in pain, and she began to tremble. She grabbed a hold of the chair, her knuckles turning white. "Oh, my God, Seth. What have we done?"

What have we done? Seth started shaking as hard and fast as Katie and a wave of nausea rolled through him. "Just... just let me think for a minute." He took deep breaths to keep the panic rising in him from spilling out.

"It's my fault. It's all my fault." Katie grabbed the rest of her clothes and ran to the bathroom. The slam of the door was followed by the crash of objects being hurled around the bathroom.

Seth felt like a man torn in two. Making love to Katie had been the best experience of his life. Hell, he'd never felt anything half as wonderful. But was the strength of that feeling enough to give up millions of dollars?

And the person he wanted to talk to the most, the one he trusted above all others, was the woman who might be taking away his fortune. What had he done? What had *they* done?

Hearing Katie's soft sobs, Seth pulled himself out of his stupor. He couldn't allow her to bear the entire responsibility for their actions. He'd wanted her. He still wanted her. Going to the bathroom, Seth raised his knuckles, intending to knock when the door suddenly jerked open.

Her eyes were puffy and red, but she had one of those determined looks on her face. "It never happened," a fully-dressed Katie declared. Then she sat on the bed and pulled on her socks and boots as if the day was nothing more than routine. She kept muttering to herself. "It never happened."

Denial. The most basic of the defense mechanisms. He sighed in resignation of having to live with the reality of their actions. "Boss, it happened. We've got to deal with it."

"No. No dealing with it. It never happened. No one knows, Seth. And no one has to know."

Katie was throwing him a lifeline, much as he had done for her once upon a time. There wasn't anyone who knew they'd been together, and no one ever had to discover the truth. Brian and Sam were in Indianapolis, Chris was at the Mitchell farm, and Ross had traveled back to Chicago. Katie was probably right. No one had to know.

But he'd remember. He'd *always* remember.

Love or money?

Katie watched Seth closely to gauge his reaction. He couldn't possibly know the depth of what she felt, nor would she ever allow it. Her body still burned from his touch, and the love she felt for him smothered her until she could barely draw air into her lungs. Her heart was breaking in its positively insane desire for Seth to throw aside his inheritance and claim her as his own.

Things like that only happened in fairy tales or romance novels. She lived in the real world, and the real world revolved around money. Katie silently vowed she would never be responsible for taking a fortune away from the man she loved. Seth had a life of his own before he became her groom. He was forcibly taken away from a world where he enjoyed the very best of everything, and he'd made the best of it because his fortune would be waiting in the end. If she could do nothing else, Katie would give Seth back his life. Even if it killed her. "Let's get the horses fed. Then you can take the truck to the track to clean up and I'll catch a shower here. We can get to the hospital by lunchtime," Katie said as nonchalantly as she could manage.

Let it go, Seth! Just let it go!

"Fine. Let's get to work." His tone was so flat, he could have been discussing as mundane as a shipment of grain.

Katie's heart shattered into a million pieces and littered the floor around her.

Chapter 19

"I hate hospitals," Katie muttered to herself.

The smell of a hospital had burned into Katie's memory with startling clarity—the smell of pain and grief.

She'd been so young when her parents died. Many of the memories she once had of them had all but faded away. She still found it hard to remember exactly what they looked like, unsure if what she saw in her mind were truly memories of them or just recollections of pictures she'd seen. She couldn't remember the sound of their voices or the touch of their hands.

But there was one thing she would *never* forget, one thing that would always remind her of her family. The disinfectant smell of a hospital.

She'd been lying on a gurney all by herself when she'd heard the policemen talking. She'd been in so much pain, but she still heard every word, every syllable. They must not have realized she rested just behind the thin curtain. To hear her beloved mother and father had died from two men talking so casually they might have been discussing their plans for lunch was something Katie could never, would never forget.

Seth held the door open, obviously waiting for her to go through.

I can't. I just can't. She looked away and hoped he wouldn't see the hurt clearly reflected in her eyes.

"Katie? Brian is all right. It's going to be okay."

She swallowed hard and nodded with every intention of moving across the threshold, but her feet remained firmly glued to the sidewalk.

Seth released the door and moved to her side. "Katie? What's wrong? Do you want to talk about it?" He wrapped his arm around her shoulder and led her to a metal bench that overlooked a bed of pink petunias.

The despair of the past mixed with fear of the future. *Love always seems to leave. Always.* It took her a few minutes to find the words to explain the tangle of her thoughts. "I feel like I'm six years old again and waiting for someone to tell me my parents are gone."

"I'm so sorry." Seth reached for her hand.

Katie wanted to pull away almost fearing any more physical contact with him, but she desperately needed his comfort at that moment.

"There was a car accident. I don't remember it, but I remember being in the hospital. I hate the smell, like... disinfectant. It always makes me think of that day. I never saw my parents again." Katie took a deep, steadying breath. "Grandpa came to be with me that night. I stayed in the hospital for a few days, but he never left my side. He was all I had left."

Seth squeezed her hand. "What can I do to help?"

"I need to pull myself together, that's all," she replied before taking her hand from his and wiping away the tears that had formed in her eyes. "Let's go. Sam's waiting. If they have a gift shop, we need to get some candy. Brian loves anything chocolate." She chuckled at a thought. "I'd kill for a chocolate rabbit right now." She followed him toward the entrance.

Seth laughed as he opened the door. "A chocolate rabbit?"

"Yeah, like the ones you get on Easter. I *love* chocolate rabbits," she replied, happy to have something more pleasant to discuss. "Grandpa used to buy me tons of them when I was little. They always make me happy."

"I like the marshmallow chicks better." He followed her into the hospital.

* * * *

After a quick stop at the gift shop, it took thirty minutes to locate Brian's room in the enormous maze of Methodist Hospital. Katie knocked softly on the door.

"Come in," Samantha's sleepy voice answered.

Katie wasn't prepared to see Brian stretched out on the hospital bed. He looked much thinner and very fragile as he slept. A sheet was draped over his injured leg as it rested on what looked like an enormous pillow. The whole thing suddenly moved, and both Katie and Seth jumped in surprise.

"It's a machine that keeps the knee moving," Sam explained. "It rotates every couple of minutes."

Sam was lying on a large reclining chair that had been unfolded to make a bed. She pulled the blanket off her legs as she sat up. She had dark circles under her eyes, and it was obvious she was exhausted.

"I'm sorry, Sam," Katie whispered. "We didn't mean to wake you."

"No worries. I was up. I can't seem to sleep. Every time I close my eyes, some damn alarm goes off. And the nurses are in here constantly to take his blood pressure or temperature." She glanced over at her husband and a small, thin-lipped smile crossed her face. "He sleeps through the whole thing."

"Where's your mom?" Katie asked.

"She went home this morning. She's got a farm of her own to run, after all. Once she knew Brian was fine, she headed back."

Katie nodded and tried not to stare at Brian lying there like some broken doll. "You need to get your rest too, Sam. So what's the news?"

"The doctor who worked on him takes care of Indy 500 drivers when they wreck. According to the nurses, he's the best orthopedist in the country. He said Brian will be fine, but he can't bear weight on it for something like six weeks. He'll be on crutches for a while."

"Don't worry about the stable," Katie said, hoping to offer something for Sam to hold onto to make the whole ordeal a little easier to bear. "Chris is moving there. He's going to keep things up and running. I called Rachel, too. Sam, don't scowl at me. She's a bitch, but she knows horses. Chris will keep her in line."

"Katie, I can't afford—"

"Shut up, Sam. Chris is on my payroll and he'll stay that way. You already pay Rachel for paddocks, now you can pay her for mucking out stalls. It'll all work out."

Sam shook her head as tears came to her eyes. "I can't let you—"

"Hush, Sam," Katie replied. "It's already done."

"Thank you." Sam wiped away the tears. "I'm sick of crying. I hate to cry. Must be the hormones."

"Must be," Brian said in a weak voice.

"Welcome back." Seth gave Brian's shoulder a friendly pat.

"I feel like shit."

"Probably because you look like shit," Sam commented in her usual frank manner before she leaned over and smoothed Brian's bangs away. She kissed her husband's forehead. "I love you."

Sam's words were a whisper that made Katie's heart ache. She longed to say them to Seth and to have him declare his feelings for her. If he had feelings for her. She envied the closeness of the Mitchells, feeling smothered by the force of it. Glancing over at Seth, she battled the need to reach out for his hand.

Brian pointed at the sack Katie held. "That for me? Better be chocolate."

Katie laughed and handed him the sweets. "What else would I bring?"

* * * *

The ride home was tense, the emotional toll of the day high.

Seth tried to make conversation. "Brian looked good."

Katie snorted a laugh. "He looked like hell... but he's going to be okay. That's the most important thing. Sam will have her hands full keeping him on crutches."

"He's pretty stubborn," Seth added, feeling a bit lame that he had nothing better to say. They needed to talk about more important things. They'd made love—violated the explicit tenants of Sterling Remington's will. He finally decided someone needed to broach the subject. "You know, I've never done that before."

He watched a mischievous smile play on her lips. "Oh, I took your virginity?" She placed her hand over her heart. "What an honor."

"No. I didn't mean..." He laughed at her response. "What I *meant* is that I've always had safe sex."

"Nice to know. So have I. At least the one time..." Katie closed her mouth without finishing the thought.

"Was it with Mike?"

"How do you know about Mike?" She didn't seem surprised, only curious.

"Jacob told me."

Katie nodded but said nothing. Getting anything personal out of her was agonizing, like playing tug-of-war with an NFL linebacker.

"I take it you don't want to talk about him."

She shrugged, but the expression on her face didn't appear nonchalant. The pain was obvious. "What am I supposed to say? The guy played me. Used me."

Seth wondered if Katie feared he would treat her the same. "How long were you engaged?" It amazed him he could feel so much naked jealousy over events that occurred before he even met Katie. Even thinking she'd almost married another man made his blood boil.

"Less than a month. Everyone tried to warn me, but I just couldn't see it. His over-inflated ego needed more attention than one woman could give. I should've listened to Sam. The woman is too smart for her own good." She shrugged again. "But I thought I was in love." Katie glanced over at him. "Stupid, huh?"

"I know a lot of guys like that." *I used to be a guy like that. What kind of guy am I now?*

"You dumb ass!" Katie suddenly shouted.

Seth wondered for a moment if she'd read his thoughts. "I beg your pardon?"

She pointed at a teenager in the red sports car. "Nothing. Just a small problem I have with road rage." Katie threw a nasty scowl at the other driver. The teenager flipped them the bird as he sped away.

"I see." It took him a moment to work up his courage. "Look, Boss, we've been dancing around it all day, but we need to talk about this. You know, you could be pregnant." Part of him actually hoped for a moment she *was* pregnant. It would solve his problem of deciding between Katie and his inheritance. But, damn, that would be one expensive child. Did the will have a contingency for grandchildren?

Katie shook her head even as she stared at the road in front of her. "I'm not pregnant, Seth. No way."

"What was it you said to me once?" He put his index finger to his lips as if needing a moment of reflection. "Ah... Must be nice to be all-knowing."

"Yeah, yeah. Ha ha," she replied in a sarcastic voice. "I'm not pregnant. I know it."

Seth eyed her warily. "How could you possibly know?"

She looked so unhappy, he wished he hadn't asked at all. "I had some bad internal injuries in the accident. Grandpa says I almost died. After the surgeries, I've got lots of scar tissue all over my insides. I've always had problems with my periods." Her words were slow, labored. "My doctor said it's likely that... that I'll have a really tough time ever having kids. He... he doesn't think it's possible." Her sadness tore at him like a knife in the belly.

"I'm sorry. Must have been hard to hear when you're so young."

"It *was* hard. But I've gotten used to the idea, I guess. Besides, I'm not sure I want kids anyway. Doesn't exactly fit with my lifestyle," Katie said in a flat, rehearsed tone that made Seth doubt her sincerity.

He remembered her tears at The Place when the Mitchells had announced their impending parenthood and wondered if she was lying to herself about wanting children. Or was she lying to him? "I didn't think I'd ever want kids."

"Didn't?" she asked.

Seth shrugged. "People change, I suppose. But kids are like big anchors. All they do is weigh you down." He didn't realize how cold he sounded until the words were already out of his mouth. *I wonder if that's how Pops felt about me?*

They rode in silence for several miles before Katie spoke up again. "Seth, we have to go back to the way we were. It happened, but it can't happen again."

Seth had been toying with an idea. "You know, it's only five years. Once I get my money, we'd only have to wait five years to be together."

Katie's face grew hard, determined. "No. No way. When the season's over, you're going back to your life, and I'm going back to mine."

"But it's only—"

"No, Seth. I don't care if it's only one damn day. We don't belong together. We live in different worlds. Besides, you don't love me."

Seth winced at her chilly pronouncement. *But do you love me?* He couldn't find the courage to ask.

She drove her truck through the entrance to Dan Patch and pulled up next to the dorms. "Qualifiers tomorrow morning. Will you be ready?"

"Absolutely."

"See ya in the morning," she said as he stepped out of the pick up.

"Yeah. See ya, Boss." Damned if he wasn't adopting her twang. He shut the door behind him and watched her drive away.

When she had talked about her infertility, Katie's voice had held such a tone of despair it made Seth's heart ache for her. His father had shared the stories of how long it had taken for his mother to get pregnant. Seth wondered if that was why he'd been so indulged as a child.

Katie would make a fantastic mother. The woman was patient, kind, and so full of life. An image of a red-headed boy flashed through his mind. The child toddled toward Seth, arms raised high. Seth could almost feel the little boy in his embrace. He shook his head to remove the compelling picture of what could never be.

Katie was right. Seth had never really loved anyone before, and he wasn't entirely sure he'd ever know how.

But if he didn't love Katie, then why did it hurt so much when she left? Why did he count the minutes until he was back at her side?

Tomorrow, Seth would try to qualify Spun Gold. For Katie's sake, he hoped he could succeed. It had all seemed exciting and fun until he'd witnessed Brian's accident. Now, the seriousness of racing was firmly etched in his mind, and he'd acquired a healthy dose of respect for the men and women who sat in the race bikes day in and day out.

He was glad Katie didn't ask again if he was ready to drive in a qualifier. Because this time, his response wouldn't be nearly as smug.

Chapter 20

The morning dawned warm and dry. Seth couldn't seem to quell his nervousness—or was it excitement?—at the prospect of steering Spun Gold around the mile oval in an attempt to qualify the colt for a real race.

The sires stakes opening races were quickly approaching, and if Gold didn't qualify soon, Katie would miss out on the lucrative series of races. Sterling Remington had hoped to give her a winning horse, and Seth was determined to see that everything his father wished for came true.

Seth and Katie moved around the chestnut, preparing for the race. Gold seemed more reserved than normal, and Seth hoped that was a good sign. Perhaps the animal understood the seriousness of the situation.

During the warm-up, Seth took the time to give a thorough look to every inch of the track. He searched for any spots that seemed uneven or any place the surface was too deep, anything that could possibly cause the inexperienced colt to fall again.

Katie grabbed Gold's bridle as he came through the exit chute. "How'd he feel?"

"Smooth as velvet. I think he'll be good," Seth replied.

Once they had the colt back in his paddock stall, all they could do was wait until their race was called. Seth paced nervously as he fiddled with the chin straps on Chris's helmet.

"You'll do fine," Katie reassured. "You know Gold better than anyone. If you tell him what to do, he'll do it. I've watched you train him. I know what you can do."

"Thanks, Boss. But I've been thinking. You were right before." She arched an eyebrow. "You know, in his first qualifier." He saw the understanding dawn on her face with her smile. "He probably should race under cover. I'm not going to take him to the front of the pack."

Katie nodded. "I think that's a good choice. He'll race well if you tuck him behind a couple of 'em and watch the outer flow."

"I'll do it your way," Seth replied before he was interrupted by the judge calling the horses for Gold's qualifier. "Show time."

Katie helped Seth lock the race bike onto Gold's harness. The colt stamped his front hoof a couple of times. Seth soothed his pet before Katie grabbed the horse's bridle and led Gold to the track.

Seth was settled firmly in the sulky with his excess reins tucked under him by the time they reached the entrance chute. As Katie released the horse to his control, she caught his eye. "I believe in you, Seth."

His chest swelled with pride. No one had ever expressed that kind of confidence in him or had ever made him feel like he was worth a damn. He swore he would do everything right because this race was for her. "Thanks, Boss."

Urging Gold to his natural gait, Seth felt a calm settle over his body and his thoughts. Everything he did seemed almost mechanical, matter of fact. All of his nervousness had evaporated with Katie's words of praise.

As the starter called the horses, Seth eased Gold up behind the gate. The colt tested the strength of his driver as he pulled against the reins. "Easy, boy." Seth gently let the horse know who was in control, and Gold settled into a smooth pace.

Katie stood by the fence, holding her breath as her lips moved in silent prayer. For all the times she'd seen Brian drive, she should have been used to watching someone she cared about race. But she couldn't believe the wealth of emotions that hit her from every side when she saw Seth straddling her horse in that small sulky. The terror of knowing the man she loved was so vulnerable overwhelmed her. How could Sam stand seeing Brian put himself on that track? Samantha Mitchell was obviously a much stronger woman than Katie had ever imagined. Her own heart pounded a fast, heavy beat as her stomach churned.

The gates folded and the qualifier began.

Katie gripped the fence, turning her knuckles the same shade as the wood's whitewash. Chris had come to stand by her side, but she couldn't even take her eyes away from the track long enough to acknowledge him.

She watched as Seth settled Gold in the middle of the pack through the first turn. Adrenaline had to be flowing through Seth, but he seemed to keep his cool. He tossed a quick glance over his shoulder as he watched the movement of the outside horses begin on the back stretch.

Katie suddenly saw the perfect opportunity. "Move him outside, Seth. Move him out *now.*" As if he heard her instructions, Seth eased Gold out between two horses moving into the outer flow. The colt responded without hesitation.

Chris elbowed Katie. "Sweet! He's getting a second-over trip."

She nodded, well aware of the strategic advantage Seth now held. "Will he know what to do with it?"

Gold's pace remained steady and fast, and the colt showed no signs of taking a bad step. The pack moved through the last turn. Katie held her breath as she watched Seth maneuver Gold for the stretch drive. He handled the horse as easily as if he'd sat behind one his whole life.

To her stunned disbelief, Gold crossed the wire first in a very respectable qualifying time of one minute and fifty-seven seconds. She squealed her thrill and relief as she hugged Chris. "He did it! He did it!"

"Looks like you've got a winner there, Katie!"

She nodded as she tried to calm the frantic rhythm of her heart. "It looks like I've got two!"

Jogging over to the exit chute, Katie received several congratulations and pats on the shoulder from other trainers, even from a couple of the guys who told her women shouldn't train horses. Seth eased Gold off the track, and he received the same. Katie was shocked that he also received several requests to drive in later qualifiers, all of which he accepted with a proud, broad smile. While she was thrilled for him to be so accepted and appreciated, part of her wished he would never sit in a race bike again. Ever.

With Gold safely back in his paddock stall, Katie quietly worked to remove the equipment. Seth finally made an appearance, but he didn't make a move to help her. "Can you finish up, Boss? Ricky wants to talk to me about driving his filly in the tenth qualifier."

She felt like someone had hit her in the gut. "Are you sure you want to drive for anyone else? I mean, after all, you know Gold." Katie tried to calm the shaking timbre of her voice. She didn't want to appear too emotional, even if she was. "You don't know anything about those other horses."

"Of course I want to drive. God, it's like flying. It's like I can see what the horse is going to do before he does it," Seth replied. The look on his face reminded her too much of Brian's expression whenever he drove. She'd lost

Seth—lost him to the track. "What's wrong, Katie?"

She wanted to scream at him and was sorely tempted to throw something heavy at his head. *What's wrong? You could break your neck, you stupid...* Katie shook her head. "Nothing's wrong. Go on, Seth. Go drive your qualifiers."

"Thanks, Katie." He smiled and turned to run back up the bark-lined aisle.

* * * *

Katie didn't see Seth again until much later when she was trying to load Gold in the trailer to head back to the farm. The chestnut had returned to his usual uncooperative mood and stubbornly refused to get inside.

Seth walked up behind the horse and smacked him once on the rump. "Come on, Buddy. Time to go home." The colt walked calmly into the trailer.

"I hate you," Katie grumbled.

"I know," he replied with a wink. "Can I ride back with you? I left some stuff at the farm."

"Sure. I'm going to take a shower and catch a nap before I ship in Jack tonight, so you can drive yourself back."

"A shower, huh?" He wiggled his eyebrows. "I could join you."

Katie could feel the heat spread across her cheeks. "Seth, shh. Someone might hear." She glanced around nervously before crawling into the driver's side of the truck. Lord, he was being dense. Track people gossiped with unequalled relish, and Seth had almost committed a fundamental error. She finally attributed his slip to still being under the influence of the endorphin rush that had come with the qualifying races.

Back at the farm, Katie took care of Gold's needs while Seth turned a few of the horses out into corrals. By the time chores were completed, she was exhausted. The last few days had been physically and emotionally draining. If she allowed herself to close her eyes for more than a few seconds, she knew she'd fall asleep on her feet.

"Seth?" she asked as she tossed him her keys. He caught them and gave her a confused frown. "Don't forget to come and get Jack and me in time to get him to the paddock."

"Sure, Boss. Go take a nap. You look beat."

"Gee, thanks a heap." Katie trudged wearily to her room. All she wanted was a hot, relaxing shower and to sleep for the next twelve hours. Unfortunately, she figured she would have to settle for a warm trickle and a two-hour nap. She slammed the door behind her.

Katie carelessly dropped her clothes in a trail as she shed them on the way to her bathroom. By the time she entered the shower stall and coaxed the water to reach a temperature somewhere above lukewarm, she heaved a sigh and stepped into the stream of water. She was so weary that all she could do was place both of her hands on the wall and let the water cascade over her head and back.

At least the water warmed enough to relax her, and Katie finally decided the limited hot water supply would give out quickly, so she reached for the soap. She heard the shower door swiftly open and close and saw a familiar masculine hand beat her to the sticky white cake sitting in the soap dish. She wasn't even surprised.

Seth had intended to leave, had even gotten as far as putting on his seatbelt and starting the truck. But an image of Katie came into his mind that set his blood on fire. Just remembering what had passed between them made him hard and flooded him with need. He wanted her. Desperately. He thought about driving to the store for condoms, but from what Katie told him, pregnancy wasn't an issue. And he had no doubt her blood was as clean as his. He didn't want to wait.

It had been simple enough to slip back into her room. His clothes fell on top of her path of garments as he had shed them rapidly and hurried to join her in the shower. He needed her again; he'd make her need him too.

Without a word, Seth molded his body to her back, wrapped his arms around her waist and worked the soap between his hands, building up lather, letting each twist of his wrist brush against the underside of her breast. All the time he rained kisses over the back of her neck, her ears, her shoulders.

Seth rubbed his slippery hands over her breasts where he toyed for a while as he continued to nibble on her sensitive neck. When he slid one hand between her legs, she trembled. His fingers played intimately with her, coaxing her to the passion he knew bubbled and churned just below her calm exterior.

His lips found all the tender spots, his hands knew all the right places.

Her heart could never refuse him. Katie put her palms against the wall to brace herself against his onslaught. The pleasure he sent through her made her legs weak, made her want things that she shouldn't have, and made her dream of things that could never be. When she felt as if she could stand no more, she turned in his arms, cupped his face in her palms, and kissed him with every ounce of love she felt. Then she pulled away and gave him a coy smile.

Taking the soap from his hands, she rubbed it between her palms to work up some suds before she set the bar aside. She let her hands slide from Seth's neck down his chest where she massaged small circles. She seductively splayed her fingers across his flat stomach and then slipped her palms around his hips to cradle his backside. That heavenly butt. Katie's hand roamed back to his hip. Nervously biting at her bottom lip, her fingers traced a path down until she found the courage to wrap her hand around his erection. Seth hissed in his breath in response. "You didn't like that." She immediately pulled her hand away.

"Are you kidding? I loved that." He pushed her shoulders roughly against the wall. His mouth claimed hers in a kiss that demanded all she had to give. He grabbed her by the waist and lifted her off her feet. "Put your legs around me, Katie." She did as he asked, and he plunged into her.

She grabbed his shoulders, squeezing her legs tightly around Seth's waist as he thrust into her again and again. *Love me, Seth. Love me as much as I love you.* The tension came quickly, pulling her to paradise. When her body found its release, she shouted her joy.

Katie's voice pushed him over the edge. His body answered her call as he buried himself deep inside her in one last stroke.

They both panted for breath. "Wow," was all Katie could say as she slowly descended to reality and carefully put her feet back on the slippery floor.

"Not good with Mike?" Seth asked in a conceited tone as he gently smoothed her wet hair away from her temple. He kissed her forehead.

"Dreadful. God, I'm tired." She turned to rinse the remainder of the soap off before opening the shower door to step out. She wrapped a towel around her body, poked her head back inside the shower stall, and smugly smiled. "I should probably tell you that you've only got about thirty seconds of hot water left."

Seth tried to give himself the fastest shower of his life, but by the time he finished, the water had rapidly retreated from warm to tepid to icy. His teeth were chattering when he opened the stall door. She handed him a dry towel.

Standing in front of the mirror with her own towel firmly wrapped around her, Katie worked a small brush through her wet hair. "You know, you should've gone back to the dorms."

"I know," Seth answered as he dried his body. He noticed Katie staring at his reflection in the mirror before she averted her eyes. He chuckled at her modesty. "It's not a crime to look."

"You're awfully vain."

"So I've been told." He chuckled. "Some tipsy redhead once sang me a song along those lines."

Katie frowned at him for a second then Seth watched her lips curve into a sassy smile. A damned alluring one at that. She started to sing "I Want a Lover Who Won't Drive Me Crazy." He laughed.

Seth sauntered over to her and tugged on her towel until it began to fall from her body. Katie stopped singing, squealed, and reached for it. He grabbed her shoulders to keep her from moving. "Lady, do you know how beautiful you are?"

She blushed profusely, retrieved her towel, and wrapped it around herself like a terrycloth cocoon before walking from the bathroom. "I'm getting dressed and catching a nap."

Seth draped his towel around his waist and then ran his hand over her backside as she left. "How about we skip the clothes and just take the nap? Or better yet, how about—"

"Seth, go back to the track."

"Fine." He strolled across her room and opened the door.

"You can't leave like that!"

"Oh, your towel. I forgot." Seth replied as he unwrapped it from around his hips, rolled it into a ball, and threw the cloth across the room at Katie. She caught it midair.

It was becoming a highly entertaining game to see how often he could make her blush. It was even more rewarding when he could fluster her enough to make her nibble on her bottom lip.

Reaching for the doorknob, Seth waved at her. "See you later."

"Get back here!" Katie grabbed his boxers and jeans from the floor and tossed them to him.

"But these are dirty, and I'm clean." He caught the garments and held them at arm's length, wrinkling his nose.

"Tough. I'm not bailing you out of jail for indecent exposure."

Katie fished through the drawers of her bureau and grabbed a t-shirt and some pink panties before retreating with them to the bathroom to dress. Seth hoped those were all she planned to wear when she came back out. He'd never known a woman who looked as sexy as Katie in a t-shirt.

He slipped his boxers on and plopped down on her bed. The frame groaned in protest. He could hear the sound of her blow-dryer and figured she'd be busy for a few minutes, so he stretched out on the quilt to relax until she finished.

When Katie finally walked out of the bathroom, she found her biggest problem sound asleep on her bed. But she was too tired to protest. Nobody would know anyway, so what did it matter? She got into bed, snuggled up to his back, and molded herself to him.

Katie couldn't find it within herself to condemn him for wanting his family money. He had never known anything but affluence, and it would be cruel to expect him to give it all up for her way of life—especially when he probably thought her way of life was beneath him. She was smart enough to understand; her heart had the most difficulty with the whole situation.

In the few moments before letting much needed sleep overtake her, Katie listened to Seth's deep, even breathing. It felt so right to lie by his side, just as it had felt so right to share her body with him. At least when he left, there would be some wonderful memories she could keep close to her broken heart.

Closing her eyes, Katie sighed. "I love you, Seth," she whispered. "I love you more than I've ever loved anyone." It felt so good to finally say the words aloud—even if he would never hear her. He could never know how much she cared. She wouldn't saddle him with that burden.

Chapter 21

"Just bide your time and let him make his move in the stretch," Katie cautioned Josh Piper as she led Monterey Jack to the entrance chute. "Don't get in a speed duel on the front end because he likes to go hard at the gate." Josh adjusted the reins, but he didn't appear to be listening as he turned to look over his shoulder. Katie tried to rein in her temper, but it wasn't easy. *I miss you, Brian.* "You've got to keep him in line, Josh. If you get away sixth or better by the first turn, I'll be happy. Save him for the stretch. Are you listening to me?"

"Yeah, yeah. Gotcha, Katie," Josh replied, buckling his chin strap on his red, white, and blue helmet.

Seth and Katie stood against the fence and watched the start of the race. As the wings folded neatly against the sedan, Katie's breath left her in an indignant gasp. "No!" Despite her warning, Josh let Jack take him to the front of the pack.

Seth whistled when the first quarter time posted. "Twenty-six seconds. Ouch. Jack is done."

Katie flashed Seth an angry glare. "Tell me something I don't know. Damn him! I told Josh not to..." She kicked the bottom of the fence. "Stupid freakin' cowboy."

Watching the race was agony. Jack put in a good effort, but because his strength had been sapped too early in the race, he faded to fifth by the finish.

"A damn postage stamp," Katie grumbled in disgust as she stomped toward the chute to wait for her horse and to yell at the man who would no longer be her driver.

"Postage stamp?" Seth asked as he followed her.

"The check will be so small it'll only be worth enough to buy a damn postage stamp. You can't keep a stable running on fifth place checks." She kicked at the dust around her feet. "I'm gonna kill Josh."

As the animals returned to the chute, the race official announced the claim through the loud speakers. "Monterey Jack claimed for eight-thousand. Goes to Light Speed Racing. Picked up by Taylor O'Riley."

Katie stomped her foot. "Shit! I *knew* he'd get back at me for claiming College Mascot!" Then she suddenly realized the more personal implication of the claim. She glanced back at Seth and instantly recognized how hard he was taking the loss of his favorite horse. The pain was clearly etched on his face. "Do you want to take him to the test barn? All claims go—"

He shot her an angry scowl. "Through the test barn. I know. I'm not an idiot, Katie. I was there when you claimed Mascot."

"But it'll give you a chance to tell him goodbye."

"No!" Seth shouted before stomping off toward the paddock. "I *hate* goodbyes."

Katie let him go because she understood. He wasn't the only one who hated goodbyes.

* * * *

Katie tended Jack in the test barn and dutifully handed him over to Taylor O'Riley when her labors were done and after Jack had produced his urine sample. She bore no grudges; she'd been on both sides of the claiming game many times. It was business, but her heart ached for Seth, for what he'd lost tonight. The first claim was always the hardest, and she knew that he held a special place in his heart for Jack.

Walking back to her truck, Katie saw Seth leaning back against the empty trailer, obviously waiting for her. She could tell from the pinched expression on his face his emotions were still running high. "You don't have to go back to the farm tonight. I can finish chores up myself," she offered.

"I quit."

"Don't be silly, Seth. You can't quit. You don't have a choice," Katie calmly replied. She wasn't prepared for his vehement reaction.

"I don't give a shit! I quit! I can't do this anymore! Any moron can just come in and take away your favorite..." He stopped talking and pushed himself away from the trailer.

"I know it hurts. It always hurts to lose someone you love." She couldn't stop the catch in her voice.

Claiming could be rough, but Katie wondered if the whole situation might be affecting Seth on a more personal level, as it was her. Her heart hoped that his distress offered proof the man could love something, someone, after all.

Don't be absurd, Katie. Seth doesn't love you.

The irony dawned on her like a slap upside the head—Seth was her "claimer." She might hold him for a while, but she could never keep him. The Remington heritage would always have a higher claim on him. And just like she let Monterey Jack go, she would have to let go of Seth. That thought made her chest feel so tight, she couldn't breathe.

"We don't have anything in tomorrow. Can I take the day off?" Seth asked, appearing to be reining in his temper.

"Big plans?"

"Yeah, something like that."

"And you're not going to tell me?" Katie was surprised at the pitiful hurt in her own voice. She had no claim on this man—could never have any claim on him. Why should it hurt so much if he had plans that don't include her?

"You'll think it's stupid." Seth stared intently at the ground.

"Try me."

"I want to go see Brian. I was going to ask to borrow the truck. I thought I'd take that stack of race tapes you've got in the tack room and go watch them with him. He can give me some driving pointers." Seth shrugged. "Maybe he might like seeing proof of how good he really is. I imagine he's a little discouraged right now."

"Can I go with you?"

She was pleased to see the smile that formed on his lips. "Of course, Boss." Then he grew quiet for a moment and stared at his boots again.

"What? You want something, but you're afraid—"

"Can I go back to the farm with you? Please?" he blurted out. "Can you believe that bastard took *my* horse?"

Katie realized he was still hurting and didn't want to be alone. But she also knew exactly what would happen if they ended up at the farm. While she wanted nothing more than to make love with him again, it was the wrong thing to do. "Seth we can't..."

He shook his head. "I know, I know. I just need to hold you, to have someone to talk to. Please?"

The hurt in his voice melted away any resistance she could offer. "Get in the truck."

* * * *

Back at the farm, Seth spent some time with Spun Gold. At least this horse wouldn't get claimed right out from under him. He'd make sure Katie never put the colt in a claiming race. At least for the rest of the season. Seth had to remind himself that he would have no say in anything Katie did after that. Not for the next five long years. If ever again.

What kind of future could they possibly have?

Katie hadn't even entertained the idea of waiting, not that he could blame her. It dawned on him exactly what he had been asking and the message he'd given her. He'd made it pretty clear the money was more important. *God, Remington. That was cold.* She had every right to refuse him. Hell, she probably should have hauled off and let him have it with both barrels.

Seth leaned his shoulder against the wall, watching Katie flit from stall to stall checking water buckets. He wondered at the changes that had occurred in his life. How the hell had he allowed himself to love a horse? The great and wealthy Seth Remington, practically in tears over losing a damn horse! Good God, what would his friends say?

What friends? The Boys' Club? There wasn't a single member who knew anything about true friendship. All they cared about was partying hard and using people as a means to their own selfish ends. He knew they'd react with pure disdain. After all, he'd been a charter member.

Friendship meant being there when a friend needed you most, just like Katie had been there for Brian and Samantha. Seth still couldn't believe she was going to keep paying Chris's salary. He'd seen her books because he'd done most of her computer work for her. The financial situation had improved since the stable had been doing well at the track, but Katie wasn't wealthy by any stretch. She was barely solvent. Her generosity was foolhardy, but he loved her for it all the same.

"I love her for it," he whispered.

Seth suddenly realized that against any kind of common sense, he had fallen in love. Against any kind of logic, against all odds, he'd fallen in love with Katie Murphy. Desperately and passionately in love with her.

So what exactly do you plan to do about it, Remington?

Every fiber of Seth's being screamed at him to go to her, to pick her up and carry her to her bed. His body was already responding to the thought of touching Katie again, to the memory of what they had shared. She even made him forget the pain of losing Monterey Jack.

Twice he'd risked everything for her. From the time he'd been old enough to know about sex, his father had instilled in Seth the need for a Remington to be extraordinarily careful. Women would use him if he wasn't vigilant. They'd try to get pregnant just to get their greedy little hands on a chunk of the Remington fortune.

Seth had always practiced the safest sex. Yet when it came to Katie, the notion of contraception hadn't so much as crossed his mind. In fact, he was deeply hurt to think a child couldn't possibly come from the times they made love. His heart ached, yearned for Katie and the red-headed boy they would never have together.

A baby! Since when did a playboy like Seth Remington ever care about something as insipid as raising a family?

All he ever cared about was money. And then Katie came into his life. He was risking his father's hard-earned wealth for her, and for that moment of time, it seemed worth *every single penny*.

Pushing himself away from the wall, Seth took long, fast strides to catch her. Katie stood next to Miss Daisy, gently patting the mare's neck. Seth grabbed Katie's hand and pulled her out of the stall.

After he latched the door, he looked down into her inquisitive green eyes, and Seth wanted to drown in them. He wanted to forget where he ended and be where she began. He cupped her face with his palms and pressed a rough, deep kiss to her lips then invaded her sweet mouth with his tongue. When he finally pulled away, he could see both passion and concern in her eyes. "Seth, we can't—"

"Is that all you ever say? Maybe I need to be a little more... persuasive." With an enormous grin, Seth backed up a step, balled his hands into loose fists, and hit his chest as he grunted his best caveman imitation. "Seth need woman."

Katie laughed. "You're nuts."

He grabbed for her. She ducked under his arm and swerved out of his reach. He hit his chest again and added a frustrated growl. "No. Woman do what Seth say. Man boss." He continued grunting, stalking her up the aisle as Katie laughed and backed cautiously away.

"Stop it!" she shrieked with a giggle in her voice. But Seth continued to pursue her, pausing every few feet to pound his chest and grunt for effect. He finally backed her into a shower stall. There would be no more retreat.

Seth bent down, picked her up, and threw her over his shoulder like a sack of feed. She squealed and laughed. "Put me down. Come on, Seth. Put me down."

He knew she didn't really mean it. "Come, woman. Seth make woman happy. Seth take woman to bed." He grunted as she giggled and slapped her palms on his back.

He walked out of the wash stall and came face to face with Chris.

"Seth! Put me down." Katie said with another laugh. Seth bent over to set her back on her feet and spun her around so she could see they had a visitor.

"Sorry. Looks like I'm... interrupting you guys," Chris said with an enormous grin and a wink. "I just came by to get some of my stuff."

Katie appeared horrified, and Seth could tell she was desperately trying to come up with a way to cover the damage. As if she could.

"We were just... just... finishing up so I could take Seth back to the dorm."

Oh, yeah. He's going to buy that one, Boss.

Chris chuckled. "I know what you were doing. It's not my business—"

"No!" She clutched at Chris's arm. "You don't know anything. Chris, you need to forget this. Please," Katie pleaded.

"What's the big deal? So you guys like each other. So what?" Chris asked in obvious confusion.

Katie grabbed her truck keys from her pocket and handed them at Seth. "Go home. Just come back tomorrow and we'll get chores done before we go see Brian." When Seth didn't move, she stomped her foot. "Go!" He nodded and made his way out of the barn.

Katie stared at Chris for a moment, but all she could think about was how to make the last few minutes rewind so she could fix this mess. If Chris let news of her relationship with Seth slip to the wrong person, it could cost

Seth his fortune.

No fraternization, Katie. Remember?

"What exactly *is* going on?" he finally asked. "Shit, Katie. I was joking when I asked if he was on work release from the prison. He's not—"

"No, Chris. It's nothing like that, but you've got to trust me here." She squeezed his arm, hoping to impress the seriousness of the situation. "Nothing, I repeat, *nothing* is going on between Seth and me. Please just believe that and let it go. It's really important."

Gathering his eyebrows into one thick line, he jerked his arm away. "Katie, you know I don't gossip. I won't tell anyone. But it hurts that you won't tell me what's up with him. You used to call him 'Crash,' but now he's always 'Seth.'"

He stared at the floor as if trying to gather his thoughts, and Katie's heart began to pound like a jackhammer in her chest. How could she protect Seth now? How could she protect his fortune if other people found out they'd slept together?

Chris finally looked back at Katie, and she was taken aback by the brotherly concern mirrored in his eyes. "I didn't pry when he got here, and I didn't drill you with questions, but I know something is up with this guy. What'd you mean the night Brian got hurt when you asked if Seth *had* to be in your barn?"

Katie weighed the potential danger posed by Chris being kept in the dark and inadvertently letting something slip versus a small violation of the confidentiality clause. The scale came down heavily on the side of friendship. "Let's go in my office. I'll tell you what I can, but you've got to *swear* to keep it secret."

"Cross my heart."

She had no choice but to trust him.

Chapter 22

Seth tossed and turned on his small and uncomfortable dormitory bed for the majority of the night. Besides the sultry weather making it entirely too hot for him to sleep, his mind could find absolutely no peace.

The stories his father had hammered into his head from the time he'd been a child echoed through his mind. Seth's grandfather had built the business from the ground up by tinkering with electronics before they were such a dominant part of everyday life. Sterling became one of the pioneers in the manufacturing of dependable computers people could afford, and his foresight earned his company more money than many third world countries claimed as their entire gross national product.

And what exactly have I done with my life? "Not a damn thing."

Remington Computers was supposed to be Seth's legacy to pass down to future generations, and he'd thrown it all away because he'd been attracted to a pretty girl.

His father had always encouraged him to make a name for himself. Seth was sure once the news got out he'd slept with Katie, no one would *ever* forget the name "Seth Remington." After all, he would forevermore be the man who screwed away his fortune. Literally. He would surely be the butt of jokes for years to come.

Seth tried to find some comfort by telling himself Katie would take care of the problem. She would talk to Chris and get him to keep their secret. She would surely smooth it all over.

With a grunt of disgust, he rolled over, kicked off the sheet, and tried to find a more comfortable spot. He was hiding behind her skirts. *So much for being my own man.*

By the time the first rays of the sunrise began to shine through the dirty window of his cramped room, Seth had found very little rest.

He retrieved some clean clothes and slammed the dresser shut. Then he got dressed and drove to the farm, dreading to hear what Katie would have to report.

When Seth walked into the barn, she was already feeding the horses. Several of them nickered and stomped their feet, waiting for their turn.

Seth went to grab an armload of hay and began to follow Katie and her wheelbarrow full of sweet grain. He pitched a flake into each stall.

"What did Chris say?" he finally found the courage to ask, not entirely sure he wanted to know the answer.

"He'll be fine. I told him enough that he knows not to talk about... anything."

"Honest?"

"No, Seth. I'm lying to you. Chris is working for the *National Enquirer*. You're the next front page story."

"Smart ass," Seth said, feeling his tension finally beginning to ease. "You know what the will said."

"No one is gonna know. No one will take your money away."

"Depends on whether you think I seduced you or not. That's what the Old Man said. I couldn't seduce you."

Katie chuckled. "We'll just call it spontaneous combustion and forget about it. Okay?"

A curt nod was his reply, but Seth knew forgetting making love to Katie was an impossibility.

They hit the road to Indianapolis less than thirty minutes later.

Neither was really in the mood to rehash their precarious situation, so they made idle chit-chat and listened to one of Katie's albums while Seth complained about her selection of music.

"Look at this," he said as he flipped through her stack of CDs. "Barry Manilow and Billy Joel. Is that all you listen to?" He stopped and held up a CD case. "Oh, wait. Here's a new one. Who the hell is Michael Bubbles?"

"It's pronounced Boo-blay, you dingbat. Michael Bublé. He happens to sing some of my favorite songs."

"Will you sing one for me on Monday?"

Katie shook her head. "I'm not going back to The Place until Brian and Sam can go, too. And I sure as hell won't sing for you."

"Why not? You didn't have any problem singing some Carly Simon for me," Seth said with a wink and a laugh.

Katie furrowed her brow. "You're never going to let me forget that, are you?"

"Never. Hey, don't miss that turn off if we're going downtown," Seth cautioned as he continued to inventory her music. "You need to take better care of these. They're all scratched up."

"Yeah. I wear them out. That Barry Manilow CD," Katie said, pointing to the case Seth held, "is the third one I've had of the same album."

"One of these days, I'll introduce you to some *real* music. Ever heard Metallica?"

"I can't play stuff like that," she replied with a chuckle. "It spooks the horses."

* * * *

Once inside the hospital, Katie and Seth discovered Brian had been moved to a new room. They made the long trek to a new wing of the enormous campus to locate him.

"I hope his room has a VCR like the last one did. Otherwise, I wasted my time hauling these along." Seth nodded toward the sack of video tapes he held.

As Katie was disparaging ever finding Brian's room, they turned the corner and she caught sight of Samantha talking to one of the nurses. Katie waved and Sam returned the gesture. Sam said a few more things to the nurse before walking down the hall to greet them.

Katie gave her friend a hug. "How's he doing?"

"It's awful!" Sam complained. Katie shot her a worried look. "Sorry, it's not what you think. He's just so damn stubborn about everything. He won't let anyone help him, and all he does is bitch about going home." She nodded toward the sack Seth was totting. "What have you got in there?"

"I brought some race tapes. I was hoping Brian could offer the rookie some tips," Seth replied.

"Maybe you can get him out of his sour mood. He lives to drive, but he won't be able to for probably six months or more. Maybe he can be your mentor." Sam gave him an enormous smile. "I heard you did a snap job on Spun Gold. Joe Perry says he'll let you qualify all his two-year-olds."

"Yeah. I'm getting a lot of qualifiers. But I really want to..."

Katie easily followed his train of thought and decided to quickly derail the ridiculous idea she knew he was proposing. "No. No way! You're not driving in a race. You can't even get your P license unless the officials waive the six-month rule, and you'll be long gone by—" She suddenly stopped the flow of information. *Watch your mouth, Kathleen.*

"Come on," Sam said to Katie. The stern glare Sam shot Katie's direction declared the time of the inquisition had at long last arrived. "Let's drop Wonderboy here off with Brian, and then we can go get a cup of coffee in the cafeteria."

Brian seemed to cheer up considerably when Seth produced the cache of videotapes, and in only a few minutes, the two men were deeply engrossed in watching Brian's glory days and discussing racing strategy.

Samantha and Katie slipped out the door and meandered down several winding corridors before they finally arrived at the cafeteria. After acquiring some coffee, the women sat down at a small table.

Katie shifted her cup in her hands as she waited anxiously for Sam to broach the subject of Seth. She knew from the look in Sam's eye that the woman had a million questions on her mind. The confidentiality agreement chafed Katie again, and she wasn't sure how she could honor it any longer—especially when she so desperately needed to share her burdens with her best friend.

"So are you ever gonna tell me what's going on between you two?" Sam finally asked.

"It's complicated." Katie continued to stare at her cup.

"Bullshit. Just open your mouth and tell me about this guy."

"I... I can't." Katie could feel the flush spreading over her cheeks.

Samantha leaned in studying Katie's face. Her eyes suddenly flew wide. "Oh, my God! You slept with him, didn't you?"

Katie had never been able to hide much from Sam, and it wasn't surprising she already knew.

"At least tell me he was better than Mike."

Katie couldn't stop a laugh at the notion Mike might even be in the same league as Seth. "*Loads* better." Her face felt like it had caught fire. "God, Sam, this is embarrassing."

"For pity's sake, why? It's not like we haven't always shared stuff." Sam leaned into the table and lowered her voice. "How about I tell you one of the reasons Brian's pissed off is because we'll have to wait a long time to have sex again?"

"I kind of figured," Katie replied. "How are you feeling? Getting enough rest?"

"Too much. Not much to do all day around here except watch TV and eat." Sam lifted the hem of her shirt to expose the small tummy that had begun to show the child she was expecting. "Look at this. I'm gonna be in maternity clothes soon."

"I think you look wonderful. I envy you." Katie glanced away.

"I'm sorry, Katie. I didn't mean to hurt your feelings." Sometimes Katie thought Sam could read her mind. "Besides, your doctor didn't say it was hopeless, did he?"

Katie shook her head but scoffed at the notion anything in her life would ever come easy. She was a Murphy after all. "No, he didn't. *Highly* unlikely, but not entirely hopeless. Not like that's a lot to hang my hat on."

They sipped their coffee quietly for a few moments.

"So when are you gonna tell me about Seth Remington?" Sam asked with a mischievous smirk.

Katie slapped her palms on the table. "You know! Oh, my God, *you know*! How? Who... who told you?"

Sam's eyes were full of impish laughter. "I told you, there's nothing to do here except eat and watch TV. Brian was flipping through the channels and found some late night gossip show. *The Tattler*, I think. And there was Seth's face on the screen. The stupid show is offering a huge reward for anyone who can locate him. Brian thought we should call, but I wouldn't let him." She chuckled and waved her hand as if to push aside the notion. "He was teasing anyway. I think he actually likes the guy."

Katie swallowed hard, trying to get a grip on her spinning thoughts. "What else did they say?"

"He disappeared after his dad's funeral, and no one has seen him since. No wonder. Who in the hell would expect to find a guy with that much money living in Indiana and shoveling horse shit? He doesn't look the same either. He's really tan now, and his hair is a bunch shorter. The only reason we caught it was the name. How common is 'Seth'? How'd he end up with you?"

"Do you remember when I told you that Sterling Remington wanted to put a horse in my barn?"

"Yeah. You thought he'd changed his mind. I remembered that when I saw the TV show," Sam said before she picked up her cup and sipped her coffee. "What happened?"

"He got sick. Evidently, he rewrote his will right before he died to leave me Seth."

Sam chuckled as she put her cup down. "Mighty thoughtful of him. So you own the guy now?"

"Ha ha," Katie replied in a flat voice. "Aren't you hysterical? Mr. Remington left me Seth as a groom for one season, and I got Spun Gold as payment. Unless Seth works hard, he won't get a dime of his inheritance. And I've got to decide if he gets it or not. He's not supposed to influence me, so we're not supposed to get too… close."

Sam nodded her understanding before she got up, grabbed one of the coffee pots standing on the drink station, and refilled her cup. She settled herself back into her seat and grew serious, taking on that motherly tone she liked to get from time to time. "Katie, this guy is bad news. You thought Mike was bad, Seth is worse. He spends money like there's no tomorrow. He wrecked a bunch of cars."

"Crash," Katie whispered. But she already knew all those things about Seth.

"Yeah, Crash. He also had a fiancée. Some blond bimbo named Muffy or Fluffy or some other rich girl name." Sam grinned at her own ironic sense of humor.

"He was engaged?" Her Seth? Engaged? Katie's heart beat a wild rhythm in her chest as her thoughts tumbled and churned. *Engaged?* What else was Seth hiding?

Sam's smile evaporated as her features took on her obvious concern. "He hasn't really told you much, has he? Look, I understand that Mike was the fifteen second failure in the sack..."

Katie laughed, happy to have the momentary distraction. "He had other... *shortcomings,* too." She held up her fist and then extended her pinkie.

Sam laughed loud enough for people to turn and stare. "Okay. *Way* too much information!" She quickly turned sober again, fast enough Katie could hardly keep up with her friend's changing moods. "Why'd you sleep with

Seth?"

Katie glanced away, not wanting to see condemnation in her best friend's eyes. "It's complicated."

"You sound like a broken record. Tell me, damn it!"

"It was after Brian's accident. I didn't want to be alone, and he was just supposed to stay and... you know... hold me. But I thought it was a dream at first, and then I didn't want to stop." Katie realized her tale made it sound like she'd been a passive player in the game. She immediately corrected that ridiculous notion. "I knew what I was doing, Sam."

Sam reached for the sugar. "At least tell me you used some protection."

Katie could feel the heat spread across her cheeks again. "It only happened twice—"

"*Twice?* C'mon, Katie! You've gotta stop this!" Sam sounded as incredulous as she looked.

"I know, I know, but... Sam, I love him," Katie finally confessed. "I really love him. What am I gonna do?" She tried desperately to stop the tears gathering in her eyes.

"First of all, you're gonna stop sleeping with the guy," Sam ordered as she picked up her spoon to stir her coffee.

Katie nodded her agreement. "You're right. I have. I mean, I will. He seemed different on the ride here. We used to talk about everything, but after last night—"

Sam threw her spoon on the table. The resulting clatter brought a few more rude stares. "You slept with him last night too?"

"Sam, shh."

Her tone and her volume didn't change too awfully much. "What are you guys, a couple of rabbits?"

"I didn't sleep with him last night. Well, we were about to. Chris came to the farm and almost caught us and... Well, it kind of cooled things off. I had to tell Chris some of the story." Katie wiped away her stray tears with the back of her hand. "If anyone finds out he slept with me, he could lose his money. You can't tell anyone, Sam."

This situation kept getting worse and worse. She knew Chris wouldn't spread the story, but if anyone else figured any of it out, Seth would be front page news in the span of time it took for a satellite to bounce the story all over the country. And Katie was positioned to get nothing but a broken heart out of the whole affair. Seth would lose his inheritance; she'd lose Spun Gold.

"I won't tell anyone, but Katie, you've gotta get this guy out of your head," Sam said as if the task was something easy or even possible to accomplish.

"I love him, Sam. The Seth I know doesn't sound like the guy you heard about. Maybe he's changed. Maybe—"

"Maybe he's cozying up to you to get his money. Where does rich lawyer man come into all this?" Sam asked before sipping her coffee and letting her intense gaze drill holes through Katie's fragile composure.

"Ross is the lawyer overseeing the will. I still haven't figured out why he got College Mascot."

"Yeah, right." Sam rolled her eyes. "You know damn well why he got that horse, Katie. He likes you. A lot. You've got this rich hunk of a lawyer head over heels for you, but you go and sleep with a guy who'll disappear soon." She frowned. "I'm sorry, Honey. I didn't mean to make it sound like—"

Katie shook her head and gave a pathetic chuckle. "Don't be sorry, Sam. It's the truth. Seth doesn't love me. I sure know how to pick them, don't I?" The tears spilled over her lashes again, and she was helpless to stop them. "First I fall for the White Knight who loves 'em and leaves 'em. Then I fall for Richie Rich who'll do the same damn thing. What am I going to do?"

Sam put her hand over Katie's. "I know what you're gonna do. You're gonna run your stable and treat him like any other employee. You're gonna protect yourself, and I don't mean condoms. Katie, you're gonna protect your heart. Even if you do love the guy, you're *not* sleeping with him again."

Katie nodded, but all the sage advice was easier said than done.

Sam clearly knew her well enough to understand what Katie's silence meant. "I mean it, *Kathleen.*"

"I understand, *Samantha.*"

* * * *

By the time the women returned to the room, Seth and Brian were deep in discussion over one of Brian's racing moves as they played, rewound, and then watched the same tape several times.

"I still can't believe you found a hole there," Seth said pointing at the screen.

"They parted like the Red Sea," Brian said with a laugh.

"Sounds like you guys are having a good time," Sam said as she walked over to plant a kiss on her husband's forehead. He patted her growing belly in return. The gesture seemed so intimate, it made Katie's heart clench in envy.

"I'll leave the tapes for you," Seth said to Brian. He turned to Katie. "Ready to go, Boss?"

She gave a resigned nod. "We really should be leaving. Is there anything I can get for you two?"

"No, thanks," Brian replied. He patted the sack lying next to him, but Katie caught some mischief in his gaze. "The tapes are great. Thanks, Seth."

Katie's eyes flew wide and she watched intently to see if Seth caught the implication of Brian using his name. Seth didn't bat an eyelash. Sam appeared to be having problems suppressing a laugh as she turned her head and faked a small cough. Men could be so dense.

"Anytime. You'll make the calls?" Seth asked.

Katie watched an enigmatic look pass between the two men and quickly realized just what was being conspired. "Oh, no. *Hell*, no! He's *not* calling the race officials. Seth, you can't drive—"

"Sure he can," Brian interrupted. "He's had a ton of qualifiers, and they've waived the six-month rule before. You can't keep having cowboys like Josh Piper drive your horses or you'll end up in the poor house. Plus, no one really wants to sit behind Spun Gold since he threw me. Seth should drive him."

"Thanks for all the support, Brian," Katie mocked. It dawned on her that Brian had not only accepted him, but the guy liked Seth.

"No problem, Kiddo."

They exchanged farewells, and Katie and Seth found themselves back in her truck making their way out of Indianapolis.

Katie briefly debated telling Seth about *The Tattler*, but quickly brushed the idea aside, sure very few people would even see the ridiculous show or recognize Seth if they did. She had more important things on her mind. "Seth, look. I'm going to have Mark Masters drive Spun Gold this week. It's for two-year-old horses that are still maidens."

"Maidens?"

"Haven't won a race yet. Mark is really good with temperamental horses. If things don't work out, we'll talk about a P license. Okay?"

Seth appeared to be mulling it over for a moment. "Fine, but I'm letting Brian go ahead and talk to the officials. I've got more than twenty-five qualifiers under my belt, and they might let me get my P license if Brian calls in some favors. If Mark screws up, then you'll let me drive Gold in the first leg of the sires stakes?"

"Fine. But only if Mark screws up."

Chapter 23

"Let's get chores done," Katie told Seth when they arrived back at the farm.

She watched him check the training board. He made a couple of notations for Spun Gold before turning back to her. "I'll get the turn outs. You check water buckets." His voice held too much authority to please Katie.

"Who died and made you emperor?"

Seth just smiled at her as he led the first horse out of the barn.

As she filled the water buckets, Katie noticed Gold had managed to push a large portion of hay deep in his water again. She smiled, thinking the horse was as much trouble as his trainer. She jokingly scolded the horse as she took the pail off the hook. Walking to the end of the barn, she heaved the dirty water out toward the grass. Unfortunately for Seth, she hadn't realized he would be turning the corner at the same moment, and she drenched him in a dirty mixture of water and hay. His hair, face, and shirt were soaked, and bits of hay clung to his cheeks and forehead.

Katie dropped the bucket and tried to sputter an apology before she started to laugh.

Seth picked a wet cloverleaf from his face and flicked it toward her. "If you thought I needed a shower, all you had to do was tell me."

"I'm... I'm sorry. " Katie tried to apologize between gasps of breath. She laughed so hard her sides ached. She wrapped her arms around herself, trying desperately to bring the ridiculous giggles to an end. "Really... I'm sorry."

With a growl, Seth ran to the hose Katie had dropped on the floor, picked it up, and aimed the nozzle at her.

"Don't!" Katie tried without much success to quell her laughing fit. "Don't!"

Seth pulled the nozzle's trigger and sprayed Katie before she could jump at him to grab the hose. When she had it firmly in her grasp, she turned it on him and sprayed his back as he ran away. Chasing him down the length of the barn, Katie continued to drench him with water.

Once he reached the wash stall, she ran out of slack, but Seth was newly armed with the wash stall's long hose. The duel commenced, leaving them both dripping wet.

"Truce!" Katie squealed.

"You put your hose down first."

"You first."

"Look, Boss, you started this whole thing. Remember?"

"Yeah, but it was an accident." Like a criminal caught by the law, she held her hands up in surrender, pointing the nozzle away from Seth. "Okay, fine. See? I'm putting it down now." She bent down to place the hose on the floor.

The second she released the nozzle, Seth sprayed her again. "Oops. Accident. My fingers slipped. Sorry."

Katie ran over and grabbed the hose out of his hand. "Yeah, I'm sure it was an *accident.*" She looped the hose around the wash stall's hanger as Seth went back to wrap up the hose she'd abandoned.

Katie stood in the middle of the aisle, feeling the water dripping from her. "Just look at me."

"Oh, I'm looking. I'm looking." His gaze raked her from head to toe, and he gave her an exaggerated growl.

She glanced down and felt her face flush hot as she realized her shirt was plastered to her body like she was a participant in some wet t-shirt contest. Thank heavens she had on a tank top underneath. "Pervert."

Seth laughed at her.

She twisted the hem of her shirt. "Come on. Let's go out in the sun and get dry."

Grabbing a clean horse blanket off the rack, Katie took Seth's hand and led him to her truck. She jerked the tailgate open and crawled into the empty bed where she spread out the blanket before plopping down in the middle.

Seth stood in the grass and watched as she took off her shirt to reveal a tight pink tank top that clung to her chest. She smiled, hoping he was still looking. The lecherous smirk he shot her way sent a shimmer of warmth through her. He didn't look too shabby himself with his shirt clinging like a second skin.

Keeping her hands off him wasn't going to be easy.

Katie wrung her t-shirt out and hung it over the side of the truck to dry in the sun and then pulled off her boots and socks. She finally stretched out on the blanket to sunbathe. "You coming?" She patted the space next to her.

He snorted a laugh. "You actually said that to me with a straight face."

"Said what?" Her face flushed hot. "Oh my God, you've got a dirty mind."

"I'm not the one tossing out invitations like that in broad daylight."

Seth jumped into the truck bed and took off his shirt and boots before he joined her on the blanket. Katie took one look at his muscular body and sighed in appreciation. Then she desperately hoped Seth hadn't heard her. He might be the most handsome man she had ever seen, and she couldn't help but admire that body. But his ego sure didn't need any more stroking, and it was embarrassing to think she behaved no better than some hormonal teenager.

Lacing his fingers, Seth put his hands behind his head and closed his eyes. "This is nice. I can't remember the last time I got to relax."

"Oh, come on. I don't work you *that* hard."

"I'm talking about before I came here. I couldn't go anywhere without some freakin' cameraman following me around. If anyone knew who I was—"

"They don't. You just fit in here—like you were born to it. Even if they did know your real name, horsemen protect their own. They might stab each other in the back sometimes, but God forbid an outsider go after one of us." She stretched her arms over her head as she enjoyed the warmth of the sun, hoping he didn't notice she was getting another eyeful of that muscular chest. Her self-control was tenuous at best as her fingers itched to reach out and touch him.

"You know what the best thing is? I can be myself. People don't expect me to automatically screw up."

"Well, maybe. I mean, we *do* expect you to screw up," Katie teased.

Seth rolled over and tickled Katie's ribs, and she howled in laughter. "Stop," she gasped, but he gave her no quarter. Between laughs she finally squealed, "You'll make me pee my pants."

"Ugh. Okay, I'll stop." Seth raised his hands in surrender. Then he lowered his palms to hover above her breasts. "Besides, there are other things I'd like to touch."

She hesitated a moment as desire warred with common sense. Finally, she brushed his hands aside. "Just like a guy. Always thinking with your..." She fixed her eyes on his groin.

Seth's chuckle sang like a melody floating in the air. Looking up at him, all Katie could feel was need. His dark hair had a kiss of late afternoon sunlight, and he was so tan and downright... gorgeous. It seemed the most natural thing in the world to give into her desire. Katie leaned up, splayed her fingers through his hair, and pulled him down to her. Their mouths danced across each other, soon to be joined by the caress of their tongues. Seth finally raised his head and stared at her. Those hazel eyes of his were hypnotic.

All Katie could think was how much she wanted him to make love to her. Her body warmed, desiring something she couldn't have. All he had to do was crook his finger, and she'd follow him straight to her bed. Hell, she'd probably rip his clothes off before he shut the door. She never thought she would turn into the type of woman who ran after a man with her tongue hanging out. Embarrassment washed over her. *I'm getting to be worse than Rachel.*

Seth wiggled his eyebrows. "You know, there's nice big pile of hay in the barn. Isn't that what hay is for? Rolling in?"

Katie smiled at his charm and pulled him back into a deep kiss. When his tongue pushed into his mouth, she sucked on it and was rewarded with his throaty growl. As her tongue swept into his warm mouth, he returned the favor. She lost herself in his kiss, in his touch, in the love she felt for him. It had never been like this with Mike.

Mike. Just thinking about him was akin to having a bucket of ice water thrown over her. She'd always been a fool where men were concerned. "Seth, we can't—"

"I know, but, God, I want you, Katie. I want you so bad." The words sent a shiver through her. She wanted him too.

She was seriously reconsidering her answer when Seth pulled himself away from her. With a groan, he grabbed his shirt before jumping out of the truck.

Katie sat up on her elbows and called after him. "Don't forget to pick up Gold's water bucket and fill it."

He hit her in the face with his wadded up, damp t-shirt.

* * * *

Chris took a table at Cyber Café and pulled a chair up to one of the available computers. Ever since his talk with Katie, he'd been deeply curious about the man who shared her stable.

The story seemed almost too ludicrous to possibly be true. Why would a guy with that much money want his son to do manual labor all summer?

Chris felt protective of Katie in a brotherly fashion, and knowing she'd become deeply involved with Seth Remington caused some major concern. It was plain Katie loved the guy. The fact was written all over her face every time Chris saw them together. But if what she told him was true, Seth would be packing his bags at the end of the season, and they would probably never see him again.

Katie's going to get hurt. No way around it. Chris decided the time had arrived for a fact-finding mission.

As he sipped his mocha latte, Chris rifled through the images and stories concerning Seth. He sure didn't like what he discovered. It was hard to reconcile the caring and concerned groom Chris had come to know with the selfish, superficial playboy depicted by several different sources.

When a website for the news show *The Tattler* popped up, Chris saw Seth's image looking back from a rendition of an old-fashioned reward poster. The producers were offering ten-thousand dollars to anyone who could disclose the true whereabouts of the missing heir to the Remington fortune.

Seth would never make it through the season. Someone would want that bounty. Although he looked different with his short hair and deep tan, he couldn't hide forever.

"Whatcha looking at?" a familiar voice asked over Chris's shoulder. He immediately clicked the mouse to close the browser.

"Nothing. Just checking out races for this week," Chris replied as he turned around to face Rachel Schaeffer. "I'm heading back to the Mitchell farm. You need a ride?"

"Nah. My suspension is over, so I'm going back to the track tonight. Gonna see if I can pick up a paddock to scare up some pocket money."

"I forgot. So do you wanna paddock the tenth for me? I was gonna do it myself, but I've got three in, and I could use the help." Chris picked up his cup and stood up.

"Yeah. The tenth is fine. I'll see you tonight."

Rachel watched as he threw away his paper cup and walked out the front door before she sat down at the computer Chris had vacated.

Rachel pulled up the Internet browser and located the history of website visits the computer had made. She brought back the page Chris had closed in such an awful hurry.

"Well, well. What have we here?" She smiled at her lucrative discovery.

Rachel's first instinct was to whip out her cell phone, call the toll-free number, and claim her reward. But as she thought it through, she decided to try for the big brass ring. Compared to the Remington fortune, *The Tattler* bounty was pocket change.

First, she'd find a way to get Seth Remington for her own. Rachel was positive she could wrap him around her finger if she put her mind and body to the task.

And if for some reason that plan failed, then she would gladly negotiate with *The Tattler*.

* * * *

"I'm sorry, Katie," Mark Masters said as he jumped off his race bike and began to release it from the harness. "He got rough gaited, and I was afraid he'd run if I pushed him too hard."

Katie nodded. She'd watched Gold's race, and she knew Mark had done an admirable job keeping the colt from breaking gait. Even after giving the horse a good stretch drive, the best he'd managed was fourth place. "You did fine with him. Thanks, Mark."

Seth led the chestnut back to his paddock stall, and Katie followed closely behind, lost deep in her thoughts. It was becoming all too obvious the only person who could seem to manage the stubborn horse was Seth, but the thought of him racing terrified her. "I know you want to drive, but what if Gold falls again? What if there's another accident?" she asked as she hooked the cross-ties.

"I know him best, Boss," Seth replied as he removed the colt's equipment. "He behaves for me. And it's the sires stakes. That's what you got him for, remember?"

She still couldn't believe the judges had actually granted him a P license. There would be no living with his ego now. "I remember." Katie helped strip the horse's knee boots. If Gold could make it to the final leg of the stakes, the purse was fifty-thousand dollars. If he won, she could support her stable for months. Maybe she could even put a nice down payment on some acres she'd seen for sale near the Mitchell farm.

Despite the temptation of the money, Katie still wanted to dissuade him. "You don't even have colors, and it's too late to get them now." She would be sure to give Brian a piece of her irritated mind the next time she saw him. If he hadn't made that call to the judges...

"That's what you think," he replied with one of his enormous, smug smiles.

Katie looked over at him and frowned. "When did you get colors?"

Seth continued to grin. "I've been planning to drive all along. I've had them for a while, actually."

She didn't believe him. "Can I see them?"

"When you let me drive Gold next week."

Before Katie could respond, her cell phone rang. After a short conversation, she flipped it shut and smiled at Seth. "How would you like to get Monterey Jack back?"

His face lit up with a hundred-watt smile. "James still wants him?"

"Yep. O'Riley hasn't won squat with him, so he finally put Jack back in at eight-thousand, and James said to get him back."

Leading Gold out of the stall, Seth walked past Katie. "You'll let me drive next week?"

She frowned again, feeling like she rode some ironic emotional roller coaster. Up, down. Happy, sad. Passion, pain. God, the ridiculous ride was draining.

There just wasn't another good driver for the colt. She would have to let Seth have his shot. "Yeah," she said with a resigned sigh. "I'll let you drive. I'm going to get a claim form for Jack. Can you get Gold washed and cooled down?"

"Absolutely. That's why you pay me the big bucks, isn't it?" Seth teased as he moved the colt down the bark-lined hallway toward the bath stalls.

* * * *

Once he had the colt secured in the bath stall, Seth picked up the hose and sprayed Gold with warm water. He filled the wash bucket with soap and water before dropping the hose and grabbing the sponge. As he stooped to work the soapy sponge over the colt's front legs, he heard someone step up behind him before she placed a hand on his shoulder. "Hello, Handsome."

"Hello, Rachel," Seth replied without looking up. He shrugged his shoulder to brush her hand away. "Your suspension finally over?"

"Yeah. I really missed you, Crash," Rachel purred.

"Sure you did," he said as he stood up and threw the sponge into the big bucket.

"Do you wanna go out after races? I know a place where we can have lots of privacy."

"No, thanks. I've got to get my colt back." Seth grabbed the hose and rinsed his horse. Gold flapped his lips, so Seth let the water spray into the colt's mouth. He chuckled as his pet played with the stream of water.

Rachel reached down and grabbed the wooden scraper and ran it over Gold's body. The horse kicked the back wall.

"He doesn't like strangers, Rachel. Let him be." Seth consoled Gold with soothing words as he rubbed a towel over the horse's face and neck.

She threw the scraper in the bucket. "You sure you don't wanna go out? We can go anytime, doesn't have to be tonight."

"I'll think about it," Seth lied. He gathered his supplies and led Spun Gold back to his stall.

Rachel watched him as he walked away. "You *better* think about it," she whispered. "Or else."

Chapter 24

"God, it's hot," Seth said as he mounted a box fan on the bars of Monterey Jack's stall. He stopped to run his hand over his forehead and then shake the dripping sweat off his fingers. "How can you stand it all the time?"

Katie shrugged. "I just do. Chris calls days like this 'mugly.' It's so damn hot and humid, it's worse than muggy."

The first leg of the sires stakes arrived on a typical July day, and she helped Seth finish installing fans for all of the horses. The machines whirled in a noisy chorus as the couple completed their morning chores.

Seth's mind seemed entirely preoccupied with the upcoming race, and his work that morning was atypically haphazard and sloppy. Katie gathered his nerves were getting the better of him, so she corrected any mistake and moved on without scolding him.

She understood his anxiety. It was one of the reasons she'd never opted to try and drive competitively. She couldn't possibly handle that kind of pressure. Split-second decisions at that speed would be impossible for most people, and her driving abilities simply weren't special enough. She admired Seth for at least having the guts to try.

"Do you want me to drive you back?" Katie asked once the work was finished. "You could probably use a nap. You'll want your mind sharp."

"Yeah, but I'll never get a nap in this weather. The dorm will be hotter than a damn oven," Seth complained.

"I know, but..."

"It's all right, Boss. I'll go back."

"No. You can stay here Seth. At least I've got the window unit. It's better than nothing."

"What about you? You could use some rest too."

He was right, but she just didn't trust herself to lie side by side with Seth in the same bed. Nothing had happened between them since the night Chris discovered them, but the only reason they'd been able to maintain their distance was out of sheer determination on both their parts. And more than a few cold showers. She had taken so many, she'd stopped worrying about her pathetic water heater. Their mutual desire remained palpable each time they were together.

"I promise to keep my mitts to myself. Can't we just take a quick nap together?" He wiggled his eyebrows. "Or will you have a problem keeping your hands off of me that long?"

Katie rolled her eyes, even though his words held an embarrassing ring of truth. "I'll just have to control myself." She strode across the barn to her room and Seth followed.

Sitting on the bed, she took off her boots and socks. She desperately wanted to shed her jeans, but she didn't trust either of them to keep to any boundaries if she wore nothing except panties. She did pull her t-shirt over her head to strip to her tank top. She was too hot to care if he saw a bit of shoulder.

She watched Seth as he sat at the desk and removed his boots, socks, and jeans in short order. Then he jerked his shirt over his head and dropped it in the heap of clothes sitting by the chair.

"You promised," Katie cautioned as she stretched out on the bed.

"I know, but I can't help it if you think boxer shorts are sexy." Seth lay down next to her. "Can I at least put my arm around you? If we don't roll on our sides and spoon, I'm going to fall out of the bed. I didn't know anyone actually made a mattress this small." He chuckled for a moment. "Or this lumpy."

"Fine." Katie turned to face the wall. Seth molded his legs to the back of hers and draped his arm across her waist. She jumped when he let his hand drift up to give her breast a stroke. She slapped at his arm. "Stop that."

"Oops. Sorry. Won't happen again, Boss," Seth teased before he wiggled his pelvis against her bottom. Evidence of his desire pressed against her.

"For the love of—"

"All right, all right. I'll be good."

"Just go to sleep, Seth."

Despite the temptation of being so close, after only a few minutes Katie could feel Seth's breaths caress her neck in a slow, steady rhythm. She closed her eyes and listened to the air conditioner drone a humming lullaby.

Katie's eyes bolted open. She tried to roll over to see if she really heard the door open, but Seth's heavy arm and the leg he had draped over hers held her firmly in place. In her sleepy haze, she listened for any sound that would tell her if someone was in the barn, but she heard nothing but the normal noises. With a yawn, she closed her eyes again and drifted back to sleep.

* * * *

As soon as Katie woke up, an overpowering wave of nausea roiled through her. She struggled to get Seth to move enough so that she could jump off of the bed and sprint to the bathroom. She barely made it in time.

Seth stood in the doorway rubbing the sleep from his eyes. "You all right, Boss?"

Katie turned her head and shot him an exasperated glare. "Do I look all right?" She brushed her hair back and threw up again.

He grabbed a washcloth off the towel rack. He ran water over it, wrung the cloth out, and stooped down to wipe her sweaty face. "Déjà vu."

"Thanks," Katie said, flushing the toilet. "I'm better now. Must be nerves."

"Or those two candy bars you ate for lunch. You know, you eat some strange stuff."

"Can we not talk about food?" Katie groaned. She walked to the sink and splashed cold water on her face as her stomach seemed reluctant to settle down. *If I brush my teeth, will the mint make me sick again?*

Seth went back to the office. When she finally trudged out of the bathroom, he was getting dressed. "Feeling better?" he asked as he finished buttoning his jeans.

"Yeah. Like I said, just nerves." She grabbed a green polo from the drawer and pulled it over her head. "Are you ready to make your debut?"

"Absolutely."

* * * *

Seth jogged toward the dorms as soon as Katie parked the truck and trailer. Gold was in a cooperative mood and gave her little trouble as she unloaded him from the trailer and deposited him in the paddock.

Busying herself with lugging the colt's harness bag, Katie barely caught a glimpse of Seth slipping into the driver lounge, toting a garment bag and a helmet box. There was too much to do paddocking her horse to pay much attention to any of the usual swirl of racing activity surrounding her, but she was dying to see what his new colors would look like. She hung the canvas bag on the hook, went into the stall, and stooped down to unwrap the shipping bandages from Gold's front legs.

Ross began to talk to her over the stall's door, and Katie jumped in surprise. "Ross, you scared me to death!" She placed her hand over her heart.

"Sorry."

"How have you been?" she asked looking up at him. "I haven't seen you in so long."

"I know. I'm sorry about that. Things are crazy at the office. I appreciate how much you've been doing with Mascot. He's sure racing well, and we're both making good money." He leaned on the metal gate and fell silent.

Katie watched as his face grew serious. "What's up?"

"We need to talk."

She paused the unwrapping for a moment. Something was definitely wrong; she could see it in his eyes. "Those four words *never* start a good conversation. What do you have to tell me?"

Ross shook his head. "Not now, Katie. We'll talk later."

She didn't like the stern "lawyer" tone in his voice. "What is it?"

"I need a little more of your attention, and I know you're too busy right now. It can wait."

"How about after the race?" she suggested as she stood to retrieve the harness from the bag.

"Yeah. That'd be fine. Good luck with the colt. I'll be back later." He started to leave, and then turned back with a skeptical frown on his face. "Is Seth really driving tonight?"

Katie laughed and nodded. "Yeah. Surprised me, too. Who would have thought?"

"Not me, that's for sure. He's really not the same guy we met in

Chicago, is he?"

She shook her head. "No, Ross, he's not. Not at all."

Ross's features grew pensive for a moment, and several emotions clearly displayed in his eyes. "Katie, has Seth been...? Has he tried...?"

She could hear the concern in his voice but was confused as to what exactly caused him so much worry. "What? Has Seth tried what?"

He shook his head. "Never mind. I'll see you later."

"See ya, Ross."

Once she was sure Gold's equipment was in place, Katie paced nervously as she waited for Seth to bring the jog cart. She fretted and fussed as it drew closer and closer to the colt's warm-up time and was just about to go search for her wayward rookie driver when she saw him. Seth strode confidently up the aisle, pulling her jog cart behind him. He was so handsome that she almost forgot to breathe.

My colors! Seth's jumpsuit was a duplicate of Katie's green and white design, right down to the white shamrock and green stripe. The only alteration was the letter on each of Seth's sleeves as her "M" had been replaced with his "R." His pristine helmet held a compilation of green and white striped designs and shamrocks.

Katie's heart swelled near to bursting with love. She wanted to shout her joy, to declare to the world how proud she was, how deep her adoration flowed. *My colors! He's wearing my colors!*

When he finally reached the stall, she threw herself into his arms and hugged him. He dropped the jog cart, wrapped his arms around her, and lifted her off her feet. He was kissing her an instant later.

She didn't care that they might be making a spectacle of themselves for the entire paddock to see. Ignoring the gossip she knew swirled around them like wafts of smoke, all Katie cared about was that the man she loved had chosen to wear her colors. Her colors! The gesture meant more to her than anyone could possibly understand.

Seth pulled his lips away and put Katie back on her feet. She couldn't trust herself to talk without breaking into joyful tears, so she mechanically went about the tasks required to hook the jog cart up to Gold's harness, letting the normalcy of the actions slowly guide her back to Earth. She led the colt to the entrance chute as Seth took the reins in hand. "Thank you," Katie finally said in a voice so clogged with emotion she barely recognized it as her own.

Seth simply nodded, but she caught him taking a couple of hard swallows, and she wondered if he was as choked up as she seemed to be. He finally slipped on his protective yellow glasses and drove the chestnut out onto the track for his warm-up laps.

Katie stood at the fence, feeling such enormous pleasure that it enveloped her like a comforting cocoon. She watched Seth on the track in his beautiful colors, driving her stakes horse. She felt as if she could take on the world single-handedly. She would slay every dragon, exorcise every demon, and fight every damned reporter. And she would win.

Chris came to stand beside her. He elbowed her and pointed at Seth. “Did you get those for him?”

Katie shook her head. “No. He got them all by himself. I take it you didn’t know either.”

“No, I didn’t. But the day I ordered mine, he went back to the shop. Must have ordered his then. Why do you think he chose your colors?”

She felt a tear spill over onto her cheek. She quickly wiped it away. “I don’t know, but I’m happy about it anyway.”

“Katie, the guy likes you. Hell, I think he even loves you. I’ve seen you guys together, remember? What are you gonna do when he leaves?”

“I don’t know. That’s a long time away,” Katie answered, shaking her head and waving her hand to dismiss the negative thought. “I don’t want to think about it now.” She wouldn’t let worry spoil such incredible moment in time. No matter what happened in the future, she would never, never forget this night.

“Gotta run,” Katie called to Chris as she hurried to meet Seth who had finished his two miles.

As he guided Gold off of the track, she caught the colt’s bridle. “How’d he do?”

“Smooth as a baby’s bare butt. I think he’ll be good,” Seth replied as he deftly dismounted and walked beside the jog cart.

“How’d *you* do?”

“Got a lot of funny stares. One of the trainers meowed like a cat and snapped his whip when he drove by.”

Although Katie tried not to smile, it was a difficult task as her mind formed pictures of the encounter. She tried to smooth Seth’s ruffled feathers.

"I'm sorry they're giving you a hard time."

"I'm not. I chose these colors. If people want to blow shit my way because I..."

Katie waited anxiously for Seth to finish the thought, but he never did. "I'll take care of Gold," she finally said. "Go relax in the driver's lounge until the race."

"You don't need me?"

Katie narrowed her eyes even though the insult was probably not intentional. "Oh, I think I can handle it from here, *Rookie*. Good God, I knew this would be bad for your ego."

Once she had secured her colt in his stall, she paced nervous circles around the paddock, seldom acknowledging the other horsemen. The races progressed at what she thought was an excruciatingly slow pace. She checked her watch more than a dozen times as the minutes seemed to drag into hours. When the official finally called for the race before Gold's, she returned to her horse to complete the final few tasks that would prepare him for the first leg of the Indiana Sires Stakes.

Pulling Katie's green sulky behind him, Seth made his way to Gold's stall. He leaned the bike up against the wall and appeared to be waiting patiently for his race to be called. If he was nervous, he did a good job of hiding it. She, on the other hand, was pretty sure she would throw up again.

"It'll be fine, Boss. You okay with this?" Seth asked. It seemed odd to have him be so reassuring.

"Just don't do anything stupid. For the love of God, *please* don't be a cowboy."

Seth nodded and grabbed the race bike when the officials called them forward. Katie led Gold from his stall and helped Seth attach the bike firmly to the harness. She double and triple checked all the equipment before taking her colt's bridle and leading the way out of the paddock to the post parade.

Seth jumped on the race bike, swung his legs to center, and tucked the excess reins under him before donning his glasses. Although Katie knew adrenaline had to be raging through his system with the intensity of a summer thunderstorm, he maintained a cool and calm outward demeanor. He didn't show an ounce of fear.

She released the horse to his control, patted his shoulder, and gave him some last minute instructions. “Remember, race him off the pace. Good luck. Be safe.” She almost said “I love you,” almost let it roll off her tongue without a thought, but she caught herself in the nick of time. He sure as hell didn’t need to be worrying about something as bothersome as her unrequited feelings during his first major race.

With a nod, Seth entered the track as Katie’s eyes tracked him with the precision of radar. She was well aware that she and her driver were the talk of everyone at the track. To use a rookie driver in a race as important as the sire stakes was unheard of and considered by many to be downright stupid. Earlier in the evening, one of the veteran drivers had even called her an “idiot female” right to her face.

Of course, the little dog and pony show that Katie and Seth had performed earlier in the paddock would surely be fodder for the gossip mill for weeks to come.

Gripping the fence, Katie’s knuckles went white as the starter called for the horses. “Keep him safe, God. Please keep him safe.” The animals eased behind the gate as they increased to full pacing speed. The gates folded and the race began.

Katie chewed nervously on her bottom lip. Seth was starting from one of the outside spots and had to settle for easing Gold into the middle of the pack as they advanced through the first turn. Several horses pushed into the outer flow. Seth couldn’t seem to find a chance to steer Gold away from the rail. Boxed in with nowhere to go, she knew that he’d have to bide his time and hope for a way to get through traffic in the stretch.

“That’s it, Baby. Be patient,” Katie whispered. “Save it for the stretch.”

As the pack entered the last turn, Seth forced Gold to the outer flow, eventually taking the horse wide outside two stalling horses. She could see the colt straining to be let loose to race at his top speed. “Keep a hand on him, Seth.” As if heeding her warning, Seth patiently waited until the top of the stretch to give the horse his head. It was now simply a matter of which of the horses had the most left for the long journey home.

As soon as the racers passed by the paddock, Katie ran to the TV to stand next to Chris.

“Ouch! That’ll leave a mark!” Chris pushed her hand away. She hadn’t even realized she punched his arm. Chris pointed to the television. “He found a higher gear, Katie! Look at that colt go!”

Seth weaved through traffic, moving first left then right before he found an unobstructed path to bring the horse to the wire. She suddenly froze. Her limbs were nothing but dead weight, her mouth dry as cotton. "He's going to... to... *win*."

Once the way became clear, she saw Seth whistling and hitting his whip against the metal sulky, urging Gold to give one last push. With a surge, Gold crossed the finish line only a head in front of his closest rival.

Katie was too shocked to even react, too stunned to move. *He won. He actually won.*

Chris finally gave a tug on her arm to get her attention. "C'mon. Get in the van."

He jarred Katie back to her senses. "Thanks!" she shouted and then ran for the van. As the vehicle buzzed down the track to reach the grandstand, she jerked the door open and jumped out before the van even came to a full stop. She jogged out to meet her horse and driver.

"How'd I do, Boss?" Seth asked with a haughty grin as he swung his legs to dismount the still moving race bike.

"Not bad... for a rookie," Katie teased as she grabbed Gold's bridle to lead him into the winner's circle.

Katie reveled in the moment, wanting to capture the time and suspend all that would come. She could hear the race announcer's voice commenting on how both Spun Gold and Seth "Crash" Reynolds had broken their "maiden" in the same race. She also caught a mention of Kathleen Murphy being both trainer and owner of the winning colt. Her spirit swelled with pride and satisfaction. This moment should last forever.

Seth slid back on the race bike and patted the frame next to him. Katie sat down and wrapped her arm around his waist. They returned to the paddock together, listening to the whistles and cheers from the crowd as they passed by. Trainer, driver, and horse victorious.

There had never been a time in her racing life that Katie was so happy to go to the test barn.

* * * *

Having shed his colors and changed into his civvies, Seth caught up with Katie as she led Gold from the test barn back to the trailer. "Ready to head home?"

"I figured you'd want to stay here and celebrate."

Oh, yes, he had plans to celebrate. Lots of plans. But they didn't involve the track. "I'd rather be alone with you," he said as he took Katie's hand in his. *What a night. What a damn fine night.*

Ross came striding from the paddock toward them. "Damn it." Seth dropped her hand before he gestured at Ross with his thumb. "Why's he here?"

"Oh, I forgot all about him. Can you get Gold in the trailer? Ross needed to talk to me." She handed Seth the lead rope.

"Sure. Whatever," Seth replied, doing nothing to disguise the annoyance he felt. He jerked the rope away from her and ignored her narrowed eyes. "Tell him I'm behaving myself, being a good boy." This was his night, not Ross Kennedy's, and Seth resented the lawyer drawing even a moment Katie's attention.

"I'll only be a few minutes. But you don't have to wait for me. If you want to go back to the dorm—"

"You'll need help with Gold when you get back. I'll just ride out with you."

Katie probably recognized the flimsy excuse, but Seth hoped that her heart dominated her brain on this special night. She cocked her head and watched him for a moment before she finally nodded. "Fine. I'll be right back."

As Katie took Ross's outstretched hand, Seth seethed as he watched them walk away together. "Did you see that? Can't keep his hands off her," he grumbled to Gold. "Touching what isn't his." The colt nudged Seth with his nose and was rewarded with a pat on the neck. "Come on. Let's get in the trailer."

* * * *

Ross finally found one of the few private spots near the paddock and turned to talk to Katie. "We've got a big problem. Do you ever watch *The Tattler*?"

"That sleazy gossip show? I'd never watch something like that."

"They've put a bounty on Seth's head." The calm look on her face told

Ross she didn't grasp the gravity of the whole situation. "If someone knows where he is, the show will pay ten grand. I don't think we're going to be able to keep a lid on this much longer."

"Surely no one cares that much about where—"

Ross shook his head. "I forgot that you don't watch much TV. Believe me, any of those low life reporters would give his right arm to know where Seth Remington disappeared to."

Katie's face finally registered some alarm. "What happens if they show up here?"

"Run. Get away from them and protect yourself. If they find out about you two..."

She went wide-eyed before she regained control. Her words came out slow, measured, clearly sizing up the situation before she'd react again. "What do you mean, Ross?"

"I was at the farm this afternoon, Katie. I saw you two sleeping together," Ross calmly replied. He wasn't about to let her know that she'd broken his heart. That was entirely beside the point. Now they were talking business.

"We didn't... You can't... Seth can't lose his money."

"I'm probably a damn fool for ignoring what's going on between the two of you, but I'm not going to tell anyone." A cold fear suddenly gripped him as he allowed himself to view the whole situation with something other than his wounded pride. Katie was too trusting to know the awful things that could happen where that amount of money was concerned, and he realized no one was looking out for her. "Unless Remington is twisting your arm about the inheritance. He's not, is he? If he's pushing you..."

She shook her head and appeared too stunned to utter a reply.

Ross put his hand on her shoulder. "If he's not pressuring you to give him the money, I won't jam him up. But Katie, I'm worried about you."

"Why? What are you afraid of?" She either honestly didn't understand or was simply too deep in denial. He knew he needed to set her straight.

"You love the guy, but we both know there can't be any kind of future for you two. He's going to break your heart."

"Seth wouldn't—"

"Katie, you're being naïve. You need to live in the real world for a while. I know you think he's changed, but do you really think a guy like

Seth Remington will give up that much money to live in a barn?" Katie obviously knew the answer, but from the pained expression on her face, he figured that she didn't want to believe it. Ross pressed the point. "Sure, he's having fun now. But a guy like that is used to nice things, fast cars, big parties. Nothing in Indiana can compare to Chicago. I don't want to hurt you, but you need to hear it from someone. No matter which way you look at this, it can't end well. It just can't."

As tears gathered in her eyes, Ross wondered how many times she might have heard the same warnings from her friends. And how many times had she ignored them? "If the press swarms, I'll come for Seth. If they get to you, call me. I'll send some help."

"You make it sound like he'll be in danger."

"He might be. You might be. You've never dealt with the paparazzi before. They're vicious. Just call me if they show up. I'll protect you."

Ross noticed Seth taking quick strides toward them. "Congratulations, *Crash*."

"Thanks, *Matlock*." Seth turned to Katie. "You guys done?"

Katie nodded. "Thanks, Ross. I appreciate you coming to let me know." She stood on tiptoe and kissed his cheek. Of course, he had to bend down a little to accommodate her. Lord, the woman was tiny.

Ross didn't have the courage to tell her that he could have passed the information along in a phone call. He'd made the long trip because he wanted to spend some time with her. After seeing her lying in Seth's arms, Ross figured he'd lost the war before he even had the opportunity to wage a battle. The notion of losing a woman as special as Katie to a man like Seth Remington, someone who would surely hurt her, was almost unbearable. A hit below the belt. Katie deserved better. Much better. "I'll be in touch," he finally said before walking away from the couple.

"What did he want?" Seth asked.

"Nothing important," Katie replied. "Let's go." She took his hand to lead him to her truck.

* * * *

They arrived at the barn, and Seth tended to Gold while Katie checked water buckets and then made notes on the training board.

Watching her contemplating the week ahead, Seth remembered Katie's face when she saw his colors. Her reaction had been more than he'd hoped it would be. He'd ordered them as a way to thank her for mentoring him, for teaching him everything she could about the sport. For making him a man his father would admire. But things had changed when he fell in love with her.

And God help him, he did love her. When he'd strode into the paddock, those colors became a declaration of that love, the only declaration he could make.

Despite all that could happen because of it, he loved her anyway. Why couldn't he just say the words? Three ridiculous little words that wouldn't really change anything or held the power to change everything.

Damn you, Pops! Why do I have to choose? Didn't you ever consider that I might fall for her? Maybe if you'd only made the no-contact rule a year...

Seth walked up behind Katie and wrapped his arms around her waist. She leaned back against him and closed her eyes. He kissed the top of her head.

"I've been waiting forever for someone like you," she whispered as she put her hands over his and let her fingers caress his skin.

Just like I've been waiting forever for you.

But all they'd ever have was now.

He put his chin on her head, inhaled her scent like a wine's bouquet. "Aren't you going to say 'Seth, we can't'?"

"We both know damn well why you came back here tonight." She tossed the black marker at the board before she turned in his arms, put her hand behind his head, and pulled him into a deep kiss. He responded with enthusiasm.

Seth kissed her and let his tongue claim her mouth with enough passion to make her sag against him. He squeezed her, trying to draw her to him until he finally lifted her off her feet. Katie wrapped her legs around his waist, and he carried her to her room. He didn't put her down again until he kicked the door shut.

In a flurry of undressing, clothes flew through the air to land in piles on the floor. He tried to push her onto the bed, wanting her with an intensity that made him close to desperate, but she resisted. Seth suddenly realized that she wanted control, wanted to take the lead, wanted to make love to him this time. The idea of his shy Katie taking charge was more intoxicating than pure alcohol. God, how he burned for her. Burned with a fire that would lay waste to anything separating him from her, to anyone who dared keep them apart.

Seth stretched out on the small bed as Katie quickly straddled him. The anticipation became blissful torture. She rained kisses on his face and neck, ran her hands down his stomach. She wrapped her fingers around him, and this time, she didn't immediately let go. Seth wasn't sure just how long he could handle the torture as she moved her cool fingers over his erection.

Nothing had ever made Katie feel as free as Seth's acceptance of her touch, her kiss. He didn't do anything to stop her. He didn't make her feel inexperienced or timid. He didn't tell her she had so very much to learn. He didn't tell her sex better with other women. He simply responded to her with honesty and passion.

Katie suddenly released him and rose to settle over him. "Now, Seth. I want you *now,*" she purred as she eased him inside her. Her fear of losing him gave her desire a hint of desperation. She wanted to reach out and grasp every single moment she had left to savor his touch, to know the feel of him deep inside her. To love him while she still could.

Their bodies moved together in a frenzy to find release. Higher and higher, reaching for stars just out of their grasp. Katie's body spasmed in pleasure, and she threw her head back and sang his name like the last, splendid note to a sad song.

The sound of her voice, the feel of those tremors surrounding him, knowing that she enjoyed him, brought Seth to his own climax as he held her hips and drove into her one last time.

Katie collapsed on his chest and reveled in the myriad of feelings coursing through her. The love she felt for Seth was too deep, too impossible to survive. Could a person die from a broken heart? If he left, *when* he left, Katie knew she would perish. Ross's words echoed through her mind in admonition and recrimination.

It can't end well. It just can't.

Seth rubbed her back and whispered sweet nothings in her ear. She let each word surround her heart to cushion it for the coming fall. Where could her love for this man possibly lead except to heartache? He whispered how beautiful she was and how much she had pleased him.

But he never once told her that he loved her and that said it all.

Chapter 25

"They're here!" Katie squealed in delight.

She and Chris had walked in The Place together. Seeing Brian seated at a table with his injured leg resting on a pillow-covered chair, she felt her heart swell in happiness. Her friends were finally back where they belonged—they'd come home. Samantha had promised they would be there, but Katie had been afraid to hold out too much hope that it would truly happen. She had desperately missed her friends and their Monday nights together. She hurried to the table and stooped to give Brian a hug before she took a seat next to Sam.

"Where's Seth?" Brian asked.

"He took my truck this afternoon to run an errand, but he wouldn't tell me where he was heading. Haven't seen hide or hair of him since," Katie answered before she turned to the waitress and ordered a ginger ale.

"Think we can get you to sing since he's not around?" Chris asked.

"I don't know..."

"Ah, come on, Katie. You haven't sung in so long. I missed it," Brian encouraged. "For me? For little ole' injured me?"

Chris chimed in and tipped the scales. "If you don't, I will." A wicked smile crossed his face. "And I'll do Hank Williams, Jr."

"Oh, for the love of... *Please,* Katie. Go sing," Sam begged.

"All right, I'll go." She walked to the stage and looked down at the karaoke machine. Feeling a bit melancholy, she knew exactly which tune to choose. After punching in her selection, she pulled the barstool to the middle of the stage and picked up the microphone. Leaning on the stool, she waited as the song played through its soft jazz opening.

Katie sang the old Ray Charles standard "You Don't Know Me." The tune had haunted her, repeated in her head since the moment she realized that she had fallen in love with Seth but couldn't tell him how she felt. Katie let the sweet melody flow from her as she used the music to express the emotions griping her heart. Singing gave her a way to hide in plain sight. Tears formed in her eyes as she sang of watching the love of her life walk away and being powerless to stop it. The song ended much too quickly for her to find any comfort.

If there was applause, Katie couldn't hear it. The only noise filling her ears was the rapid pounding of her heart as it reached a terrible conclusion. Seth would be leaving. Soon. And there wasn't a damn thing she could do to prevent it. She hadn't told him about the bounty being offered by *The Tattler*, but she knew it was just a matter of time before his identity was revealed.

Love never stays.

Katie stood up, put the microphone on the stool and went back to her seat.

Seth had been standing in the shadows of the restaurant's entrance when he looked up and saw Katie sitting center stage. He'd ducked back behind the partition to watch her as she sang.

When she finished the song, Seth couldn't seem to find enough strength in his legs to move as he came to a startling revelation. *Katie loves me*. He heard it in every note of her song and in the emotions she weaved with her voice. *She loves me.* Why should the revelation make his knees knock, his head swim, and his heat pound a swift cadence? Placing a hand against the partition, Seth steadied himself.

Love or money? The words echoed in his ears like some voice from above.

Running his fingers lightly over the small black velvet box hidden in his pocket, Seth realized that he was leaning heavily toward the side of love. Katie gave him strength—perhaps enough strength to walk away from his legacy. *Love or money?* At least the heat of the summer was far from the time when he would have to make the choice.

"Hi, everyone," Seth called as he finally stepped out from the shadows. Katie eyed him distrustfully, and he knew she wondered if he had witnessed her little musical spectacle. He kissed her cheek and took a seat next to her.

As Chris took his turn on stage, singing his threatened country song, Katie's cell phone rang. "Saved by the bell," she joked as she checked the caller ID and then flipped the phone open. She couldn't hear the caller's voice with all the noise surrounding her, so she stood up and hurried out of the restaurant. “James? The horses are fine. Monterey Jack is settling back in. Wait, I can’t hear you. Hang on, I’m going outside.”

When she reached the door, she pushed it open to head to the parking lot and its peace and quiet. “Sorry, James. Hard to hear with all that racket. What’s up?”

“Katie, you need to be careful. Look, we know your groom is Seth Remington. We’ve known since we met him.”

“How did you...?” Just how many people knew who Seth was and where he was? And how many of those who knew would be dialing *The Tattler*? “How, James?”

“Everyone in Chicago probably knows him, but he and his friends used to come to one of my restaurants a lot. He looks a little different, and I honestly didn’t recognize him. But Susan did. Some reporters were snooping around here earlier today. They must’ve been checking out his old haunts. I overheard one of them mention Indiana. Susan said I should tell you.”

“No,” Katie gasped. “How could they—?”

“I don’t know, but they’re turning over every rock searching for him.”

Katie felt the fear wash over her. This problem was more than some stupid tabloid show. Seth had become a hunted man, a man with a rising price on his head. “Why didn’t you call for the reward?”

“You know we wouldn’t do that to you,” James replied, sounding more than a little offended. “Susan and I figured he was just trying to get away from his life or something. Trust me, weirder things have happened. Is there anything I can do to help?”

“No. But thanks for the heads up. And thanks for protecting Seth. If you hear anything else, you’ll call?”

“Sure thing. See you, Katie.”

“Thanks again, James.” She snapped the phone shut.

Every inch of her skin crawled, every pore burned. Katie could almost feel each tiny grain of sand as it slipped through the hourglass marking what little time she had left to share with Seth. Anger and frustration washed over her and she shouted her feelings to the empty parking lot. “Damn it! It’s not fair! It’s just not fair!” It took her several minutes to compose herself enough to go back into the restaurant.

Katie knew that Samantha could sense her apprehension the second Katie returned to the table. Sam had that hard look she got when she was just about to lecture someone. When Katie shook her head at her friend's stare, she hoped Sam would decide to wait for a private opportunity to start the interrogation.

Seemingly oblivious to the women's exchange, Brian turned to Seth. "How many did you win this week?"

"Four. Three were Katie's," Seth answered with a note of pride in his voice as he reached for a slice of pizza.

"You're getting a lot of drives now. I'm jealous. You're gonna steal half my trainers away."

"Never. I'm just keeping the bike warm for you." Seth snorted a laugh. "I think Josh Piper hates my guts."

Brian nodded and chuckled. "He should. You're taking most of his drives."

Seth leaned back and put his arm across the back of Katie's chair. "You're exaggerating. But if he wasn't such a freakin' cowboy and listened to his trainers, they wouldn't come to me."

Katie listened as the two men talked harness racing. Between gossiping like a couple of old women and speculating on upcoming race strategies, they both seemed well occupied.

The Place quickly grew too warm in Katie's estimation, and the food was beginning to look less than appetizing. She sipped her ginger ale, hoping to settle her growing nausea. When she glanced over to see Chris munching on a chicken wing soaked in greasy barbeque sauce and greedily licking each of his fingers, it was more than Katie's queasy stomach could stand. She put her hand over her mouth, jumped up, and ran for the restroom.

Katie spent the next five minutes holding her hair back while she threw up.

"You all right in there?" Sam called through the bathroom stall door.

Great. What a wonderful time for twenty questions. God, she was tired of throwing up.

Sam handed some damp paper towels to Katie as soon as she opened the door. "Thanks." Katie wiped one of the cool cloths across her hot face.

"Not feeling well?" Sam skeptically arched her eyebrow.

"I think it's the heat. I've thrown up every day this week." Katie cupped her hand to gather some water trickling from the faucet. She sucked it into her mouth before swishing the water around and spitting it back in the sink.

"Bullshit. Have you taken a test yet?"

Katie gaped at Sam. "No. I couldn't be... I can't..." *No. No. No.* Her thoughts reeled at the implications as she held onto the sink for support.

"Yes, you could. C'mon, Katie. You're a smart woman. Didn't you even think about it?"

"But I can't have... I'm not supposed to..." Katie couldn't finish. The truth slammed into her with the force of a freight train. *Oh, my God! I might be pregnant!*

Sam patted her on the shoulder. "Miracles happen every day. You gonna tell him?"

Tell Seth? He'd hate me for the rest of his life. "Hell, no. Look, I need to know for sure first. You know what the doctor said. Sam, you can't tell anyone. Not even Brian. He'd go straight to Seth."

"You have to tell him sometime."

Katie shook her head. "No. I can't. Don't you see? He'd feel obligated to—"

"He *is* obligated."

Katie felt tears stinging her eyes. Her anxiety could easily become a full-fledged panic attack. She knew she had to persuade Sam to keep a lid on the news or everything would go straight to hell. "Sam, I can't. He'll lose his inheritance. Do you think I could live with myself if I cost him all that money? He'd hate me. He'd hate us."

"Calm down. I think you're selling yourself short, Katie. The guy likes you." Sam glanced at herself in the mirror, but those reflected eyes still stared back at Katie.

"Likes, Sam. Not loves, *likes.* I won't make him give up his money for me because I might've been stupid enough to get pregnant."

With a heavy sigh, Sam turned away from the mirror to look at Katie. "You know, he was there too. You didn't make a baby all by yourself."

"You don't understand. He'll think I tricked him. Don't you see? People have probably used Seth his whole life to get to his money. He'll think I got pregnant on purpose. You've got to promise you won't say anything."

"You have to—"

"Please, Sam. *Please.*"

Sam sighed again. "Fine. It's against my better judgment, but I promise." She shot Katie a motherly glare. "But I'm coming by with a test tomorrow when Brian is at physical therapy, so you better make sure Seth is out of the barn by noon."

"He won't even come in tomorrow. It's his day off."

Sam snorted a laugh.

"What?"

"Everyone knows he spends every night with you now, Katie."

Katie opened her mouth to form a denial, but quickly closed it again when she realized how pathetic any attempt to refute Samantha would sound. At that moment, she hated everyone at the track. All they ever did was poke their noses where they didn't belong. Just like the damn reporters. "There's no air conditioning in his dorm."

"Yeah, right. I'm sure that's why he stays. You promised you'd stop sleeping with the guy, remember?"

"Sam, please don't scold me. I love him." Katie grew silent as she stared at the floor, trying not to cry. After several long moments choking back her tears, she finally looked back at Sam. "Promise you won't tell? Not even Brian?"

"Not even Brian." She turned her profile to Katie and patted her rounded belly. "You do realize you won't be able to keep it a secret forever, don't you?"

Katie nodded and jammed the wet towels in the trash can. "But I can keep it a secret for *now.*" She opened the bathroom door to leave and Sam followed her back to the table.

Seth looked up at Katie with trusting, caring eyes. He didn't know she'd betrayed him. He arched a skeptical eyebrow. "You got sick again, didn't you? Are you okay?" She could see the concern on his face and it warmed her heart. God, how she loved him.

She pulled out the chair and sat down. "I'm fine. Don't eat the buffalo wings though. I think they're bad."

Chris immediately threw the wing he was gnawing on back on the plate. "Great. Now you tell me."

"You want me to take you home?" Seth asked as he put his arm around her shoulder and pulled her closer.

"Not yet. Really, I'm fine."

The karaoke died out and the lights dimmed for dancing. Seth stood up and offered his hand to Katie. "You up to dancing, Boss?"

Katie looked up from where she sat and stared at his handsome face. He was perfect in every way she could possibly imagine, and her heart ached with love for him. The future shouldn't exist, shouldn't interfere. Her world should just be Seth, and horses, and babies. But it wasn't.

He would leave soon, that much was clear. But it wouldn't be tonight. She decided to enjoy the present and let tomorrow take care of itself.

When Katie didn't make a move as she kept staring intently at his face, Seth became self-conscious. "Is there pizza sauce on my face or something?" He wiped his hand over his mouth.

"No, you're fine. I'd love to dance." Katie reached up to take his hand.

Seth had wanted to take Katie into his arms since the moment he heard her sing. He led her to the dance floor and pulled her into his embrace. She slipped her arms around his neck and laid her cheek against his chest. Giving no concern to the number of onlookers, Seth nuzzled his nose in her hair. He always loved the way she smelled. So sweet, so soothing. Shampoo and spring clover.

Holding her close, Seth felt contentment like he'd never known. His realization that Katie loved him made him whole. This woman loved him for who he was, not for his money or his damn name. She knew she could never share his wealth, and yet Katie gave him every part of herself. Body and soul.

Before he met her, Seth had enjoyed the chase. Yet he always quickly tired of a woman once he caught her. If he managed to get her into bed, it brought a swift end to the attraction. But each time he made love with Katie, it only got better and better. He could hardly wait to get her back to her room, their room to give Katie the present he'd carefully chosen that afternoon.

The song ended too fast for his taste, but Seth took Katie's hand and led her back to the table. When he pulled her chair out for her, Katie shook her head. "I'm really tired." She looked over at Chris. "Can you drop Seth off at the dorm? I want to go home."

"I'll take you home," Seth insisted.

"Can't Chris just—"

"No, Katie. I'm taking you home. You don't look well, and I want to be sure you're okay. No arguments." Seth grabbed her purse from the back of her chair and slung it over her shoulder. "Good night, everyone."

Katie kissed Brian on the cheek and Sam stood up to give her a hug. "Don't forget I'll be there tomorrow," Sam whispered before she turned her loose.

"I won't forget," Katie promised before Seth put his hand to the small of her back and ushered her out the door. He had not a clue as to what the women were talking about, but figured they'd share it when the time was right. If it was even worth sharing.

"Give me the keys," he ordered when they reached her truck.

"Who died and made you emperor?"

"Oh, come on, Boss. I'll drive. You don't feel well. Do you need to stop and get some antacids or something?"

"No, thanks. Let's just go home," Katie replied as she crawled into the passenger side of the truck.

* * * *

They reached the farm, and Katie wondered if she should tell Seth what James, Sam, and Ross had told her. She knew it would be the wisest thing to do, but wanting to keep Seth with her for however long they had left, she decided against it. He turned off the engine and followed her inside the barn.

"Good night, kids," Katie called to the horses as she turned off the main lights. Most of the animals had already bedded down for the night. Gold stuck his head over his stall door and nickered. Seth went over to give the chestnut an affectionate pat on the neck.

Using Katie's keys to open the office, he held the door for her. He kicked off his shoes, and Katie raised her eyebrow. "You're not going back to the dorm?"

"Not tonight. You might need me." After dropping the keys on her desk, he looked entirely absorbed in thought for several long moments. His gaze finally came back to her. "Your stomach has been a mess lately. You don't think you might... I don't know... be pregnant?"

Katie held her breath. Now's the time, she told herself. Now. There would never be a better opportunity. When she finally opened her mouth, she was positively amazed at what came out. "No. No way. I think it was the chicken."

Coward!

"You're sure?"

She nodded like a damned bobble-head. "Positive. I told you, it's impossible." *You really blew it this time, Kathleen!*

"You know, it's nice not worrying that you'd try to get pregnant to get your hands on my money."

Katie walked to the chair and dropped her purse. "Gee, thanks. I think."

"Don't take it wrong. I just mean I can trust you."

She wanted to cry. Or throw up. Or both.

He gave her a concerned frown. "You look a little green again. Maybe you're getting an ulcer. Go to bed."

"I'm fine." She tried to squash the horrible feeling that she had betrayed him.

"Quit arguing." Seth gently pushed her to sit down on the bed and kissed her forehead.

Katie sighed. He really did care about her. What would he think of her if he knew that she might be carrying his child? Would he hate her? Would he think the baby was part of a plot to snare a portion of his inheritance?

He'll hate me. I know he will.

Kneeling down on the ground beside her, Seth pulled a velvet box out of his pocket. "I got you something. It's not much, but it'll have to do. For now. One day, I'll drape you in diamonds." Seth flipped the box open to reveal a small silver necklace with a shamrock-shaped pendant. Engraved on the face of the shamrock were the intertwined letters "K" and "S."

"Do you like it?"

"It's beautiful," Katie whispered, letting her fingertips brush the shamrock.

Taking the necklace out of the box, he reached up to fasten the chain around her neck. She could feel the cool of the metal against her skin, and she tried without success to keep the tears from pooling in her eyes. "Thank you, Seth."

"You're welcome. Now slip those pants off," he teased as he pulled her shoes from her feet.

"Seth..."

"I know, I know. 'Seth, we can't.' Get your mind out of the gutter. You need to get some sleep."

Katie shed her jeans. She pulled both arms into her t-shirt, took off her bra, and shoved both arms back into the sleeves without showing an inch of skin.

"You've got some unusual talents there, Lady." He smiled at her and patted the pillow.

"You're staying?" Katie asked, her need blatantly evident in her voice. Did she sound as pathetic as she felt?

Seth nodded. "Don't I always?" He turned off the light and kicked off his shoes. Stripping down to his boxers and t-shirt, he slid into the bed beside her.

As they lay in the dark with Seth's strong body pressed against her back and his legs molded to hers, Katie's mind twisted and turned like the winds of a winter storm. *A baby. There might really be a baby.*

She was going to have Seth's child.

It was nothing short of a miracle. But would he see it that way? Or would he see it as—what was the word he used?—an anchor? Katie guessed that he would feel trapped. How could he feel otherwise? She was torn between utter joy over the prospect of being a mother and mind-numbing despair over what Seth would think of her once he knew her condition.

He could never know.

"Tell me about your family. Except for your dad, I don't know anything about them," Katie whispered in the dark.

"Not much to know."

"Tell me about your mom."

Katie could feel his body stiffen for a moment, then he relaxed again. "She got shot trying to protect me from a lowlife who was robbing a convenience store we stopped at. I was only four. I can't even remember her face very well."

"If you don't want to talk about it—"

"No, it's all right. I have impressions... feelings... that seem like memories. I think about her whenever I smell vanilla. Pops said she always made me chocolate chip cookies. Maybe that's why."

Katie's heart ached for the little boy left behind by his mother's tragic death. It was too close to her own story for her not to empathize. "What was she like?"

"Pops told me she was the strongest woman he'd ever met. He always said she was the glue that held him together. He told me I'd be lucky to find a woman half as wonderful as my mom." She could feel him rubbing his nose in her hair. "I got her looks. The hair, the eyes. They're hers. I think that hurt my father. To see her in me. I didn't see him much after that. Spent most my time with nannies."

"He must have been devastated when she died," Katie said as she stroked his arm.

"It was rough. He worked all the time. Probably a way to dull the pain."

"Tell me about your friends."

He seemed to ponder the term for a moment.

"Seth?" Katie asked as she turned her head to glance over her shoulder.

"I didn't really have friends. I had people who mooched off me. Friends are people like Brian and Chris. Even Sam. They're there when you need them." He pulled her a little closer. "Go to sleep, Katie."

A few minutes passed before she whispered to him again. "What are you going to do when the season is over?"

"That depends on you."

"On me?"

"It depends on if you give me my money or not."

Chapter 26

Katie tried to throw herself into mundane chores to forget the problems weighing on her mind.

The test will be negative. The doctor had said "impossible" when describing her chances at ever being a mother. There was no way she could be pregnant. Her vomiting had to be the flu.

By the time Samantha arrived, Katie had sent Seth on a run for supplies, hoping the distance of the store and the length of the list would keep him well occupied. Sam's truck pulled up at the scheduled noon meeting time. Katie watched her friend jump out of the vehicle, clutching a small white pharmacy sack.

"Moment of truth." Katie swallowed hard and then nibbled on her lower lip.

"Oh, come on. It's not life or death."

"Easy for you to say. What do I have to do?"

Sam opened the box and handed Katie a white plastic stick. "Just pee on the small end of this and set it on the sink. We'll check it in ten minutes."

"You know, Sam, it's not likely that I'm—"

"Oh, for the love of... Will you *please* just go and pee on the stupid stick?" Sam pointed toward the office.

Katie obeyed and then sat on her bed, staring at the clock. Sam sat down beside her to join the vigil—the longest ten minutes of Katie's life. Seconds became minutes, minutes became hours. If only her time with Seth passed in the same leisurely way.

"It's time. Do you wanna look or should I?" Sam asked.

Shaking her head, Katie stood up on trembling legs. "I'll look." She took several steps toward the bathroom before turning back. "Sam, if it's positive, you can't tell anyone."

"But you'll have to tell Seth if—"

"No, I don't. Sam, you promised, remember?" Katie said in a calm, steady voice that couldn't possibly be her own. She'd never been so frightened in her whole life.

"Just go check the damn stick."

Taking a deep breath and letting it out in a ragged sigh, Katie went to the sink and picked up the prophetic piece of plastic. A big blue plus had formed in the result window.

"What kind of test did you buy?" Katie called, her voice breaking as her heart skipped a rough cadence. "One of those generic ones? This is obviously wrong."

"Who the hell cares what kind it is?" Sam shouted back. "What's it say?"

Maybe it's a crappy test. Maybe I need another one. Maybe... I'm actually pregnant.

For a moment, she didn't know whether to be ecstatic or suicidal. Her hands shook. She swallowed the bile rising in her throat.

"I'm going to have a baby," she whispered.

She could give Seth something no one else ever had, something that didn't require a famous name or an obscenely large fortune.

And he had given her a gift she thought could never be.

This baby was their own little miracle. What had that fortune cookie said? *Where there is love, expect the impossible.*

"Well?" Sam asked as she walked to the bathroom door and leaned against the frame. Holding up the stick, Katie showed her friend the result. "Katie, that's wonderful!" She gave her a quick hug. Then Samantha morphed back into her more typical straightforward nature that smacked a little of I-told-you-so. "So you're pregnant. What are you gonna do about it?"

"I don't know. I really don't know." Katie could almost see Seth's reaction in her mind's eye. He'd never believe she hadn't done this on purpose.

Sam could obviously see the fear in Katie's eyes because she tried to offer some consolation and support. "You know, I think it's great. Our kids can grow up together. They'll be the best of friends. We'll turn them both into track rats."

"Yeah, sure," Katie said without a single ounce of conviction. How could something so wonderful cause such apprehension? After abandoning hope of every having a child of her own, she wanted to revel in the news, to shout it out loud. But the notion of Seth's scorn was almost more than she could bear.

"I hate to leave you, but Brian is gonna be done soon. Are you gonna be okay?" Sam asked.

Katie nodded. "Yeah. I'll be fine. Please keep your promise, okay? I'll tell him, just not now. Please?"

Sam pulled her friend into another hug. "I promise, but you've gotta make me a promise too. I want you to see a doctor to get checked out. And get some prenatal vitamins. Okay?" She patted Katie's back.

"I will. You can give me your doctor's name and number."

Turning Katie loose, Sam nodded and started to walk out of the office before she suddenly turned around with wide eyes. "You better go get the box and that stick and let me take them with me. Otherwise—"

"Oh, my God! He'd find them!" Katie ran to the bathroom to retrieve the evidence. When she returned, she shoved the sack at Sam. "Thanks."

"No problem, Honey. I'll save the stick for the baby book. Call me if you need anything."

"I will."

"You're gonna have a baby, Katie."

"A baby." *I'm going to have a baby.*

* * * *

Rachel promised herself that she would only give Seth one more opportunity to come around. As she sat alone in the Cyber Café, she stared at the screen of her computer and smiled. *The Tattler* had upped their bounty to twenty-thousand dollars. She licked her lips in anticipation.

Although she'd hoped to either land Seth Remington or try to get pregnant by him to force eighteen years of guaranteed support, the stubborn guy just wasn't cooperating.

And I'm almost out of tricks.

She had trotted out all of her previously successful seduction techniques, the ones that allowed her to wrap many a man around her little finger. Seth seemed immune to any of her advances. She might have figured the man was gay if it hadn't been for the way he acted around Katie. She had seen stallions more subtle around a mare in heat. The guy obviously needed to be kept away from Katie if Rachel wanted any chance at success.

Katie Murphy—the bane of Rachel's existence.

Rachel let the irritating memories bubble to the surface. She'd been forced to share everything with Katie from the time she'd been an adolescent. Jacob always insisted that Katie live with them every summer, but it was Rachel who had to share her room. Not that Katie was there often. She usually followed Jacob from county fair to county fair or spent most of her time at the Schaeffer farm in the barn with the horses.

But that was entirely beside the point. Katie's mere presence had been a burden. The redhead had pulled Jacob Schaeffer's attention away from his only child. He'd all but adopted Katie from the moment he met her. Whenever Rachel asked to learn to train, Jacob had always pushed her aside with comments about her habit of sleeping late or her desire to spend time with her friends rather than logging hours in a barn. He always told her to be more like Katie. Like perfect Katie.

Is it my fault I'm a night owl? It wasn't fair that he always found time to teach Katie about training. In fact, he lived for it. Rachel had quickly tired of being told that she was never as good as Katie at anything. The memories made Rachel's jaw clench. Then she relaxed as a new set of recollections flooded her mind.

When she turned fifteen, Rachel finally found something that she was much better at than Katie. *Men*. Since it had been Katie's goal to take away the father that Rachel loved, Rachel made it her business to take away any man that Katie loved.

In high school, if a guy showed Katie any kind of attention, Rachel worked her charms on him, and few high school boys could resist her attention. But that only lasted a couple of years before Katie got her G.E.D. and left school to train.

Katie's one serious relationship had been with Mike Knight when he was still driving mainly in Indiana. Even though it took some time and creativity, Rachel had brought that love affair to an abrupt halt. Katie could really pick 'em. The White Knight was handsome, and he seemed to have real affection for Katie. He had resisted for almost a month before he finally gave in to what Rachel had to offer. It had been a stroke of genius to plan an encounter with Mike so that Katie would just *happen* to stumble across the couple in his truck in the throes of passion. The look on Katie's face had been worth all the effort.

Sweet victory! Rachel still savored her triumph.

Of course, she never bothered to sleep with the man again. He had way too little to offer a woman. In more ways than one.

When Seth Remington first arrived, Rachel wanted him the minute she saw him. Those dark good looks made him the type of man who she usually targeted for a lover. It only made him all the more desirable to realize that Katie wanted him too. But then the rich lawyer suddenly appeared, and it had taken a while to sort out which hunk Katie really liked. Not that Rachel would have been disappointed with either of them. Or both of them. She let a wicked smile form on her lips.

The suspension for fighting didn't help. It kept her away from the track just when she was sorting through the messy details. The whole assault incident had been humiliating as well as costly, and all simply because Rachel had arranged a one-night stand with the woman's driver boyfriend. The guy sure as hell hadn't been worth the black eye or the cracked tooth she'd received in the ensuing fight.

Thank heavens Chris had inadvertently handed her such a fantastic and possibly lucrative new option.

Now she wanted to land the Remington fortune by landing Seth. *This should've been easy*. But Katie obviously had her hooks deep in this one. At least *The Tattler* remained Rachel's ace in the hole.

Then an interesting idea dawned on her. Perhaps if she got Katie out of the picture, then Seth would turn to a new woman in his time of need. Rebound sex was always the best—one of the reasons she never felt any guilt over breaking up a relationship or two. Or ten.

Rachel decided that the time had arrived to change her focus. With the past she shared with Katie, Rachel knew exactly what to do, how to hurt her rival the most. With an evil smile, she flipped the switch to turn off the computer.

Rachel grabbed her empty cup, pitched it in the trash, and left The Cyber Café. She had work to do.

* * * *

The night of the second leg of the sires stakes seemed ominous. Dark clouds gathered in the west and cast a shadow over racing activities. Although rain had yet to fall, thunder rumbled in the distance. The wind whipped the dust into small clouds that swirled around the horsemen's feet. Drivers scurried about looking for their rain gear in case they had to change in the middle of the racing program. Grooms scoured the paddock, locating mud fenders for the race bikes.

A storm was coming.

Katie felt nauseous again. She wondered why everyone called it "morning sickness" when it only seemed to hit her in the late afternoon and early evening. Seth was so wrapped up in driving that he wasn't around to notice the time she sprinted for the paddock ladies' room, and she was grateful for that small stroke of luck.

She would have to tell him about the positive test soon. He had a right to know he was going to be a father. Katie just didn't know how to break the news to him without it appearing like she'd cleverly set a trap meant to ensnare a piece of his fortune.

Ignoring the situation was easy enough. She just went on autopilot and did her work. When Katie wasn't reminded of the pregnancy by feeling queasy or throwing up, it was a simple thing to wallow in denial.

He would hate her when he found out. She couldn't bear the idea of Seth looking at her with condemnation in his eyes. This blessing from God, this baby, wouldn't make him as happy as it had made her. Katie spent the whole evening so worried that she was constantly wringing her hands and on the verge of tears.

Seth reached the stall with the jog cart, leaned it up against the wall, and stepped into the stall. Running his hands over Gold's harness, he seemed to be checking her work. Already emotionally overwrought, Katie couldn't help but take offense. "I checked the harness, Seth. I taught you everything you know, remember?"

"I know," he replied as he patted Gold, "but it never hurts to check it again."

"Kiss my..." Katie swallowed the next word and glared at him.

"Did you say something, *Honey*?" he asked with a wry smile.

"You're getting too big for your damned britches, you know that?" She fit the head number under the bridle.

Seth chuckled. "That's why you love me. You know how drivers are." His wink and the implication of his words shut her up.

Katie assumed he'd had a slip of the tongue. How could he possibly know she loved him?

Leading Gold out of his stall, Katie helped Seth hook up the jog cart. She guided the horse to the entrance chute. "Can you smell it? It's going to storm," she said as she hooked the last strap. "Did you find the mud fenders?"

Seth nodded. "I dropped them by the race bike over by the door." He steered his colt onto the track while Katie disappeared to find the race bike and fenders and bring them to Gold's stall.

By the time Seth completed his two miles, Katie stood waiting for him by the exit chute. "How'd he do?"

"He's smooth as glass. I really hope the rain holds off. It's been so dry this summer, I've got no idea how he'll do on a sloppy track. I'd rather not find out the hard way."

Katie nodded and led Gold away after Seth removed the jog cart. "I'll see you when they call his race. Good luck in the next one."

"Thanks," Seth said over his shoulder as tucked his whip under his arm and ran to his next drive.

The thunder continued to announce the approaching storm, but the rain bided its time. As her race was called to the track, Katie proudly led her colt to the entrance chute. Seth met her at the paddock entrance and deftly slid onto the sulky. She listened to the announcer's voice droning through the post parade information and realized that she still cringed whenever she heard the name "Crash Reynolds."

She had never been able to say it even once without making a mistake. Seth was a Remington, a fact she had never been able to ignore.

Waiting by the fence, she watched him jogging Gold as he waited for the starter to call the horses. He passed close enough to the fence to give Katie a cocky smile before the car rolled around to urge the drivers to prepare for the start. Katie said her usual prayer to keep Seth safe and took her customary white-knuckle stance against the fence rail. She didn't think she would ever become accustomed to seeing Seth that vulnerable as he straddled the powerful animal. She marveled again at Sam's inner strength.

Seth guided Spun Gold through a textbook example of harness racing strategy. Getting away sixth at the start, Seth eased his horse out into the outer flow for a perfect second-over trip. By the time the horses reached the stretch, Seth took the colt outside of traffic and never looked back.

The win was officially recorded as five lengths.

* * * *

Just as the photographer took the winning picture, rain began to fall in big, lazy drops. Fans ran for the grandstand as horsemen began to change into rain gear and add their mud fenders to their race bikes.

Seth was glad he was done for the night so his colors wouldn't be soiled by the mud. He figured he'd have to get around to ordering rain gear sometime soon. *Maybe Katie and I could get a new race bike, something fast. And maybe Katie and I could...*

It never ceased to amaze him how carried away he could get in planning for a future that could never be.

As the clouds unleashed their fury and the rain drenched the track in sheets, Seth watched Katie jog alongside Gold as they headed toward the test barn. He ran for the paddock to change in the drivers' lounge. Rachel intercepted him at the door the instant he exited in street clothes.

"Crash, I'm so glad to see you. I really need your help," she pleaded. "There are some papers my lawyer sent over, but I don't understand them. Could you look at them? Maybe tell me what they mean?"

Just being around Rachel made him uneasy. She was too predatory, too sordid. "Rachel, I'm not a lawyer. Can't you—"

She interrupted him. "I know, but people around here are so... so... hick. You're smart. Please?"

"Fine. Can you bring them back here in a couple of minutes?" Seth glanced at his watch to let her know he'd be watching the time very carefully.

She gave him a coy smile. "They're in my truck. How 'bout we run out there together?"

Seth hesitated. Gold would be done in the test barn soon. *That horse always pees like a... racehorse.* He figured that he and Katie would leave for the farm right away. He knew she still didn't feel as well as she should, and he wanted her to get some rest. A visit to a doctor might be wise in the near future. Seth looked at his watch again. "I'm not sure I've got enough time."

"Please? If I screw this up, I might have to do some time in jail. I didn't do anything wrong. She came after me. It'll only take a minute. I'm parked right by Katie. Please?"

Casting a wary glance toward the test barn, Seth couldn't see Katie on her way back, so he acquiesced. "Let's make it quick."

Rachel grabbed his hand and pulled him out into the pouring rain. He jerked his hand back, but followed her as they sprinted toward the far parking lot. Her truck was parked very close to Katie's truck and trailer, so at least he'd know when Katie was ready to head for the farm.

Rachel unlocked the driver side door. "Get in!" she yelled, and Seth dove out of the driving rain into the truck cab before scooting over to the passenger's side as she slid in beside him.

"Where are the papers?"

"In the glove compartment. Hang on, I'll get them." Rachel leaned over and placed her right hand on his lap. She fiddled with the latch to the glove compartment with her left. "Stupid thing. It always sticks." She let her hand slide slowly over his thigh.

Having experienced many better attempts at seduction by women much more skilled than Rachel, Seth knew exactly what she was doing. Her touch made his skin crawl. "If you don't have the papers..."

The glove compartment magically opened and Rachel grabbed a thick white envelope. "Here they are." She handed the papers to Seth. Rachel draped her right arm across the back of the bench seat as she leaned in to read over his shoulder.

Glancing at the legal papers, Seth couldn't see anything at all confusing. They seemed to be a simple explanation of a plea agreement that would give Rachel nothing more than a small probation period for her disorderly conduct. "What don't you get, Rachel? These seem pretty straightforward."

Rachel was busy staring out the rear window. "I'm sorry, what did you say?" She looked back at the papers.

"What don't you understand?" Then he noticed she was sliding closer and closer to him. "Rachel, I'm not—" He stopped talking when he realized she wasn't even listening to him again because she was peering through the back window.

"Come on. Over here. Look over here," Rachel whispered as she leaned even closer to Seth.

"What are you talking about?" Seth asked before turning around to look out the window at whatever drew Rachel's attention.

A flash of lightning illuminated the scene. Katie stood as still as a statue in the middle of the parking lot, staring directly at him. The rain washed over her in sheets, but she simply remained there unflinching.

"Shit, Rachel! What in the hell are you trying to do?" Seth fumbled for the door handle.

"Oh, come on, Crash. It's just a little joke between old friends. Why don't we go get a drink or something?" Rachel ran the hand that had been on the back of the seat across his shoulders and up through his hair.

Seth finally forced the door open. He jumped out of the truck and ran for Katie as she sprinted for her truck. By the time Seth reached the passenger side of the pickup, Katie had locked all the doors.

Pounding on the window, Seth yelled, "Come on, Katie! Let me in! It's not what you think!"

"Go to hell!" she screamed back as she started up the truck.

"Boss, please! Open the door!"

"Go back to your whore!" Katie jammed the truck in gear and punched the gas pedal. Seth had to jump back to keep from having his feet run over by her wheels.

"Goddamn it, Katie!" He chased after the truck, hoping to catch her when she stopped at the guard shack. Unfortunately, Rachel had come out of her pickup and threw herself directly in his path. "Get out of my way!" Seth yelled as he tried to push Rachel to one side.

She grabbed at his arm, dragging at him like an anchor. "Come on. Stay here. Get back in my truck. You're soaking wet."

Katie's truck had already started moving again. There was no way to catch her now. He turned on Rachel. "You bitch! You did that on purpose!"

Rachel stood in the rain and laughed aloud. She looked a bit crazed, and he was almost afraid of her. "Of course I did, you idiot. I *hate* Katie Murphy."

The rain continued to pour over Seth as he considered what he next move should be. He thought about walking to the farm, but the storm was intensifying. It would be dangerous walking the winding back roads on the dark, rainy night. "Stay the hell away from me. And stay the hell away from Katie."

Rachel stood her ground and continued to laugh—an evil and menacing sound that was followed by streak of lightning and a loud clap of thunder. Seth finally ran back toward the paddock to see if he could catch a ride to Katie's farm.

Rachel crawled back into her truck and pulled her cell phone out of her pocket. Flipping it open, she searched through her list of saved numbers to find the most important one of all. Punching the correct buttons, Rachel put the phone to her ear to listen for an answer as she pushed her dripping hair away from her face.

"Thank you for calling the twenty-four hour tip line for *The Tattler*. We're the number one entertainment news show on cable television. Do you have a news tip for our show?" a cheery feminine voice asked.

"Do I ever! How would you like to know where Seth Remington is right now?"

Chapter 27

Seth finally returned to his dorm room soaked to the bone and angry beyond rational thought. There was no way to get out to the farm. He'd tried to call Katie's cell, but she wouldn't answer.

As he stripped his wet clothes off and threw them on the floor, he railed at himself for being stupid enough to fall so easily into Rachel's trap. Then he damned Rachel for being a narcissistic bitch who had obviously plagued Katie for years. And finally, he cursed Katie for not waiting long enough for him to even have a chance to offer her an explanation.

Seth flopped on his bed and punched his pillow. When that didn't help, he threw it across the small room. Explanation or not, Katie would never believe him. After the story Jacob had told him about Rachel and Mike Knight, she must have been experiencing a horrible case of déjà vu when she witnessed Seth and Rachel together in that truck. What had he been thinking trying to help her?

Seth figured that he would give just about anything, including the Remington fortune, to be able to pluck those sickening moments out of Katie's memory. To undo the pain that he knew she must be feeling.

No, his Katie was smart and sensible. After she cooled down, she would calmly and carefully listen to his explanation.

And then she would toss him out on his ear.

* * * *

Somehow, Katie managed to get back to the farm and mechanically tended to the needs of her horses. She praised Gold for his performance and produced several carrots as his reward. As long as she kept busy, she didn't need to think too much. Unfortunately, there wasn't nearly enough to do to keep her occupied for very long.

Despite her best efforts, the horrible thoughts swirled in her mind. The nightmare played over and over again as she saw Seth in Rachel's truck with that heinous bitch touching him as if he belonged to her. She'd never forget the look of triumph in Rachel's eyes because she'd seen it once before. The only saving grace was that at least Katie hadn't witnessed Rachel and Seth locked in an intimate embrace as she had when she discovered Rachel and Mike together.

Rachel Schaeffer. Katie shook her head in frustration. What had she ever done to deserve such contempt? She had always stayed as much out of Rachel's way as she could manage whenever she'd been at the Schaeffer farm. She didn't borrow her clothes, use her make-up, or steal her boyfriends. Those activities had all been Rachel's style, not Katie's.

Seth Remington floated through her thoughts. Men could be such morons, always thinking with the wrong head. *He can't want Rachel. He can't.*

There had never been any warning, no reason whatsoever to believe he was unhappy or dissatisfied. Seth had given Katie absolutely no sign that he wanted another woman. Then she reminded herself that Mike had given no suggestion of his desire to fool around either. Things had seemed to be going along just fine when she'd stumbled across him with Rachel sitting firmly on his naked lap.

No. Seth wouldn't do this to me. It was all a mistake, just a huge, horrible misunderstanding.

If it *was* a mistake, then why had Seth been in Rachel's truck? And why did Rachel have her hands all over him?

Katie was quickly losing the argument with herself.

She hadn't cried. She'd been too angry at first. The entire trip home, she had screamed at the top of her lungs, calling Seth every terrible name she could think of as she pounded the steering wheel with her fists hard enough she was surprised the airbag hadn't exploded in her face. None of her shouted words seemed entirely bad enough to fit him. She'd had to invent a couple of new ones. Her throat was raw and hoarse by the time she reached the farm.

Once the anger subsided, numbness set in and lasted until Katie had Gold ensconced in his stall with a large bucket of grain and his beloved carrots.

When she shivered from being cold, wet, and angry, Katie finally dragged her exhausted body and battered heart to her room. The intense storm brought an unusual summer cool down that made her air-conditioned room feel like the inside of a refrigerator. She walked to the wall unit and flipped the power switch off. The noisy machine groaned in protest before sputtering to a halt. Picking up her cell phone, she wanted to check for any messages from Seth, but she realized she'd let the battery run out. She jammed it into the desktop charger.

Katie wrapped a towel around her wet hair like a turban. She stripped out of her sodden clothes and threw them in the hamper. Pulling on dry underwear, she donned one of the flannel shirts Seth had left behind. His scent still clung to it. Katie buried her nose in the sleeve to breathe in the comforting essence. After rubbing as much moisture as she could out of her hair, she threw the towel over the chair and promptly ran out of things to do. She no longer had a means of avoiding thinking about everything that had happened.

Pain washed over her in mammoth waves the minute she finally sat down on the bed. Tears quickly turned to ragged sobs that spasmed through her body. Katie lay down on the bed and pulled her knees to her chest as she wailed her anguish.

Oh, Seth. Why? What did I do wrong?

With her grief finally spent through tears, Katie latched onto one rational thought. *Seth would never hurt me like this*. There was absolutely no way he could be that duplicitous; it just wasn't in his nature. While she might have viewed Mike Knight through younger and more naïve eyes that had missed his over-inflated ego, Katie believed she could clearly see Seth's true character. She knew him well enough to know the truth. The more she thought about the whole sordid situation, the more she recognized that it smacked of a Rachel Schaeffer custom maneuver. Rachel had been doing all the touching, hadn't she?

Katie suddenly realized that she had been set up.

"Damn her!" she shouted as pain rapidly turned to anger. "That bitch!"

She wished for a moment that she had as much courage as the blonde who had taken a chunk out of Rachel in the paddock. If Katie found herself within arm's length of Rachel, the woman would be sporting a nice black eye and a fat lip.

She thought about getting dressed to hurry back to the track dorms and fetch Seth. But the hour was late, and Katie was physically and emotionally exhausted. The rain came down in torrents and thunder rumbled at regular intervals. With a yawn, she decided to wait until morning. She and the baby needed some rest and a few more hours to calm down.

Besides, he deserved to wait. Since Seth had been stupid enough to fall for one of Rachel's tricks, she figured it would serve him right if he had to sit and stew in his own foolishness for the night. Maybe he'd learn a lesson. Having him stay away might also bring a halt to some of the track gossip that constantly swirled around them.

The patter of the rain on the metal roof lulled Katie into a troubled sleep. She dreamed of a swollen, raging river that separated her from Seth. No matter how hard she searched, she couldn't find a way to cross the water. As she stood on the bank, wringing her hands, Seth simply turned around and walked away. He never even looked back to offer a farewell.

She knew why. Like he'd told her when they'd lost Monterey Jack, Seth hated goodbyes.

* * * *

The unusual noises woke her.

Katie was used to hearing the customary morning sounds of the crickets chirping a busy tune, the birds whistling their melodies, and the gentle movement of the horses as they milled about in their stalls. She wasn't, however, accustomed to the sound of vehicles traveling down the gravel road at such an early hour.

Katie stretched and yawned. *I suppose I should get up and see what's causing the commotion.* Maybe there was a hay delivery she'd forgotten, or perhaps the man who owned the farm was working the deep ruts left by the rain out of the gravel drive with some noisy equipment.

Still clad in Seth's green flannel shirt, she pulled a pair of old jeans out of a pile of clean laundry and lazily donned them before walking barefoot out of the office to the large barn door. She knew she looked a sight. The sleeves of the shirt hung past her hands, the flannel shirt fell below her knees, and the jeans had more holes than a piece of Swiss cheese. Of course, it wasn't like she was expecting company.

Calling a morning greeting to her horses, she threw the latch and yanked the door open. She was immediately assaulted with a multitude of bright lights and the flashes of many cameras.

"Miss Murphy, is Seth Remington here with you now?" the first reporter shouted, pushing a microphone at Katie's face.

Once the feeding frenzy started, several other reporters joined in a chorus of questions. There were so many people talking at once and flashes popping every few seconds that Katie quickly became dizzy and disoriented.

"Katie, how long have you been involved with Seth Remington?"

"Did Seth Remington run away to be with you?"

"Miss Murphy! My show is offering a substantial reward for any news—"

"Is Seth Remington here with you? Can I talk to him?"

Katie stood in the doorway, dumbfounded and overwhelmed. Cameras came at her from every direction, and the voices grew louder and louder in their quest for information. She was too frightened to even move.

"Where is Seth Remington?"

"Are you two planning on marrying?"

"Can we have an exclusive interview?"

The questions and flashes continued to assault her. When the noise of her horses reached her ears, Katie finally broke out of her mental fog. The animals were obviously terrified of the clamor. "Go away!" She grabbed the door and pulled it shut.

Gold began to buck in his stall, and Katie hurried to the colt to soothe away the fear. "It's okay, Baby. It's okay." She wasn't sure if she was trying to convince the horse or herself. It was still hard to see well with blue spots constantly dancing before her eyes.

A cold fear descended. The worst had happened. Seth couldn't hide any longer. The rest of the world knew where he was now.

He would have to leave.

Running back to her office, Katie grabbed her cell phone from her desktop charger. She dialed the familiar Chicago number.

"O'Connor, LaGrange, Rowland, and Associates. How may I direct your call?"

"It's Katie Murphy. I need to talk to Ross Kennedy. *Now,*" Katie replied. *Please be there. I need you, Ross.*

"Just a moment, Miss Murphy, and I'll ring his office."

Katie began to pace in agitation as she waited for what seemed an eternity.

"Ross Kennedy."

"Ross, it's Katie. It's awful! There are reporters everywhere. I can't even get out of the barn. I'm scared for Seth. We need you. Please."

"Stay inside," he ordered. "I'll send some security guards to get them off your doorstep. You're at the barn?"

"Yeah, the barn. I need to get to Seth at the track, but I can't get out!" Katie knew she was practically screaming, but she just couldn't stop herself. She tried to take some deep, steadying breaths. They didn't help.

"You can't leave. You don't even want to *try* to get through those reporters. But, Katie, listen to me. Even if you could make it out, you can't see Seth now. Hang on a second." She could hear his voice yelling for his secretary. She caught bits and pieces of a faint conversation about looking for security firms the law office employed.

Katie wasn't in a patient mood. "Of course, I can see—"

"No, you can't. The minute they discovered his identity, the no-contact clause went into effect."

"I don't see how—"

"Just listen to me. Okay?" She could hear how pissed he was, but she didn't really care.

"Fine," Katie replied in as flat a voice as she could manage under the circumstances. "I'm listening."

"I helped write the will, remember? We put a directive in that would protect Seth if the media got to him before the season ended. The minute they found him, the five year no-contact rule began." Katie could hear him shuffling through papers and talking to his secretary. "Sheila, call this one. Now."

Katie couldn't even utter a word to show that she'd heard him. This wasn't happening. It couldn't be happening. What about the baby?

"Katie? You still there?"

"Yeah, I'm here," she replied as she looked around the room for her truck keys. This was bullshit. She was going to the track to get Seth.

"Do you understand what I'm telling you?"

She stopped to think it through. "There's got to be a loophole. I need to talk to him, Ross. Just for a minute. Please."

"The rule is ironclad. You can't have any contact with him now because he can't influence your decision about the inheritance. I'm sorry, Katie. Don't even try to call him."

"He doesn't have a phone, and you can bend the stupid rule, Ross."

Ross was still pissed. She could hear it plainly in his every word. "I've looked the other way with you two on a lot of things. That was bad enough. But if I let you violate the no contact rule, I could be disbarred. He'll lose his inheritance and you'll lose your horse and your bonus."

"I don't give a shit about the bonus, Ross, and you damn well know it." She didn't know how much it was, and she really didn't care. Her love for Seth had never carried a price tag. Even in her wildest fantasies, they'd left the inheritance behind to make their way in the world together. "Screw the damn money!"

"I know it doesn't matter to you, Katie. But what about Seth? You can't honestly believe he'd walk away from all that money. You're not being fair to him. I'm sorry, but you just can't see him."

"Please," Katie whispered.

"No, Katie," he replied in that stern lawyer voice she hated. "I'm sending security as soon as I can. I'll be down to get Seth today. Stay away from him." Ross hung up the phone.

Katie folded her cell phone shut and then threw it across the room. "Damn it! What am I supposed to do now?"

* * * *

Seth awakened to a pounding on his door. In his sleep-fogged mind, he figured Katie had come to apologize for her hasty, rude exit. He figured he would make her wait a minute or two before he answered.

The pounding didn't cease. "Mr. Remington? You in there?" a baritone voice asked.

He rolled out of the lumpy bed and opened the door to two tall, beefy local cops.

"What's up, guys?" Seth asked with a yawn as he leaned against the doorframe and tried to blink the sleep out of his eyes.

"We have a problem." One officer pushed his way into the room. He walked to the window and pulled the cord to hoist the dusty blinds.

Seth squinted and shaded his eyes with his hand at the intrusion of the bright light. "What?"

The cop pointed to the window. "Look."

As his eyes adjusted to the sunlight, Seth saw his biggest fear come to life—a carnival of trucks and cars were parked all along the enormous chain-link fence separating the grounds of the track from the outside world. Reporters stood at various places along the fence while cameras pointed at them, taking in their live broadcasts and recorded footage.

The bastards had found him.

Remington. The cop had used his real name.

"Shit! They can't get inside, can they?" Seth asked turning back to the officers.

"Not without a racing license, they can't," the larger of the two answered. "We've already thrown a couple of 'em off the grounds when we caught 'em trying to sneak in."

"Good." Seth's mind swirled around the implications of the situation until one troubling thought pushed its way forward.

Katie! What if the bloodhounds had found out about Katie? What if they were already at the farm, bullying her? She sure didn't deserve an attack by the paparazzi. "Look, I need to get out of here," Seth said as he reached for his clothes.

"I'm sorry, Mr. Remington. You can't leave right now. You'll have to stay put until a...," the smaller cop stopped to pull a paper from his shirt pocket and read it, "Mr. Kennedy arrives. He's gonna have private security to help get you outta here."

Seth sat on the bed and jammed his legs into his jeans. "I'm not waiting for Ross Kennedy. I need to get to Katie Murphy's farm. The reporters might already be there."

"Sorry. Chief said we can't let you leave the grounds. We're having a hard enough time containing those reporters. You can go to the kitchen or the barns, but that's it," the larger officer explained as he lowered the blinds to cover the window. Both cops left the room a moment later.

Seth slammed the door behind them. It wasn't going to end like this. It couldn't end like this.

He leaned his back against the closed door and rubbed his fingers over his forehead as it dawned on him he hadn't had one of his tension headaches in a good long while. A monster of one was forming now.

"Oh, Boss. I'm so sorry," he whispered to his empty room.

Chapter 28

Katie felt like an animal being kept in too small a cage. She'd spent the better part of the morning trying to get news about Seth from people in and around the track, but no one had seen him.

The horsemen did, however, relate stories of the crowds of reporters and local townspeople gathering outside the track to try to get a glimpse of the infamous Seth Remington. Every person she talked to asked Katie how long she had known his true identity. A few of them acted like they didn't even know the man—the same Seth who had worked alongside them for months. To a couple of ignorant people, he was now nothing more than an oddity.

Her horses were still agitated, but Katie could do little except soothe them. She threw an extra flake of hay in every stall to give the animals something to do. Unfortunately, the clamor wouldn't die down. Moving from stall to stall, she comforted the most disturbed of her horses with a soft word or a tender touch.

She could overhear some of the correspondents talking as they gave their reports, and the implication seemed to be that Seth had fled his luxurious home in a deep depression over his father's death. Katie's name was used several times, but not in a very flattering manner. She was evidently the siren whose seductive song had lured him to her side. *As if.*

In her mind's eye, Katie could see the pictures of her taken that morning while barefoot, sleepy-eyed, and rumpled in Seth's enormous shirt and her own ragged jeans. She knew those embarrassing images played on televisions all over the country. People tuned in and gawked at her while they ate their breakfasts and drank their coffee. In that instant, she vowed to never again watch a celebrity news show or buy a gossip magazine. "Damn vultures."

Just before noon, Katie was digging through what little food she had in her refrigerator when she heard a loud rumble coming from outside. She jumped on her bed to look out the small portion of the window not covered by her air conditioner. Two large black Hummers were coming up the white gravel drive followed closely by a local black and white police cruiser and Ross's silver Lexus.

The cars came to a stop and several muscular uniformed men jumped out of the Hummers to huddle with the two police officers who had exited their vehicle. The group then marched toward the reporters as a united front with Ross leading the way.

Katie hurried to the barn door to listen to the hullabaloo. From the bits and pieces she could take in, the reporters were told that they were trespassing on private property and were ordered to retreat to the public road. Many of the reporters argued something about the First Amendment, but after some time passed, the barn finally grew quiet. When the door suddenly opened, Katie squealed in surprise.

"Hi, Katie. I'm sorry about all this," Ross said as he walked in and closed the door behind him.

"Are they gone?"

"Not gone, just moved. They can't come down the drive at all, but they'll probably hang around the road until they realize there's no story here."

Katie walked over to one of the trunks lining the aisle and flipped open the lid. "What a nightmare. Was it like this all the time for Seth?"

"Not *all* the time. But they were there often enough, especially when he did something stupid. Or when there was a big event like his father's death." Ross sat down on one of the closed trunks.

Katie's heart went out to Seth. "I can't imagine how awful it would be to have those reporters following you everywhere. He must've felt like an animal locked in a zoo."

Ross gave her a sympathetic shrug. "Couldn't have been a lot of fun."

"I'm really behind now. I've got three to jog and two to train. I need you to go get Seth for me. He always jogs Gold after a race," Katie said as if the day was nothing but routine. She rifled through the trunk for supplies.

"Katie, I already told you—"

She slammed the trunk shut and whirled to face him. "You don't understand. I *need* him! I don't have any help. Sterling Remington wouldn't want me left high and dry like this."

Ross folded his arms over his chest. She knew a lecture was coming, but she sure wasn't in the mood to hear one. "Don't even start with me, Ross."

"I know you're frustrated, but you can't see Seth anymore. I'm sorry. The estate is going to pay for a replacement groom for the rest of the season. You'll have your pick."

Shaking her head, Katie tried to control her temper. None of this was Ross's fault, but right now he was directly in the line of fire. "That's not good enough, Ross, and you know it. Seth is my second now. Where am I supposed to find another good second this time of the year?" Her anger grew by the minute. Not only was her heart breaking into little pieces, but her business would suffer greatly once Seth left.

Desperately trying to rein in her fury, she resisted the urge to throw something at Ross. "Why can't you understand? Why can't you do something to stop this?"

"Seth isn't coming back. Not unless he wants to give up his inheritance. How much plainer can I make it? Plus there's Spun Gold and your bonus to think about."

"I told you, I don't want the stupid—"

"It's a hundred-thousand dollars, Katie."

"A hundred... thousand... Dear God." She could buy her own farm. She could get a top notch horse. She could... lose Seth forever. "I don't want it, Ross. I don't want a damn penny of it."

He shook his head and frowned at her. "You don't mean that."

She nodded. "Damn straight, I do. If Seth can give up—"

"Damn it, Katie. You've got to stop it. You know he's not going to walk away from that much money. I'll help you find a new second. I'll help you—"

Katie angrily interrupted him again. "Oh, I forgot. You've got a horse now, so you're an expert in racing. You can snap your fingers and poof! A new second who also happens to be a fantastic driver will just appear like a genie from a freakin' bottle."

Ross sat in silence and she hoped that he could feel her rage and frustration swirl around him, wishing that it would prod him into taking action. All he finally gave her was a resigned sigh.

"You've got every right to be angry. None of us anticipated how deeply Seth would mix himself up in your life. All he was supposed to do was work for you for awhile." He shook his head and breathed another sigh. "I'm so sorry, Katie."

Katie put her hands on her hips and waited for Ross to say something else, but he just looked at her with his big, brown calf eyes. As if she didn't have enough problems, now she had to worry about hurting his feelings, too. "Oh, for God's sake. Just go." He didn't move. "Go on. Just go back to Illinois." She waved him away with her hand. "I'll get some help on my own. You've caused me enough trouble."

"I'm sorry, Katie. I really am. I know how you feel about the guy. I do. But he'd be walking away from a fortune." He shook his head again. "You couldn't have expected him to give it all up and work with horses the rest of his life."

But that was exactly what she had expected. In her heart, Katie always dreamed that there could be a happily ever after where she and Seth would buy a small farm and raise horses and kids. Just like Brian and Sam.

"Look, I've got to go get Seth at the track and take him back to Chicago. I'll drive back down tomorrow and we'll go shopping for some help."

She snorted a rueful laugh. "Don't bother. I have friends. I'll make do. Tell Seth..."

Katie paused for a moment to ponder her message. She suddenly realized that Seth's future, his fortune, rested entirely in her hands. She could easily take his money away by claiming he hadn't worked hard enough to earn his inheritance. Surely, he'd stay with her then. But that would be a lie. Not only did Katie know that, but everyone at the track did as well. She had lost him.

Had she ever really had him?

"Katie? What do you want me to tell Seth?"

Tell him that I love him with every piece of my heart. Tell him I'll always love him—'til the day I die. And tell him I'll always love his baby.

"Just... just tell him he earned his money," Katie said as she tried to sniff back the tears forming in her eyes. "And tell him to have a nice life."

Ross opened his mouth as if to say something but didn't follow through. He hopped off the trunk, turned on his heel, and walked toward the barn door. Right before he ducked outside, he called back to Katie. "I'll be back tomorrow."

She didn't even look at him as she lifted a harness bag and began to organize equipment to take Gold for a jog. Katie promised herself she wouldn't cry until she was sure Ross was really gone.

* * * *

Ross sat in his car, staring at the barn and thinking about how his legal work for the Remington family had set Katie up for this gigantic fall. While he wanted desperately to offer her some type of comfort in this hour of her need, he couldn't. Katie had to face harsh reality. The sooner, the better. He promised himself that he'd do anything he could make it up to her. But the one thing he couldn't do was give her the one thing she wanted most.

Seth Remington.

Only Seth could make that choice for himself.

Turning the key to start the Lexus, Ross jammed the car into gear and eased out onto the gravel road to begin his trip to Dan Patch Raceway. He wondered for a moment what Seth would do.

Was it possible that he would choose to stay with Katie? Or would he want his inheritance? Had the man really changed as much as Katie claimed?

Ross wasn't entirely sure which choice he hoped Seth would make. Regardless, Ross promised himself he'd be there when Katie needed him.

He'd help her pick up the pieces.

* * * *

"Samantha! Come here! Quick!"

When she heard Brian shouting from the living room, Sam dropped the pan she'd been washing back into the sink and sprinted toward her husband, thinking he'd hurt himself. She stopped short when she saw him sitting on the edge of the couch with his injured leg stretched out in front of him. He stared intently at the television.

"Look. It's Katie," he said as he pointed at the image of their redheaded friend being mobbed by reporters outside her barn door.

"Oh, my God." She leaned over the back of the sofa and gawked at the television. "Oh, Katie."

They listened for a few moments as the talking-head reporter droned on about Seth Remington and the woman he'd been living with for the nearly six months since his disappearance. The live report was interplayed with file footage of Seth in some of his early and clearly more entertaining moments. Standing next to some publicity-crazed starlet. Surveying the damage from one of his wrecked sports cars. Bailing a member of the Boys' Club out of jail.

Sam was so transfixed on the show that she barely heard Chris come in the kitchen door. "Hey! Where in the hell is everybody?" He jogged into the living room. "Have you guys seen—?"

"Shh," Sam scolded as she pointed to the television.

"I guess you have." Chris plopped down next to Brian.

When the story finally ended, Sam looked at her husband. "I've gotta get to Katie. She's all alone out there."

Brian nodded. "I'll go too." He started to push himself to stand.

"The hell you will. What are you gonna do, beat them off with your crutch? You'd just get hurt."

"I'm fine. I can help. Jesus, Sam. She needs me."

"And what exactly do you think you can accomplish except getting your leg busted again? We're gonna help her. I promise. But you have to take care of that leg."

Brian slumped back onto the couch and nodded.

Her cell phone rang. Sam grabbed it and glanced at the caller ID before she hurried to answer it. "Katie! Oh, my God. Are you all right, Honey?"

Sam tried to take in everything Katie was saying, but it was hard to hear between the sobs and the hiccups. She finally gleaned enough information to gather that Ross Kennedy had come to Katie's aid and made most of the reporters give her some space.

"That's a good idea, Katie. I'll be there tomorrow, but call me if you need anything." She flipped the phone shut.

"What's a good idea?" Brian asked.

"She's calling her grandfather and Jacob Schaeffer to see if they can help her for a while. Seth is going back home, and she's screwed without any help." Then the whole awful, ugly truth of Katie's situation hit. "Oh, my God. Katie is gonna be devastated." And all alone and pregnant.

That son of a bitch.

Brian hit the arm of the couch with his fist. "I *knew* this would happen! I should've... I don't know... protected her. I should've tried harder to keep that guy away from her. If I hadn't gotten hurt, he would've never been her second."

Sam patted his shoulder, wondering just how pissed he'd be when he learned about Katie's condition. "She's a big girl, Brian. She had to make her own choices."

"How do you think I feel?" Chris asked. "I *was* her second. I should've been there. But you guys needed me. How could I be two places at the same time?"

"It's nobody's fault," Sam consoled. She sure didn't need the men going into a mental meltdown. "Brian, you didn't get hurt on purpose. And we *do* need you, Chris. You helped save our farm."

Brian started to get up. "I'm heading out there."

"I'm going too," Chris piped in.

Sam put her hands on her hips. "Just stop it. You guys can't go. She told me to keep everyone away. Ross got a restraining order to keep the reporters off the farm, but they're camped out on the frontage road. Katie said she didn't want us to try to get through to see her. It'll only make things worse."

"Fine," Chris grumbled. "Whatever. I'm going back to work. Let me know if there's anything I can do."

The slamming of the kitchen door echoed through the house as he left.

* * * *

When he arrived at the track, Ross presented his owner's badge to the track security and was allowed to pass through the gate. Seeing the police cruiser sitting in front of the dormitories, he pulled his car up alongside and parked.

Two uniformed officers leaned against the black and white sedan. Neither spoke when they saw him, so Ross broached the topic. "Where's Seth Remington?"

"You Ross Kennedy?" one of the cops asked. "Got any ID?"

Ross flipped the owner's badge hanging from his lapel. "Right there. Couldn't get in here without it. Now where's Seth?"

"Still in his room," the officer answered as he gestured his thumb toward the dorms.

"Thanks. We'll be leaving shortly. I imagine the reporters will hang around awhile, but they'll get bored quickly. I don't think they'll be a problem in a day or two."

The second officer smiled. "They're not a problem now. We haven't had this much excitement around here since that rock star's bus overturned on the interstate."

"I think the track likes the publicity," the first officer added. "Oughta be a good crowd tonight." He elbowed the other officer and they both chuckled.

Ross walked into the dorm and went to Seth's room. When he knocked, there was no answer. "Remington?" he called as he knocked again.

After a few moments, he could hear sounds of movement and the door suddenly jerked open. Without any greeting, Seth demanded, "Take me to Katie."

Ross heaved a deep sigh. He felt like he had just gone through this same scene back at the farm. "I can't."

"I don't give a shit what you think you can or can't do, *Matlock*. I want to see Katie. *Now.*" Seth pushed Ross aside and walked out of the door. Slamming it shut, he headed down the hallway toward the stairs.

"Wait! You can't go to Katie!"

Seth threw him a hard glare and disappeared down the steps. Ross sighed again and shook his head. What a goddamn mess. He chased after Seth.

By the time he caught up with him, Ross saw him leaning against the Lexus with his arms crossed sternly over his chest, impatiently tapping his foot.

Ross walked up to an obviously pissed off Seth. "I went round and round with Katie this morning. You two can't—"

The look of panic in Seth's eyes took Ross by surprise. "You saw Katie?" Seth interrupted. "Is she okay? Are the reporters—?"

"She's fine. I took care of the media. She's got security out there protecting her now."

"Good, then let's go. Gold will get sore if I don't jog him." Seth turned to open the car door.

"Wait. Seth, please just wait a minute and listen to me." Ross pushed the door closed.

"What? What's so damn important that we can't talk about it on the way to the farm?"

"You can't see Katie anymore. The second the reporters found you, the clock started ticking. You two can't have contact for five years or you lose your inheritance," Ross explained for what he felt was the millionth time that day. The guilt he felt wasn't as overwhelming when facing Seth instead of Katie, but it still lurked around, prodding and poking at his conscience.

Seth glared at Ross. The longer Seth stood unflinching, the more uncomfortable it made Ross. He finally tugged at the tie that had suddenly become way too tight around his neck. For a moment, Ross could have sworn that he was looking at Sterling Remington.

The time had come for Seth to make a decision, unpleasant as it was. "You've got two choices. You either go back to Chicago with me and take over Remington Computers, or you have me take you to the farm and you kiss away something like ninety-five million dollars in personal assets. Not to mention the company's holdings."

Seth didn't even blink.

Ross leaned against the car next to Seth and waited patiently for the man to make up his mind while he thanked God he would never find himself in such a precarious predicament. Seth Remington was now Solomon, and the day of the dreaded decision had arrived.

Seth finally glanced over at Ross. The hurt in Seth's eyes came as a shock. "Katie and I... Well, we kind of had a fight last night. It was a big misunderstanding, and if I don't talk to her, I can't straighten it out. Can't you give me five minutes with her? Just five minutes? Or I can send a message with you? You'd take it to her, wouldn't you?"

Ross shook his head. "I want to help. I really do, but the instant you come within a mile of that farm, every reporter will blast your face all over the media. If I broke the no-contact clause, I'd be disbarred for breaching my fiduciary responsibility to your dad's estate, and you'll lose your inheritance. I'm sorry, Seth. You contact her at all in the next five years, you forfeit the money."

"Did she say *anything*?"

Ross nodded. "She said to tell you that you earned your money and... She said to have a nice life."

"She'll need some help if I leave. She'll have to get a new second, and if

I don't drive—"

"She knows. I'm already working on it."

Seth didn't appear at all appeased. "Can't I send her a note or a letter? Something?"

"If you want to put a ninety-five million dollar stamp on it," Ross said with a wry chuckle that he quickly squelched when Seth glared at him again with Sterling's eyes. "Look, Seth. I think there's something else you need to know."

"Then you'd damn well better tell me now."

Ross cleared his throat. "If you see Katie, you're not the only one who'll lose a shitload of money."

Seth arched an eyebrow. Ross now had his client's full attention.

"Sterling left her a bonus of a hundred-thousand once the season was over. Since the press found you early, she still gets the bonus. You two see each other in the next five years, the estate will take it back. Do you really want to take that much money away from her?"

The look on Seth's face confused Ross. He saw vulnerability, and it surprised the hell out of him. But Seth's expression rapidly began to change. Next, Ross saw hurt—plain and simple pain. And then anger.

"She knew about the bonus." Seth calmly stated the fact. The composure didn't register on his face. What Ross saw there was nothing short of fury.

Ross nodded. "She knew. Not the whole time or just how much, but she knew there was a bonus."

"Have a nice life." Seth repeated Katie's farewell.

Ross suddenly understood what was causing Seth's turmoil. "Oh, no. You're wrong, Remington. You're wrong. She didn't choose the money over you. Katie would've given it up if you'd just—"

"Bullshit!" The fierceness of Seth's voice frightened several birds which had been dissecting a small pile of manure several yards away.

"You're not being fair to Katie. She's not like that, and you damn well know it."

"Have a nice life," Seth repeated again.

"You know she didn't—"

"The hell she didn't. She *knew*. You told me she knew. Well, she made her choice, *didn't she*? And it sure as shit wasn't *me*."

Ross shook his head at the man's stupidity. If Seth didn't know Katie any better than that, he deserved to lose her.

He watched Seth stare at the nest of reporters milling about outside the fence aiming their telephoto lenses at them. Seth's spine suddenly straightened. His face became a mask that hid the softening Ross had always seen whenever Katie was near. The selfish heir to the Remington Computer fortune had returned.

"We need to get you away from the press. What are you going to do?" Ross asked.

Seth had no idea why he wasn't exploding. He wanted to scream. He wanted to hit something. He wanted someone else to hurt as deeply as he did. Perhaps the explosion was contained because he was too numb to deal with what he'd discovered about Katie.

She was supposed to be different. The Old Man had chosen her because she was different. She wouldn't have used him for money. Not like everyone else he'd ever known. No one else had every loved him for who he was, for the person he was deep down inside. At least until he came to Indiana, to Dan Patch Raceway. To Katie. And he'd stupidly thought he belonged to her and her world.

But he was a fool, a damn fool. She didn't love him. Not like he loved her. *Love or money?* When faced with Seth's dilemma, the decision he'd struggled with every hour of every day, Katie Murphy had easily chosen money and thrown away his love.

"I'm going home. Tell Katie to... to... *have a nice life*. I hope she enjoys her money. I'm sure as hell going to enjoy mine." Seth opened the Lexus, slipped inside, and slammed the door.

Chapter 29

Katie saw the RV pull up next to the barn and steered her horse off the track to go meet it. The side door of the vehicle opened and Jacob Schaeffer stepped out, put his hands to the small of his back, and stretched. She knew the instant he saw her heading his way because he grinned and walked toward her.

Jumping off of the jog cart, Katie forced a nervous smile. God, she didn't feel like smiling ever again. "It's good to see you."

"You, too," he replied as he grabbed Jack's bridle and led him into the barn. "You all right, Red?"

"I'm fine," she lied. "Thank you so much for coming. I'm trying to get some help, but..."

"Nonsense. I'm here for as long as you need me," Jacob insisted as he cross-tied Jack and began to strip the horse's equipment. "Seems kinda familiar, don't it?"

Katie gave him a weak smile. "Sure does. Did you talk to Grandpa? When's he coming?" She doffed her protective glasses and helmet.

Jacob nodded toward the barn door. Kevin Murphy was just walking through it. "He's already here. Came with me."

"Grandpa!" She immediately ran to throw herself into his arms. "Oh, Grandpa." She grabbed the front of his shirt, buried her face in his chest, and finally let her guard down long enough to cry in front of someone else over the whole horrid situation. She needed the security she felt as he hugged her tightly to him.

"Shh. It's okay now, Sweetheart. Grandpa is here." He rubbed her back and stroked her hair. "It'll be all right, Kathleen. It'll all be all right."

After several long moments, she got herself under control and pulled away. She sniffled a couple of times before drying her tears with the sleeve of her shirt. There was so much she wanted to tell him, but there would be time enough for that later. Right now she had a stable to run. Her stubbornness would allow her to work despite the heartache threatening to paralyze her at any moment.

Like old times, Katie and Jacob fell into their routine of caring for the horses. They mostly exchanged racing gossip, but when Jacob asked about his daughter, Katie didn't want to spread tales of Rachel's exploits. "Don't you talk to her, Jacob?"

"Not in the last six months. She ain't got much use for me, and I don't like what she does most the time. She causin' you trouble again? Girl can't seem to keep her nose clean."

Katie couldn't bring herself to tell Jacob about Rachel's paddock fistfight or her cruel interference with Seth. She loved Jacob too much to hurt him. "She's fine. She gets plenty of work."

Jacob nodded and thankfully let the touchy subject drop.

* * * *

Ready to head to the track with the one horse she had racing that evening, Katie peeked into the RV to tell the men she was leaving. Jacob and her grandfather were relaxing and watching ESPN. "Are you sure you don't want me to get you guys a motel room?"

"Why on earth would you wanna do that?" Jacob asked. "Got everythin' we need right here. Even got a satellite dish on the roof." He gestured with his thumb at the ceiling.

"We're fine," Kevin reassured. "You sure you don't need help tonight?"

"No thanks, Grandpa. I've only got one. I just hope they don't fine me for a late driver's change when..." Damn, but it hurt to even think about Seth. How was she going to face the people at the track?

"We need to sit and have a long talk, Kathleen," Kevin said in that voice of his that told her he was demanding, not suggesting.

"We will," she lied as she turned and walked out of the RV. The last thing in the world she wanted to do was have a long talk with anyone, but she wasn't about to share that with her grandfather. It bothered her to keep an important secret like her pregnancy from the man who had raised her, but Katie still wanted to keep the information to herself for the time being.

There was already plenty of change to deal with for a long time to come.

* * * *

Brian, Sam, and Chris came to visit the next day. Katie had just finished jogging the last of the horses and was putting equipment away while Jacob washed the animal in the bath stall.

Sam ran up to Katie and pulled her into a hug. "How you doing, Honey?"

Katie didn't want to cry anymore, but she couldn't seem to stop herself. "I'm fine." She scrubbed away the errant tears with the back of her hand.

"Bullshit. Talk to me, Katie."

Brian and Chris stood awkwardly staring at the ground as if to keep from eavesdropping on the women's conversation. Katie loved them both for being there, but she wasn't sure she wanted them to hear all she wanted to say to Sam. Ever perceptive, Sam said, "Let's go in your office." She was already heading that way before she even finished the sentence. Katie dutifully followed.

Once inside the small room, Sam plopped down on the bed as Katie took the chair. "How you doing?" Sam asked again.

Tears began to roll down Katie's cheeks. "I hurt, Sam. I hurt every second of the day. How could he... how could he... just *leave*?"

"I don't know, Katie. I just don't know."

The more she thought about the whole situation, the angrier Katie got. "For money. For freakin' money! Can you believe it?"

"Katie, I think he should've—"

"Don't you pick on him." Katie wagged her finger at Sam. "He had every right to go back. I'd have taken the money too."

"Are you bi-polar? 'Cause I can't tell if you're mad at him for leaving or mad at me for being pissed at him for leaving."

"Both!" Katie stood up and paced the room as she railed. "It's just not fair. I can't even sleep unless I use his pillow 'cause it smells like him. Every place I look, he's there. The barn. My room. Everywhere." Some of his clothes remained tucked into the drawers next to hers. His razor still sat side by side with hers in the shower. Her heart clenched as pain washed over her. Her hands dropped to cover her stomach, and she knew a part of Seth would always be in her life. But she wanted him to share this new life, this miraculous child with her. *I love you, Seth. How could you leave me?*

Sam nodded.

Katie straightened her spine. "Does he think I'll take him back in five years? Well, he can kiss my ass. No way I'll take him back. I'd never know if he loved us or the money best."

"You didn't tell him, did you?" Sam finally asked in a quiet voice that helped Katie find some calm.

Katie stared at Sam for a moment before she sat back down. "No. No, I didn't. And I'm glad. He'd hate us if he knew. You know what the worst thing is?"

Sam shook her head.

Katie closed her eyes and let her anger ebb. "I still love him. God help me, I do. With all my heart. I always will." She couldn't push aside her feelings for him. No matter what he'd done, Seth would always be the love of her life.

Why does love always leave?

Sam brushed away the tears that pooled in her eyes. "What do you wanna do now?"

Katie lifted her chin and tightened her resolve. "I'm going to run my stable. I think I'm going to ditch some of the horses. I've got Spun Gold, and I can keep the horses I have with James and Susan. They pay their bills. You know, if Gold finishes fifth or better, he'll be in the finals for sire stakes."

"What do they go for? Fifty grand?" Sam whistled her opinion of the size of the purse. "That would get you set for the time you can't work because of the baby. You know, you could always move in with Brian and me. We've got room."

Katie shook her head before Sam even finished. "Thanks, Sam, but I need to be on my own. Plus, you've got your own baby on the way. You don't need me hanging around. You know, if Gold wins, maybe I can buy that land out by your farm." She finally confessed her last secret. "I'm supposed to get a hundred-thousand from Sterling Remington's estate for taking Seth. God help me, Sam, but I don't want it."

Sam's eyes showed her surprise. She whistled again. "You earned it, Katie."

"If I took it, I'd feel like a whore."

Sam shook her head. "That's bullshit thinking. You didn't earn it on your back, and you damn well know it. You earned it for helping him. And you did, Katie. You helped him."

Katie stared to tear up again. "Not enough."

"Do you have the money now?"

She shook her head. "Not for a few weeks according to Ross."

"Fine. Don't think about the money right now. Think about your stable."

Katie sniffed back tears and nodded. "And the sires stakes."

"And the sires stakes."

It appeared that Brian and Chris had grown impatient when the women heard the tentative knocks on the door. "Come on in!" Sam yelled. Brian worked through the door on his crutches and settled next to Sam on the bed. Chris simply stood in the doorway, looking subdued.

"You okay, Katie?" Brian asked. Then his face contorted. "I'm so sorry. It's my fault. If I hadn't gotten hurt—"

Katie wasn't about to let that nonsense go on for a moment longer. "Stop it, Brian. It's nobody's fault."

"Do you need me to come back?" Chris asked.

"No, I'm good. Thanks, guys. You don't know how much it means to me that you're here." Katie stared at her friends for a moment before realizing that she needed their love and support every bit as much as the air she breathed. The time had come to share the entire story with the men so that they could absorb the shock and then be there for her in her time of need. She owed them the truth.

Katie glanced at Sam for a moment, and her friend must have understood. Sam nodded and let a weak smile cross her lips.

"Guys, I need to tell you something," Katie said, barely above a whisper.

They both looked at her.

She sighed. *You can do this, Katie. They won't hate you.* "I'm pregnant."

The two men gawked at her with wide eyes for several suspended seconds.

Brian threw his crutches across the room. Chris kicked the doorframe.

Katie tried to calm them. "C'mon, guys. It's not that bad."

"I'll kill him," Brian said through clenched teeth.

"Kill him? Hell, I'll *geld* him," Chris added as he punched his fist into his hand.

"That bastard left you, knowing you were pregnant?" Brian shouted.

"I didn't tell him." Katie wanted to cry again, fearing that she'd probably destroyed any fondness the men had ever had for Seth. "He didn't know. I didn't want him to lose all that money because of us. I couldn't force him to stay." *He didn't want to stay.*

"Stop it, you two," Sam scolded. "You're not helping her by getting all pissed off and acting like damned cavemen. Can't you just give her some support? We're her family." She stood up and walked across the room to hug Katie.

Brian watched the women for a moment before he struggled to his feet and hopped on one leg over to wrap his arms around Katie and Sam. Chris followed suit on the other side, completing the cocoon of a hug. The four friends clung to each other for a few moments.

Jacob came strolling into the office and gaped at the tight embrace of the group before he finally smiled. "You folks should really get a room."

* * * *

After a wave of morning sickness, Katie shakily emerged from the bathroom. Kevin sat in her desk chair and had parked himself directly in front of the bathroom door. She couldn't possibly avoid him any longer.

"Sweetheart, I do believe it's time for that talk."

She felt trapped and more than a little embarrassed. "Grandpa, I really don't want to—"

"Kathleen, I don't *care* what you wanna do. Are you pregnant?"

She nodded and stared at the floor, unable to bring herself to meet her grandfather's eyes.

"What are you gonna do?"

Katie walked past him to sit on the bed as he swiveled his chair and continued to watch her with those intense green eyes—the eyes he'd always used during her childhood to stare holes through her whenever she had been naughty. "I'm not sure yet. I do know that I'm going to cut down on my stable."

He nodded. "That's wise, but you know that's not what I'm asking.

What are you gonna do about your... situation? You know, you can always come home."

"This *is* home. I need my friends. I need Sam. I love you, Grandpa, but I'm a big girl now," she explained while feeling great relief at his apparently calm acceptance of her pregnancy.

"I understand. Are you gonna ask that goddamn bum for help?"

Katie vigorously shook her head. "No way. I don't want him to know." She couldn't bring herself to tell Kevin about the bonus.

"I can't say as I think that's entirely the smart thing to do."

"What if... What if he wants the baby?" She finally admitted the one fear that threatened to swallow her whole.

He looked shocked. "You're afraid he'll take the child away?"

Katie hadn't realized she was gripping the blanket with white knuckles until she let go. "He's got all that money, Grandpa. If he knows... He might think he could give the baby a better…" She shook her head.

She saw the understanding in his eyes. "His money can't give this baby anything that would replace its momma. We'll protect you. Somehow."

Keeping the news from Seth wouldn't be an easy task, especially if he watched racing, but she nodded and sniffled. Perhaps if she simply ignored the problem... "Thanks, Grandpa."

"You'll let me know if you need help? I want you to see a doctor."

"Yeah, I will. I've got an appointment with Sam's in a few days."

Kevin still appeared concerned. "Do you need money, Kathleen?" She winced at the name.

"No, I'm good. Look, Grandpa, I've got stuff to do," she lied in hopes of ending the humiliating conversation.

Kevin nodded. "I can tell from that look on your face that you're done talking, but promise you'll let me know if you need me, if you need anything at all."

Katie nodded and ran out of the room.

* * * *

Few reporters still hung around the end of the frontage road near Katie's barn. Most must have realized that long distance shots of Katie doing nothing more than sitting in a jog cart and spinning mile after mile were wasted footage. One by one they disappeared.

She arrived at Dan Patch Raceway several days after Seth's disappearance, and she wasn't surprised to see that only one reporter still remained camped outside the track. How nice to know that it only took a handful of days for her to become old news.

As she led Heathcliffe to the paddock, Katie was relieved to see that most things appeared to have returned to normal. People who usually waved or called a greeting still did so, and she returned the words or gestures. What a comfort to be among the familiarity of the track and its inhabitants—both human and equine.

Katie walked back up the long paddock toward the race office to deal with her last late driver change and suddenly found herself face to face with Rachel Schaeffer. The woman grinned like a Cheshire cat. Maintaining much more control than she felt, Katie pushed past her to talk to the officials. When her business ended, she strode purposefully out of the office without exchanging a word with the troublesome woman.

After a few moments of holding her head high, Katie sprinted to the bathroom where she cried and vomited at the same time. Seth Remington and Rachel Schaeffer—the causes of her distress. *Damn them both.*

Katie walked out of the bathroom to find Rachel standing outside the door, leaning against the wall and obviously waiting for her. "So he left, huh? Such a shame," Rachel said with an evil smile and a "tsk tsk."

The only thing keeping Katie from pulling Rachel's hair out by the roots was the fear of something happening to her baby in the ensuing brawl. Otherwise, she would've gladly risked the suspension. "What's it matter to you anyway? It's not like he ever gave you the time of day."

"But I got him in the end, didn't I?"

"Go to Hell, Rachel. I don't believe for one minute that he did *anything* with you." Katie worked up some bravado. "How'd you trick him into your truck?"

Rachel's face suddenly registered surprise. "How'd you know we didn't—?"

"I didn't know for sure. But thanks for telling me." Katie turned to walk away. Seth had been faithful. At least where other women were concerned. He'd certainly left quickly enough when money was involved.

Rachel laughed in an eerie, grating tone. "I got the last laugh, though, didn't I?"

Katie turned back to face her adversary and narrowed her eyes. "What do you mean?"

"I'm the one that called *The Tattler*. How about that Miss High and Mighty? Now, he's gone. And you can't have him! I win!" Rachel shouted.

People around the paddock stopped to stare at the two women, and voices could be heard discussing Rachel's outburst. In only a few moments, several people had gathered behind Katie to yell at Rachel.

"You ain't working for me anymore!" a familiar voice shouted.

"You're the one that ratted him out? Do you know how much trouble you caused?" another voice rang out.

"Look at the mess you made! Don't bother paddocking for me on Friday!" another trainer bellowed.

Katie's favorite comment was the simple "Bitch!" that reverberated off the walls.

The horsemen always supported their own, and they were letting Katie know that she and Seth belonged with them. Rachel had forfeited any goodwill she had with the people at Dan Patch Raceway when she hurt their friends and took away their star driver.

Katie allowed herself a smug smile as she crossed her arms over her breasts. "I'm sure Sam and Brian won't be needing your help anymore, either."

Rachel sputtered for a moment before she evidently decided retreat was the best course of action. When she stalked out of the paddock, several people applauded.

Katie allowed herself to smile before she nodded and waved to friends as she made her way back to her horse.

* * * *

The mansion was spotless. Nothing had really changed from the time Seth had left that cold March morning.

Nothing except him.

The first day he returned, Seth had actually enjoyed all of the luxuries.

There was the shower. It didn't turn frigid because Katie had used up the precious small amount hot water. Then he remembered making love to her in that tiny shower stall and felt his heart clench in pain.

The quiet was nice. At least at first. It became too hard to sleep without the lullaby of the horses bedding down in their stalls, the drone of the air conditioner, or the sounds of Katie sighing and talking softly in her sleep.

And the bed was big enough to hold one or two of the racehorses. It seemed firm and comfortable—until Seth felt lost and alone in its magnitude.

The music was better. No more goofy love songs that made Katie sing. When he heard her melodious voice echo through his memories, his stomach tightened.

The luxuries had obviously been worth the sacrifice of leaving Katie behind. At least that's what Seth told himself to keep from falling to a heap on the floor and bawling like a baby.

Seth found himself a stranger in his own home. The staff had all been let go when Ross took over the care of the compound. There wasn't a single face that Seth recognized.

But one face haunted him day and night. A face full of sunshine and happiness with emerald eyes and framed by copper hair. The face of an angel.

Seth reminded himself that Katie had made the same choice, taken the same option. Money, not love. He wondered if she was enjoying her hundred-grand. It was probably a fortune to her.

Damn her, anyway.

Seth watched the news reports at first just to see her. There were shots of her jogging horses around the practice track and segments showing her leading animals in and out of corrals. When he saw footage of Katie sitting behind Spun Gold as she trained him, jealousy overwhelmed him. She was handling Gold. *My horse.* Then he had to be honest with himself and admit the colt had always been her horse.

Seth called Ross at least twice a day to ask about Katie, and each time Ross told him the same thing. "She's fine, Seth. Let it go."

So she's doing just fine without me. He hadn't mattered that much to her after all. He had mistakenly thought that Katie loved him.

Part of him was angry. Seth had hoped that somewhere deep down, Katie wouldn't be able to stay away, that she wanted him for more than the Remington money. Of course, in his fantasy, when she showed up on his doorstep, Ross would suddenly realize that two people in love were destined to be together and he would waive the five-year clause.

Yeah, right. Like Matlock would ever do something that compassionate.

Whenever Seth thought of Ross being able to see Katie, talk to her, and touch her whenever he wished, Seth seethed. The jealousy was incredible, smothering in its intensity. He remembered the times he'd seen Ross kiss Katie in the winner's circle or hold her hand in the paddock. He thought about the time his angel had drawn the lawyer into a passionate kiss as they sat in the Lexus. The images became more than Seth could bear.

It hurt that Katie could go on without him because he was having quite a lot of trouble going on without her and her world. He missed the track and the people who worked there. He missed the horses. He missed Mondays at The Place talking to Brian, Samantha, and Chris.

But he missed Katie most of all.

Ross had suggested that Seth go to Remington Computer headquarters and try to find a way to contribute to the running of his company. Seth figured that would be what Sterling would want. Yet the time he spent there made him feel like a fish trying to live on dry land. His degree in psychology didn't exactly prepare him for any position of importance in his own company. They definitely didn't need a good harness driver.

Most of the time, Seth would duck into his father's old office, close the door, and surf the Internet, checking on racing entries and results. He kept up with the horses he'd driven, but he constantly fretted over not being able to tell the new drivers all about the animals they had taken away from him. He had to correct himself that the horses weren't taken away from him. Seth had abandoned them as well as their trainers who had grown to trust him.

I abandoned everyone at Dan Patch Raceway.

The only times Ross would reach out to contact Seth were to remind him that some residual paperwork remained for Sterling's estate. "Are you ever coming in to sign the papers?" the lawyer would ask each time they talked. If Seth signed them, it would make it all permanent. He just wasn't able to force himself to do so.

He was torn between wanting to be rid of Ross and wanting to hold onto the lawyer like a lifeline. Ross was Seth's only connection to Katie, yet at the same time Ross became a painful reminder of what he had lost.

And Seth realized how much he had really lost when he left Katie

Murphy behind to claim his fortune.

Perhaps I'm really a poor man after all.

* * * *

It took Katie twenty minutes to fill out all of the paperwork on the clipboard the receptionist had handed her. There were forms for everything. Forms for insurance. Forms for medical history. Forms for financial responsibility. Katie was sure her eyes would be permanently crossed from reading all of the fine print. It all boiled down to one thing—having a baby was going to be damned expensive.

She handed the clipboard back to the nurse. The woman flipped through the papers. "You don't have *any* insurance?" she asked.

"No," Katie meekly replied.

"Doesn't the baby's father have any insurance?"

"The baby's father is... out of the picture." Katie tried to hold her head high and her spine straight.

The receptionist rattled off her obviously well-practiced speech. "The fee for prenatal care and a normal delivery is on a sliding scale. We'll look over your financial records and give you the price before you leave. The total fee has to be paid in full before your due date. The hospital will send you a separate bill. If you require a cesarean, you'll be charged more depending on your income. If you want an epidural, the anesthesiologist will send you a separate bill. Any questions?"

Katie felt like she'd been listening to someone speak in a foreign language. A shiver of hurt ran through her thinking about how Seth must have felt those first few weeks in her employ. "What's an epidural?"

"The doctor will explain that," the receptionist answered. "Any other questions?"

"No, I'm fine."

"Have a seat. The nurse will call you in a minute." The receptionist shut the glass window separating her desk from the waiting room.

Katie turned around and saw three women who were obviously due to deliver at any minute. For a moment, she wondered exactly what she had gotten herself into, but she comforted herself with the notion that she would always have a part of Seth close to her. That thought made her smile. Her hand drifted to her stomach.

Katie sat down and picked up one of the magazines littering the tables of the waiting area. She saw a small photo of Seth on the upper corner, and she stared at it for a minute. *I'm not going to cry, damn it.* She dropped it back on the table and chose another magazine. She had almost finished reading an article on the benefits of breastfeeding when a skinny blond nurse walked into the waiting room and called her name.

The nurse escorted her to a peaceful blue room with framed pictures of smiling babies dressed in adorable animal costumes. "Please take off all your clothes and change into this," the nurse instructed as she handed Katie a green gown. "Have a seat on the table when you're done, and I'll be back to take your vitals."

"Thanks," Katie replied as she took the gown.

Once the nurse had completed the task of taking Katie's blood pressure, weighing her, and making notes about anything from allergies to whether she took vitamins, Katie had nothing to do except wait patiently for the doctor. She sat on the paper-covered table, trying to hold together the flimsy gown and wondering what kind of sadist would design something as ridiculous as the pathetic piece of material that barely covered her.

There was a soft knock on the door before it opened. The doctor's smile immediately put Katie at ease. He had a round face, soft blue eyes, and a gray-brown beard that reminded her so much of a young Santa Claus that she couldn't help but like the man. His voice and touch were gentle as he completed a lengthy examination to be sure Katie's pregnancy was progressing normally.

After the doctor made a few notes in her chart, he went over to the cabinet and retrieved a piece of equipment that looked like a small transistor radio. "What's that for?" Katie asked.

"We're going to listen to the baby's heartbeat," the doctor replied as he picked up a white bottle and squeezed cold blue jelly on her belly. Using a small device that reminded Katie of a tiny microphone, he rubbed it gently into the goop, searching for just the right place on her stomach.

When she heard the first "whoosh whoosh" of the tiny heartbeats, she was stunned. For some reason, the experience made the whole thing real for the first time.

I'm going to be a mother. I'm really going to be a mother.

"Good strong heart tones," the doctor said as he glanced at Katie and smiled.

She nodded and swallowed the large lump that had formed in her throat.

"Everything looks really good. I'll want to see you back in about four weeks. We'll schedule an ultrasound on your next visit so we can narrow down the due date and make sure the little guy is doing well."

"It's a boy?" she asked entirely surprised the doctor could possibly know the baby's gender so early in the pregnancy.

"Can't say for sure. But the heart rate is high, so it's more in the boy range than the girl range. Of course, I've been fooled before." He chuckled. "Many, many times. Please call me if you need anything." He patted her knee and then left the room.

All of a sudden, Katie didn't feel all alone in the world anymore.

Maybe this love will stay.

Chapter 30

"Matlock! Come on in," Seth said with a sweeping gesture of his arm and a sarcastic tone. "Welcome to the Taj Mahal."

Ross stepped in and looked around the enormous living room. The place was littered with harness racing magazines, fast food boxes, and beer bottles. "It looks like a tornado went through here."

"Sorry. The maid isn't in until... never. I fired her." Seth cleared a couple of magazines off the black leather couch and threw them onto another pile of magazines on the floor. "Here, sit down. Want a beer?"

"No, thanks." Ross picked up one of the large number of CDs scattered around the room. "Since when do you listen to Clay Aiken?" He grabbed another and shook his head. "Didn't know you were a closet Barry Manilow fan. Sure you're not gay?"

"Kiss my ass," Seth replied as he grabbed a remote control from the end table. A huge flat-screen plasma television hanging on the wall came to life. "I had the Internet hooked up so I can watch the races in here. Spun Gold races tonight. Third leg of the sires stakes. I can't believe Katie is letting Mark Masters drive. What the hell is she thinking?"

Ross frowned. He hated this whole situation and was damned sick and tired of all of them being nothing more than pawns to the whims of a man long dead. Sterling Remington might have been a formidable man in the corporate world, but it had become obvious he wasn't much of a father. "Why are you watching that? You've been back for two weeks."

"Because I want to see how my... how Katie's horse does. It's a shame Brian can't drive yet. He'd give Gold a good trip," Seth rattled on as if making idle chit-chat. Ross knew that what Seth really hoped to accomplish was to fish for some new information about Katie.

Seth walked across the room to the large wooden bar, opened the refrigerator door, and grabbed a beer. "I heard College Mascot got claimed.

You made a killing on that, didn't you? What did Katie say when she lost him?"

Ross didn't answer.

Seth tried again. "How much did he get claimed for?"

"Thirty grand."

"And what did Katie say?" Seth prodded as walked away from the bar.

Ross set his briefcase on the floor, took off his jacket, and slung it over the couch arm before sitting down. "Just let it go."

Crossing the room in long strides, Seth sat on the coffee table across from Ross. "I just want to know how she is. Did she get her money yet? Did she get her hundred grand?"

Ross wondered if Seth knew how pathetic he sounded. "No contact, remember?"

"Ah, come on, *Matlock*. Have a heart."

Ross didn't bother to hide his frustration. "*Remington*, you know the rules. Why do I have to keep explaining them to you?"

"Fine. Whatever. How are Brian and Sam? You can tell me about them, can't you?" Seth asked as he twisted the cap off his bottle.

Ross sighed, realizing Seth would be like a pit bull until he got some new information. "They're fine. Sam looks pregnant. Brian is off the crutches and using a cane."

Seth nodded as he seemed to greedily soak up the information. "And did they ask about me?"

"Well, yes and no. Can't you just drop—?"

"What did they say?"

"Seth, you don't want to know." Ross felt like a kid gossiping on the school playground.

"Sure I do. I know my buddy Brian wouldn't let you leave without a message. What did he say?" Seth asked with the eagerness plain in his voice.

Ross sighed again and reluctantly answered. "He said for you to go fornicate with yourself. Not in so many words, but..." He shrugged. "You'll forgive me if I don't quote him."

Seth's face contorted like he'd taken a punch to the gut.

"How do you expect him to feel? You knew you'd have to leave eventually. It's not your fault, but they've had to deal with the fallout." Ross tried to console his client. He would have preferred to deck him.

The more Ross thought about the situation, the more ridiculous the whole mess seemed. Seth made a choice, and now he acted as if a wrong had been perpetrated on him. All of his pissing and moaning couldn't change the fact that Seth had left Katie behind. Her friends had every right to be angry at him, and now the man needed to suck it up and learn how to live with it.

The post parade began. Seth threw himself on the couch, transfixed to the television, absorbing every word.

Ross really wanted to leave, but he decided to stay long enough to see Katie's race. "You know, you really need to sign those papers."

"Yeah, whatever," Seth replied without taking his attention away from the television.

Realizing that talking was wasted breath as long as racing was on, Ross leaned back and let his head rest against the couch to watch the race. As the starters released the horses, Gold immediately sprinted to the front of the pack.

"No, you moron! He races off the pace! *Off* the pace!" Seth screamed at the television. "Katie must be having a fit."

Ross sat there and watched Seth. It was clear that he missed racing. It was even more apparent that he was utterly lost without Katie Murphy. Ross wondered why Seth couldn't seem to be able to figure out that money wasn't always the most important thing in life. Millions of dollars sure weren't buying Seth any kind of happiness.

By the half-mile pole, the outside horses challenged, but Gold dug in to try to keep the advantage. The colt hung on through most of the stretch and only faded in the last sixteenth of the mile, holding on for third.

"Damn it! Masters should've won that race!" Seth shouted as he jumped up. He turned off the television and then pitched the remote at the couch. "Well, at least he'll be in the finals. Tell Katie to think about a driver change. And tell her to tell the damn cowboy she puts in the bike to race him *off* the pace. If Masters would've won, I could've at least... at least... seen her in the winner's circle."

Ross considered Seth for a moment before he finally stood up and grabbed his briefcase. Clicking open the latches, he popped it open, fished out a magazine, and tossed it at Seth.

"What's this?" Seth asked as he caught the publication.

"Arthur's been holding onto it. It was in your father's file. You were supposed to get it before you signed the final papers for the estate, but I thought you might want to see it now. There's an interview with your father in there. You ought to read it."

Seth dropped the magazine down amongst the other discarded debris. "I damn well won't. After what he did to me? I don't care what he had to say about anything."

Ross stared at Seth for moment, allowing his anger to swell. When he finally spoke his mind, the words came out in a stream of contempt. "You're a freakin' moron, you know that? I've watched you for the past six months. You went from a man acting like a spoiled brat to a real human being. Now you're back to being a rich, miserable waste of life."

"It's not nice to talk about your paycheck that way."

"Katie was—"

Seth's eyes flashed rage. "*Don't you dare!* Every time I've asked about her, you've put me off. You can't—"

"I'll say whatever I damn well please. Katie was the best thing that ever happened to you. Hell, she's the best thing that ever happened to *me.* And you threw her away." Although he had a quick temper, Ross generally didn't resort to a physical display of anger. But at that moment, he was sorely tempted to knock Seth Remington down a peg or two. Literally.

"You think I don't know that? You think I don't sit here every damn day wondering what she's doing, who she's with? If she misses..." He cut off his words and took a long draw on his beer bottle.

"Yet, here you stay in your gilded cage. You're pathetic. You don't deserve her." Ross picked up his briefcase and grabbed his jacket. "When you're ready to sign the paperwork, call Arthur. I quit." He slammed the door as he left.

Seth watched Ross's exit and was surprised to realize that he was actually sorry to see him go. Even though Seth didn't want to admit it, Ross had always done a commendable job in taking care of his family's interests—of Seth's interests. And of Katie.

God, I miss her. There was no one to talk to, no one to tease. His angel was gone, but his heart wouldn't accept that reality. It still pined for her like a vital piece of him was missing, like a limb had been wrenched from his body. Like there was a hole in his soul.

But Katie wanted money more than she wanted me.

Sometimes Seth watched racing just to hear the announcer say Katie's name or to get a glimpse of her on camera. It was like a caress to his soul, but pain quickly followed, as it always did each time he thought of her.

He blamed his father more than anyone could ever imagine. In his mind, it had been the Old Man's fault that Seth had lost Katie.

Wallowing in his misery, Seth decided to play the one card he still had left to try to get past his problems forgetting Katie Murphy. Picking up the cordless phone, he scrolled through the stored numbers that dated back to the winter before finding the one he wanted. He dialed and waited for an answer.

"Hello?"

"Kirsten, it's Seth. I'm back."

* * * *

The minute he picked Kirsten up, Seth realized his folly. She was still as beautiful as ever. Her long blond hair bounced around her shoulders. Her face bore just enough make-up to give her a natural look. Everything about her screamed sophistication. But the second she opened her mouth, Seth wished he'd just stayed home.

The woman prattled on about people Seth hadn't seen in ages, about people he'd really cared nothing about in the first place. Kirsten must have figured her duty was to catch Seth up on all the important things he had missed while he'd been away. His ears were ringing before they even reached the trendy nightclub.

The instant he walked inside, Seth realized that Kirsten had obviously phoned several friends who now waited at one of the larger tables. She waved to them as she pulled Seth's arm, leading him toward the group. He groaned when he saw their familiar faces. The Boys' Club was there.

As Seth pulled out Kirsten's chair, he leaned over to whisper in her ear. "I wish you hadn't called any of—" Before he finished his sentence, a flash went off near his face temporarily blinding him. Through the blue dots that floated in his line of vision, Seth saw a man with a camera running for the exit. "Damn press."

Kirsten sat down as Seth took a seat beside her. He listened to the table conversation but only answered questions when he was specifically prodded to do so. There was chatter of who would travel to their warm weather condos over the winter months. Kirsten discussed several important upcoming social events. One of Seth's old friends talked about his girlfriend's abortion and what a close call it was that the unfortunate woman had actually considered keeping the baby for a few agonizing days.

He thought about his Katie, who longed to have a child but never could have one of her own. Katie, whose depth of caring would have embraced his child and loved him for who the child was rather than thinking of the baby as a burden.

How was I ever a friend to any of these morons?

Senator Kelly's son grabbed another Jell-O shot and threw it back. "C'mon, Seth. You need to try one of these."

"No, thanks." Most of the people around him were fast on their way to being drunk, and he had no desire to follow suit.

"Wanna dance?" Kirsten asked, reaching out and stroking his arm.

The gesture reminded him too much of Rachel. He brushed her hand away. "No, thanks."

After twenty irritatingly long minutes passed, Seth stood up, threw a few bills on the table, and leaned over to Kirsten. "This was a huge mistake. I'm leaving. You want me to take you home?"

Kirsten knit her forehead as she stared at Seth for a moment. "You've changed. And not for the better. Go home. I'm staying with my friends."

Seth breathed a sigh of relief as he walked out the front door.

He picked up a speeding ticket on the drive home.

Chapter 31

The cover photo on the magazine sitting under the small stack of mail immediately caught Samantha's eye. Her first instinct was to rip it to pieces so that Katie never had to see the stupid thing, but that would only be stalling the inevitable. She shoved the magazine into the vast wasteland she liked to call a purse. "You coming, Brian? Your appointment is in fifteen minutes."

She heard him yelling back from the kitchen. "Yeah, yeah. I'm coming. Hold your horses." Sam could hear him laugh at his own ironic sense of humor. It only made her realize how much she really loved the guy.

After dropping Brian off for his physical therapy, Sam drove out to Katie's farm. She stopped the truck next to the barn, pulled the magazine out of her purse, and looked at the cover again. The headline blazed "Remington Heir and Fiancée Reconcile" next to a picture of Seth leaning over a beautiful blonde. Their faces were so close that it appeared as if he might have just kissed her.

Figuring Katie should hear the news from a friend before someone else showed her the picture, Sam pushed the truck door open and stepped out, taking the magazine with her.

"Sam," Katie called from the aisle where she brushed one of the horses. "Nice to see you." Katie's gaze swept Sam from head to toe. "Look at you. You gonna have twins?" She winked at Sam.

"Quit making fun." Sam rubbed her well-rounded stomach and laughed.

"I think you look wonderful." Katie's eyes twinkled. Sam was glad to see her happy for once, and she had to squelch her guilt at being the bearer of bad news. But better to hear it from a friend.

"It'll be you running around with a belly like this in no time. Just wait another couple of months. By then you can borrow my maternity clothes. Did Jacob and Kevin get away all right?"

Katie nodded as she continued her work. "Yeah. I'm down to five horses. I didn't need the help anymore. Besides, I was tired of dealing with Dan Porter anyway. He never pays his bills. All of his horses are all in Perry's stable now."

"Good riddance." Sam walked closer to where Katie worked.

"My thoughts exactly. Thanks for taking over Chris's pay."

"I wish you'd have let me do it sooner. How you feeling?" Sam asked.

"I'm good. Still some nausea, but the doctor said that should stop in the next couple of weeks. He thinks the baby will come the middle of February." Sam watched as Katie ran the brush over the horse's back with practiced ease. "He wanted me to have an ultrasound, but I need to save up some money first. Can you believe those prices?"

Sam frowned. "You know, you should really call Ross and have him file a paternity—"

"No!" Katie shouted loud enough to startle the horse.

"Aren't you going to at least take the bonus?"

Sam watched Katie's eyes grow hard. The twinkle had evaporated. "I don't want a *dime* of Seth Remington's money. *Ever.*"

"As long as you don't have any complications with the pregnancy. Right? I mean, you'd ask if—"

Katie waved a hand. "Of course. If the baby ever needed anything important that I couldn't give him, I'd swallow my pride. But I really don't want him involved if I can help it."

"If you really feel that way, then I suppose I should show you this," Sam said, sheepishly producing the magazine from her enormous purse.

Katie took it from Sam's hands and glanced at the cover. After a few long moments, Katie flung it toward the trash barrel and went back to brushing her horse.

"Aren't you gonna say something?"

Katie shrugged. "What's to say? He's not the man I thought he was." She sniffled.

Sam walked over and put her hand on Katie's shoulder. Katie sighed and laid her hand over Sam's. "Thanks for letting me know. It helps to not get broadsided every time I go to the grocery store."

"I know. At least the publicity has died down."

Katie finished brushing the horse before taking him out of the cross-ties and leading him back to his stall. Sam sat down on one of the green trunks.

"What scheme are you cooking up now?" Katie asked.

"No scheme. Just thinking... How do you plan to keep Seth from knowing you're pregnant? I mean, the guy can add. If he sees you, he's bound to figure it out."

Katie nodded. "I know. For now, it's easy enough to hide. I'm only about seven weeks along. By the end of the season, I'll just wear loose sweaters and big jackets. Even if he still watches racing, there's no way he'll see me after that. The baby will come before Dan Patch opens again."

Sam frowned realizing it probably wasn't that easy. "You don't think he'll be back when the five years are up?"

Katie shook her head.

"But if he does show up, how do you think he'll feel when he sees a four-year-old kid running around?"

"He won't be back."

"How can you say that?"

"'Cause Seth's smart enough to realize he's not welcome anymore. I know him, and I think he knows me. He'd realize I'd consider it an insult," Katie replied with confidence Sam figured she probably didn't really feel. "If he chose the money now, he doesn't get to change in mind in five years."

"I don't know, Katie. Have you thought about what you'd do?"

"Yeah, a little," Katie replied, and then she shrugged. "But I haven't come up with much. Besides, that's a *long* way off. I can't think about it now. Things have a way of taking care of themselves anyway." Putting her brushes away, Katie turned back to Sam. "I need to go. I'm having lunch with Ross. He's looking at claiming again."

"That's okay. I need to go get Brian anyway." Sam stood up and gave Katie a quick hug. "You coming with us on Monday?"

"Yeah. I could use the distraction."

"See ya then."

"Yeah, Sam. I'll see ya."

* * * *

Katie took a seat as Ross handed her the cup of decaffeinated mocha that the barista had prepared for her. "Why do you even drink it when it's unleaded? Might as well have water," he joked. She smiled up at him, but she didn't say anything as she wiggled the mouse on the computer at their table to begin a search for Ross's next horse.

Every time he'd been around her since Seth returned to Chicago, Katie seemed to grow more and more withdrawn. She looked pale. And a bit thinner, too. She had dark circles under her eyes. His heart ached to bring back the effervescent Katie he knew hid inside her somewhere.

She deserved so much better than what had happened to her from the moment Seth Remington was forced into her life. Yet, after the upheaval of his arrival, Katie had treated Seth with kindness and taken a firm, but loving hand with a man who needed some discipline. She had succeeded in transforming the spoiled man into a valuable human being—at least for the time Seth stayed with her.

Then the fallout from the discovery of Seth's identity hit her with the force of a category five hurricane. But Katie had borne the press, as well as the devastation to her professional and personal lives, with dignity and an almost regal bearing. She had triumphed. How could he not admire her?

Ross also hoped he could still make a difference in her life, the same type of difference she'd made in his. He wanted to be Katie's knight in shining armor, if she would only let him. Unfortunately, she obviously still cared deeply for Seth. Given time, she'd forget. And maybe Katie could learn to love someone new. *Like me.*

Ross had fallen in love with her, and he blamed himself for her woes. If he had known the outcome of the whole debacle, he would have advised Katie to pass on the colt and go back to her life. But then, he would never have gotten to know her.

Such a paradox.

When Katie had quietly allowed Seth to go back to his fortune, Ross's respect for her swelled to admiration. He'd never met a woman who could be so strong, so unselfish. It just reconfirmed his opinion that Seth Remington was a fool. Women like Katie were few and way too far between. Ross wondered what he could do to help her now, even knowing that her heart still belonged to Seth. One amazing idea had been spinning in his head, but he needed to summon an incredible amount of courage to bring it to fruition.

"This one looks good," she said as she pointed to the race lines on the screen. "I'm still pissed at O'Riley, and I think I can help this horse. It'd serve him right if we claimed it." She picked up her cup and sipped her brew.

Ross loosened the knot on his tie with one hand and drummed his fingers on the table with the other. "Get whatever you want."

His heart was telling him it was now or never, and Ross wasn't sure he'd ever have a better opportunity. They were alone. She'd had some time apart from Seth. He took a leap of faith. "How would you like to get married?"

Katie choked on her drink. She sputtered and coughed for a few moments as Ross thumped her on the back. "What... what did you just say?"

"I want us to get married." Katie looked at him wide-eyed. He hurried to explain. "Hear me out. I know you don't love me, but you like me. And I... I love you. Good marriages have been based on less."

Katie continued to gawk at him but kept her thoughts to herself.

"We're good together, Katie." He groped to find a way to convince her of his sincerity. "I want to buy you a farm. We can build a training track. I'll take care of you. I promise. You'll never want for anything. Maybe we'll raise some kids and—"

Katie winced and looked away.

"Look, if it's that bad an idea..."

She kept her silence for a moment then brought her gaze back to lock with his. "No, Ross. It's actually a good idea."

"Really? Will you think about it?" He heard her heave a sigh as she stared at her cup. *Why won't she look me in the eye?*

"I need to tell you something, Ross. You're not gonna like it, and I won't tell you if you don't swear that you'll listen as a friend and not Seth's lawyer."

"I'm not Seth's lawyer anymore."

Her eyes came back to his, wide with surprise. "You're not? What happened?"

Ross picked up his spoon and stirred his coffee. There were some ethical boundaries he knew he shouldn't cross, and one was the no-contact order. He carefully considered his words to keep them within the spirit of the will. "I couldn't work with him anymore. Seth has… changed. He's lost, Katie. He wasn't listening to any advice I gave him, and... well... frankly, I think the guy is an idiot."

"Why's he an idiot?"

"Because he left you behind."

"I'd have taken the money too."

Ross shook his head. "No, you wouldn't. That's the point. You love people, not money. That's why I love you so much."

Katie looked like she actually sympathized with Remington's plight, and that reaction took Ross by surprise. "You don't know what I'd do if it were me. You can't blame Seth for wanting to go home. That money belonged to him. He had every right to get it back."

Setting his spoon back on the saucer and picking up his cup, Ross considered her comments. It was hard to believe she could be so understanding considering how the whole situation had affected her personally. "What was it you wanted to tell me?"

"You're going to think I'm even bigger idiot than Seth, but you deserve the truth."

"What?" He sipped his coffee as he watched a firm resolve settle on her face.

"I'm pregnant."

Ross dropped the cup. "Shit!" They both jumped up to reach for napkins to mop up the mess on the table.

When they finally settled back down, Ross spoke his mind. "You know that baby's the heir to the Remington—"

Her fist slammed on the table making her cup jostle. "*No!* This baby's *mine.* And you promised you'd listen as a friend and not a lawyer. I don't want a penny of his money."

Ross nodded in quick acceptance. Katie was even stronger in spirit than he'd ever anticipated. She deserved some happiness, and he would see she got it. "You know what? I'm glad. I always wanted kids."

Katie looked at him as if in a stupor. "You still want to marry me?"

"Of course. I love you."

"But, Ross, I don't love you. Is that fair to you?"

"Let me decide what's best for me. Okay? You know, I'm happy about the baby," Ross reassured with a big smile. "I think I'll make a helluva dad."

Katie jumped up. "I'm going to the bathroom." She practically ran for the restroom door.

Desperately needing some privacy to consider all the implications of Ross's proposal, Katie felt like a coward for fleeing the table like a scared rabbit being chased by a hound.

This wonderful man was handing her a solution to all of her problems. If Seth had the nerve to come to her in five years, there'd be no reason for him to believe that the child belonged to anyone except Ross. Her son would be safe from Seth's lawyers and the prospect of a nasty custody suit that she would surely lose without the Remington fortune. Would Seth do that to her? Take her child away?

She liked Ross, loved him—as a friend. But was that enough to commit to a relationship that should last a lifetime? There was no doubt that she believed Ross would make a fantastic father, but it seemed unfair to let him bear the enormous burden of parenthood for a child that wasn't his.

God, Seth, I miss you. Why did you leave me? It hurt to think that her son would never know his real father. But, then again, what made a *real* father? A real father put the needs of his child ahead of his own selfish desires.

It suddenly crossed her mind that Ross had said "kids." He would expect a normal marriage, and while Katie knew he would never pressure her for sex, it was obvious that it would have to become a part of their relationship. At least at some point.

She stared at the reflection in the mirror. "So what do I do?" The reflection didn't have the courtesy to answer. It looked every bit as confused as she felt. "Thanks a heap."

Katie finally went back and sat down. Ross peered at her from across the small table. She took a few moments to work up enough courage to say what she needed to. "Ross, I don't know if I could... I mean, would you expect...?" It was too humiliating to even bring up. Katie simply stopped talking and shook her head to banish the thought as she felt the heat of a blush spread across her face.

"I know what you're worried about. How about we just say we'll give it time? I grow on people, remember?" Ross said with a shy smile.

"Yes, you certainly do." Katie gave him a nervous laugh.

Seth won't forgive you, her heart taunted.

Seth left me, her logic answered.

In the end, Katie knew she would have to do what was best for all involved, especially her son. And if she was going to marry Ross, she decided that she would do so without waiting long enough to talk herself out of it. "How would you like to go to Las Vegas and get married?"

"You mean it? You really mean it? Ah, Katie, I'd love it. The sooner, the better. When can you go?" He sounded like a kid on Christmas morning, and Ross's enthusiasm made Katie as happy as she could be considering the unusual and unsettling circumstances.

"How about Sunday? I won't put any horses in for that day. We can fly out in the morning."

Ross pulled his phone out of his jacket pocket and flipped it open. "Sheila? I need two first class tickets from Indianapolis to Las Vegas for early Sunday morning. Charge them to my personal account. I need a nice hotel room for... hang on." Ross looked at Katie. "How long do you want to stay? We could spend a few days out there, make it a real honeymoon. Maybe catch a show or hit the slots?"

"I can't leave the horses more than a night," Katie replied, feeling guilty for what she was about to do to her friend. "Ross, are you sure you want to do this?"

"Absolutely."

The word made Katie recoil in reminder of Seth's typical cocky reply. The entire weight on the world landed squarely on her small shoulders. She tried to calm the rapid beat of her heart and swallowed the bile rising in the back of her throat.

Seth will never forgive me.

Ross finished his phone call by reassuring his obviously skeptical secretary he wasn't perpetrating some kind of bizarre practical joke. He flipped the phone shut with a loud snap.

The tears came despite her best efforts to stop them.

"Katie, what's wrong? Is it that upsetting to think about marrying me?"

Ross's concern helped Katie regain some control. "I'm... I'm... fine."

"Are you worried about money? I'll take care of you. And Arthur told me that you're going to get your check next week."

"You can tell Seth Remington where he can stick his damn money. I don't want it."

"You earned that money, Katie. I've never seen anyone as patient as you were with Seth." He reached out and took her hand in his. "Take the money.

If you don't want it for you, then I'll help you put it in a trust for the baby."

She had to think about that one. Saving the money for her son would take some of the pressure off Ross because he shouldn't have to shoulder the burden for another man's child.

Katie finally nodded. "For the baby." She'd save the money for Seth's child. And she'd marry Ross. Her heart clenched and an overwhelming wave of sadness coursed over her.

Why, Seth? Why would you throw our love away?

Tears filled her eyes and she tried to choke back the sob that rose in her throat. "Ross, I can't... I can't do this."

Ross stood up and reached for her. In one quick motion, Katie let herself be drawn into his embrace. He pulled her close and stroked her hair. "Yes, you can," he whispered in her ear. "It's best for everyone, Katie. I'll take good care of you. And I'll take care of your baby."

Your baby. Not our baby. Kate wondered if that was a bad sign, but she sniffled and nodded. "We've always made good partners. Haven't we?"

"The best," Ross replied.

But when the time came to say, "I do," could she follow through?

Chapter 32

Seth shoved a CD into the Bose stereo. The soft jazzy sound of Michael Bublé's "Home" filled the room. Seth threw the empty case down on top of the enormous stack of new music he'd acquired since his return to the Remington compound.

Barry Manilow and Billy Joel mixed with several of the singers Seth had finally decided he enjoyed. It goaded him that Ross had poked fun of his new selection of tunes. So what was the difference if a guy enjoyed a good love song every now and then?

Screw him.

The songs brought him comfort in a sorrowful sort of way as images of Katie swirled around his mind each time he listened to them. He could almost hear her voice and feel the touch of her hand with each bittersweet song.

I miss you, Boss.

Throwing himself onto the leather sofa, Seth reached for the remote control and turned on the television. He hit the mute button so he could listen to the music as he flipped through the channels to locate any kind of horseracing. There was none to be found, so he quickly turned the plasma screen back off.

He dropped the remote on the floor, but then thought better of it and decided to put it on the table so he wouldn't step on it later as was becoming his habit. Leaning down to get the pesky object, he saw it resting on the magazine that Ross had left behind. Seth reached down to pick the magazine up.

One of the teasers on the cover promised an in-depth interview with the "enigmatic Sterling Remington," and Seth's curiosity sent him searching through the table of contents so he could locate the story.

How much more damage could the Old Man do? Maybe there would be a revelation of some deep, dark family secret. Perhaps there would be some mention of how his father had managed to think up the cruel plan he'd devised for his will.

Settling back into the couch, Seth read the interview that was obviously given shortly before his father's death. Sterling bared his soul to some reporter—told her intimate things he'd never shared with anyone, including his son.

Seth's heart tightened in pain and grief at the idea of reading what his father had to say. He'd ignored the story when Ross left the magazine because his anger at his father still smothered him. But now, Seth felt that he *had* to read it, that something important sat quietly waiting for him to discover it.

And then he finally found what he was seeking in his father's own words. Straight from the horse's mouth.

The worst thing in life is living without love. When my Brenda died, a part of me died, too. I left my heart in that tomb with her. If the devil had promised to bring her back if I gave up every penny I had ever earned, I'd have asked him to draw up the contract on the spot and I would have signed it in my own blood.

Absolutely nothing is more important in life than finding someone you can love who loves you in return. If you're lucky enough to find her, hold onto her with both hands, with everything you've got. And don't you ever her let go. She's worth her weight in gold.

How many times had Seth heard the same words from people who knew Katie? Hadn't Sam said the exact same thing to him once upon a time?

Samantha Mitchell was a wise woman. A brilliant woman. She had seen things the correct way right from the very beginning.

Then the truth hit Seth with the intensity of a two-by-four slammed into his head. His heart began to pound a furious rhythm. His breath came in ragged gasps. Waves of nausea roiled through him. He suddenly knew.

Katie hadn't left him for the money, for the hundred-thousand bonus. She'd pushed him away so that he could keep his inheritance.

Even worse. She'd turned the choice right back on him. Katie had let him decide his own future.

And Seth had chosen wrong.

Dead wrong.

Only now did he finally understand. *Katie loves me! She really loves me!* Katie had loved him enough to let him go.

"I'm a goddamn fool!" Seth threw the magazine across the room before he turned and kicked over the coffee table. "Katie loves me! And I left her behind!"

So what are you going to do about it?

Seth hoped the marvelous revelation didn't come too late to fix the mess he'd made of his life, of Katie's life, of any chance they had to make a new life together.

I have to fix this! I have to!

Seth grabbed for his phone. After taking a deep, steadying breath, he dialed the familiar number and waited for an answer.

"Mitchell Stables," Samantha's cheerful voice answered.

"Sam, it's Seth Remington. I need your—" The line went dead. Seth was well aware that he deserved that response, but he wasn't about to quit trying. Not now.

Pushing the redial button, Seth waited as the phone rang several times. Sam's voicemail answered with her recorded message, and Seth waited for the perfunctory tone. "Sam, I know you're there. I'll just keep calling until you pick up. Come on, Sam, pick up! Fine. Well, you can expect me to call and leave a message every couple of minutes until you either talk to me or call me back." He hung up and nervously drummed his fingers on the countertop, waiting as time passed at an interminably slow pace. "Come on, damn it. I need your help."

After a few minutes, Seth dialed again. Sam's message greeted him and the annoying tone sounded. "Hi, Samantha. Told you I'd keep calling. How are you? How's Brian? I miss you guys more than you know. Pick up, Sam. Please pick up. Not there? Well, I'll try again, *real* soon."

Seth hated this game. For the first time in a very long time, he felt as if his destiny was back in his control, but he couldn't get through to the one person he knew could help him. Now he was a man with a mission, and he wasn't going to be stopped. He called the Mitchell number again. This time he shouted at the machine. "Sam! I'll give you a *million dollars* if you answer the phone! A million bucks, Sam! Come on! Give me a break! *Please?*"

He waited a minute or two and tried the number again. He was shocked when he got the real McCoy.

"It better be a cashier's check," Sam demanded, answering her phone without any type of greeting.

"Thank God. I... I need your help." God, that was hard to say—to admit that he wasn't an island unto himself.

"Either tell me what the hell you want or I'm hanging up. And the check damn well better be in the mail."

"I made a mistake. I never should've come back here." His heart was still pounding and his mouth had gone dry. *A mistake?* A wrecked car was a mistake. Leaving Katie was a catastrophe.

"Is that *all*? You're wasting my time."

"And I want her back." The words were choked out as tears formed in his eyes.

She snorted a rueful laugh. "Kind of late to be coming to that conclusion, isn't it? You hurt her, Seth. Just leave her alone."

"I can't, Sam. I love her," Seth finally said aloud for the first time. The simple declaration made him feel free, made him feel powerful. Hell, he wanted to shout it to the entire world! "Really, Sam. I love her. I do. I love her more than living." *I love her more than ever damn penny of the Remington fortune. I love her so much it hurts.* He scrubbed away his tears with his free hand.

He could hear Sam breathing, but she didn't respond. "Sam? I know you're still there."

"Yeah, I'm still here. You're an asshole, you know that? A big fat asshole."

"I kinda figured that one out on my own."

Seth heard her sigh.

"And you're... you're too late."

Seth's thought his heart might have stopped beating. He jumped off the couch and began to pace the room. "What the hell do you mean too late?"

"I shouldn't be telling you any of this."

"Come on, Sam. You're scaring me here," Seth pleaded.

"Katie is... Well, she's... She's marrying Ross Kennedy. They're flying to Vegas Sunday morning."

That miserable son of a bitch. I'll kill him with my bare hands.

"Seth? You still there?"

"Yeah, I'm here," he replied through clenched teeth.

"Well? Are you just gonna sit there or do you plan to do something about it?"

"I'm going to murder Ross Kennedy. He's not good enough for her."

"And you are?"

"No. But I love her, damn it. And she loves me." Then a slew of memories came flooding back, swamping Seth with ideas and a ray of hope. "I know exactly what to do, but I'll need your help. Can I count on you?"

"Only if you *swear* you won't hurt her again. I don't know if I can trust you," she replied.

Was it possible that Samantha was on his side? *Thank you, God!*

"Cross my heart. I love her. Just wait, she's in for the surprise of her life!"

"So are you, Loverboy."

Chapter 33

Katie rolled out of bed to answer the incessant knocking on the barn door. She slipped on some jeans under the big t-shirt she'd donned for bed and walked barefoot through the barn as horses nickered their morning greetings.

"I'm coming!" she shouted when the impatient pounding continued. She threw the latch and pulled the door open to be greeted by a delivery man with an enormous bouquet of flowers in a crystal vase.

"Oh, Ross," she whispered. The man was certainly sweet. She felt a surge of guilt knowing that she didn't return his feelings. A nice guy like Ross obviously deserved better than a woman who loved someone else.

I'll learn to love Ross. I will.

Taking the clipboard and signing for the delivery, Katie accepted the flowers and took them back to her room where she set them on the desk next to her computer. She ran her fingers across the keyboard, remembering the night Seth had given it to her. The crippling pain of his leaving was always there, just below the surface. Katie refused to let it rise too high. If she did, she'd lose her nerve. She jerked her fingers back and wiped away the tear that had spilled over her lashes onto her cheek.

Katie went about her usual morning ritual of caring for the horses. There was only one to jog, and three were turned out to corrals for the day. Spun Gold would race that evening. She'd be leaving the next day to marry Ross Kennedy. By this time tomorrow, she would have changed her life in a "no going back" way.

Jogging Jack around the track, she had a hard time concentrating. Somewhere in the back of her mind remained a single thread of unrealistic and desperate hope that her love for Seth would bring him back to her side before it was too late.

You're doing this for the baby. You're marrying Ross because it's the best thing to do. He would see that her son had all he deserved in life, all the things that she could never afford on her own.

"Katie Kennedy," she said, hoping to convince herself that the name fit. But it didn't.

Damn it, I don't want to cry again.

Just as she guided Jack off of the small track, another truck pulled up to the barn. Not a delivery van this time, but a refrigerated grocery truck. Katie's brow wrinkled in confusion as she pondered what could possibly be in the huge box the uniformed man carried from the big truck.

"Just a minute!" Katie yelled as she slid off the jog cart. The twenty-something guy looked around in obvious confusion as to where to deliver his burden. She steered the horse back to the barn and set him in cross-ties before turning to the courier who had dutifully followed her.

"Be sure and keep it out of the heat. Have a nice day," he said as he handed her the box and left.

Katie set the delivery on top of one of her trunks. Jerking on the lid, she was finally able to wrestle it open. Inside rested a huge assortment of chocolates. There were big chunks of fudge and several varieties of her favorite candy bars. But what surprised Katie the most was the multitude of chocolate rabbits.

Katie was both amused and bemused. She couldn't remember telling Ross about her fascination with Easter candy, but she figured it might've been an impressively good guess on his part. "Maybe he went to the trouble to ask Sam," she told Jack. The horse didn't reply.

Katie picked up one of the rabbits and sat down on a trunk. She unwrapped the treat and promptly bit off its ears. As the chocolate melted in her mouth, she sighed in contentment. Easter candy in August. It was sublime.

As she ate the rest of the rabbit, Katie absentmindedly touched the silver shamrock that always hung around her neck—a talisman that bound her to Seth. Their lives had been intertwined in the same way their engraved initials could not be separated. They had become one in their child.

When she suddenly realized what she was doing, she reminded herself to take the necklace off before she left with Ross.

Yeah, Katie. Like you'll be able to leave it behind. Doing so would be akin to having a limb removed.

After finishing her work, Katie returned to her room to take a shower. As usual, the warm water ran out too quickly to suit her, but she felt clean and a little more relaxed by the time she was done.

Wrapped only in a towel, Katie went back to her room to rifle through her drawers to find some clean clothes. She glanced over at the duffle bag sitting on the chair. In it she had packed all the things she would need for her trip, her elopement. A shiver of hurt ran through her as she wished for the millionth time that things could have been different. Katie took one of Seth's green stable shirts from the drawer and threw it on the bed next to a clean pair of jeans. She dressed and dried her hair as she fought off a slew of yawns and a wave of fatigue.

Checking the clock, she was pleased she still had time to catch a short nap before she and Gold would have to leave for the track. As she stretched out on the bed, her head had no sooner touched the pillow when she heard another vehicle approaching. With a weary sigh, Katie got up and walked to the end of the barn to see what else the day held in store for her.

Yet another delivery truck had pulled up next to her barn. Katie watched the man get out holding a medium-sized box covered in floral wrapping paper. "You Katie Murphy?"

"Yeah. I take it that's for me."

"Sign here."

Back in her room, Katie set the box on her bed and just stared at it. Ross was certainly going overboard, but the gestures made her horribly uncomfortable. She desperately wished she could return the obvious affection the man had for her.

Her hand moved over her stomach. "Oh, Sweetheart. Am I doing the right thing? God, I miss your daddy." Tears formed in her eyes. She wiped them away and shook her head. She had to be practical about this if she was going to be able to force herself to follow through. "Ross will take care of us," she said with conviction she didn't really feel. She reached for the box.

Ripping off the wrapping paper and then lifting the lid, Katie freed the contents from the container. Inside was a variety of CDs. Katie lifted several and shuffled through them like playing cards. The names were familiar to her heart. Michael Bublé, Billy Joel, Barry Manilow, and Clay Aiken were all there. All her favorites.

A caution sounded in the back of Katie's mind. Ross couldn't have possibly known which albums were the ones she'd listened to so many times that she had to replace them. She dug through the box looking for a card, *anything* to tell her who sent the present. There was nothing to be found. Her heart started to drum a fast rhythm in her chest. *Seth?*

Katie turned to the flowers and quickly ran her fingers through them trying to find a card. Again, she found no evidence of the person who ordered the gorgeous bouquet.

When she looked at the chocolates, Katie's stomach rebelled. The typical afternoon nausea was short-lived, but it deterred Katie from burrowing into the stash of candy.

What the hell is going on?

Taking a CD from the box, Katie opened it and pushed it into her small stereo. The sound of Barry Manilow's "Even Now" filled the room as Katie moved the box to the desk so she could stretch out for her nap.

Sleep never found her as a small spark of hope wound its way from her heart to her head. She tried to force it back down, but the more she fought it, the louder it became.

Maybe Seth is coming back.

Don't be absurd, Kathleen.

She rolled over to face the wall. She knew it was her imagination, but she could feel Seth mold his strong, warm body to hers, just as he had so many times before.

At the insistent beeping of her watch alarm, Katie finally pushed her weary body out of bed and pulled on her work boots. It was time to get Spun Gold to the track.

As she eased her truck and trailer off of the main road heading to the back entrance of the track, she suddenly encountered her next surprise. Flashing lights moved in a chase around the borders of a big yellow sign. Enormous red letters spelled out "I love Katie Murphy." She almost drove off the road.

Ross is going to be in a shitload of trouble when I get my hands on him.

She could almost hear the gossip that had to be rolling through the track like wildfire burning through some autumn-dried leaves.

She pulled up to the security checkpoint. "Hi'ya, Katie," one of the guards said. Then he laughed. "You didn't happen to see the sign, did ya?"

Katie frowned as her cheeks grow hot. "You guys been here all day?"

she asked as the second guard checked her license plates and filled out her information on his clipboard.

"Yeah. Since noon, but it was here when I got here." He nodded toward the embarrassing sign.

"You mean that stupid sign has been here all day? Everyone has seen it?"

The guard laughed again. "Oh, yeah. Joe told me it was here before daylight broke."

Katie wasn't sure if she should be flattered or pissed. It wasn't as if she hadn't given the gossips more than enough to chew on in the past few months. Now they could tease her unmercifully about that embarrassing sign.

After getting her colt out of the trailer, Katie led Gold to the paddock, hoping that the surprises had finally come to an end. As she walked the length of the aisle, several people smiled, nodded, or laughed as they passed her. Her face felt as if it had been sunburned.

Approaching the stall assigned to Gold, Katie noticed several people gathered around looking at a large white paper that had been taped to the gate. When they saw Katie, the crowd quickly parted to give her and her horse room enough to get through. Katie turned Gold loose in the stall and slammed the gate before looking at the message.

A large mockup of a claim form stared back at her. Where the name of the horse to be claimed was to be written, someone had used a red marker to write "Katie Murphy" in huge letters. The amount of money being spent on the claim was listed as "priceless." Katie groaned in frustration as people around her patted her on the back and laughed at the humor of the message. She reached up to rip the paper from the door and crumpled it in her fist. "I'm going to kill Ross when I see him," Katie hissed through clenched teeth before going about her job preparing her colt for his warm-up.

Chris showed up, pulling her jog cart behind him. "Hey, Katie."

"Hi. Thanks for bringing that. I need to go put on my colors."

"Good luck getting in the locker room," Chris said with a chuckle.

"Why?" Katie asked as she adjusted another piece of equipment.

"There's a crowd up front. Someone is actually setting up a karaoke machine."

She rolled her eyes. "Just great. Another birthday party. Why can't they take that stuff up to the grandstand instead of the paddock?" She made one last adjustment to Gold's harness. "Please keep an eye on him. I'm going to get my colors on. I'm getting into that locker room, one way or another."

Katie elbowed her way through the throng of trainers, drivers, and grooms who were tightly packed around the front of the paddock. She wrestled the door to the locker room open enough to slip inside.

After donning her colors and grabbing her helmet, gloves, and glasses, Katie pushed on the door. It didn't budge. She shoved harder, but the damn thing wouldn't give an inch. She pounded on the door with her fist. "Hey, you guys! Move! I need to get out!"

She was surprised to hear Sam's voice reply, "Hold on a second, Katie. We'll get you out in a minute."

"I need to warm up my horse, *Samantha*! Let me out of here! Now!"

"Just a minute, *Kathleen!*" Sam yelled back with a syrupy lilt to her voice.

Katie stomped her foot and cursed. She could hear several people outside the door laughing and talking, but she couldn't make out exactly what was being said. "Sam! Let me out now, damn it!"

The door immediately swung open, and Katie glanced around suspiciously before stepping out of the lounge.

The crowd had formed into a tight circle surrounding one of the picnic tables which had been dragged in the front area of the paddock. She looked around to try to figure out what drew their attention, but she couldn't see anything of importance. Just as she turned to head back up the aisle, Katie heard his voice and stopped in her tracks.

"Katie, wait."

She whirled around to see Seth standing in the center of the table dressed in his colors—*her* colors. The two of them probably looked like a matched pair in their jumpsuits. She had a quick flash of memory to the Raggedy Anne and Raggedy Andy that had always sat on her bed at her grandfather's home.

Seth held a microphone and grinned at her as if he'd never even left. Katie stared at him slack-jawed for a moment. Seth was back. He'd actually come back for her.

And he can just go straight to Hell. Katie's wounded pride made her put her nose in the air and turn around to go back to Gold.

"Hit it, Sam!" Seth yelled. Rock music blasted through all of the loud speakers. Katie skidded to a halt before whirling around to face him again. What in the hell was he doing? "Oh, my God. He's singing."

The strong beat of Player's "Baby Come Back" thrummed through the paddock. Seth serenaded everyone in the building. Most of the people gathered around began to sing along with him and dance in the aisles. The rock melody pounding through the speakers was infectious.

She had to admit, the guy could actually sing. Even the race officials joined in the fun as they danced around their glass-enclosed office. Katie wasn't sure if she wanted to laugh or cry, but it seemed she was doing both. Seth continued to follow along with the music, and as the people who accompanied him hit the song's bridge, the high notes echoed off the rafters.

When Seth finally ended the song, the people in the paddock erupted in applause, cheers, and whistles. He jumped off of the table and made his way to Katie through the path that the horsemen cleared for him. Pulling a small blue velvet box from his pocket, he dropped to one knee.

Katie couldn't believe what she was seeing. Her heart slammed in her chest. Her whole body trembled. She sure didn't want to be ill at that moment, but the way her stomach was tumbling, it was a distinct possibility. "What in God's name are you doing?"

"I'm making an ass out of myself for a woman." Seth gave her an enormous smile. "I love you, Katie Murphy. Will you marry me?"

Katie bit her lower lip and tried unsuccessfully to stop crying. "What about the money?"

"I made a big mistake, Boss. I don't want the money. It just doesn't matter without you. Nothing matters without you."

Katie wanted to run into his arms, but she stood her ground and squelched a sob. "I can't let you give up your money. Not for me."

Seth opened the box and laid it in his outstretched palm. Inside rested a silver ring with a diamond surrounded by a circle of small emeralds. Katie had never seen anything more beautiful. "It's not much, but I paid for it with my own money. Racing money, not Remington money," Seth explained with a note of pride in his voice.

"You *can't* give it up. It's... it's too much," Katie barely choked out. She couldn't stop the tears rolling down her cheeks.

Seth shook his head. "Don't you see, Boss? I already gave it up. Just by coming here, I gave it all away. Every damn dime of it. I want *you*, Katie, not the money. You're worth far more."

"Go home, Seth." Her voice was nothing but a whisper. "Go back home."

"I *am* home. Home is where you are. Please, Katie. I love you. Will you marry me?" Seth rose to his feet and opened his arms.

She dropped her helmet and glasses and was in his embrace in two steps as cheers erupted throughout the paddock. He lifted her off her feet and hugged her until she could barely breathe.

So many emotions flowed through Katie that she couldn't get a handle on any of them. But now she'd have all the time in the world to sort through the emotional roller coaster she had been riding since the day she met Seth Remington.

"I missed you, Baby," he whispered in her ear. "I'll never leave you again. I swear." She nodded her head against his neck. "I love you, Katie."

"I love you too, Seth."

The shouts finally penetrated the small universe the two had created for themselves. He let her body slide down his as he put her back on her feet. She was afraid to let him leave her arms. "Am I dreaming?"

He smiled. "If you are, then so am I."

Seth took a small step back, removed the ring from the box, and slipped it on Katie's left hand as their friends continued enjoy the show.

"Come on! Kiss her already!" Chris called.

"Give her a kiss!" another voice echoed.

Seth smiled at her again, showing those wonderfully white teeth. "Do we give them what they want?"

"No," she replied with a grin. "We give them what *we* want."

Seth put his hand under her chin to lift her face as his mouth settled on hers. The whistles and shouts urged them on, but she finally pulled away and sighed in contentment.

Samantha came over to them with Brian and his cane close at her heels. Seth gently pushed Katie away and turned her around. She smiled at her friends, until she saw the sly look in Sam's eyes. Seth had an accomplice. "So how much of this was your idea?"

"None." Sam nodded toward Seth. "It's all Loverboy here."

"You hurt her again, I'll kick your ass," Brian said even as he offered his hand to Seth.

"It's good to see you too, Brian." Seth reached out to shake Brian's hand.

Katie was drowning in happiness until she turned around again and saw Ross over Seth's shoulder. He'd come for Gold's race. He came to marry her.

Ross was dressed in one of his impeccable suits and leaning against the wall with his arms folded over his chest. Katie tapped Seth on the arm and pointed over his shoulder.

"Shit," he said. "I forgot all about him."

She wasn't sure if Seth knew about the planned elopement, and Katie didn't think the paddock was the proper place to discuss something so personal. She'd explain it all to Seth later, but she owed Ross an explanation now. "I need to talk to him, Seth."

Katie walked over to lean against the wall next to Ross while Seth talked to the horsemen who surrounded him, shaking his hand and patting him on the back.

What could she possibly say to someone that has been so publicly rejected? Guilt washed over her. "Ross, I'm so sorry. I didn't mean—"

"Don't be sorry," Ross interrupted. "If you hadn't agreed to marry him, I would've." He winked at her, but his eyes lacked their usual sparkle. "God, that was so... so... romantic. If I'd proposed like that, who knows?" He shrugged. "Maybe you'd still be leaving with me tomorrow." She knew he was trying to be funny, but she could hear the hurt buried in the joke.

"Can you ever forgive me?"

"I already have, Katie. You two belong together. I'm just glad the guy finally came to his senses."

She wiped away an errant tear. "You don't know how much you mean to me. I'll never be able to repay you for all you've done."

"You can find me another horse. I'm in the mood to make money," Ross said with a chuckle that sounded less than sincere.

Seth walked over to join them. He extended his hand to Ross who returned the gesture as the two shook hands.

"I guess I won't be signing those papers for my inheritance," Seth said with a smile.

"I kind of figured. Money isn't everything, is it, Remington?"

He laughed at that and shook his head. "No, Kennedy, it isn't." Katie watched Seth's face change as his brows knit in concern. "Katie won't lose Spun Gold, will she?"

Spun Gold. A fantastic colt, but the price she might have to pay for Seth's love. It was the easiest decision Katie had ever made. She would miss her horse.

Ross seemed to ponder Seth's question before he finally answered. "You came to her; she didn't break the agreement. She fulfilled her end of the bargain. I'm sure she can keep her horse. Probably the bonus, too. I'll have to get back to you on that." He reached inside his jacket pocket and pulled out a red and blue envelope that he handed to Katie. "Here's an early wedding present."

Katie opened the envelope and pulled out the plane tickets Ross had purchased for their trip to Las Vegas. "Ross, I can't take these."

"Sure you can. They're nonrefundable, and it doesn't look like I'm going to use them now," he said with a sardonic laugh. "Go on. You two go and get married tomorrow."

Pushing herself away from the wall, she turned to give Ross a heartfelt hug which he returned. "You know I'll always love you. You ever need me, just call," he whispered in her ear. He released her, and Seth immediately grabbed her hand and pulled her to his side.

Katie brushed the tears out of her eyes and nodded. Ross gave them both a wave and walked out of the paddock.

The race official's voice came booming through the speakers. "If the festivities are concluded, can we *please* get back to business? Bring the horses for the first race up to the front." The crowd scrambled back into motion as everyone went back to their tasks. Someone handed Katie her helmet, gloves, and glasses.

Seth led Katie back to Spun Gold's stall. Katie smiled when the horse recognized Seth immediately and stomped a front foot, demanding attention.

"I missed you," Seth said as he entered the stall and patted his pet.

Releasing the cross-ties, he led Gold out to the aisle, and then Katie fastened the jog cart to the harness. She jumped on the cart and adjusted her reins. "Seth, why don't you go see if you can make a late driver change? I'll pay the fine if you'll drive Gold for me."

"You got it, Boss."

"So you're ready to race again?"

"Absolutely."

* * * *

Back at the barn, Seth tended to Spun Gold as Katie finished the nightly chores. He completed his work first and then sat on a trunk, content to simply watch her.

"What are you staring at?" she finally asked, looking up from her task.

"I'd forgotten how beautiful you are."

Katie blushed and finished wrapping the hose around its hanger.

Seth stood up and crossed to her side. Scooping her up in his arms, he twirled in a circle as she squealed in clear delight.

"Are you ready for bed?" he asked and then growled deep in his throat as he kissed the spot just below her ear that she liked so much. He felt her shiver in response. As quickly as his body responded and as badly as he wanted her, he wasn't sure they'd even make it back to the room.

"Seth, we need to talk."

Seth groaned. "Famous last words." Then he suddenly stopped moving as naked fear swept through him. "You haven't... haven't changed your mind, have you?"

"God, no. Why would you think...? Oh, sorry. Bad choice of words."

Seth carried her to her room and kicked the door shut behind them before setting Katie on the bed. "So what do we need to talk about?" He sat down next to her.

She swallowed hard. "I..." She cleared her throat. "Um, we..." But she couldn't seem to finish the thought.

Seth realized that she was having a very hard time finding the right words. What could make her so nervous? Things were finally working out. She should be happy. "What is it, Boss?"

Katie gave him a weak, nervous smile. Then she picked up Seth's hand and placed it gently on her stomach. She looked deeply into his eyes.

"What do you—?" The hand he kept on her belly began to tremble as he suddenly understood just what Katie couldn't find the words tell him. "Are you sure?" he asked in a voice that cracked like an adolescent.

Katie's nibbled on her lower lip and nodded.

"When?"

"February."

"A baby. You're going to have my... my... baby." He wasn't sure his heart would ever settle back into a normal rhythm. Seth rubbed small circles on her belly as he quickly did the math. "You knew? Before I left, you knew?"

She nodded.

"Why didn't you—?"

"I couldn't," she interrupted.

She had known she was pregnant before he left, and yet Katie hadn't forced a choice from him. She'd given him enough time to discover the truth for himself, to figure out where his heart belonged. To find his way home.

God, he loved her for that.

Lifting the hem of her shirt, Seth pressed a kiss to Katie's belly before raising his head to kiss her lips. "I love you, Katie," he murmured against her mouth.

"I love you too." As Seth pulled away to look into her eyes, Katie gave him a coy smile. "Took you long enough..."

Epilogue

Easing the Lexus up the familiar gravel drive, the first thing Ross noticed was Seth out on the practice track, jogging a horse. Ross parked his car and walked toward the barn. Seth made it back to the door at the same time.

"Hi, Remington. How have you been?" Ross asked as he pulled his thick coat closed against the frigid November wind. "Damn. I forgot how cold it gets out here."

Seth chuckled. "We're good. Come inside before you freeze your ass off."

Noticing Seth wearing the grey flannel-lined jumpsuit and Elmer Fudd hat Ross had purchased almost nine months before, Ross couldn't let the opportunity pass. "Nice outfit. You look like the newest member of the Village People."

"Yeah, well kiss my ass, Kennedy. Out here, I'll take comfort before fashion any day."

"Where you racing now that Dan Patch is closed for the season?" Ross asked, following Seth into the barn and pulling the big door closed behind them.

"We were going to go to Chicago, but Katie wanted to take a couple of weeks off before the holidays. We'll probably start shipping to Balmoral Park in January. We're spending Christmas in Goshen with Kevin and Jacob. You still thinking about another horse?"

"Yeah, but not until the spring. I've got so much to do at work, I can barely keep my head above water. The press isn't bothering you anymore?"

"Nah. They disappeared with the Remington money. Good riddance."

After setting the horse in cross-ties, Seth called to Katie who peeked out of the office. "Ross!" she squealed as she threw the door open and walked up the aisle.

Ross greeted her with a hug and was pleased to see that Seth still scowled whenever he saw them together. A little jealousy never hurt. Ross put his hand on her swelling belly and smiled. "You look great, Katie. Positively radiant."

She smiled. "You look good too, Ross."

He'd missed her smile.

"So what's up?" Seth finally asked, taking Katie's hand and yanking her to his side. Ross had to contain his smile at the telling action.

"I need to close out the paperwork on the transfer of assets." He set his briefcase on one of the green trunks and popped open the latches. Retrieving a white envelope, Ross handed it to Seth. "There's one more thing for you to see."

Seth took the missive and frowned. "What's this?" He looked at both sides of the envelope. "It doesn't say who it's from."

"Your father left it for you. You were supposed to get it at the end of the season. I could've just mailed it, but Arthur insisted I bring it in person. After you read it, then we can close out the last of the requirements of the will." Ross saw Katie squeeze Seth's hand and swallowed his own jealousy. He envied their closeness.

"Why don't you go into the office and read it in private?" she suggested.

Seth stared at Katie, his gaze full of love. "We don't have any secrets anymore."

She smiled at him with no less affection. "I know. But it's from your dad. You might like the privacy. You can share it with me later."

"Thanks, Boss," Seth said before kissing her on the cheek. He headed to the office and shut the door behind him.

"How are you feeling, Katie?" Ross asked as he sat down on one of the big green trunks to watch her strip the equipment from the horse Seth had been jogging.

"I'm feeling really good. Getting kind of fat though." She turned to show her profile and pat her swelling belly. "Another month or so and I'm gonna look like a water buffalo. Did I tell you it's a boy? At least that's what the ultrasound showed."

"No, you didn't. Congratulations. Picked any names?"

"Not yet. Seth is partial to a name that he can find a jazzy nickname for. He swears the kid was bred to be the greatest driver in the history of harness racing."

Ross smiled. "How is the house coming?"

"It's coming. You know how contractors are. They tell you two weeks and mean three months. I really wanted it done before winter set in, but..." She shrugged. "It's almost Thanksgiving and we're not really a whole lot closer to moving in."

"How many acres did you guys buy?"

"We mortgaged twenty plus the cost of the house. But we have the option to buy more land when we can. The money from winning the sires stakes helped so much."

Ross nodded and smiled remembering how excited she'd been when she got Spun Gold. "I told you Sterling picked you a fantastic horse. What about the bonus?"

"We put it aside for the baby. For his college fund. Seth won't touch it otherwise." She pulled the harness from the horse and walked over to hang it on the hook. "I'm proud of him for that."

"How close will you be to the Mitchell farm?"

"Our south property line runs right up to theirs. We're going to share their practice track as soon as the barn is done." She pulled the bit from the horse's mouth. "We just figured with the munchkin on the way, the house needed to get done first."

Ross swallowed his jealousy. "I can understand that. Where's Chris?"

"He splits his time between Brian and his own stable. He's got three horses he trains now. He's still dating Angie O'Riley."

"Do I know her?" Ross asked.

"I doubt it, but she's Taylor O'Riley's daughter. That guy you love claiming horses off of. The one that hates our guts."

Ross laughed and nodded.

"They're so cute together. You should see Sam and Brian's little girl. Chelsea is the sweetest thing ever. Sleeps well, eats well, the perfect kid." Katie laughed. "Our son will probably have my temper, God help us."

The door to the office opened and Seth came out with a look a sheer bewilderment on his face.

"Seth? What's wrong?" Katie asked.

He walked to her and handed her the letter. "I think you should read this. I'll tell you, love him or hate him, you have to admit the Old Man had...

guts."

Katie read aloud the message written in Sterling Remington's own hand.

Dearest Seth and Katie,

I knew you'd choose the right thing, Seth. From the second I met her, I knew Katie was the right woman for you. The problem was that you weren't the right man for her—at least not before you learned a little about life.

Katie, when I told you I was giving you my son, I wasn't kidding. You're probably a little angry over what I've put you through, but there was just no other way to convince Seth that his life was being wasted.

I thought about simply introducing you two, but both of you would have been too stubborn to see beyond your own worlds. I needed to find a way to get you together without either of you knowing what I really wanted from you.

I'm sorry that the will seemed spiteful, but you have to be honest. If a parent tells his kid that he can't have something, it makes it more attractive. I had to make you both believe the other was forbidden fruit. Forgive an old man his desire to see you together and happy, just like Brenda and I were.

I know now that my son's life has meaning and purpose—two things my money wasn't able to give him.

Now, about the money.

All of my shares in Remington Computers will be divided among the loyal employees who helped make it the company it is today. Just consider it a form of profit sharing. Ross Kennedy has the list and will handle the division of those assets.

The compound will be sold. I know the two of you have no use for it. Take the money and buy a farm. Have a place you two can call your own. And please raise my grandchildren to love horses as much as I do.

The personal assets will be set aside for you and your children to use as you see fit. In other words, all of my personal wealth is now yours. Don't ever let it be a burden.

Love each other. Be good to each other. Nothing should ever be more important.

Love, Pops

Katie's hands were shaking as she finished reading the letter. "Ross? Did you know about this?"

He shook his head. "I hadn't read it. I just found out about it a couple of days ago then I called you. Arthur played this hand really close to his vest. He didn't even tell me. You weren't supposed to know about it until the end of the racing season."

Seth remained speechless for a few moments. "Maybe we don't want it," he said, turning to look at his wife. "Katie? What do you think?"

She took his hand in hers and gave it a squeeze. "It's up to you, Seth. I'm happy with what we have, but it's your father's money. You have a right to it."

Ross couldn't believe what he was hearing. "You mean you don't want the money?"

Katie smiled. "He's afraid it'll change him."

Seth nodded. Ross wondered if the man even knew he was stroking his wife's rounded belly. The endearing action gave Ross a flash of naked envy for all Seth Remington had found in life.

Turning back to her husband, Katie kissed him and used her fingertips to brush a caress across his cheek. "Seth, you know how much I love you. You're a good man. Nothing can change that. Whatever you decide, I'll still be here." She covered the hand Seth had on her stomach with her own. "We'll still be here."

Ross hopped off of the trunk and went back to his briefcase. He pulled out the document that would give Seth back his inheritance. "If you want the money, you need to sign this last paper. I can help with the transfer of assets. But if you don't want it, then we'll need to figure something else out."

Seth drew a deep breath. He turned to Ross with an enormous smile. "Hell, yeah, I want it. I'm not a total idiot." He turned back to his wife and chuckled. "God, Boss, think about how much fun we'll have at the next yearling auction."

THE END

www.sandy-james.com

ABOUT THE AUTHOR

Sandy lives in a quiet suburb of Indianapolis with her husband of over twenty-five years. She started writing when empty nest syndrome stared her in the eye, completing her first book the year the younger of her two children graduated from high school. Her family owns a small stable of harness racehorses and enjoys spending time at the two Indiana racetracks.

Look for handsome attorney Ross Kennedy from *Murphy's Law* in the second book in the "Damaged Heroes" series. *Free Falling* will be released by BookStrand in April 2009.

Printed in the United States
146594LV00003B/23/P

9 781606 012710